SURVIVOR'S GUILT
AND OTHER STORIES

Praise for Greg Herren

Sleeping Angel "will probably be put on the young adult (YA) shelf, but the fact is that it's a cracking good mystery that general readers will enjoy as well. It just happens to be about teens…A unique viewpoint, a solid mystery and good characterization all conspire to make *Sleeping Angel* a welcome addition to any shelf, no matter where the bookstores stock it."—Jerry Wheeler, *Out in Print*

"This fast-paced mystery is skillfully crafted. Red herrings abound and will keep readers on their toes until the very end. Before the accident, few readers would care about Eric, but his loss of memory gives him a chance to experience dramatic growth, and the end result is a sympathetic character embroiled in a dangerous quest for truth." —*VOYA*

"Herren, a loyal New Orleans resident, paints a brilliant portrait of the recovering city, including insights into its tight-knit gay community. This latest installment in a powerful series is sure to delight old fans and attract new ones."—*Publishers Weekly*

"Fast-moving and entertaining, evoking the Quarter and its gay scene in a sweet, funny, action-packed way."—*New Orleans Times-Picayune*

"Herren does a fine job of moving the story along, deftly juggling the murder investigation and the intricate relationships while maintaining several running subjects."—*Echo Magazine*

"An entertaining read."—*OutSmart Magazine*

"A pleasant addition to your beach bag."—*Bay Windows*

"Greg Herren gives readers a tantalizing glimpse of New Orleans." —*The Midwest Book Review*

"Herren's characters, dialogue and setting make the book seem absolutely real."—*The Houston Voice*

"So much fun it should be thrown from Mardi Gras floats!"—*New Orleans Times-Picayune*

"Greg Herren just keeps getting better."—*Lambda Book Report*

By the Author

The Scotty Bradley Adventures

Bourbon Street Blues

Jackson Square Jazz

Mardi Gras Mambo

Vieux Carré Voodoo

Who Dat Whodunnit

Baton Rouge Bingo

Garden District Gothic

The Chanse MacLeod Mysteries

Murder in the Rue Dauphine

Murder in the Rue St. Ann

Murder in the Rue Chartres

Murder in the Rue Ursulines

Murder in the Garden District

Murder in the Irish Channel

Murder in the Arts District

Young Adult

Sleeping Angel

Sara

Lake Thirteen

New Adult

Timothy

The Orion Mask

Dark Tide

Survivor's Guilt and Other Stories

Going Down for the Count
(Writing as Cage Thunder)

Wicked Frat Boy Ways
(Writing as Todd Gregory)

Edited with J.M. Redmann

Women of the Mean Streets: Lesbian Noir

Men of the Mean Streets: Gay Noir

Night Shadows: Queer Horror

Edited as Todd Gregory

Rough Trade

Sweat

Anything for a Dollar

Blood Sacraments

Visit us at www.boldstrokesbooks.com

SURVIVOR'S GUILT
AND OTHER STORIES

by

Greg Herren

2019

"Survivor's Guilt" originally appeared in *Blood on the Bayou: 2016 Bouchercon Anthology*, Greg Herren, ed., Down and Out Books (September 2016); "The Email Always Pings Twice" originally appeared in *Ellery Queen's Mystery Magazine* (September/October 2014); "Keeper of the Flame" originally appeared in *Mystery Week* (September 2017); "A Streetcar Named Death" originally appeared in *I Never Thought I'd See You Again*, Lou Aronica, ed., The Story Plant (July 2013); "An Arrow for Sebastian" originally appeared in *Cast of Characters*, Lou Aronica, ed., Fiction Studio Books (April 2012); "Housecleaning" originally appeared in *Sunshine Noir*, Annamaria Alfieri and Michael Stanley, eds., White Sun Books (2016); "Acts of Contrition" originally appeared in *Ellery Queen's Mystery Magazine* (November 2006); "Spin Cycle" originally appeared in *Men of the Mean Streets*, Greg Herren and J. M. Redmann, eds., Bold Strokes Books (2012); "Cold Beer No Flies" originally appeard in *Florida Happens*, Greg Herren, ed., Three Rooms Press (2018);"Annunciation Shotgun" originally appeared in *New Orleans Noir*, Julie Smith, ed., Akashic Books (2007); "Quiet Desperation" originally appeared as a Kindle Single (February 2018)

ISBN 13: 978-1-63555-413-7

THIS TRADE PAPERBACK ORIGINAL IS PUBLISHED BY
BOLD STROKES BOOKS, INC.
P.O. Box 249
VALLEY FALLS, NY 12185

FIRST EDITION: APRIL 2019

CREDITS

EDITOR: STACIA SEAMAN
PRODUCTION DESIGN: STACIA SEAMAN
COVER DESIGN BY TAMMY SEIDICK

This is for Paul, as always.

Contents

SURVIVOR'S GUILT

I'm going to die on this stupid roof.

It wasn't the first time the thought had run through his mind in the—how long had it been, anyway? Days? Weeks?—however long it had been since he'd climbed up there. It didn't matter how long it really had been, all that mattered was it felt like it had been an eternity. He'd run out of bottled water—when? Yesterday? Two days ago? It didn't matter. All that mattered was he was thirsty and hot and he now knew how a lobster felt when dropped in boiling water, how it felt to be boiled or scalded or burned to death.

He was out of water.

Not that the last bottles of water had been much help anyway.

In the hot oven that used to be the attic of the single shotgun house he'd called home for almost twenty years, the water inside the bottles had gotten so damned hot he could have made coffee with it and it tasted like melted plastic, was probably toxic, poisonous in some way. Wasn't plastic bad for you? He seemed to remember reading that somewhere or hearing it on the television a million years ago when his house wasn't underwater and there was still air-conditioning and cold beer in the fridge instead of this…this purgatory of hot sun and stagnant water and sweat-soaked clothes.

But drinking hot water that tasted like plastic and was probably, maybe, poisonous—that was better than dying of thirst on the hot tiles of this stupid stinking roof. He'd tried to conserve it, space it out, save it, trying to make it last as long as possible because he had no idea when rescue was coming.

If it ever came at all.

He'd been on the roof so long already—how long *had* it been? Days? Weeks? Months?

Should have left, should have listened to her, should have put everything we could in the truck and headed west.

But they'd never gone before, never fled before an oncoming storm, laughed at those who panicked and packed up and ran away, paying hotels and motels way too much money for days on end.

Hadn't the storms had always turned to the east at the last minute, coming ashore somewhere to the east, and New Orleans breathed another sigh of relief at dodging another bullet while saying a prayer at the same time for those getting hammered by high winds and storm surges and power outages and downed trees?

Hell, that last time the storm had gone up into Mississippi and the highways south had been damaged and blocked, keeping people who'd gone that way marooned for well over a week.

So, no, there was no need to go this time, either, because Katrina would surely turn east like so many before her had.

Stupid, so damned stupid.

He could be in a hotel room in Houston at that very moment, basking in the air-conditioning, drinking lots of ice-cold water, waiting for the water to recede and come home, see what survived, see what could be saved and what couldn't.

Ice.

He'd sell his soul for an ice cube.

But when rescue came, he'd have to explain…

No, no need to think about that now.

If—no, *when*—rescue came, he'd deal with it then.

The sun, oh God, the sun.

He'd never been this hot in his life before, at least not that he could remember.

The closest was the beach in summertime, but there was always something cold to drink, the warm gulf waters to plunge into for some relief.

He felt like he was broiling inside his own skin.

Sometimes when it became too much he'd slip back down inside the attic. The oven. The air down there so thick and humid and hot and dusty he could barely breathe, but at least he was out of the sun. The air was barely breathable, clinging to his skin, so thick and wet he felt sometimes like he was drowning.

Every so often the wind would come, blowing through the vents at either end of the attic, and it felt so good he felt like crying.

But he couldn't stay down there for long. He had to stay out on the roof, in case rescuers came. He couldn't take a chance on missing them.

If someone came for him.

Don't think that. Someone has to come, rescuers will come. If I don't believe that I'll lose my damned mind.

Maybe it's divine punishment for—

Yet another helicopter flew past overhead, the latest of many. He'd stopped waving and yelling and jumping up and down when they passed overhead, like he wasn't even there. His throat was so sore from yelling he could barely make a sound anyway. They never stopped, but he knew—he *knew* they were rescuing people. They had to be. What else was the point of the big basket hanging from the underside of the helicopter, if not for lowering down to people stranded up on roofs like he was?

He just had to be patient. It would be his turn eventually.

He just had to stay alive until it was his turn.

The whole city was probably underwater for all he knew.

At least it was for as far as he could see, shimmering filthy water everywhere.

Should have left, should have listened.

One of them would—had to—stop for him, before he died.

Meantime, roasting, baking, frying, dying in the late August sun, or was it September now?

Every once in a while he heard a boat motor passing close by. He didn't bother making noise anymore when he heard those, either. There wasn't any point. They hadn't heard him when he could still yell. Back when he could still yell, whenever that was. However long it had been.

They never heard him. They never came.

His throat hurt so badly from all the yelling he'd done when his throat could still make a sound other than a hoarse rasp, he might have damaged his vocal cords. He might never be able to talk again.

Which wouldn't matter, anyway.

If I never get off this roof.

He picked up the wine bottle again, poured the last swallow of hot red wine into his mouth. Alcohol dehydrated the body, he knew that, remembered that from somewhere. But some liquid was better than no liquid.

The sour hot wine hit his empty stomach. He hadn't eaten, hadn't had anything to eat in—it felt like an eternity. He'd passed the point of being hungry.

But he worried that since all that was left was hot wine, he might make himself sick.

If he started throwing up he might just throw himself off the roof and drown himself.

It was tempting to think about. The thought came now and then, when he was so hot he could barely stand it, when his skin hurt so bad, blistered from sunburn, that he climbed down into the stiflingly hot attic and wept but was too dehydrated for tears to form. That was when he thought about drowning himself, diving through the trap door into the water and drowning himself.

Joining her down there.

Then he would get back to his right mind and open another bottle of wine and sip it slowly.

He looked at the empty bottle in his hands and tossed it off the end of the roof.

It splashed when it hit the water.

It was the last of the wine. All that was left now was hard liquor—a bottle of hot gin and a bottle of hot cheap tequila.

He hadn't wanted to touch the liquor, so he saved it for when there was nothing else left. Every time he took a swig of the wine he got light-headed, so there was no telling what the liquor would do, on his empty stomach and dehydrated body.

He wasn't even hydrated enough to sweat anymore. He hadn't had to relieve himself since—weeks ago? It didn't matter. Nothing mattered. Time didn't matter anymore, it was all one endless nightmare of heat and humidity and the sun, oh God, the sun.

Water, water, everywhere—but not a drop to drink.

No one was ever going to come.

I can't believe I'm going to die on this stupid roof. I should just kill myself and get it over with.

No, someone would come.

Someone had to come.

Should have left, should have listened.

The sun was setting in the west in an explosion of oranges and reds reflecting off the stagnant, dark, oily water. The roof of his truck was still slightly visible when he looked down over the side of the roof, its white roof almost glowing through the filthy water. Paid for, finally, years of paying off that damned loan finally come to an end just a month ago, the pink slip arriving in the mail last week. And now it was drowned, just like the city and God knows how many people. Ruined, gone, the money he put into it wasted. He'd babied it, too—oil change every three months without fail, servicing it before it was needed, the fucking thing so well taken care of it would have lasted easily another five to ten years if he kept babying it.

It doesn't matter anyway. Everything's ruined. The city's dead. We'll never come back from this.

Thank God the old house had an attic—yes, thank God for that—the kind with a trap door with a long dangling cord that hung down in a corner of the bedroom. You pulled the cord, the door came down, and a wooden ladder unfolded. He'd left the door open when he came up, when the water came, as the house filled up, left it open thinking it might help when rescue came.

If rescue ever came.

Even though she was down there.

Someone will come, he told himself again, *someone will come for me.*

Someone has to.

If he didn't believe rescue would come, he would lose his mind.

If he didn't believe someone would come, there wasn't any point in going on, to this suffering, to this agony of broiled skin and dehydration and starvation and air so thick he could barely breathe it, the stink of the wet wood rotting down below.

And despite the delirium, despite the agony, somehow—somehow he wasn't ready to give up.

If he gave up now, the suffering of the days? Weeks? Months? Was for nothing.

Nothing.

But it would be so much easier to give up. Then I wouldn't be thirsty anymore. Then I wouldn't be hungry anymore.

If he stopped believing one of the helicopters would lower a basket for him, or a boat might come by to take him to safety, through the end of the world to whatever might still be out there, away from the water, he might as well kill himself now.

There was a rope coiled in a corner of the attic. He could tie a noose and find something, somewhere, on the roof or in the attic, to loop it around and just let his weight fall, his neck snapping, death coming quickly and easily.

That would be so much better than this slow, horrible death from heat exhaustion and dehydration on the roof.

But the sun was going down at last, and night was coming.

He'd survived another day.

It would still be hot, and humid, and the smell of the water wouldn't go away, but the night was better.

Now he had to just survive another night.

He could still see the skyline of the business district in the distance in the darkening sky. There were no lights anywhere. Thick black plumes of smoke billowed in several places he could see, but there hadn't been an explosion in a while.

Or gunfire. He hadn't heard gunfire in a while.

Night wouldn't relieve the relentless humidity, but at least being out of direct sunlight would be better, give his blistering and salt-crusted skin some relief.

There might even be a breeze.

And he could stay out on the roof, not have to climb down inside to get away from the vicious rays of the sun.

No air moved in the attic, the heavy wet air almost suffocating in its thickness.

He could smell his own stink, and sometimes imagined he could even smell his flesh frying in the hot sun. His skin was burned, red, raw, but he couldn't breathe the fetid stale dead air in the hot attic all day. A cold shower to bring his skin temperature down was all he could think about, or packing himself in a tub of ice. That wasn't going to happen any time soon.

Ice. The thought of it made him want to weep.

Should have left. Should have listened.

She'd been right.

"We need to go," she'd said on Saturday, whenever that had been, however long ago that had been. She'd never been afraid of storms before, never wanted to leave. This unease, this nervousness, was something new, something he'd never seen before in her. There had been storms before when he'd wanted to go, and she'd laughed in his face, mocked him, and they hadn't gone. She'd been right those times.

He liked that she was afraid of this one, that it made her nervous. She seemed off balance, for once, not sure of herself.

"It won't come this way, you know they always turn east before landfall," he'd replied, dismissing and laughing at her, shutting her down every time she watched another emergency news conference, or when the Weather Channel ran another worst-case scenario for the city, as everyone began packing up and heading west for Houston, north for Jackson, and the city began to empty out. He mocked her panic, her nervousness, enjoying this new side of her he'd never seen before, and was determined to take advantage of it as long as it lasted. He sent her to the store for supplies. Batteries and bread and bottled water and peanut butter and protein bars and hell, might as well get some liquor, too.

Liquor never went to waste, after all, and it didn't spoil.

She came home hours later, complaining about how crazy the Walmart had been, everyone talking about evacuating and the city being destroyed, whining the way she always did when she didn't get her way.

"You know they say that every time," he'd replied, sure of himself, smug he'd held firm and not given in, cracking open a beer and flipping away from the Weather Channel with its constant predictions of doom and aerial views of the traffic snarl on the highways out of town. He found a baseball game and relaxed in his easy chair.

Probably no work on Monday, he'd thought as she clattered around in the kitchen angrily, muttering to herself, *so might as well kick back and have a nice little mini-vacation.*

Some mini-vacation this had turned out to be.

The sun usually set around nine in the late summer, didn't it?

His watch was down on the first floor, under the water. The power had been off before the nasty filthy dirty murdering water had started filling up the house, drowning everything as far as the eye could see. Days, time, had all lost all meaning for him. The only thing that mattered was night or day. He didn't sleep well—could anyone under the heavy hot wet blanket of humidity?

He didn't really care anymore. Nothing really mattered other than the sun was going down and his skin would have some blessed relief.

And he would hear her again, whispering.

We need to go, Mike. We can't stay here.

Every time the sun went down. Every time it got dark.

It's a big storm. At least the power will go out and do you want to be here without the a/c?

Sometimes he thought he might just be going insane.

If he wasn't already, that was.

He wasn't sure of anything anymore.

We can stay with my sister in Houston, we don't even have to pay for a motel, Mike, can't we go, please?

The water lapped against the side of the house.

Water, water, everywhere.

Through the attic door into the downstairs, he could see things floating when he looked. Furniture, books, cushions, once even the dresser was there.

He hadn't seen her down there in a while.

He was always afraid he'd look down and see her face, floating just below the surface, her eyes staring at him.

Should have closed her eyes.

He wasn't sure where she was and he didn't care.

Sometimes he would see her, walking on the surface of the oily water, pointing her finger at him, complaining, whispering, *we should have left, I wanted to go, this is all your fault, you know, like everything is always your fault you can never do anything right this is why I never listened to you...*

And he would wake from his fevered sleep, shivering even though it was so hot, even though the air was so damp and heavy and warm it just pressed down on him until he thought his bones might break.

His lips were so damned chapped. His skin was red and hurt, blisters here and there on the peeling baked skin. He wanted water to drink, something to eat besides chips and crackers and peanut butter and bread. He wanted off the roof. He wanted a bed. He wanted to be away from New Orleans, it didn't matter where as long as it was far away from the drowned city. Sometimes he wondered if the entire world was underwater, that it wasn't just New Orleans that drowned.

Someone would come, he knew it. He just had to hold on, stay alive no matter how horrible it got. He wouldn't die on the damned roof of the house he'd never liked in the first fucking place.

She'd wanted the house. Once she saw it when they were

driving around looking, this was the house she wanted, even though it was on the wrong side of the Industrial Canal, even though it was in the Ninth Ward. "It spoke to me," she'd insisted, "and it's cheap! We can fix it up ourselves. It'll be perfect!"

He'd given into her, even though he didn't want to live down here. She was right about the price—it was less than they'd been thinking they'd spend, and the monthly mortgage payments were a lot more affordable than any of the other houses they'd looked at. It wasn't until later, when they'd moved in, that it even occurred to him that it was the only place they'd looked at in the Ninth Ward. When he brought it up to her, she'd admitted she'd found it on her own and fallen in love with it, colluded with the Realtor to get him to see it.

They'd worked on him until he'd given in.

It wasn't the last time she'd gotten her way.

We need to go, Mike. It won't be safe here. I'm scared.

She always got her way, didn't she?

Not this last time.

Which was why he was up on the roof. Because just once he didn't want her to get her way, wanted to stand up for himself and not give in for once, put his foot down for good and MEAN it.

So, really, in a way, it was her fault.

And if someone did finally come, if someone ever did come to rescue him, he was never coming back to this godforsaken place.

Because she would be here, waiting for him. She would never leave him alone, not as long as he was here, even if the house was bulldozed and he built a new one.

Mike, we have to go, it's scary, it's a big storm, we've got to go.

He lowered himself back down through the hole in the roof, carefully avoiding the jagged edges of the beams he'd hacked through with the ax to make the hole in the roof, so he could get out there, out of that suffocating attic, away from the rising water. He switched on the flashlight, looking for the liquor, and saw there was actually another bottle of the red wine after all—it had rolled off to the side, and he hadn't noticed before. There was no need to switch to tequila just yet. He fought with the corkscrew, chewing the cork up, little flakes floating down into the wine but he didn't care, he could always spit them out, and took a slug out from it. The sourness made him wince but it was wet, and that was all that mattered.

He heard a splash.

That wasn't from outside.

The trap door to the lower level was open, a large rectangle of dark with the long shadows creeping across the floor.

He took a deep breath and backed away, not losing his sweaty grip on the green bottle. He'd closed it before he went back out on the roof, hadn't he?

He couldn't remember.

Hadn't he decided to close it, in case he saw her down there in the water again?

He could hear his heart beating.

He focused on keeping his breathing even, taking deep breaths, ignoring the rising fear creeping up his spine.

I just forgot to close it, is all, I meant to close it but maybe it didn't latch, that's all there is to it, just close it now. She couldn't have gotten up here. I'd have heard her.

She's dead, you idiot.

But that wouldn't stop her, would it?

Just close the damned door. All that's down there is water. You're making yourself crazy. She's dead, dead, dead. Just close the door and you won't have to worry about her.

But he couldn't move, wouldn't move, he kept standing there and staring and trying to remember if he'd closed it or not. He would swear that he did, but he wasn't sure of anything anymore. The heat, the humidity, the damned bugs and the sun and the monotony, the way everything kept changing in his mind, the way he couldn't remember how long he'd been up on the damned roof, how long it had been since the water rose, since he'd climbed up the damned ladder to the attic, since he'd taken the hatchet and chopped his way out to the roof.

The shadows were getting longer. Soon it would be completely dark.

Mike, we have to go really, it's a big storm and what will happen to us if the levees fail?

"Shut up shut up SHUT UP!" he yelled, or tried to, but all that came out of his sore and parched throat was a croak.

He took a step forward, swallowed, and took another.

One after another until he was standing next to the dark opening, looking down into the flooded house.

She wasn't there.

Shaking now, he reached for the flashlight and flicked it on, pointing it with trembling hands into the darkness.

The oily dark water reflected the light back up at him, the filthy water swirling around in what used to be his bedroom.

Their bedroom.

He closed his eyes and said a prayer before opening his eyes again.

No, she still wasn't there.

The last time he'd looked down and seen her—when was that? It didn't matter, it was after the water came and he'd gone up to the roof—she was still there, face up floating in the water, her dark hair fanned out in the filthy water, eyes wide open and staring up at him accusingly.

You killed me. We should have left, but we stayed and you killed me.

He knew he couldn't really hear her, she was just in his head, but still—he kept the light shining down there, swinging back and forth. He heard another splash somewhere down there—maybe it was a gator? There wasn't any telling what was down in that water.

During the day, he could see the river levee in the distance—maybe it had held, but there was no telling where the water had come from. That didn't matter anyway. All that mattered was that it was there.

So maybe…if the bayous and canals or even the swamps had filled with water, it wasn't out of the question there could be gators in the water-filled city.

But wouldn't he have heard something if a gator had gotten her? Some loud splashing or something?

She's dead so she couldn't fight it but still a gator wouldn't have been able to get her underwater without making some noise?

He'd seen snakes a couple of times, making S curves to move forward in the water outside, but not inside the house.

The house.

What was left of the house.

The plasterboard was probably dissolving from the wet, and there was no mistaking the smell of wet, rotting wood. Hell, black mold was an issue even when the house wasn't underwater—how many times had he had to climb a ladder to wipe down the ceiling around the air-conditioning vents with bleach to kill it?

Yeah, this house had been a good investment.

Even if the water somehow got pumped out—and it didn't look

like that was going to happen any time soon—the house was ruined. It would take a lot of money to make it habitable again.

Maybe this time New Orleans would be left to drown.

He turned off the flashlight and backed away from the hole. He took another slug of the hot, cloyingly sweet wine.

She'd wanted to evacuate Sunday morning when the Weather Channel and all the weather broadcasters had gone into full-scale panic mode. "The mother of all storms," the mayor had called it. He just shook his head at her fears, her complaints, his mind was made up and that was that. "They say this every time," he'd scoffed at her, "remember Ivan? Georges? I can't even remember how many times they said it was the end. If you're so damned scared, *you* go. I'm staying put."

She wouldn't go by herself. He knew that.

And why get in the damned truck and be stuck in stop-and-go traffic, eight hours to go the seventy stinking miles to Baton Rouge just to hole up in a hotel somewhere that jacked up their room rates to gouge the evacuees only to have the stupid storm turn east like they always did at the last minute and New Orleans would be fine.

Yeah, no way.

They weren't going anywhere.

They'd lost power sometime in the early morning before the full fury of the storm came, and when it did come, it wasn't that bad. Howling winds and crashes outside, sometimes the house itself shook, but then, after what seemed like an eternity, it was over.

It was over and they'd survived.

He'd gone outside. Some tree branches were down, debris everywhere he looked, a big live oak down the street had been uprooted and smashed through a house. Everyone else was gone, evacuated, holed up in a hotel or shelter somewhere west on I-10.

They had a few hours before the house started filling up with water.

He'd lost his temper when she started panicking. He just meant to slap her but he hadn't meant to slap her so hard, it was an accident, she slipped in the water and hit her head on the table and went limp, and before he knew it the house was filling up with water and she was dead and he had to get up into the attic, had to make sure food and liquid was up there—

He reached over and looked down into the darkness. He shone

the light down, his heart pumping, as he waved the beam of light around.

Nothing but floating furniture.

No sign of her.

He heard something.

Was that an outboard motor?

Bottle of hot wine still in one hand, he tucked the flashlight into the waistband of his shorts and climbed back out onto the roof.

It was definitely an outboard motor, and getting closer from the sound of it.

The flashlight dimmed in his hand and went out.

Swearing, he shook it as he tried to yell, but his vocal cords were too fried, his throat too raw.

Miracle of miracles, the flashlight came back on, and he started waving it in the direction the motor sound was coming from.

Oh please God oh please God oh please God

He was almost blinded as a strong spotlight shone in his eyes.

"Hey there," a voice called as the motor idled, close by, near enough for him to see if not for the damned spots in front of his eyes. But as the bright red shapes began to fade, he could see someone swinging up onto the roof, and heard footsteps, and something cold and icy and wet was put in his hands. He almost wept, it felt so good, the cold against his hot skin. "Have some water, man. My name is Pete LaPierre, me and some buddies came down from Breaux Bridge to rescue some people—they told us we couldn't and we thought, damned if we don't have our own boat, all we need is some water to put it in and here we are."

He twisted the cap off the water and poured some of it down, the coldness stinging his throat. He dropped the wine bottle he'd forgotten, heard it hit the roof and roll down the side and splash when it hit the water. He didn't care, this cold water was like he'd died and gone to heaven, he just wanted to cry—

"Are you the only one here? No one else around here, down in the attic? You must have been pretty lonesome."

He took another drink of the water, slow and steady, and felt a cramp forming in his stomach—*too much cold too fast*—and he breathed in and out for a moment, waiting for the cramp to pass, pressing the cold plastic bottle against the hot skin of his forehead.

He shook his head no.

"Come on, then, let's get you out of here." Pete LaPierre clapped him on the back, and he followed him down the side of the roof and dropped down over the side into the boat. It wasn't much, just a fishing boat with an outboard motor and a large cooler filled with ice and water and beer and—

"You need you a hot shower," Pete said, and he revved the motor, steering the boat away from the little house and away through the dark night, using the spotlight to make sure there was nothing beneath the surface.

He looked back at the house.

He might never ever see it again.

He slumped down in the boat and took another drink of water.

Someone was pressing a sandwich on him, one of Pete's buddies, but he just waved it away.

They might not ever find her.

He exhaled, and watched the stars pass by overhead.

THE EMAIL ALWAYS PINGS TWICE

Y‌ou always say that, don't you?" Her mother's voice on the phone grated on Emily Hudson's nerves the way it always did. "You never listen to me, and that's why you *always* get in trouble. You moved in with this guy way too fast. You don't really know anything about this guy. He could be a *serial killer* for all you know."

Emily closed her eyes and could see the triumphant smirk on her mother's face. Even though she knew she shouldn't engage, didn't want to, wasn't going to, she heard the words coming out of her mouth. "Yes, Mom, you're right, as always. I'm a complete idiot—it's a wonder I can tie my shoelaces. Of course Joey's a serial killer—I just didn't know how to break it to you before. Thank you *so much* for giving me the chance to come clean." She closed her eyes and swore at herself, *idiot—why do you do that?* Her voice shook a little bit as she tried to save herself. "Really, Mom, would it kill you to be supportive just this once?"

She bit her lower lip, thinking, *and here we go.*

Sure enough, she heard the sharp intake of breath, followed by the exact same words in the injured tone Emily had been hearing as long as she could remember, that she sometimes heard in her sleep, "That's right, Emily, I'm a bad mother because I worry about my child. Why, I'm just about the worst mother who ever lived. Everything is *my* fault, isn't it? How have you managed to put up with me all of these years?"

Emily pressed her index fingers to her temples as the headache started.

"Just like it was my fault you were fat," her mother was saying. It was the same old song, the same old lyrics, the same old harmony. Over and over on an endless loop, her entire life—it was even one of her earliest memories. *Mom's Greatest Hits*, featuring the chart-topping "Everything's My Fault Because I'm Such a Bad Mother."

She stopped listening, tuning out the voice in her ear like she always did. She took some deep breaths and watched a squirrel run along the side fence through the kitchen window. It was late afternoon and starting to get dark out. The crepe myrtles on the other side of the fence were swaying in the wind. A thunderstorm was on its way—there were already tornado watches on the north shore and the west bank.

Yet on and on her mother's voice droned in her ear.

Don't engage her again, just wait till she stops talking, Emily told herself, *otherwise she'll just keep going. And maybe, just maybe, someday I'll learn not to set her off.*

Her sister Teresa no longer spoke to their mother—and on the rare occasions she spoke to Emily, urged her to cut her off, too.

And, really, would that be such a bad thing?

She seized the chance to take back control of the conversation when her mother paused for breath. "Mom, you're being unfair and you know it," she said, sitting down at the kitchen table, drumming her fingertips on the table top. "You haven't even met Joe yet." *Nor are you likely to anytime in the near future if this is how you're going to be,* she added to herself. *And Joe's definitely a keeper—I'm not going to let her fuck this up for me. Not this time. This time is going to work, and it's not going to be like last time.*

"I just worry about you. I mean, I don't want you to make the same mistakes—"

Emily cut her off before she could get going again. "Really, Mom, I'm okay. Joe's really good to me, he's a good guy—he really is, Mom."

"But what do you *really* know about this guy?" Her mother persisted, like she always did. Once she sank her teeth into something, she was worse than a dog with a fresh steak bone. "You met him what? Three months ago? And already you're living with him? That's just a recipe for disaster." The unspoken word *again* hung in the silence.

"Oh, look at the time!" Emily said, forcing enthusiasm into her voice. "Okay, Mom, I have to go. I'll call you in a few days. Love you." She clicked the phone off without waiting for a response. She closed her eyes and took a deep breath, leaning against the counter and putting the phone down. *She means well,* Emily told herself, like she had so many times before.

I don't know why she can't just be happy for me, Emily thought, rubbing her temples and willing the slight headache to go away. *She always expects the worst, always. But being married to Dad as long as she was would make anyone like that, I guess.*

She pushed thoughts of her father out of her mind before they stirred up any memories, and poured herself another cup of coffee. The house was silent other than the rustling of the wind. The silence was kind of nice. She liked quiet, had forgotten how peaceful silence could be. She sat down at the table and looked out the window. A squirrel sat up on his back legs on the top of the fence and stared at her, whiskers twitching.

Moving in with Joe was the right thing, she reminded herself, *and Mom is wrong about him. And she didn't drive me to Twinkies this time.*

That made her smile.

Her cell phone pinged, and a few seconds later so did her laptop.

It's probably spam, she told herself, taking another sip of her coffee and glaring at the offending electronics. The only emails she ever got were work-related. She'd taken a few days off to finish unpacking and get settled. Joe was on a sales trip through northern Louisiana and wouldn't be back home until late tonight—he wanted her to have a few days in the house by herself, "to get used to it, so it'll start feeling like home to you." *And it's working,* she thought, *it's such a lovely house.* She looked back out the window. The squirrel was gone, but a couple of birds were there now.

Her eyes came back to where her laptop and her phone sat on the table.

She reached for her laptop and opened it.

You really need to stop being so anal about email, she reminded herself with a little shake of her head as she touched the space bar, waking the computer up. *Hi, my name is Emily Hudson and I have a problem. I am obsessive compulsive about email.* She always tried to keep her in-box empty.

She rolled her eyes at herself as her email program opened. She frowned—the sender was clearly a spambot; the return address was a Yahoo account, but all numbers. She moved the cursor to the Delete box but read the subject line, and she froze.

Joey Valletta isn't who you think he is.

She bit her lip. *What the hell?* She put her fingertip back down on the touch pad, ready to click and delete it—but hesitated again.

You're being silly. Go ahead and open it, read the email. It's nothing—someone just trying to cause trouble, like an ex-girlfriend or something.

Joey had warned her about an ex who might be a problem. She hadn't taken the breakup well and he'd finally had to get a restraining order against her—but that was back when he lived in Baton Rouge. He'd been living in this house in New Orleans for almost six months now. When he'd told her about the restraining order, she'd wondered if that was why he'd left Baton Rouge, but hadn't asked.

You should go ahead and read it, if it is from her—Joey should know. Maybe I'll need to get a restraining order, too. But how—how did she get my email address?

Goose bumps rose on her arms and she shivered. She glanced back out the window.

You're being silly, no one can see in—the fence is too high. If you can't see their windows they can't see yours.

It was going to take getting used to not having any curtains or blinds on the kitchen windows. The glass was tinted, so the UV rays were blocked, Joey had said. "That way the kitchen can have lots of natural light but not get overheated by the sun." The back wall was all glass, looking out onto the wooden deck where the hot tub was.

She bit her lower lip and stared back at the computer screen.

I should just save it for Joey, let him deal with it. If it's her—better to let him deal with it, right? It's probably really ugly and all it's going to do is upset you.

Conflict had always made her sick to her stomach.

When her parents would fight when she was a little girl, she got physically ill every time. When other kids at school had teased her or mocked her, she got away from them as quickly as she could—especially after what happened to her father.

She pushed her chair back and stood up. She took a deep breath and closed her laptop. *I can do this,* she told herself as she walked back into the living room. Moving boxes were stacked around the furniture. She picked up a box cutter and sliced the tape open on a box labeled *books.* She smiled as she looked down at the yellow spines staring back up at her. Her Nancy Drew collection was the only thing she had left from her childhood, and those yellow spines were like old friends. She placed *The Secret of the Old Clock* on the top shelf of the bookcase. Joey had bought several bookcases for the living room, clearing a space for them before she'd moved in. He was thoughtful that way—he'd bought an armoire for his clothes so she could have the entire closet, bought a bigger dresser and left three drawers for her, and condensed his things in the bathroom down to a small section of the counter. This type of consideration, this kindness without having to think about it, was one of the reasons she'd fallen so deeply in love with him so quickly. Like her mother, her best friend Allison thought they were moving too fast—*you haven't even known him six months*—but she dismissed Allison's concerns as plain old jealousy. Allison had been dating her guy for three years, after all, and was still waiting for a wedding ring—a ring Emily was sure wasn't going to be coming along any time soon.

If ever.

She started carefully setting the books on the shelves in order, one at a time, looking at the cover before lining it up with the others on the top shelf. The yellow spines, lined up perfectly, had always meant home to her.

In the kitchen, she heard her phone and computer ping again.

She rolled her eyes and focused on the job at hand—but only managed to get volumes 20–25 on the shelf before giving in to her compulsion. She walked back into the kitchen, picked up her phone, and saw there was a new email in her in-box—from the same series of numbers.

Enough, even if it is the psycho girlfriend, enough is enough.

She was about to click on the new one so she could delete it when she read the subject line.

Joey Valletta killed my sister.

She dropped the phone. It bounced off the counter and hit the floor.

She picked it up with shaking hands and opened her laptop.

She sat down at the table. The wind was blowing even stronger and it was really getting dark outside. Her heart was beating so loud she could hear it in her ears, could feel the skin on her face getting warmer.

She clicked on the second email—the one with the horrible subject line.

Look I don't have anything against you I don't even know you but I think you should know you're living with a killer Joey Valletta killed my sister but he went by Joey Valenzuela then. You can do a Google search for Joey Valenzuela Tracy Goodwin and see what comes up. I thought you should know it's my Christian duty to tell. You need to know.

She felt numbness spreading through her mind, the corners of her vision going gray as she stared at the ugly words on her computer screen. She swallowed. *No, that can't be true. She's crazy, whoever this woman is, she's crazy. Delete it and forget about it.*

Yet somehow, she couldn't bring herself to do it—or to open the original email.

Her mind was racing. She wanted a Twinkie, a candy bar, something sweet, anything really. But there wasn't anything like that in the house.

There's a mom-and-pop grocery on the corner.

"No," she said out loud, squaring her shoulders and taking a deep breath. "I don't need sugar or chocolate or anything. I'm a strong woman and I can handle this without sweets. I don't need sweets." She nodded. Feeling better, she opened her web browser and typed the names in. She frowned at the screen. *Go ahead, click the Search button. Do it, prove this bitch wrong.*

Her cell phone rang and she jumped with a slight cry. She swallowed and laughed at herself—*oh, yes, Emily, you're really handling this well.* She shook her head and picked up the phone. Joey's face smiled up at her from the screen. She moved the tip of her index finger along the Answer bar and said, "Hello, baby."

"How's the unpacking going?" he asked.

The sound of his voice was so reassuring that she cursed herself for being such a fool. It was a crank email, that's all—and she'd been stupid for letting it get under her skin that way.

Joey wasn't a killer, he was the sweetest man on earth—and she was damned lucky to have him.

"I'm almost done and making myself completely at home." She laughed. "I warned you I was going to take over your house. How's the trip going?"

"Good." She could almost see him beaming. "I've picked up a couple of new clients, and the new drug—everyone's interested." Joey worked as a sales rep for a drug company, which took him out of town fairly regularly. That was how they'd met, actually—he'd come to the clinic where she worked. She hadn't been in a place emotionally where she wanted to date anyone—all she wanted to do was go to work and go home. She'd had enough of that—and now that she'd lost the weight and had gotten back control of her weight—*and her life*—again, the last thing she needed was to get involved with some other man. But Joey began wearing her down— and now, a little over three months after she'd agreed to go out with him the first time, she was moving into his house on Constance Street. "Anyway, I had a bit of a break and wanted to check in with you."

"I'm just missing you," she replied, "and wishing you were coming home sooner."

He made a kissing noise. "I'll be home later this evening," he said. "But I really do wish I was there already with you. I love you, Emily."

"I love you, too," she said, but he'd hung up before she finished saying it.

She put her phone down and smiled at it. *I never thought I'd fall in love again*, she thought, sitting down at the table. The last of the afternoon light was fading. *But this? This is almost too perfect. A beautiful house, a great guy—who would have ever thought I'd end up like this? Especially after—*

She closed her eyes and chewed her lower lip, forcing that thought behind a door in her mind. Once the door was shut and sensibly locked, she opened her eyes with a smile.

The names she'd typed into the search engine stared back at her on the laptop's screen.

Joey Valenzuela Tracy Goodwin

Don't do it, she told herself. *Whoever's emailing you is just trying to cause trouble. Just walk away, don't look this up. You deserve to be happy, remember? You deserve this.*

A voice that sounded remarkably similar to her mother's answered.

Sure, just turn a blind eye, don't wonder, don't find out anything about him you don't want to know. Just like the last time, right? Isn't that how you do things, Emily? Turn a blind eye to what's right in front of your face? And then you have no one to blame but yourself when it all goes south. Isn't that right? How much trouble would you have been saved if you'd just—

"Shut up," she whispered, her lower lip quivering just a little bit.

Her stomach growled.

She got up and walked away from the computer. She poured herself another cup of coffee and drank it. The caffeine always helped with the hunger pains, even though her mind was racing through images of cheesecake slices and chocolate bars, donuts and Twinkies and cupcakes.

Walking away from it won't make it go away, the voice taunted. *Your mother's right, you deserve what you get.*

"Fuck you, Mother," she said out loud, and resolutely sat down at the kitchen table again.

She clicked on the Search button, not caring if she would regret it.

The first link was to an article in the *Shreveport Times.* The headline simply read "Boyfriend Wanted for Questioning in Murder of Bossier City Woman."

Her heart climbed up into her throat, but she couldn't stop now. Pandora's box was open. She clicked on the link.

> *Police are looking to talk to the boyfriend of murder victim Tracy Goodwin. Goodwin's body was found in a country ditch, heavily mutilated, yesterday afternoon by some hikers.*
>
> *Goodwin, 27, was reported missing by her sister, Melanie Mathews, just hours before the hikers made their grisly discovery in the countryside. Goodwin was last seen by her sister when the two women had lunch together two days earlier.*
>
> *Goodwin was involved with Joey Valenzuela, a drug company rep from Houston...*

Emily got up and somehow walked through the house to the front door. She opened it and sat down in the swing on the front porch. She clutched her hands together in her lap and started swinging back and forth. The neighborhood was still and the streetlights were coming on. A car drove by but she didn't look up.

It isn't him, she told herself, over and over again. *Sure, the name is similar, and the job is the same, but he would have had to change his name and that's not so easy to do, why would he do that, it's the ex-girlfriend, he said she was crazy, you don't get restraining orders against sane people, so that must be it, she's just trying to cause trouble, and the name similarity, that's what gave her the idea to pull this bullshit.*

She took a couple of deep breaths and stood up. "You aren't going to cause trouble for us, bitch," she whispered under her breath. "I won't let you have that kind of power over us."

The wind was picking up a little, and the air was heavy with moisture. There was definitely a storm on the way.

She went back inside. She sat down at the table, and with a steady finger she scrolled the page down till she saw the pictures that ran with the article.

Tracy Goodwin had been a pretty girl. The photograph looked like it had been taken at one of those places in a mall, where someone would do your hair and makeup, put you in a sexy outfit and try to make you look glamorous. She had blond hair and a pert nose, full lips and a heart-shaped face ending in a pointy chin.

Emily swallowed. Joey Valenzuela was definitely the man she knew as Joey Valletta. That was his smile, his hair, the carefree look he always had on his handsome face.

Her hand shook as she clicked on the mouse to close the window.

He'd *lied* to her.

What else has he lied to me about?

"Just like before," she whispered without thinking, and her stomach clenched. She managed to make it to the kitchen sink before the hot coffee came spewing out of her. She stood there, bent over the sink, until her stomach stopped heaving. She turned on the water and washed her face, rinsed out her mouth.

She took a deep breath and walked into the room Joey used as his office. His computer sat there on the pristinely organized and clean desk.

Don't do it, she told herself as she sat down at the desk and pressed the button turning on his computer, *once you do this there's no turning back.*

The password box opened on the screen.

She stared at it for a few moments, her emotions warring inside her.

That's it, I don't know his password, turn off his damned computer and delete those emails, he's not a killer, not my Joey.

She closed her eyes and remembered. She could see it as

clearly as if it were happening at that very moment. Joey was sitting behind his desk while she stood in the doorway watching. He was smiling at her as he booted up his computer. He wasn't wearing a shirt, his strongly muscled upper body lightly dusted with curly black hairs.

She placed her fingers on the keyboard and slowly mimicked the movement she remembered of Joey's fingers and with her right pinkie hit the Enter key.

She opened her eyes and watched as the computer booted up and came to life rapidly in front of her.

Sign off, shut the computer down and forget about it, you don't want to do this, you don't even know what you're looking for.

There was a folder on the desktop labeled JOEY. She clicked it open, and a list of folders opened before her.

She scrolled down.

Her blood froze for a moment, and a cry came out of her mouth.

There was a folder named TRACY.

No, it's not the same thing, it's just a coincidence, it's not too late, shut the computer down and get out of here.

She opened it. It was all JPEG and PDF files, all named with series of numbers. She pulled her hand away from the mouse like she was burned. But the numbers urged her on, like they were saying *Click on me, you know you want to, what will it hurt, click me open, you'll wonder.*

She took a deep breath and planted both hands on the desk. She pushed and the desk chair rolled backward. She got up and walked out of the office, hesitating at the door.

I have to trust him.

Easier said than done.

Remember what happened the last time you trusted a man?

"Shut up," she whispered.

You don't get a happily ever after, the voice whispered, *women like you don't. Why do you think you even deserve one?*

"Shut up," she said aloud, more firmly this time, focusing and forcing the voice out of her mind. Her therapist didn't think it a coincidence the voice sounded like her mother.

But she had to know. She couldn't pretend there wasn't a file folder on his computer named TRACY. Maybe the emails were a prank, and nothing more. But the truth was she had to find out; otherwise that voice would always come back the way it always did.

And you know what happens when the voice comes back.

Resolutely she walked back over to the desk and sat back down. She clicked on the folder again and opened the first JPEG file.

The smiling face she was looking at was definitely the same girl from the online article she'd found.

But you knew that already, didn't you, Emily?

She was smiling at the camera. Her hair was wet, and drops of water glistened on her tan skin. She was wearing a blue bikini, and in the background the clear blue water of a swimming pool glittered in the sun. She was holding a sweating bottle of beer. She looked like she didn't have a care in the world.

Emily swallowed and clicked on the next picture.

They were all similar. Tracy was always by herself in the photos but was always smiling. Sometimes she was dressed more formally, other times more casually. She scrutinized each picture, unaware of how much time she was spending on each one until she reached the final one.

When it opened, she recoiled and pushed instinctively with her feet.

The chair rolled back and didn't stop till she hit the wall with a low thud.

She tried to look away, told herself to stop looking, but she couldn't.

The picture on the computer screen kept drawing her back, as repulsive as it was.

Tracy was naked, her body bruised and bleeding, a gag in her mouth, her arms and legs bound together. She was stretched across a bed, and her eyes were absolutely terrified.

There's an explanation for this, there has to be, maybe the person who killed her sent this to him.

And her mother's voice: *Sure, that's why he kept it in a folder with the nice pictures of her. Because that's just what people do, Emily, right? Is that what YOU did?*

She closed the program, shut the computer down, and walked back out of the office. She could see the crepe myrtles along the fence bending in the wind. It was very dark outside, and as she watched, the rain started coming down.

She felt like she'd been punched in the stomach or had tossed back too much tequila in a short period of time. Dazed and confused, sickened and horrified, she felt a weird numbness as her mind leapfrogged from one thought to another without stopping, and she—

She didn't know what to do.

She somehow managed to get down the hallway into the kitchen. There were no sweets in the house, no candy bars, no snacks, no nothing—she wouldn't allow them, and Joey—

the murderer

—had agreed with her, he wanted to try to live a healthier lifestyle and eat better, at least that was what he told her.

She opened the cabinet where he—*they*—kept the liquor and grabbed a bottle of Bombay Sapphire. She poured herself a glass of gin with a few ice cubes and took a long belt. Her heart was beating so loudly she could hear it, and her hands shook as she put the glass back down on the counter.

You've got to get out of here, you don't want to go through that again, you don't DESERVE to have to go through that all over again, get out, just grab your things and go, you can come back for the rest—

Her computer and her phone both dinged again within seconds of each other, and she barked out a half scream.

She finished the gin left in the glass and refilled it before sitting down at the table and touching the space bar. The rain was beating against the windows, wet leaves from the crepe myrtles blowing against the glass and sticking. The laptop screen came to life again, and sure enough, there was yet another email from the string of numbers. The subject line on this one was *IMPORTANT!!!*

She clicked it open.

I know you don't know me from adam but I am worried about you any woman who gets involved with Joey is in danger from him I know you don't believe me but if you googled Tracy Goodwin you found out what he did to my sister they couldn't prove anything so he got away with it he moved to New Orleans and changed his last name it's not the first time he's done it google Pamela Marshall in Lake Charles and you'll see what I mean.

Her hand shaking, she opened another tab and went to Google; she typed in the name and hit Return.

It wasn't the first link that came up—it had to be one halfway down the results page.

Lake Charles authorities are looking for elementary school teacher Pamela Marshall, 27, reported missing by her live-in boyfriend, Joey Valentine...

There was a picture of Pamela Marshall. She was blond and smiling at the camera, her bangs hanging wistfully over her forehead, her smile not quite reaching the eyes. She didn't look like Tracy Goodwin other than the shape of her face, and the hair, and maybe the innocent look in her eyes.

Joey Valletta.

Joey Valenzuela.

Joey Valentine.

She closed the laptop and staggered into the bathroom just off the kitchen. She looked at herself in the mirror.

Blond hair, blue eyes, a heart-shaped face.

He certainly runs to type—but then they always do, don't they?

She splashed more water on her face, her hands trembling. The rain was coming down harder now, and she shivered as a blast of wind shook the house.

She took a deep breath and pulled herself together.

She walked back out into the kitchen and watched the sheets of rain beating against the windows. The gin bottle still sat on the counter. She put it back in the cabinet, cursing at herself for being stupid enough to drink some.

She froze as she heard the front door open.

"Emily, honey?" Joey called. There was the sound of his suitcase hitting the hardwood floor. "Are you home, honey?"

Act natural. She forced a smile on her face and ran lightly on her bare feet to the front of the house. She closed her eyes and threw her arms around him, kissing his cheek even though her skin crawled at his touch. He smelled slightly of peppermint and cologne. "What are you doing home so early? I would have made dinner."

He squeezed her. "You sounded weird on the phone, so I

canceled the rest and drove home..." He shrugged. He smiled. "I didn't like the thought of you being here lonely. Is everything okay?"

You mean, besides the fact that the man I just moved in with is a serial killer with a thing for blondes?

"Just lonely," she replied, amazed at how calm her voice sounded. "Well, that's not entirely true. I got some weird emails today—but I mean, they were probably from that crazy ex of yours, like you told me, but still." She managed to keep smiling at him, even though all she wanted to do was run away as fast as she could.

"Geez, Emily, I told you to delete those without reading them." He let go of her and pried her arms from around his neck. "All she wants to do is upset you. Why would you read that shit?"

"I know." She turned her back to him so he couldn't see her face, and walked back over to the box of books. She grabbed a handful and placed them on the shelf. "I wanted to see what she would actually say, Joey. I'm sorry—from now on I'll just delete them, I promise." She placed another handful of the yellow-spined books on the shelf. She frowned. Number 28 was missing. She turned back around and forced another smile on her face. "It didn't really upset me, Joey, so don't worry about that. The language was just—well, a shock. That's all."

His eyes narrowed. "And that's all? What did she say?"

"Oh, she"—*careful now, girl, be careful*—"just was nasty. You don't really want to know. Besides, I deleted them and now I know what to expect. From now on, I'll just delete them unread, I promise."

"Okay." He picked his suitcase up again, yawning. "I think I'm going to take a long, hot bath." He winked at her. "You want to join me?"

She smiled. "Get the water ready." Emily turned back to the box, frowning. *Where is Number 28?* "I'll be there as soon as I finish this box."

She swallowed as she heard him walking through the house, the sound of his suitcase being set down in the—*their*—bedroom, and the sound of water running in the bathtub.

You know what you have to do. You've done it before.

"That was different," she whispered as she set another six books on the shelf.

Not really. He wanted to kill you, too, didn't he? Just like your father.

She could hear Joey whistling in the bathroom, the water still flowing into the tub.

I don't want to think about that now.

The water ceased. "Come on, honey, the water's ready," Joey yelled.

She put some more books out on the shelf. At the very bottom of the spine of *The Clue in the Crossword Cipher* was a tiny, almost imperceptible brown spot. She licked the tip of her finger and rubbed it until it disappeared. She smiled at the book and walked into the bedroom. She could see through the bathroom door—Joey was already in the massive bathtub. She could see his strong, powerful, hairy arm draped over the side. She walked across the bedroom.

Thunder shook the house—*just like before, just like with her father and with—*

She walked into the bathroom. The tub was full of suds, but Joey was leaning against the end with his eyes closed. His shoulders were out of the water, and some suds were clinging to the bottom of his left ear. The dark olive skin was smooth, the cleft in his chin she loved so much marred by a little scab from his razor just below it.

He opened his eyes with a lazy smile that quickly faded as his eyes opened wider. "Emily, don't—" he half-shouted as she tossed the hair dryer into the bathwater.

She closed her eyes until it was all over, and when all the sound had faded again and the only thing she could hear was the rain hitting against the house, she opened them.

Joey's eyes were open and staring.

She took a deep breath and walked back into the kitchen. She picked up her cell phone and dialed a number.

"Mama? You were right again. But I took care of it."

There was silence on the other end. And then, "You remembered to make it look like an accident?"

"Yes, Mama."

"You'd better be calling 9-1-1 then, dear." There was a click on the other end of the line.

Emily took a deep breath and dialed. And while she waited for the operator to answer, she watched the rain splashing against the windows and running down. She put her free hand against the window, and felt sad.

Maybe next time.

KEEPER OF THE FLAME

So what if it was only ten in the morning?

It was also Las Vegas.

Why *not* have a glass of Chardonnay?

It wasn't like she'd be the only one drinking.

Her stomach was still churning from last night's vodka—although it was technically morning when she'd finally stumbled into the elevators marked Habitat. The sun was mere hours from rising in the east, over the mountains she could vaguely see through the window of her room on the twenty-fourth floor of the Flamingo Hotel while collapsing onto the bed still wearing her black sandals, the tight black skirt, and the odd top she'd bought at some chic boutique that looked like an odd assortment and collection of black elastic bandages artfully stretched and strategically arranged over her breasts and shoulders. She'd set her phone to start ringing at nine, so she'd have time to shower—but it was closer to ten when she'd rolled out of bed and glared at her reflection in the mirror, said the hell with it, splashed some water on her face, brushed her teeth, and gone out the door.

Actually, a glass of wine was sounding more and more perfect by the minute.

The blogger who wanted to interview her was meeting her at the patio bar at eleven—so why *not* get a head start? There were even slot machines built into the bar, under glass—it was Las Vegas, for Christ's sake, where weren't there slot machines—so she could throw some money away, drink some white wine, get that hangover firmly chased away before the interviewer showed up so she could be reasonably coherent...maybe he wasn't a blogger, she really couldn't remember what he'd said, it was for either a blog or website or some other kind of nonsense like that.

It wasn't like it was for a real newspaper or a magazine, like in the old days.

She hated all of this new stuff, anyway.

It didn't seem real.

Blogs and e-magazines and e-news. Who cared? She longed for the old days, back when you could make the cover of an industry magazine and take it in to be framed and mounted and then hang it in your living room, when all of your colleagues and contemporaries would see it on the newsstands or get it in the mail and have to give you compliments to cover their own seething jealousy, wondering what you'd done to get the cover. Back when a reviewer actually knew what they were talking about, could parse sentences and paragraphs and themes and character development; when a print review meant *something*.

Now any idiot could log into a website and type out some meaningless, senseless drivel and click Post and it was there forever, badly typed, mixing up *there* and *their* and *they're*, sentences not making sense to anyone with more than a third-grade education, and worst of all, completely missing the point.

They always missed the point.

Thank God, she thought, not for the first time, *Daddy didn't live to see this insanity.*

She glanced down at her reflection in the glass over the slot machine set into the bar. She ordered a glass of Chardonnay without looking up, reaching into her purse for the appropriate credit card (one of the two or three that weren't over the limit already) to fit into the appropriate place to swipe and authorize. Her blond hair, unwashed, hung past her chin almost to her shoulders, but it looked fine. Americans were too obsessed with cleanliness anyway, she thought as she pushed her dark glasses back up her red nose. Her skin was fair, to go with the blond hair, and she'd convinced herself over the years that the perpetual red flush of her nose, cheeks, and chin came from exposure to the sun. She offered that explanation to anyone and everyone, babbling on about lotions not being strong enough to protect her delicate, sensitive skin, and if her teeth were gray and crooked, again, Americans were too obsessed with perfection, and why should she spend money to try to fit into the impossible American beauty standard?

Americans didn't appreciate anything except superficiality, anyway.

Daddy hadn't been a big success in the States, after all, which was why she'd grown up in the UK, born there, her mother from Glasgow, a part-time student and bookseller who'd met him at a signing and swept him off his feet. The British had always appreciated Daddy's genius, even if American readers didn't.

Peasants, really, with their love of writers who were at best typists.

Then again, it was no wonder Daddy had never broken big in the United States after his promising start. After what that horrible editor did with Daddy's third book—well, that bastard had pretty much destroyed Daddy's career in the United States just as he was on the verge of breaking big, becoming a household name, someone who elevated the genre to literature.

Instead, he was practically forgotten in the States.

She took a sip of her Chardonnay and pressed the button to start the slot machine spinning. That was another thing she hated, didn't think was an improvement over the old days—the way slot machines were now all digital. They still made the same sounds they used to when they were mechanical, but it was just canned noise, a simulation intended to replicate the sounds they used to make. She wasn't sure she trusted the digital slot machines the way she had the old ones. She hadn't been to Vegas in—how long had it been? She was fifteen or sixteen, Daddy was still alive, they'd come for a convention—she couldn't remember which one—and she didn't have a fake ID, but Daddy had told her to dress sexy and no one would question her. He was right, they didn't, she just wore a low-cut top and an underwire push-up bra and a short skirt and no one questioned her as she put the money Daddy had given her into the machines and waitresses brought her cocktails whenever she wanted another one. She'd had beginner's luck, too—Daddy had only given her a couple of hundred dollars, and at one point she'd been up several thousand dollars before she'd lost it all at the craps tables. But it had been wonderful not having to ask Daddy for more money…he'd been so proud of how well she'd done…always been so proud.

She was working her way through her third glass of Chardonnay and had almost gone through her third hundred-dollar authorization on her credit card when she heard someone say her name.

"Colleen?"

She pressed the Play button on the slot machine, turned her head, and tilted her dark glasses up so she could get a good look at this blogger or reviewer or whatever he was. He was young— maybe in his early twenties, but to be fair anyone under thirty these days looked like a child to her—with an awful lot of hair, thick and frizzy, framing his round, bespectacled pale face. He looked soft and doughy, like he'd never taken a lick of exercise since getting out of required gym class in high school, earnestness positively radiating off him with his nervous, excited smile and his glasses, which looked to be almost as smudged and dirty as her own. He was wearing what looked like a vintage Mötley Crüe T-shirt from the 1980s—*whatever happened to Vince Neil*, she wondered, when she was a girl she'd lusted after him madly—and long, dirty-looking shorts reaching past his knees in a weird plaid pattern mix of earth tones, browns and oranges and beiges. His white calves were dusted with curly brown hairs, some of them ingrown. He shifted his weight from one foot to the other nervously.

Well, it wasn't *her* job to make him comfortable.

"Jacob?" she replied icily, letting her glasses drop back down to her nose, and turned her attention back to the spinning screens on the bar. Another loss. She bet again, the last few bucks authorized, ignoring him and letting him stand there, staring at her bare shoulder while she watched the screens spin, blurring images of bananas and cherries and apples and God knows what else whirring past her eyes. The wine was kicking in, and she was feeling more like herself again, the headache and the nausea gone and the edges of her mind blunted, softened, sanded down by the cheap wine. Once the whirring stopped and she'd lost again, she slid down off the seat. "Let's sit out on the patio," she said to him over her shoulder, "and get me another glass of Chardonnay."

There weren't many people out on the patio—maybe because it was over ninety degrees and there was a big fire going in the open air fireplace in the direct center. There was a steady stream of people up and down the stairs just on the other side of the low wall where stools were set up for people to sit, young men and women in bathing suits so skimpy there didn't seem much point to them, all in various stages of precancerous tanning. *Young men these days spend too much time on their bodies*, she thought, looking back through the tinted glass, wondering where Jacob was with her wine. The hot, dry air was making her thirsty, wasn't good for her skin, aggravating the rosacea that spread across her cheeks and chin and her nose.

That snooty doctor she'd seen—where was it, it didn't really matter—had insisted to her that alcohol made it worse. She knew what he was really saying, that it wasn't rosacea at all but too many years of too much alcohol.

She hadn't gone back to him, instead found a sympathetic woman who knew just exactly what she was dealing with, who knew how hard it was on a girl to have rosacea, how terrible it was to have everyone think you drank too much and sit in judgment—

"Here you are," he said breathlessly, sitting down across the table from her and placing the glass of wine in front of her. He hadn't gotten anything for himself, and sweat was already beading up on her reddening forehead. He fumbled with his shoulder bag—was there anything worse than a man carrying a purse, because really, that's what it was—and pulled out a pad of paper with a pen clipped to the front. "I can't tell you what this means to me, I've been a fan of your father's ever since I was a kid and first read *The Last Gleaming*—"

"He was particularly proud of that one," she said, cutting him off, remembering that she shouldn't call him *Daddy* in front of this young man, from the blog or website or e-zine or whatever it was called.

She'd made that mistake once, and the article hadn't been kind.

She'd not been sorry when that rag had ceased publication, which was nothing more than they deserved.

Daddy was still alive as long she kept his legacy going, as long as new readers found his books.

He started talking about himself, as she'd known he would, even though she'd tried to make it clear she wasn't interested in his story. They never listened, even when she told them point blank she didn't care. They always told her everything, way more than she cared to know. How they found her father's work, which one was their favorite, why it meant so much to them, and so on and so on until she could almost scream. She knew their stories, she'd heard them all so many times, knew everything there was to know about them once they told her which one of her father's books was their favorite.

Since *The Last Gleaming* was his favorite, she knew Jacob was a loner, someone who grew up feeling unloved and unwanted by his parents, might have had a step-parent who mocked and belittled him constantly, who drew solace from a cruel world by withdrawing into comic books about super-heroes, eventually moving his way into more of an interest in darker fiction. For some boys there was a direct correlation between super-heroes and dark fiction, the two genres caught up in a strange dance of connection, an almost latent misogynistic thing where women were just things, objects of attraction, there only to serve as visual stimulation.

And they would never understand why they couldn't get a date for their prom, why girls just smiled awkwardly when asked for a date and said no.

"So, why do you think your father never achieved the success in this country he enjoyed in Europe?"

There it was, the Holy Grail of questions, tacked on the end of an overlong rumination of why he was such a major fanboy of her dearly departed father. They always asked, every last one of them. They'd never dared ask when he was alive, of course, they only dared after he was gone, when she'd taken it upon herself to keep his memory alive, to maintain his legacy, his brilliant body of work that had influenced so many others who'd come after him, so that his brilliance could continue to inspire and influence future generations of writers, as long as she lived.

"As long as I live," she'd whispered to her mother, dying in that hospital, her skin like tissue paper in Colleen's hand, her mother somehow finding the strength to make sure Colleen knew, that Colleen would keep the flame of her father's genius alive, make sure he would never be forgotten.

She answered Jacob's question automatically, by rote, because it was all part and parcel of the script of her father's life, one she had told so many times she could do it without thinking, the words coming out of her chapped lips as she watched the people beyond Jacob, the plump young woman with the Bride-to-Be sash across her full figure, the plastic penises hanging around her neck on a string, and the cheap tiara on her head smiling at a pair of handsome young men whose board shorts hung from hip bones, what someone back in school had told her was called the "girdle of Venus," deep lines that ran from their hip bones toward the center, disappearing into the tops of their shorts, the chests waxed smooth and tanned, and she couldn't help but think, as she told once again the story of the evil editor at the evil publisher who'd succeeded in destroying her father's career in this country, forcing him into exile in the United Kingdom where he met her mother and rebuilt his life, managing to still get published in North America but never quite getting the respect and success his talent deserved, all because of one editor's jealous and vicious vendetta.

She was getting close to the bottom of her glass, and she was about to order Jacob to get another when he looked at her, confused, and said, "But *why* would David Garrett do that to your father? What did he have to gain? He risked his own career and reputation by ruining your father's book." He shook his head. "And I've never been able to find anyone who could answer that question. I know you weren't born yet when it happened, but why do you think Garrett turned so viciously against your father?"

No one had ever asked her that before, no one had dared question the Gospel According to Colleen Fitzgerald in all the years she'd been telling the story, just as no one had questioned her mother while she was still alive. It was merely taken as truth, just as when Colleen had put the book back together from pieces—well, it wasn't really pieces, was it, no matter what she said in the introduction? She'd really rewritten it, hadn't she, basing her rewrite on things her father had said over the years in interviews, on things he had said to her and her mother while he was drunk, when he was drinking. But no one would want it if Colleen had written it, so she pretended, hadn't she, that she'd found drafts and bits and pieces in his papers, and from that she had pieced the destroyed book back together, written an introduction about her painstaking efforts to rebuild the masterpiece David Garrett had wrecked, cornered a small press publisher at a convention after the estate's agent had no luck finding anyone who wanted the book, and gotten him to publish it and even pay her a pittance in advance...

She gaped at him, her mouth open, as her mind—more addled with wine and last night's vodka than she'd thought—tried to find an answer, couldn't, and finally just said, when the silence was getting too long and maybe a tad awkward, "I don't know. You'd have to ask him."

He nodded, his eyes narrowed in agreement with her. "Well, he's dead, of course."

"Of course." She exhaled carefully, so he couldn't see her relief.

For a moment, she'd forgotten—*need to switch to water, no more wine with this one, he's a little more sharp than I thought he'd be*—but that was right, Garrett had died even before Daddy.

Which was why the story worked, was never questioned.

Maybe there were still people around from back when it happened, back when *Dusk of a Summer Evening* was first published, but they'd never said anything, never called her brazen bluff.

The Gospel According to Colleen Fitzgerald was allowed to stand unchallenged.

She'd told the story so many times she now almost believed it herself, believed the tale of a bitter editor determined to derail the career of a rising star in the crime noir genre.

"No one must ever know," her mother had said, dying, in that hospital bed, the beeps and chirps of all the machinery hooked up to her, "promise me, Colleen. Promise me you'll protect him."

"It's always—it's something I've always wondered about," he stammered, his pale face flushing almost to a red hue to match her own, "I mean, it doesn't make sense. Why would an editor risk his career like that? And Dave Garrett went on to edit a lot more great books before he died."

"He wasn't stable," she heard herself saying, so far away that she might have thought it was someone at another table if she didn't recognize the timbre of her own voice. "Stable people don't kill themselves, you know."

Stable people don't kill themselves.

"Can't we keep it quiet?" her mother, talking again, Colleen sitting in a chair, her arms wrapped around herself, to try to keep herself from shaking, so cold, so cold she felt like she would never be warm again. "Can't we just say it was a heart attack?"

The police, the doctor, both fans of Daddy's, had agreed. He'd clearly done it himself, his toes still lodged in the trigger mechanism, his hands on the barrel of the rifle he'd fit into his mouth. And so the story went out that he'd died suddenly, of a massive heart attack while working on his latest book, dead in front of his typewriter, and no one questioned it, never, but it had been weeks, months, before Colleen could sleep through the night without waking up gasping, her chest heaving, before she could get the image of the blood spatter and the bone and hair and gristle—and the *brains*—all over the wall behind his desk.

There hadn't been a note, but Colleen knew why.

Oh yes, she'd known.

That was why she'd sent Jimmy away once and for all, returned the ring, canceled the engagement. It was her fault he'd done it, unable to bear the things she'd said to him when Daddy had said she couldn't marry Jimmy, couldn't go away.

The last things she'd said to Daddy had been unspeakable, and the moment she walked out of the room he'd gotten the rifle down and put his mouth on the barrel and his toe on the trigger.

No, she couldn't marry Jimmy after that.

She couldn't marry anyone after that.

Jimmy.

Her heart constricted. She hadn't thought about Jimmy in years.

"Is it possible that what Dave Garrett did to your father might have had something to do with his daughter's breakdown?" Jacob was saying, and she couldn't do anything but stare into the bottom of her glass, now empty, wishing she had more Chardonnay—no, she needed vodka, she was beyond wine at this point, not even a Xanax or a Klonopin or anything she carried in her makeup kit would help her at this point.

He was so, so close, this stupid young man, just another one of Daddy's fanboys, no one had ever gotten so close before.

No one has ever cared enough before.

"What do you mean?" Another bride-to-be, this one a lot thinner than the previous one, boyish hips and a flat chest, standing on the top step, shading her eyes against the hot afternoon sun, looking for someone.

"The timing," Jacob said, fumbling with his notebook and the file folder he was holding, trying to find the right paper, whatever evidence it was he thought he'd found that might explain the mystery behind the publication of *Dusk of a Summer Evening.* "Jenny Garrett—his teenage daughter—she had a breakdown that summer, had to be committed to a mental hospital, when her father was working on your father's book." He frowned. "But that doesn't make sense. He was working on other books, and they—they didn't turn out to be disasters." He was still fumbling with his papers, his moon face beaming suddenly when he found the paper he was looking for. "In your introduction to the reconstructed version, you said your father had said that Garrett had destroyed it, gutted it, added things that weren't in the original form…but didn't your father see galleys?"

No one ever thought to ask that. That's the part of the story, the Gospel my mother and I peddled for years, the story no one ever questioned.

The galleys.

There had been galleys, of course, she'd seen them. The galleys Daddy had signed off on, agreed to before fleeing the country once and for all.

She hadn't, of course, allowed the library where Daddy had gone to college to have them for their collection of his papers.

If the galleys had gone there, the proof was there for anyone who cared to look, dared to call her on the lie.

Daddy had signed off on the galleys, had approved them.

He'd never discussed the book publicly, refusing to answer questions about it.

That had been the agreement between Daddy and his editor.

"He signed off on the galleys," she said, looking at his doughy face, worried because she'd had four glasses and wanted another, wasn't at her sharpest, was going off script and was making a mistake, but that had always been her fear, her mother's fear, that a copy of the galleys might turn up somewhere. Ensign never cared, Garrett was long dead, but they might—there might be a set of them somewhere. "They told him fixing it all, making it right, taking out all the stuff that had been rewritten without his knowledge would be too expensive, and he—he," she made it seem like she was floundering, pushed the glasses back up the red nose, made her voice break as she continued, "needed the money. They told him they would keep the rest of his advance to pay for resetting the galleys if he insisted on it…and he was afraid, his agent was afraid…that he'd get a reputation for being difficult…"

Difficult. Yes, that was Daddy's problem.

Jenny Garrett.

She'd seen a picture of her once.

Jenny had been a young girl, almost thirteen, when she'd been sent away for good. In the picture she was laughing, a big smile on her heart-shaped face, her long black hair in braids hanging from either side of her head, wearing a white T-shirt with JENNY in black block letters across the flat girl's chest, just starting to sprout breasts that summer at Disney World, the Mouse-ka-ears pressed down on her head. She'd been pretty, braces on her teeth and dimples in her cheeks, the only child of Daddy's editor and his wife, the two people who'd been closest to Daddy before he fled to England and met Mummy. Dave Garrett, who'd pulled Daddy's first book out of his slush pile and given him a two-book contract, pushed him forward and brought him to the attention of the important reviewers and critics, introduced him to the right people, smoothed his way, preparing him to be the next Ross Macdonald, James M. Cain, Raymond Chandler. That was who the reviewers compared him to, and maybe the books didn't sell quite as well as Dave Garrett and Ensign Books might have hoped, but the second one sold more than the first one did, and there was a third book contract...only a one-book contract, to see if the third sold as much as the second, hedging their bets before plunking down enough cash for a fourth and a fifth.

The third book, Daddy always said, *is the make-or-break one.*

She wondered sometimes, when she let her mind go that way, if Dave had already started suspecting, if that was why the second contract was only for one book rather than two. But she'd heard it from other authors enough—*the third book will make or break you*—for her to think Dave hadn't wondered anything, hadn't suspected anything, at least until *Dusk of a Summer Evening* was in his hands.

Jenny had never come out of the mental hospital. She'd died in there.

Daddy's agent from that time was dead, and everything he'd had in his files about Daddy he'd returned when he'd fired Daddy as a client. He'd suspected the truth but couldn't prove anything, of course—knew enough to know he didn't want Daddy in his stable anymore. But he'd delivered the manuscript to Dave Garrett at Ensign as Daddy had written it, had envisioned it.

She hadn't reconstructed the book from bit and pieces of early drafts. She'd simply rewritten it from the original, final manuscript, which she'd always kept locked in the safe in the house she'd grown up in. She knew enough of Daddy's style to fake it, she knew how to write the way he did—and any slips in style or word usage or language could be easily explained away as early draft, or pieces she'd had to fill in. She had aspired to be a writer herself one day, when she was grown, follow in Daddy's footsteps and make it big the way he'd come so close to but never quite reached.

"Your reconstruction of the book was quite masterful," Jacob was saying. "I just wish I had the chance to ask Dave Garrett why he did what he did to the book. I don't understand why no one ever did."

He'd believed her.

"I guess we'll never know," she replied, having to use both hands braced against the table to push herself to her feet. "Maybe we could continue this another time? I'm—I'm not feeling so well."

It wasn't a lie.

His face, really rather kind in its extreme level of plainness, looked concerned as he bumbled out platitudes and wishes for her health and of course, just let him know what was convenient and he could understand if she would rather finish it by email, it was just knowing she was in town and he couldn't let the chance pass by to meet her, his favorite writer's daughter, and she was smiling and nodding as politely as she could manage, which wasn't terribly polite at all because what she really wanted to do was scream.

Jimmy.

And she was inside, out of the heat, weaving her way through and around pedestrians and groups of people, heading for the Habitat elevators, past the blackjack tables and slot machines, past the showroom and people carrying drinks, the bile boiling in her stomach.

She got into the elevator and hit the Close Door button, alone as the doors closed in the startled faces of a pair of bros with veiny bulging muscles who smelled of sweat and testosterone and stale beer, and as the elevator climbed ever upward she cursed at herself for agreeing to meet him, for drinking so much the night before and having all that wine before meeting him.

It was the alcohol's fault.

It was the alcohol that opened those doors she usually kept shut in her mind.

She slid her keycard into the door twice before the light flashed green and she heard it unlock. She stumbled into the bathroom and splashed cold water into her face, making it to the toilet as the wine and bile forced its way up and out of her mouth, coughing and gagging and spitting, the nasty sour taste in her mouth, her teeth feeling raw against her tongue.

She rinsed out her mouth, brushed her teeth, waited to see whether she was finished vomiting before walking, staggering out into the bedroom.

The half-empty vodka bottle sat on the nightstand where she'd left it when she passed out the night before, her laptop open and asleep on the desk.

He couldn't know, he couldn't have known.

No one would ever know.

No one could ever know.

Jimmy. Oh, God, Jimmy.

Her eyes filled with tears as she reached for the pill bottle.

"What," her father had said to her when he'd shown her his original, submitted draft of *Dusk of a Summer Evening*, "could be more noir than the despoiling of innocence?"

She poured some vodka with shaking hands into the enormous coffee cup with Flamingo written in pink script on the side, the handle in the shape of a flamingo. She shook out a pill—hell, why not take two, she'd earned them—and washed them down with the vodka. It wasn't cold—she liked her vodka cold—but the ice in the bucket had melted and she didn't have the patience to get more and wait for the vodka to chill down.

She sighed and leaned back against the pillows.

She was engaged to Jimmy, sweet Jimmy, with the reddish-brown hair and the snub nose and the cheerful disposition, that she'd met in a pub after his rugby team had won some game and she was over in a corner by herself reading, and they were roughhousing and he almost fell on top of her, smiling that boyishly handsome smile at her, and said, "Sorry, miss," and her heart had almost melted.

Jimmy, who could always make her feel safe and warm and loved.

Who could always make her laugh.

Jimmy had wanted to ask Daddy for her hand, ever the traditionalist, and she'd said no, it was better if she talked to Daddy first. She'd told him, there, in his office in the house in Dover, so close to the sea with the shriek of gulls forever in the background, yes, she'd told him that she was going to marry Jimmy and Daddy just had to be okay with it. He hadn't said anything, just gone over to the safe and gotten the manuscript out and handed it to her.

She'd read it that night, unable to stop reading, drinking wine as she turned page after page.

It was a masterpiece.

It was the book that would have launched Daddy once and for all, made him a literary superstar.

But, Jesus—if she, who had never met her, who'd only ever seen her picture—could recognize Jenny Garrett, had Daddy honestly thought Jenny's own father wouldn't?

She'd thrown the manuscript at him, with the rubber band stretched around it tightly again, her own anger unabated, her fury lashing out at him one last time before she stormed out of his office, and he went to get his own gun.

She looked at the bottle of pills and shook out some more.

Jimmy.

She washed down another five or six with another gulp of vodka, took another four or five.

And once the bottle of pills was empty, she leaned her head back against her pillow and closed her eyes. It was long past time.

She should have done this years ago.

And as she slowly felt herself slipping away, the last words she'd screamed at her father echoed in her brain.

"I thought I was special!"

A STREETCAR NAMED DEATH

There was a crowd of people, like always, grouped around the corner of Canal and Carondelet.

Barry Monteith sighed and crossed Canal to the neutral ground. It was a miserably hot August afternoon, and his socks were already soaked through with sweat. He mopped the wetness off his forehead and tried not to go to the bad place. It was hard—without the crutch of a cigarette or a Xanax or a drink to ease the stress balling up between his shoulder blades or the pinpoint of pain forming behind his right eye. He pulled his iPhone out of the pocket of his slacks and found a playlist of calming, soothing mellow music and hit Shuffle. But even the silky voice of Gladys Knight didn't seem to help much as he crossed from the neutral ground to the far side of Canal and joined the crowd of sweaty people gazing down the street hoping to catch sight of a streetcar coming.

He leaned against the brick wall of the Foot Locker and closed his eyes, wishing death on the incompetent mechanic who still hadn't found out what was wrong with his car. *If a streetcar doesn't come along in five minutes I'll try flagging down a cab,* he decided, wondering if there was enough time to run across to the Walgreens and buy some aspirin. *Breathe in and out, nice and slow and deep, listen to Gladys sing, and think happy thoughts. The car will be fixed tonight and I'll be able to pick it up on my way to work in the morning and everything's going to be just fine.*

He opened his eyes and smiled. There was a streetcar stopped at the light at Common Street just a block away. *See? When you think positive thoughts, good things happen.*

Wordlessly the crowd started forming a line. He joined the queue, and in a few minutes paid his dollar twenty-five and made his way to the back of the streetcar. He always sat in the back, because it was easier to get out the back door at his stop. He closed his eyes, enjoying the cool breeze coming in through the window as the streetcar clanged and went around the corner onto Canal. He leaned his head against the window and looked around at his fellow passengers. The car was crowded, but no one had sat on the small wooden bench next to him—and there were several other empty spots. His eyes met those of a young black man with dreadlocks wearing the filthy white smock and black-and-white checked pants native to kitchen workers. The young man shrugged slightly and closed his own eyes, slumping farther down on his own bench.

Barry felt better. Gladys Knight switched over to an old Olivia Newton-John song that had been a hit when he was in junior high school a million years ago. He smiled to himself. Junior high school had been hell when he'd been living through it, but all these years later the memories didn't sting anymore, didn't have any power over him.

Everything, he reflected, *becomes less painful over time.*

The streetcar lurched to a stop, and he looked out onto the sidewalk. There were maybe three or four people lining up to board—so he wouldn't have the seat to himself for much longer. He looked up to the front of the car as the first person climbed up the steps and paid. He turned to walk down the aisle, and Barry's blood froze.

It can't be, he thought as he stared with his mouth open and his right hand coming up to his throat. *I must be seeing things, it can't be him.*

But it *was* him.

It had to be.

He looked older—with a shock Barry remembered it had been over eight years—and he was leaner, more muscular than he had been when he was just seventeen. But the face—there was no mistaking that face. The square jaw, the wide-set green eyes, the thick pouty lips, the prominent cheekbones—it was him. It couldn't be anyone else. Barry could remember thinking, somehow, through the burning bitter hatred, what a shame it was that such beauty was going to be wasted.

The green eyes looked around the interior of the car, lighting on Barry for just a moment before moving on without any sign of recognition. He was wearing a black T-shirt with Who Dat written across the front in gold print and glitter, over drooping jeans rolled up into cuffs at the ankles. There was a strange tattoo on his left inner forearm, and he slid into an aisle seat several rows in front of Barry.

Deep breaths, Barry, he reminded himself as his heart pounded in his ears and his stomach churned up burning acid, *stay calm. It might not be him,* he thought over and over again as he worked his iPhone out of his pants pocket. Olivia Newton-John had given way to Roberta Flack, but he hit the button on the bottom of the phone and pressed the Safari icon. The little wheel spun around and around as the streetcar started moving again. A heavyset black woman slipped down into the seat with him and grunted a hello. He didn't acknowledge her presence, just kept staring at the screen on his phone, willing it to finish loading before he lost his patience and his temper and threw the fucking thing out the open window.

It finally did load, and he pulled up Google, typing with trembling fingers the name *Ricky Livaudais,* having to back up to correct typos several times before he finally got it correct and touched the Search button.

A list of links came up when the streetcar stopped at Poydras Street and more people got on board, standing in the aisles since there was no place to sit.

None of them were the Ricky Livaudais he was looking for— the one sitting several rows in front of him on the streetcar.

Roberta Flack was now Carly Simon, and with a sudden jerk the streetcar started moving again.

He's out, Barry thought as the streetcar rolled down St. Charles, past Gallier Hall and restaurants, corner groceries with big signs advertising po'boys and Lotto tickets in their windows. *He's out and he's alive and he's back in New Orleans. Why didn't I know this? Why didn't anyone tell me?*

He swallowed, his eyes burning a hole in the back of the head just a few yards away from him. There was a sunburst tattoo on the back of Ricky's neck, right where it met his shoulders. The bottom rays of the sun disappeared inside of the collar of the T-shirt.

It's been over eight years, he reminded himself. *No one probably even gave me a second thought. The world keeps turning, life keeps moving, and no one remembers anything. Maybe they thought it was better I didn't know. Maybe they figured Ricky Livaudais could come back here and I'd never know. What were the odds against us winding up on the same streetcar?*

The streetcar swung around the statue of General Lee on top of its massive marble column and stopped just outside of Lee Circle. Several people got out of their seats and climbed down out of the streetcar before it started moving again, including the black woman who'd sat next to him and the Goth-looking girl who'd been sitting with Ricky.

Barry realized with a start that he was neither angry nor afraid.

In eight years, he'd never once thought about how he'd react if he came face-to-face with any of them again. They were in jail, convicted and sent away—and when he'd walked out of the courtroom after their sentencing, he'd put them out of his mind like they'd ceased to exist.

But now, staring at the back of Ricky's head, he felt—nothing, really, just an odd sort of curiosity.

I'm probably just numb from the shock.

The streetcar came to a stop at Melpomene. The light was red, and Ricky stood, walking to the front of the car. Before he realized what he was doing, Barry got up and went to the back door. The green light was on above it as he stepped down, but he waited until he saw Ricky step down onto the pavement before he pushed it open and got off the streetcar two stops too soon.

The light turned green and the streetcar lurched across, continuing on its path uptown.

Why did I get off? Barry wondered as he watched Ricky cross the neutral ground and start across St. Charles.

Because you want to see where he goes, that's why. If he hadn't gotten off so close to your own stop, you wouldn't have.

Carly Simon was now Melissa Manchester as he followed Ricky across the street.

I just need to see where he's going, that's all, I should know where he lives, he told himself as he watched Ricky's slender frame head down Melpomene Street toward the river. *If I'd gotten off first that would have been the end of it, but he got off in my neighborhood so I need to see where he's going. I need to know where he is if he's living in my neighborhood. I have a right to know where he's at, don't I?*

Ricky crossed Prytania Street, but the light had changed by the time Barry got to the corner. He had to wait, as rush hour traffic drove by in both directions, his eyes on the retreating form as he got farther and farther away. By the time Barry could cross, Ricky was crossing Melpomene at the corner at Coliseum, and was soon out of sight.

But when Barry got to the corner, he saw Ricky crossing the park, waiting at the curb to cross Camp Street. He hurried across the street as Melissa Manchester became Bette Midler. He watched from under a live oak in the park as Ricky went through a black wrought iron gate on the other side of Camp Street, climbed the front steps, slid a key into the lock, and opened the front door.

He lives less than two blocks away from me, Barry thought, feeling the panic rising from deep inside. He put a hand up against the tree and closed his eyes, listening to his heart leaping inside his rib cage. He focused, as the long-ago therapist had taught him, on the sound and rhythm of his heart, slowly imaging it softer and quieter, until it was the sound of waves lapping against a white sand beach, beautiful clear green water cresting softly with white foam. Once his heart was beating normally again, he crossed Coliseum Street and walked on the other side, never taking his eyes away from the fuchsia Victorian and the big green door Ricky Livaudais had disappeared behind.

Before he knew it he was unlocking his front door and stepping into the air-conditioning inside. His orange striped cat howled and wrapped himself around Barry's legs as he stood there, leaning back against the door. He slid the dead bolt into place and put the chain on. Breathing deeply, he fed the cat and sank down into an easy chair. The phone was blinking, so he pressed the message button.

BEEP. *"Hi, this message is for Barry Monteith. This is Lawrence Schindler. It's been a long time, hasn't it? I hope this is still your number. I have to apologize for not contacting you sooner, but I only just got the notice myself and I thought you should know they've released Ricky Livaudais. Yes, he was sentenced to eleven years but he got out early for good behavior. I'm sure this is a shock to you—it was to me, too—but he has done his time, Barry, and I hope you can remember that, appreciate it. I know it's hard but you have to let the past go. He's free, he's paid his debt to society and there's nothing anyone can do about it. He was just the driver, remember— the others won't be eligible for parole for at least another seven years, if then. If you need to, you can call me at—"*

Barry depressed the Erase button. There was no need to call Lawrence Schindler.

He walked into the kitchen and, for the first time in four years, poured himself a drink.

The vodka tasted good. Tasted, in fact, like another glass.

That would have been the end of it, really, if it weren't for the fact that it seemed he ran into Ricky Livaudais everywhere he went. Standing in line to buy toilet paper at Walgreens, the front doors would open and there he would be, walking in and picking up a shopping basket, sliding it onto his tattooed arm before disappearing down the aisles. At Zara's Grocery, when Barry walked in to buy lettuce and vegetables for a salad, there he was at the cash register, buying a loaf of bread and a pack of cigarettes and a really cheap bottle of gin. When he walked to the Burger King when he didn't feel like making dinner, there Ricky was at the soda fountain, filling up an extra-large plastic cup with Coke before picking up his greasy bag and walking out the front door.

Everywhere he turned, Ricky was there in some kind of sleeveless T-shirt and those damned droopy-drawer baggy jeans and a baseball cap turned sideways on top of his head.

And whenever their eyes met, there was no recognition in Ricky's. He would just turn away and go about whatever it was he was doing.

It was frustrating, infuriating. He wanted to scream at Ricky, *How dare you not know who I am?*

And every time he saw Ricky, he'd come back home and pour himself a glass of vodka, watching television but not seeing or comprehending what was on the screen as he slowly drank the vodka down, letting it cool his body and his temper, settle his mind down and let him relax.

And yet somehow he always found himself on Coliseum Street, walking slowly along while his music played into his earbuds, his eyes glancing every so often to the big fuchsia house, wondering what Ricky was doing, if he was home, sitting on his couch planning on destroying someone else's life.

He certainly had an aptitude for it.

Three weeks after Barry saw Ricky that first time on the streetcar, he began frequenting the coffee shop at the corner of Race and Magazine. He would get a cup of coffee and walk back up Camp Street to the corner at Melpomene. Some mornings he'd stop in front of the big fuchsia house and stare at the green door, wondering if Ricky was awake yet, if he was drinking coffee inside, wondering what he would say if the green door opened and Ricky came out suddenly and unexpectedly.

One morning he walked up the sloping driveway and looked into the parking lot behind the big wrought iron fence, wondering if any of the cars back there were Ricky's—but reminding himself that it was unlikely—hadn't he first seen Ricky on the streetcar?

But maybe his car was in the shop—mine was, wasn't it?

He heard a door opening in the rear of the house and he hurried back down to the sidewalk, glanced down the street, and ran across to the park on the other side, sitting down on a cement bench in the shade of an ancient live oak tree. He watched as a young woman with reddish-blond hair climbed into a green Honda about the same age as the live oak, opened the gate with a remote control, and drove down the slope and out onto Camp Street. She gave him an odd look when she stopped at the foot of the drive, and he panicked for a moment.

He got up and walked back home, deciding it was time to forget about Ricky Livaudais.

That was the smart thing to do, after all.

He went about the business of living his life for three days before Ricky invaded his world again. Barry's routine was always the same: He got up every morning and went to the gym, worked out, came home, ate breakfast, and went to work. He then came home every night and fed the cat, relaxed without the vodka, and was, in general, feeling rather pleased with himself when he ran into Ricky Livaudais in the most unusual place.

It was a Friday, and his boss's birthday. "Meet us for drinks tonight," his boss insisted. "You never do anything with us anymore. It won't kill you."

He agreed, not really wanting to but figuring it would do no harm to go to the Brass Rail. He met his coworkers and their friends there at nine, and at nine thirty on the dot the door back behind the pool table opened and several young men wearing only underwear came out to peddle their wares and dance for dollars. He'd never really cared for the Brass Rail—he knew it was snobbish to feel the way he did about the bar, but he couldn't help it. There was just something enormously sad to him about the place, the dancers, and the patrons who parted with dollar bills to grope the lithe young bodies of the dancers. In other bars the dancers didn't get to him the way the ones in the Brass Rail did. There was something seedy and sad in their neediness. They didn't turn him on—rather, they made him feel kind of sad.

But he was relaxing and having a good time when he froze with his vodka tonic halfway to his lips.

Ricky Livaudais was climbing up onto the bar in red bikini briefs.

At first, Barry was certain he was seeing things. It couldn't be—not Ricky Livaudais, surely not. But as he watched him start shaking his narrow hips from side to side on the other side of the bar, he saw the sunburst tattoo at the base of his neck and knew it was him. There was another tattoo—the word Destiny written in blue ink and old English lettering—across his lower back just above the waistband of the red bikinis. And there was the tattoo on the inner forearm.

Yes, it was most definitely Ricky Livaudais.

Ricky slowly started moving across the top of the bar, making way for another, more muscular young man to climb up where he'd just been dancing. Beyoncé began wailing through the speakers about divas being the female version of hustlers, and he couldn't take his eyes away from Ricky as he coaxed and teased dollar bills from men around the bar.

He wasn't the handsomest stripper, nor did he have the best body, nor did he have the biggest package neatly wrapped up inside thin cotton underwear.

But there was just something about Ricky.

Barry couldn't look away, no matter how much he wanted to.

He wasn't sure what he would do when Ricky made it to where he and his friends were standing.

"That's hot," he heard his boss say as Ricky stepped over several drinks on the bar until he was standing just above them, moving his hips from side to side.

He swallowed and looked up.

His eyes locked on Ricky's, and Ricky looked confused.

Ricky knelt down. "Do I know you from somewhere?" he said above the music, which was now Lady Gaga bitching about getting a telephone call on the dance floor. Ricky's knees were spread, only inches away from Barry's arms on either side. Ricky's head was tilted to one side, his eyebrows furrowed together.

You murdered my boyfriend, Barry wanted to scream at the top of his lungs. Instead, he shrugged. "Maybe." He managed to sound calm and nonchalant, just another gay man in a gay bar talking to a stripper in red underwear. "You do look kind of familiar to me." A smile spread across Ricky's face, and Barry was sickened to realize how handsome he actually was. The green eyes lit up, and the stern, angry-looking features relaxed into the face of a good-looking young man, the kind of young man you'd want to wake up next to every morning. "You shop at Zara's!" Ricky said excitedly, snapping his fingers, delighted with himself for remembering. "You live in my hood!" Ricky placed both hands on Barry's shoulders. "I knew I recognized you!"

The hands on his shoulders burned him through the tight T-shirt Barry was wearing. They felt like acid devouring his flesh, insidiously eating their way into his nervous system. He swallowed, resisting the urge to throw Ricky's hands off him, to toss the cheap vodka tonic in his face, to shove him hard enough to knock him backward off the bar and maybe even crack his skull or snap his neck when he hit the floor. "I do live in the lower Garden District," Barry replied slowly. "I guess maybe I've seen you around." He was amazed at how calm and even his voice sounded, now that contact was being made. He thought he'd be more nervous, that his heart would pound so loudly others could hear it. He was proud of himself, more proud than he perhaps should have been. His hands weren't even shaking. His only reaction was the sudden dryness of his mouth and throat. He took another sip of his vodka tonic.

Ricky leaned forward and pressed his lips against Barry's ear. "How long you gonna be here?" His breath felt hot against Barry's neck, as one hand slid down Barry's torso. "Maybe you could give me a ride home?"

Barry swallowed. "How late you going to be working?"

Ricky looked around. "I can leave in an hour if I want." He swallowed. "There's too many guys working tonight for me to make much money, anyway."

"Okay," Barry replied, looking into the deep green eyes just inches away from his own. *They are*, he reflected, *really beautiful.*

"I'll be back." Ricky smiled at him, and stood back up to his full height on the bar, and started dancing his way down to the next group of men.

His coworkers teased him about his "encounter," but their jaws dropped when Ricky came walking up a little over an hour later, a bag slung over his right shoulder, ready to leave. Barry said his goodbyes to his openly envious coworkers and headed out the front door with Ricky.

"I didn't mean for you to leave your friends," Ricky said finally, when they were inside Barry's car and he was pulling away from the curb.

"I don't mind," Barry replied. "It was my boss's birthday. I don't really go out that much. I don't much care for it."

"You don't?" Ricky looked out the window.

"Since I quit smoking the smoke bothers me," Barry said with a slight shrug of his shoulders. "And I don't really like to drink all that much anymore, either. No, if it hadn't been my boss's birthday, I would have probably stayed home tonight."

"And we wouldn't have met."

We've kind of already met—you just don't remember me.

Ricky laughed. "I don't know your name, I just realized I didn't ask."

"Barry."

"I'm Ricky."

They smiled at each other while stopped at the light at Canal Street.

"It's so weird that we live in the same neighborhood," Ricky went on when the light turned green. "And that we shop at the same places and all. I knew as soon as I saw you tonight that I knew you from somewhere—oh, turn here. I live on Camp Street, close to the corner at Melpomene."

"So I should go down to Magazine?" Barry asked.

"Uh-huh."

Ricky didn't speak again until after Barry turned onto Camp Street. "Pull up here—oh, good, there's a spot right in front."

Barry maneuvered the car into the spot in front of the fuchsia house and cut the engine. "Well, here you are." He smiled brightly.

"Oh, come on in." Ricky smiled back at him, opening the passenger side door. "I know you don't smoke cigarettes, but I've got some awesome weed that'll blow your mind."

"Just for a little while." Barry hesitated with his hand on the car door handle. *Maybe he does remember me. What if this is some kind of trick? To get me inside? And he has friends waiting, so they can do to me what they did to Thomas?*

He looked back into Ricky's green eyes and chided himself for being so paranoid. He opened the car door and got out, following

Ricky through the gate and up the front steps. Ricky fumbled in the darkness for his keys, apologizing—"I can't tell you how many times I've asked them to fix that damned light"—and finally getting the door open. He flicked on the lights and shut the door behind Barry.

Almost immediately, Barry felt sorry for Ricky.

The place was big, but it was empty. There was a tiny television mounted on top of milk crates, and the furniture—originally intended to sit on a nice suburban patio—was now threadbare and decrepit. The whole place felt unlived in—transitory rather than a home. There was a battered and scarred plywood coffee table in front of what passed for a couch. There was a paper plate with chicken bones and a big grease spot sitting on it, with a dirty steak knife and fork on either side. He sat down on one of the rusty patio chairs and felt it give a little under his weight. Ricky tossed his bag into a corner and went into the kitchen, coming back with a joint and a lighter in his hand.

"The place is kind of a dump," Ricky said as he lit the joint, sitting down in a chair next to Barry's. "I've been here a little over a month." He inhaled and offered Barry the joint. He blew the smoke out with a hacking cough. "It's harsh, though." He choked the words out as Barry took a dainty hit from the joint. "Be careful."

Barry didn't hold the smoke in. "Where were you before?"

"Prison." Ricky took another hit and pinched it out when Barry refused to take it from him. "Don't freak out, man. I made a mistake—a major mistake—when I was a kid and I went to jail for eight years."

Barry looked down at his hands. "What did you do?"

"I don't know that I really want to talk about it yet." Ricky leaned forward in the chair and pulled his T-shirt over his head.

"You killed someone?"

Ricky stared at him. "No, no, I didn't. My friends did. I was driving that night." He swallowed and closed his eyes. "You have no idea how many times I've wished I stayed home that night. *No idea.* I thought—you know, I just thought we were driving around wasting time, throwing back a few beers—I didn't know they wanted to—" He slumped down. "Can we talk about something else?" He swallowed and opened his eyes again. There was a sad, almost repentant look on his face. He looked like nothing more than a sad little boy who'd done something wrong and was terribly sorry. "I can still hear that guy screaming as they beat him to death..."

He winced and his eyes filled with tears. He wiped at them, closing them again.

Barry reached over and touched his arm. His skin was damp and hot. "The guilt must be really terrible," he said softly. "I'm not sure I could live with it, you know? I mean, the pain the guy must have suffered…the people he left behind."

Ricky's eyes remained closed. "Every night I can hear the guy screaming." He shook his head and a greasy tear slid out from his right eye.

"That must be so awful for you," Barry whispered as he picked up the steak knife sitting on the plywood coffee table and shoved it into the soft skin underneath Ricky's chin. "I've heard him screaming every night since you and your bastard friends killed him, you know." Blood spurted, and Ricky's eyes opened wide for a moment. He gurgled, trying to reach for Barry with both hands.

Barry moved out of his reach and watched as Ricky's eyes went glassy with death.

Barry stared at him for a few moments as the blood pumped out and gushed down Ricky's throat, soaking his T-shirt.

He went into the kitchen and found some charcoal lighter fluid underneath the sink. He squirted it all over the body and the floor of the living room, and paused at the front door for just a moment before lighting a match and tossing it onto the couch.

The flames danced over the body.

"At least you won't hear him screaming anymore," Barry said, as he closed the front door behind him and walked down the front steps.

He got into his car and started it, driving off without a backward glance.

AN ARROW FOR SEBASTIAN

So, just how did you two meet anyway?" Lorita Godwin asked into a sudden silence that had dropped over the dinner party. Her words were only slightly slurred. She was on at least her fourth glass of red wine since we'd sat down at the table. She'd had a couple of whiskeys before dinner, and God only knew how much she'd drunk before her guests started arriving. Her eyelids were starting to droop a bit—which didn't go particularly well with the bad facelift she'd had since I'd last seen her.

Bless her heart, Lorita's parties were always rather ghastly—a fact I always seemed to forget. It was like there was some kind of curse on her. She hired the right caterers, got the right flowers, and always invited interesting people. Yet somehow things never seemed to come together properly for her. The food the caterers were serving us at this party, for example, seemed to be either undercooked or overcooked. The salad seemed wilted, and the vinaigrette seemed to be mostly vinegar.

But she always got the liquor right.

I turned my head from her to the couple she was addressing. Jake Lamauthe and his young companion, Sebastian Dixon, were sitting to her left, and directly across the table from me. I hadn't really paid much attention to either of them, frankly. Lorita always insisted on eating by candlelight, and I really couldn't see them through the long tapered red candles in the center of the table. I'd spent most of the evening listening to Lorita ramble on about this or that. The woman on my right was a bore, so I'd ignored her for the most part.

Jake was just as used to Lorita's awkward conversational gambits when she was drinking as the rest of the condemned unfortunates gathered around her dining table. He merely smiled in that strange way he had and said, "You know, Lorita, I was after him for quite some time but wasn't getting anywhere. Finally, I just had to hit him with my car to get his attention. That did the trick, and we've been together ever since."

Everyone laughed at this, and conversation around the table started up again. From the corner of my eye, though, I'd noticed that young Sebastian's laughter seemed a bit forced. As soon as everyone's eyes had turned away from him and Jake again, he compressed his lips into a tight little line and looked down at his plate before taking another gulp from his own wineglass.

Curious, I thought, and even while I participated in the mindless small talk I find so tedious yet effortless to keep up, I kept stealing glances at Sebastian, watching him and what he was doing. He seemed extremely uncomfortable, but since everyone else at the table was a stranger to him that wasn't surprising. He was a very beautiful young man. He looked like a teenager, maybe in his senior year of high school, but I figured if he was here with Jake he had to be in his early twenties. He had a rather large forehead and short-cropped dark hair over gorgeous green eyes framed by long, curling dark lashes. Most of the time, his face was empty of expression, and he only spoke when he was directly addressed, flashing a nervous smile before giving a very short answer that ended rather than advanced the conversation. His skin was pale, but his cheeks were rosy with spots of color that looked almost feverish. I assumed he was Irish, given the combination of dark hair and green eyes and pale skin. He sat very erect in his chair, and I also noticed he wasn't eating much of Lorita's food, but was just pushing it around on his plate with the wrong fork.

At one point he looked across the table at me. Our eyes met for the briefest moment before he averted his.

Very curious indeed.

I'd known Jake Lamauthe for years but wouldn't call him a friend. I'd never cared enough for him to want to get to know him better or to build a friendship. We often were at the same parties, as we knew most of the same people. We were always distantly friendly, the way people who barely know each other are at social gatherings, full of false bonhomie and cheer that didn't go very deeply. He seemed to be in his late forties and had established himself into polite New Orleans society through his exceptionally successful floral shop on Magazine Street. He'd cultivated the rich hostesses of the Garden District and Uptown, first to help his business grow—and then somehow managed to make the transition from hired help to invited guest. That took some doing in a city like New Orleans, where the lines of class were drawn before birth and rarely crossed. He was certainly never going to be asked to join Rex or Comus, of course, but he'd managed to charm his way into becoming a mainstay at parties and dinners hosted by the city's bluest bloods.

There was just something about Jake I didn't like, from the very first time we'd met, and nothing had ever warranted changing my opinion. He was an attractive enough man, if you liked that type. He'd always struck me as the kind of man who would have facelifts and color his hair—but then, he'd let it go gray and he looked better for it. But there was just something repellant about him. I could never put my finger on what exactly it was about him I'd always found distasteful—but I'd never cared enough about it to figure it out. We were socially polite to each other, and I used his services on those rare occasions I felt the need to host a gathering of some sort in my home. To give credit where it is due, he was a master when it came to floral décor. I myself was absolutely hopeless with flowers.

The dinner conversation continued to swirl around my head as a cater waiter cleared away plates and brought in dessert dishes of orange sorbet. His name was Luke, I think—he'd worked a dinner party at my house the previous month. I had chatted him up in that dreadful, nerve-wracking hour before my guests arrived, when I am always terrified no one will actually show up. Luke was a master's student in literature at Tulane—he had actually heard of me and was familiar with my work. I smiled at him as I deflected a rather invasive question about my next book from Dolores Devlin, who was seated on my right—Dolores was always tactless when she drank gin, which was a regular occurrence, unfortunately. I turned away from Dolores and looked directly across the table. Sebastian was watching me without expression and we looked directly into each other's eyes again. This time he didn't look away but met my gaze fearlessly, as though daring me to speak to him. The pinkness of his cheeks in the candlelight made him look slightly feverish. Our eyes remained locked as Dolores chattered mindlessly away, not even aware that she'd lost my attention. I wondered which one of us would look away first, but then Lorita tossed out another one of her peculiar conversational gambits my way, and courtesy forced me to turn and address my answer to her.

After the dessert plates had been cleared and Lorita began ushering her guests into the drawing room for brandy, I excused myself and slipped out the French doors onto the terrace for a quick smoke. As I lighted my cigarette, I heard the streetcar clang past on St. Charles Avenue. It was nice and peaceful out there. I sat down in a chair in the darkness and stared up at the stars, wondering how much longer I had to wait before escaping this abysmal party without appearing rude. I heard the French doors open behind me. I turned my head and watched young Sebastian come down the two steps.

He walked on the balls of his feet, which gave him an odd rolling gait that coupled with his immaculate posture gave him the appearance of being uncomfortable in his own body. His arms didn't swing as he walked, and his shoulders remained solidly in place. "Hello, Sebastian," I said, and blew a plume of smoke up to the sky.

He smiled at me, and even in the darkness I could not help but marvel at how truly extraordinary his beauty was. The smile— so rarely in evidence throughout the interminable dinner party— exposed remarkably white and even teeth, and dimples that deepened in the rose-shaded cheeks. "You're a writer." It wasn't a question. He sat down on the other side of the table from me and pulled out his own pack of cigarettes—Marlboro Reds. He tapped one on the edge of the table before lighting it.

I nodded. "Did Jake really hit you with his car, or was he trying to be clever?" I asked, stubbing my cigarette out against the sole of my shoe.

The smile disappeared, the expressionless mask slipping back into place. "Yes." He took another puff from his cigarette and didn't look at me. "Although he makes it sound like he ran me over. I was in my car. He pulled out in front of me."

"That's quite a story." I lit another cigarette. From inside the house I could hear a jazz recording I didn't care for—Lorita's musical taste was nearly as bad as her parties—so I was in no hurry to go inside and rejoin the other guests. I blew out smoke. "You don't like the story."

"It's how we met." He shook his head. "I just don't like the way he tells it to people. Sometimes, though, I wonder—" He cut his words off when we heard the sound of the doors opening again.

"There you are, darling." Jake put his hands down on Sebastian's shoulders proprietarily, and he stiffened almost imperceptively in response. "You mustn't pester David, Sebastian—writers like their solitude, don't they, David?" Jake's eyes glittered, and he swayed a little bit.

I could smell the whiskey on his breath and knew he was drunk.

"I'm sorry if I intruded," Sebastian replied, looking down submissively.

"Let's go inside, shall we, dear?" Jake gave me a malevolently triumphant smile of ownership as he guided Sebastian back up the brick steps and inside the house. But just before they went through the doors, Sebastian looked back at me over his shoulder.

It was a look of quiet desperation if I'd ever seen one. I lighted another cigarette, and by the time I'd finished it and rejoined the party, Jake and Sebastian had already made their apologies and left.

"I think Jake was a little drunk," Lorita slurred to me in what she thought was a whisper but could clearly be heard by everyone in the drawing room.

That look haunted me over the next few days. I would be working on my book—I was in the corrections and revisions phase, which is always tedious—and when I'd stop to think for a moment, I'd see that look on his face again. I wasn't sure what it meant—and I replayed our interaction several times trying to figure it all out.

There was something about young Sebastian that had somehow lodged itself like a splinter into my psyche.

It was possible I'd misread the look and it had been something else entirely. Or nothing at all, for that matter. But the more I thought about it, the more I was certain he was appealing to me for help, which didn't really make much sense. Why me, and help from what? I cursed myself for not bothering to get to know Jake better in the past, or for at least not paying better attention. Several times I picked up the phone to call Lorita—she collected gossip the way some women collected shoes—but always stopped myself before I could dial. Lorita would naturally want to know why I was asking about Jake and Sebastian, and I didn't have an answer that would satisfy her curiosity. Once I'd hung up, she would start to wonder about why I was asking, what I was up to, as she poured herself yet another whiskey, and would eventually come up with her own explanation for why I was asking. By the next glass of whiskey she'd be convinced it was all true. And after refilling her glass a third time, she would be telling anyone who would take her call about my obsession with Jake Lamauthe's new lover.

And that was not something I cared to have spreading through the Garden District like bubonic plague.

Besides, even I myself didn't understand my curiosity about Sebastian.

It really came down to that haunting look he'd given me on the terrace.

I'd been alone two years—nearly two—since Robert had left. Certainly, Sebastian was a beautiful young man, but there were plenty of beautiful young men in New Orleans. If I wanted to see beautiful young men, all I had to do was drive down St. Charles Avenue in the late afternoon. The neutral ground between the streetcar tracks would be filled with beautiful shirtless young men jogging, their muscular torsos gleaming with sweat in the late afternoon sun. No, my fascination with Sebastian was a curiosity about the strange look on his face when Jake told the story of how they'd met, the way he'd stiffened ever so slightly when Jake touched him on the terrace, and that final, odd look he'd given me when they'd gone back inside.

I was thinking about that look as I climbed the stairs to my gym three days later, and wondering if I had crossed that thin line from curiosity to obsession, when I ran into Sebastian coming out. His hair was wet with sweat, his soaked white tank top clinging to his muscled chest like another layer of skin. I could see his hard little nipples and every cut muscle in his stomach. He was wearing aviator sunglasses so I couldn't see his eyes as he brushed past me and mumbled a barely audible "excuse me." He either didn't recognize me or didn't want to talk, so I just continued up the stairs.

I made it up another three stairs when he called my name. I stopped and turned to look back at him.

He'd pushed the sunglasses up on top of his head and he was smiling, his dimples deepened in the rosy cheeks and the even white teeth gleaming in the late morning sun. Again I marveled at the difference in his face when he smiled. He started back up the steps toward me. "It's me, Sebastian." He held out his right hand. "I'm sorry, I was in a hurry and then I realized it was you."

I took his moist hand and shook it. "Nice to see you again, Sebastian." I smiled. "I didn't know you worked out here."

"I just started recently." The smile didn't falter in the least. "I didn't know you worked out here, either. How often do you come in?"

"I try to get here at least three times a week." It was a lie—I hadn't been that regular since Robert left.

"Is this the time you usually come in?" he asked, frowning as he looked at his watch. I nodded, and he went on, "Well, maybe we could work out together? I have to run right now, but say Wednesday? At eleven?"

"Sure."

"Great." He turned and went down the stairs at a gallop, and I watched him go out the door before continuing on my way up to the second floor.

That was how Sebastian and I started working out together. In the two days before we met, I kept telling myself that he was just a nice kid who seemed like he needed a friend, that it would benefit me to have someone I met regularly at the gym so I could get rid of the spare tire stubbornly starting to form around my waist, and so on. That Wednesday morning, I couldn't focus on the pages I needed to revise, and kept pacing, looking at the clock and the slow creep of the hands around until it was finally time for me to get to the gym.

He was waiting for me, sitting at the counter reading the newspaper. He was wearing another white tank top like the one he'd worn the other day, with long baggy red basketball shorts that reached just past his knees. "I was afraid you wouldn't come," he said with a big grin.

"Why would you think that?" I replied, curious.

He shrugged. "I don't know—I really don't get out of the house much, and I don't really have any friends." He beamed at me again. "I hope we can be friends," he added shyly, not able to look me in the eyes.

I was touched, and felt sorry for him. It couldn't be easy being involved with Jake Lamauthe, I figured as we went through our workout. I'd never liked him, and he'd gone through any number of "boyfriends" since I'd first met him. They were always younger, always rather pretty if a little vapid, and they never stuck around for very long.

I found myself looking forward to meeting Sebastian at the gym—I didn't get out of the house myself very often, other than errands and the gym. And while he was reticent at first, he eventually became more talkative. Not so much about Jake, of course, but more about himself. He was from Nebraska originally (*Of course*, I thought when he told me, *the corn-fed good looks and the apple cheeks*.) but had left for New Orleans when he turned eighteen to make his way in the world. His parents were very conservative, as was everyone else in the small town where he grew up, and he knew then he was different, not like the other boys he played football with or who were on the wrestling team. College wasn't an option, and after graduation everyone expected him to go to work in the pork processing plant.

"The whole town smelled of stale blood," he said, making a face, "and I just wanted to get away. And New Orleans seemed like a magic place, you know? So I came here."

"And you met Jake, and now you live in a big house in the Garden District." I smiled, removing the forty-five-pound weight plates off the bar we'd just finished using. His face darkened, but I pretended not to notice.

I also pretended not to notice other things—like the frequency of the ugly bruises or black eyes he would always try to explain away as nothing. "I tripped" or "I'm so clumsy" or "I'm always bumping into things" was the catechism I came to expect from him whenever he showed up trying to cover up another one. Jake was bigger than he was, of course—Sebastian was lean with no extra body fat on him anywhere. He couldn't have weighed more than one hundred and fifty pounds dripping wet, while Jake was a big man, easily topping the scales at two hundred and twenty pounds. I know Jake came to the gym in the evenings after he shut down the store, and he worked with one of the trainers—I used to see him when I'd come in to do the elliptical machine in the early evenings when I was stuck on whatever book I was writing—the mindless concentration of a cardio machine often helped me work through whatever problem I was having with my writing. I'd never heard that Jake was violent— but there was something about him I'd never cared for. Perhaps I'd always sensed there was violence just below the surface of his smiling and of-so-friendly façade.

Many nights I would lie in my bed, staring at the ceiling, wondering if I should say something about them or offer to help him get out of Jake's house. It was unusual. If Sebastian were a woman there would be no question about it; I would say something, I would do whatever it took to get her away from her abuser. I would talk to her, sit her down and explain how the violence never stops, it never goes away no matter how much your man says it will or how sorry he is. It only stops in death.

But he was a man involved with another man, and I didn't know if the bruising and the black eyes might be a part of some kind of kinky role play they both enjoyed. I didn't know if my intervention would be welcomed or seen as an incredible intrusion and invasion of privacy. And I liked Sebastian. The workouts were the highlight of my week. Every Monday, Wednesday, and Friday I would wake up and be excited because I was going to see him at the gym. I didn't want to do or say anything that would jeopardize that.

If he needed my help, I figured he would ask for it.

He was an adult, right?

The book was finally finished, and I printed out two copies and burned a CD the way my publisher always wanted. I drove down to the Fedex office on Tchoupitoulas, and when the package was on its way to New York I went into the PJ's next door to treat myself to an iced mocha as a reward for turning the book in only two months past deadline.

As I stood in the line, the guy working the register seemed vaguely familiar, and as I moved steadily closer to the counter as each person in front of me placed their order, I tried to remember where I knew him from. New Orleans is a small town, and this kind of thing happens all the time—you see someone in a different context than you're used to seeing them in and it drives you crazy until you remember. This guy, for example, may have used to work in a restaurant I frequent, or worked out at my gym for a while at the same time I did, or maybe was just one of my readers and had come to a signing. He could just be a fan who had become my friend on Facebook, and I was used to seeing his face on my newsfeed.

When I reached the counter he smiled at me. "David! I haven't seen you in a while! How are you?"

"Good," I replied, trying to hide that I had no idea who he was. "And you?"

He smiled, and winked at me. He leaned over the counter a bit and said, "I live in a roach-infested studio apartment and work here for next to nothing, but I am so much happier than I was!"

And in that instant, I knew immediately who he was—he was

Sebastian's predecessor in Jake's life. "I'm glad," I replied, genuinely pleased for him but with all kinds of questions racing through my head.

"I'm going to UNO for the next semester," he went on, oblivious to my fumbling for something to say. "Getting the hell away from Jake was the smartest thing I ever did."

"It was that bad?" I heard myself saying.

"You have no idea." He rolled his eyes. "What can I get for you?"

"Large iced mocha," I replied, and handed him a five dollar bill.

I'd planned on drinking it in the car on my way home, but instead I picked up a *Gambit Weekly* and sat down at a table. I pretended to read it while I watched him. *Here's your chance to find out about Jake and what goes on in that house*, a voice whispered inside my head, *and clearly he has no qualms about keeping Jake's secrets.*

I watched as people came and went, drinking the mocha as slowly as I could, even as the ice melted and watered down the flavor. Each time I drummed up the nerve to go talk to him, someone would walk up to the counter to order, or the girl he was working with would start talking to him, or his cell phone would ring.

I finished the mocha and tossed it into the garbage. Figuring it wasn't meant to be, I started for the door to the parking lot when I heard him call my name. I turned and he came out from around the counter. In his hand was one of the store's business cards, and he pressed it into my hand. "Call me sometime," he said with a big smile. "It would be nice to catch up."

I thanked him and asked, "Do you mind telling me what was so awful about being with Jake?"

"He was very controlling," he replied, his face darkening. He shrugged. "He didn't want me to work—didn't really want me to do anything besides go to the gym and be there in the house ready to do whatever he wanted me to."

"I see," I replied, trying to summon the nerve to ask the question I really wanted to ask. In my mind I could see the multiple bruises on Sebastian's arms and legs. *Did he hit you? Was he violent?* But I couldn't say the words.

"Call me." He reached out and touched my shoulder gently, a smile on his pretty face.

I nodded and he went back behind the counter. It wasn't until

I looked at the little card when I was in my car that I realized that I still didn't remember his name.

Alone, in my house, I wondered what to do.

It was clear Jake wasn't right in the head, and I worried about Sebastian. The bruising could only mean one thing. I didn't believe for a minute he was that clumsy—watching him at the gym I could see he was graceful. Despite the awkward way he stood, his movements were always fluid. Besides, I never once saw him bump into anything at the gym.

Apparently, he was only clumsy in Jake's house.

Would my intrusion be welcome? I was his only friend—he had told me that often enough. There was no one else he could turn to, no one else he could trust.

But he could just walk out, I reminded myself. *No one is ever trapped anywhere, not in this day and time.*

He could always come to my house.

Tomorrow, I decided, *at the gym I will say something, offer him my house.*

But he didn't show up at the gym the next day, and he didn't answer when I called.

It was curious, I thought as I went through my own workout, lost in thought and not really paying attention to what I was doing. It wasn't like him. He never missed the gym—he'd often said it was one of the few times he could get out of the house. I worried and I wondered, and finally gave up on the workout as a lost cause and went home.

"Darling, have you heard?" Lorita breathed when I answered my phone later that afternoon.

"Heard what?" I replied absently, thinking she was slurring her words already and it was only two in the afternoon.

"Darling, Jake went and shot that boy of his!" Her voice dripped with malice, and as the news went through me I couldn't help but wonder how long she had hated Jake Lamauthe.

"Shot him?" I replied.

"Shot him dead," she said, not even bothering to hide her glee. "He claims it was self-defense, of course, that he caught the boy stealing from him and he attacked him, but apparently the police aren't buying his story."

"They aren't?"

"Supposedly they struggled over the gun, and it went off—at least that's what Jake is saying." Her voice sounded smug. "But the police don't believe it for a moment. Apparently his cleaning woman told them Jake used to smack the boy around."

"How do you know all this?" I asked, playing with the pen on the table next to the phone. "And when did all this happen?"

"Last night, around two in the morning." I could hear ice clicking together as she took another drink. "His cleaning woman, you know, also cleans for Binky Claypool, and she told Binky everything this morning."

And now everyone in Uptown knows, I thought. "I have to go."

"But—"

I pushed the Off button and put the phone back down.

Poor Sebastian, I thought as I filled a glass with gin. *Maybe— maybe I should have said something.*

I drank alone in the dark for the rest of the day, unable to forget that haunted look on his face.

HOUSECLEANING

The smell of bleach always reminded him of his mother.
It was, he thought as he filled the blue plastic bucket with hot water from the kitchen tap, probably one of the reasons he rarely used it. His mother had used it for practically everything. Everywhere she'd lived had always smelled slightly like bleach. She was always cleaning. He had so many memories of his mother cleaning something; steam rising from hot water pouring from the sink spigot, the sound of brush bristles as she scrubbed the floor ("mops only move the dirt around, good in a pinch but not for *real* cleaning"), folding laundry scented by Downy, washing the dishes by hand before running them through the dishwasher ("it doesn't wash the dishes clean enough, it's only good for sterilization"), running the vacuum cleaner over carpets and underneath the cushions on the couch. In her world, dirt and germs were everywhere and constant vigilance was the only solution. She judged other people for how slovenly they looked or how messy their yards were or how filthy their houses were. He remembered one time—when they were living in the apartment in Wichita—watching her struggle at a neighbor's to not say anything as they sat in a living room that hadn't been cleaned or straightened in a while, the way her fingers absently wiped away dust on the side table as she smiled and made conversation, the nerve in her cheek jumping, the veins and cords in her neck trying to burst through her olive skin, her voice strained but still polite.

When the tea was finished and the cookies just crumbs on a dirty plate with what looked like egg yolk dried onto its side, she couldn't get the two of them out of there fast enough. Once back in the sterile safety of their own apartment, she'd taken a long, hot shower—and made him do the same. They'd never gone back there, the neighbor woman's future friendliness rebuffed politely yet firmly, until they'd finally moved away again.

"People who keep slovenly homes are lazy and cannot be trusted," she'd told him after refusing the woman's invitation a second time. "A sloppy house means a sloppy soul."

Crazy as she seemed to him at times, he had to admit she'd been right about that. In school after school, kids who didn't keep their desks or lockers neat had never proven trustworthy or likable. It had been hard to keep his revulsion hidden behind the polite mask as he walked to his next class and someone inevitably opened a locker to a cascade of their belongings. He'd just walked faster to get away from the laughter of other kids and the comic fumbling of the sloppy student as he tried to gather the crumpled papers and broken pencils and textbooks scattered on the shiny linoleum floor.

Take Josh, for instance. He'd been cleaning up after Josh for almost eight years now. Josh didn't appreciate the rule of everything has its place and everything in its place.

But he wasn't going to have to clean up after Josh again. Just this one last time.

Steam was rising out of the bucket, making his forehead bead with sweat. The hot afternoon sun was coming through the big bay windows in the kitchen. No matter how low he turned the air-conditioning, the kitchen never seemed to get really cool. But the heat and humidity was part of the price of living in New Orleans, like he always said, and the floor was a disgrace.

He lifted the bucket out of the sink after adding more bleach. The fumes made his eyes water and his back was a bit sore, but the floor needed to be scrubbed. That meant hands and knees and a hand brush. It had been a while since he'd taken the time to do the floor properly. He poured some of the water onto the floor and watched as it slowly spread and ran to the left side. The tile was hideous, of course. He'd bought the house despite the green-and-white-and-beige patterned tile in the kitchen, faded and yellowed from years of use. It was one of those projects he figured he'd have time for at some point, either pulling up the tile and replacing it himself or hiring someone to come in to do it. He'd been in the house now for five years and still hadn't gotten around to it. He pulled the yellow rubber gloves back on up to his elbows and got down on his knees and started scrubbing with the brush.

He liked the sound of the bristles as they scoured the tile. He'd gotten used to the ugly tile, he supposed as he ran the brush over them, not really noticing when he used the kitchen. Maybe it was time to do something about the kitchen. The window frames were yellowed from age, and the walls themselves, a pale green that sort of went with the ugly tile, looked dirty. There was no telling when was the last time the kitchen had been done, and as he looked around as he scrubbed he could see other things he didn't seem to notice before—the thin layer of grease on the stove top around the dials and timer, the filth accumulated under the vent screen over the stove, the yellowing of the refrigerator, the spots all over the black glassy front of the dishwasher. The windows also needed to be cleaned.

"Your home will never look clean if the windows are filthy," he heard his mother saying as she mixed vinegar and water to use, "but a dirty house will look cleaner if the windows are clean. And you can't let the windows go for long, else water spots and the dirt will become permanent, and the dirt will also scratch the glass. And you can never ever rub away scratches on glass."

Should have put that on her tombstone, he thought with a smile as he dunked the brush back into the bucket and moved to a new spot.

Not that she had one.

"She'd be ashamed of this kitchen," he said aloud into the silence. His iPod had reached the end of the playlist and he hadn't stopped what he was doing to cue up another. He'd wiped dust off the iHome stereo system on the kitchen counter before starting the music up in the first place. "But she didn't work full-time, either."

That made him smile. His mother hadn't worked nine to five, maybe, but she had worked.

She was always very careful to make sure she wore gloves when she cleaned, and to make sure she wore a gauze mask over her face, her hair pulled back and tucked into the back of her shirt. Cleanliness might have been next to godliness, but she wasn't risking her skin or her hair to do it. His earliest memories of her were of her brushing the thick bluish-black hair that she always wore long before going to bed, putting cleansing masks on her face and creams on her hands. Her beauty rituals were almost as complicated as her cleaning habits. Every night without fail, she sat at her vanity and removed her makeup before putting on the mask of unguents that she claimed kept her skin youthful and her pores clean. When money was tight she made it herself, from cucumbers and aloe and olive oil and some other ingredients he couldn't remember—but when times were good she bought the most expensive products at the most expensive department stores. Once the mask was firmly in place she brushed her hair exactly one hundred times, counting the strokes as she went. Once her hair was lustrous and silky, she rubbed lotions and oils into her hands, trimming her cuticles and filing her nails, and then retreated to the bathroom to scrub the mask from her face. Her skin always glowed as she got into bed.

And she was always able to find some man willing to help out a pretty widow lady and her son.

"I do what I have to do," was all she would say to him when she went out for the evening, lightly scented, with minimal makeup applied, just enough to hide some things and draw attention to others. "Remember to not let anyone in if they knock, okay?" She would kneel down beside him or, when he was older, go up on her tippy-toes to give him a kiss on the cheek.

He only met the ones who lasted more than a few dates, the ones who had money or might lead to something. He was never sure—still wasn't—what exactly she got up to with the men. She wasn't a prostitute, or at least didn't consider herself to be one. But she hustled the men somehow, got money and jewelry and presents from them, certainly enough for them to live on. She always had cash, never had credit cards. Sometimes the men would give her a car to use, but they never took it with them whenever they moved on. Sometimes when they moved on it was in the middle of the night, in a rush, hurriedly packing everything they possibly could and heading for the train station and catching the next train out of town. They never wound up anywhere that didn't have a train station or an airport.

She wouldn't ride the bus.

"Why do we have to change our names every time we move?" he'd asked her once, on a late night train out of St. Louis, as the cornfields of Illinois flew past, barely visible by the light of a silvery half-moon. He was maybe nine or ten at the time, old enough to ask some questions, old enough to start wondering why they moved around so much, old enough to wonder why they had no family, no roots, no credit cards, no home.

She'd smiled at him, leaning down to kiss his cheek, smelling vaguely of lilies-of-the-valley. "We don't want people to be able to find us, do we?"

"I don't even know what my real name is anymore," he'd grumbled.

She laughed in response. "I think in this next city you'll be David," she tapped her index finger against her pointed, catlike chin, "and I'll be Lily. What should our last name be?"

They'd settled on Lindquist that time, for some reason he couldn't really remember now, and they'd chosen Pittsburgh as their new home, their new city, their new adventure. They'd rented a little two-bedroom cottage in a suburb, and she'd put him into the local school. There was enough money so they didn't have to worry for a while, and he liked it there. He liked the cozy little suburb with the nice kids in the neighborhood and the nice teachers in the school and the friendly neighbors who liked to give him cookies when he brought them their newspaper up from the curb. He liked it there so much that he hoped they'd stay there for a while. He liked being David Lindquist. He was making friends, and sometimes, after he'd gone to bed and turned out the light, he'd pray to God—any god—that they'd be able to stay there, put down roots, and not ever move again.

They were there three months before she started getting itchy, when afternoon coffees with the neighbors and discussions about what was happening on *Days of Our Lives* and gossip about other women in the suburb began to bore her. She'd said they wouldn't have to worry about money for a long time, but he should have known better than to think she would become another housewife, that being the widowed Mrs. Lindquist who kept such a clean house and was raising such a nice son and always had time to listen to anyone who had a problem would begin to bore her. She started going out in the evenings, after he'd gone to bed—she never said anything, always checked his room before she left, so he would pretend to sleep until he heard the front door shut, then he'd look out the window and see her getting into the taxi waiting at the curb. Maybe it was because she had money socked away that she got so careless this time, that she didn't cover her tracks as well as she usually did.

It was three in the morning when a cry woke him from a dream about *Star Wars*, when he got out of bed and went into the living room where a big man he'd never seen before had his mother pressed up against the wall and was choking her. She was trying to get away.

He didn't mean to swing the baseball bat so hard.

"You've killed him," she said finally, her throat raspy and her neck bruised from his thick hands. She staggered a bit as she stepped over to the body, kneeling down and feeling for a pulse in his neck. She looked up at him, her hair disheveled, her face wild. "I'm glad you killed him."

"We need to call the police—"

She pressed her index finger against his lips to stop him from speaking. "We never call the police," she whispered, a half-smile on her bruised lips. "Never call the police." She staggered into the kitchen and came back with one of her kitchen towels. She wrapped it around the man's head, tying it into a knot. "Help me drag him into the bathroom."

The little cottage had two bathrooms, one in the hallway that he used and a private one off her bedroom, which he never got to use. It seemed to take forever, and the dead man seemed to weigh a lot more than he should, but they finally got him to the hall bathroom and into the tub. "There," she panted, "we can leave him there for now." She pushed him back out of the room and into the hallway, shutting the door behind her. "You can shower in my bathroom tomorrow morning. We need to clean up the living room." She laughed, a harsh, cynical laugh. "Thank God I didn't pick a house that's carpeted."

More of her wisdom—never pick a home with carpet.

"I haven't thought about Pittsburgh in years," he said with a laugh, as he dumped the dirty bucket of water back into the sink and reached for the mop. He dragged the mop through the bleach water on the floor, wringing it back out into the sink before mopping up more of the water. The floor where he hadn't mopped yet looked even dingier in comparison to where he'd already cleaned, and his back was already starting to ache a little bit. But now that he'd started, he couldn't not finish.

"Always finish what you've started" was another one of her sayings.

He'd come home from school that next day to find her sitting in the living room, coolly cutting up credit cards into a big mixing bowl sitting on the coffee table. A leather wallet was on the table next to the bowl, along with an expensive-looking gold watch and a man's ring, also gold. A wad of cash was on the other side of the bowl. "Almost finished," she said, her tone almost gay as he shut the front door. She nodded toward the wad of money. "Almost two thousand dollars, David!"

He didn't say anything, just walked down the hallway to the bathroom. The door was open, but there was also a horrible antiseptic smell coming from there he could smell long before he got to the doorway, where it was so bad his eyes watered. But the bathtub was empty.

"Caustic lye," his mother said from the end of the hallway, her hands on her hips. "You'll want to stay out of there for a few days. You can just use my shower until it's safe."

"What—what happened to him?" He managed to stammer the words out.

"I told you, caustic lye," she replied with a roll of her eyes. "Now do your homework, I'm going to start making dinner."

No one ever came looking for the man, and after a few more days of terror whenever he saw a police car or heard a siren, he began to settle back into life as David Lindquist. He never knew who the man was—he stopped at the library on his way home from school for a couple of weeks to look through the newspaper without her knowing, but there was never anything in there about him, or if there was, there was no picture. It was almost like he'd never existed, and there were times he wondered if the man ever had, if he hadn't maybe dreamed hitting a man in the head with a baseball bat to stop him from strangling his mother. But then he would remember the sound of the bat connecting with bone, the way the skull had given, the gurgling sound the man made in his throat as he went down.

He hadn't dreamed that.

They left Pittsburgh at the end of the school year, saying goodbye to all of their friends and neighbors at a going-away barbecue, selling all the furniture and things and once again taking a night train out of Pittsburgh. He didn't want to go—she said they were going to keep the Lindquist names for now, but not to get used to them—he was starting to grow and he was starting to notice boys, and there was a boy in the neighborhood he really, really liked. But there was no arguing, no point in asking if they could stay longer. When she made up her mind to move on, she made up her mind, and that was that.

This time it was Atlanta where they landed, and she found a nice little house to rent in a quiet neighborhood.

It was in Atlanta that she found a man who wanted to marry her.

It was in Atlanta where he changed from David Lindquist to David Rutledge, taking the name of his mother's new husband.

He'd liked Ted Rutledge, who was a lawyer for a lot of big companies and had a huge house in a rich suburb of Atlanta. The house they moved into was huge—six bedrooms, six bathrooms, every room enormous and immaculate and beautifully decorated. She couldn't keep the house clean herself, but a team of cleaners came in once a week to clean from ceiling to floor—and she watched them like a hawk, not tolerating any slacking or missed spots. Ted had a big booming laugh and always seemed to be in a good mood. But he also worked a lot, and even though his wife liked spending his money...about six months after the wedding he could tell his mother was getting restless again. He could see it in her eyes, the twitching of that muscle in her jaw, the way she sometimes stood in the window and stared out at the street across the vast expanse of grass that passed as a front lawn.

"Don't mess this up, Mom," he warned her one morning before he left for school, "this is a good thing and we should make this work for as long as we can."

She'd just smiled at him and nodded.

"You never could trust in your own good luck, could you, Mom?" he said as he poured more water onto the kitchen floor.

He stood back up and leaned back, his hands on his lower spine as it popped and cracked.

But she'd lasted much longer than he thought she would.

He was a senior in high school, straight-A student, letterman on the football and baseball teams (he didn't care much about playing sports, but it meant a lot to Ted) when he came home from school one day and found them both.

"They'd been fighting," he said numbly, still in shock, to the police officer who'd come in answer to his call, the call he couldn't really remember making. "I don't know about what. I know my mom was going out at night while he was at work but he never seemed to mind, not that I know about."

His new guardian, Ted's law partner, told him much later that it seemed like she'd killed Ted and then turned the gun on herself. He just nodded, the same way he nodded when he was told how much money there was and that it was probably best to sell the house and get rid of everything, all those bad memories. He just nodded and went to live with his new guardian until it was time to go away to school.

No one ever wondered about the deaths.

No one ever wondered if maybe it wasn't just a little bit strange that she'd waited until after her son went off to school before shooting her husband over his breakfast and then turning the gun on herself.

No one ever figured out that he'd walked into the kitchen that morning with one of Ted's revolvers in his hand, came up behind where his mother was sitting and fired the gun into Ted's face, and before she even had time to react, put it to her temple and pulled the trigger himself. No one ever wondered if he'd then taken the gun, put it into her hand, and fired it again at Ted's chest, so she'd have powder residue on her hand.

No one knew that she'd caught him with a boy, seen him in the pool kissing Brad Brown, and that once Brad had gone home they'd both told him he was going to be sent somewhere to be cured.

Sometimes you have to make your own luck, like she always said.

He finished the floor and got back to his feet. The sunlight was already starting to fade a little bit, but the floor was finally clean. He glanced around the kitchen. Once the floor dried he was going to have to come back in and clean some more, get those spots he'd been noticing. The grease on the stove back, on the vent, the spots on the front of the dishwasher—he couldn't just leave them like that. He'd never be able to sleep knowing the kitchen was so filthy. And he needed his sleep.

Tomorrow was going to be a big day for him.

He walked into the living room and gave the room a critical once-over. There was a cushion on the couch that needed fluffing, and the magazines on the coffee table weren't centered quite right. The TV screen shone in the sunlight, and there was no dust on any surfaces. He fluffed the pillow and moved the magazines, fiddling with them a bit until they were just right, the perfect distance from each edge of the table.

He sat down on the couch and looked around. He loved this house. He was glad he'd found it, had made it his own. He'd carefully selected every thing in the house, and everything was in its perfect place, as though it had been specifically made to go there. Ten years—it had been ten years since he'd bought the house, had moved in, made it his home.

And now it was all his again.

He'd miss Josh, of course. You live with someone for long enough, and you're bound to miss him when he leaves, no matter how bad things have gotten between the two of you.

Josh had been like his mother, he realized, and that was part of the initial attraction. Josh was a hustler, with no family and no past, just like she was. Josh was good looking with his green eyes and thick brow and bluish-black hair and slavish devotion to his appearance. But like his mother, Josh wasn't a whore. And they'd lasted for eight years, eight years with minimal strife, very few fights, very few disagreements. As long as Josh got to go to the gym and lie by the pool in the briefest of bikinis and had money to buy nice clothes, Josh was very agreeable. There was enough money so that neither of them had to work, of course, and he didn't care if Josh wanted to go out to clubs at night. He didn't even care if Josh met people and slept with them, as long as Josh was there for him when needed. And he always was. Josh never pouted if he had to change his plans and stay home as directed.

He'd almost loved Josh, really. It wasn't even like he hated him, either.

He'd just tired of him, the way his mother had always gotten bored.

If he had to put his finger on the time when he decided it was time for Josh to go, he couldn't.

It was just one of those things, like his mother always used to say when she'd decided to move on.

This morning, when he woke up, he knew that it was going to be today. He just knew it, somehow, and that knowing was what made him think of his mother for the first time in years.

It felt right.

He wished he didn't have the ties for a moment, the house and the car and the credit cards and the bank accounts. He could understand her wanderlust now, the need to just cut all ties and start all over again somewhere new, the need to be free from anything and everything, the ability to just pack some things and just go, walk away from your current life. He was tied to this house now, he was tied to being David Rutledge, didn't know if he could just change his name and start all over again somewhere else the way she used to do.

It might not even be possible now—with computers and cell phones and tracking and Homeland Security. It had been easy back in the day to start all over again without too much fear of someone from the past tracking you down.

No, he knew it was a foolish thought—even if he moved away to some remote place in Central America, someone would be able to hunt him down eventually if they were so inclined.

No one ever suspected a thing about his mother and Ted, had they?

No one would suspect a thing about Josh, either.

"Once the floor dries," he decided, "then I'll use the lye."

The floor was now nice and clean, spick-and-span, gleaming.

Not one trace of blood had escaped his eyes. He'd gotten it all up.

Yes, no sense in taking the lye into the back bathroom now and tracking up that nice clean floor until it dried—not after all the effort he'd spent scrubbing it clean, like Mom always did.

Besides, it wasn't like Josh was going to get up and walk away from his resting place in the bathtub, was he?

And no one was going to miss him, anyway.

It was going to be nice living alone again.

ACTS OF CONTRITION

Help me, Father," she cried. Her brown eyes were wide open with terror. The rain was falling, drenching them both, soaking her white T-shirt so that it clung to her body. Her dreadlocked hair was dripping with water that ran down her face, streaming from her chin as she gripped his arms with her black-fingernailed hands. She reached for one of his hands and drew it to the crevice between her breasts. "Please, Father," she pleaded again. He didn't pull his hand away from her cold chest. He knew in his heart he should, but somehow he couldn't. He let it rest there, feeling her frantic heartbeat through her cold wet skin, and closed his eyes. This is a test, he reminded himself, a test. But still he left his hand there, betraying the collar he was wearing, betraying his God. He tried to pray for strength, for guidance, but all he could think about was the feel of her skin beneath his hand. *Push her away, reprimand her for her temptation, do something, anything, don't just stand here with your hands on her...be strong, find strength from your love of God, but don't just keep standing here...*

His hand remained where it was.

And she began to laugh, her lips pulling back into a smile of triumph. Her eyes glowed with triumph.

"Fallen priest, fallen priest," she chanted between her laughter. "You're going to hell, aren't you, Father?"

He pulled back from her, staring at her face as it changed. She wasn't Molly anymore, the sweet young runaway he was trying to help, she was something else, something evil. The hair on the back of his neck stood up, and he opened his mouth to scream, but nothing came out.

"Fallen priest, you're nothing but a fallen priest." Her voice deepened and she took a step forward, her lips still curled in that horrible smile. She tore at the collar of her T-shirt, ripping it downward and exposing herself. She grabbed his hand again and pulled it to her breasts.

"Get thee behind me, Satan," he finally managed to choke out, provoking her to more laughter. It echoed off the alleyways, and a light went on in a house a few yards from where he was standing. "Stop," he whispered, glancing at the lighted window.

"What are you so afraid of, fallen priest?" She leered, her lips pulling back even farther. "That you'll be exposed for what you are?" And she laughed again, throwing her hand back and sending the sound upward, to the spires of the cathedral, and more lights were going on up the alleyway.

"Please," he said, and pulled his hand away from her. Where the knife came from he had no idea. One moment there was nothing and in the next it was there, in his hand, the sword of the Lord. It glowed with a righteous cleansing blue fire. It pulsed and throbbed in his hand with an almost unimaginable power. Tears filled his eyes as he raised his hand. "Please," he whispered again, not wanting to do it, knowing he had no choice. He brought the knife down into her chest. Black blood splattered, spilling down her stomach and onto her wet denim skirt. Yet still she laughed, and he brought it down again, tears flowing down his face and mingling with the rain. *She must be cleansed, she must be cleansed, she must be cleansed*, he thought as he kept swinging his arm. *She must be cleansed...cleansed... cleansed...*and he hacked at her, the blood spurting and splashing, mixing with the rain, and yet still she laughed...

He sat up in his bed, wide awake and shivering, his body damp with sweat, his short graying hair plastered to his scalp. He wiped at his face. It was still raining, the windows fogged up. He sat there, hugging his thin arms around himself trying to get warm. The digital clock on the nightstand read 9:23 a.m., but it was still dark as night. Lightning flashed, so near it was merely a sudden bright light blinding him, followed almost immediately by a roar of thunder that rattled his windows. It had been raining for days, one storm rolling in after another, filling the gutters and streets with water, swirling as the city's pumping system desperately tried to keep up. The ground was soaked, the big elephant ferns outside his door waving in the wind and drenching him every time he walked outside. He tried to slow his heartbeat by taking deep breaths, and he slowly felt warmth creeping through his body again. He threw back the covers and swung his bare feet down to the cracked linoleum. He walked over to the opposite wall.

The walls of his apartment were cracked, the plaster buckling. The ceiling was covered with brownish water stains, and he could hear the steady plopping of water landing in the pots and pans he had set out in the kitchen to catch the leaks.

In the center of the wall was a huge crucifix. Jesus's face was turned imploringly to the sky, blood running down the sides of his face from the crown of thorns, his beautiful features twisted in agony. Blood leaked out of the wound in his side, his ribs pressing through the pale skin. The nails in his hands and feet were drenched in red. He grabbed the worn rosary from the small table and clutched it. He carefully lit the votive candles, then sank to his knees and began praying. His knees ached from contact with the hard floor. The Latin words rolled off his tongue easily, feverishly, as he counted the beads with his fingers. After a few minutes, when his heart had slowed to a normal pace and he felt calm again, he finished his prayers and crossed himself. He rose to his feet and walked to the window. He wiped the condensation away and looked out into the street.

Such a horrible dream. He still felt chilled, rubbing his arms to increase the circulation. Was it a sign from God, he wondered. The feelings—of lust and desire—the girl aroused in him had been dormant for so long. He knew they weren't wrong, but after so many years of self-denial through prayer, his vows were ingrained so deeply in his head he couldn't shake them off that easily. There was no reason for him to feel ashamed of his feelings or to deny them, but even though he was no longer a priest, he kept his vows. Maybe she was a test, sent by God to test his dedication to him. He'd been released from his vows for nearly five years now, so perhaps it wasn't really a test of some sort…but then again, God moved in mysterious ways. Maybe he was supposed to save her.

No one knows the mind of God.

She was one of the street people, a runaway. One of the disposable teenagers, the thrown-away children who somehow made their way to the French Quarter to hang out in coffee shops or in doorways, cadging change and cigarettes from passersby. She couldn't be older than fifteen, he thought, but then again, as he got older he found it more and more difficult to judge the age of the young. It was possible she was older. He had found her—was it only three weeks since that evening he had found her asleep in one of the back pews at St. Mark's when he'd gone in to pray? At first he'd thought it was just a bundle of rags someone had left in one of the back pews. Then the pile had moved, and he jumped, startled. It had only been three weeks. He hadn't stopped thinking about her since that moment she'd sat up in the pew, coughing.

Three weeks only.

"What's your name?" he'd asked, slipping into the pew beside her.

She just smiled and said, "Call me Molly, Father." He opened his mouth to correct her, but closed it again without saying anything.

It was the smile that brought the memories back, memories so strong he had to catch his breath. There was something about her that reminded him so strongly of Carla Mallory…the girl he'd loved when he was young, before he'd answered the call and entered the seminary. She'd been so angry when he told her his plans. Her pretty face had contorted with rage before collapsing into tears. *But I thought you loved me*, she'd accused him, *I thought we were going to get married.*

"The streets are dangerous, Molly," he'd said to her, putting thoughts of Carla firmly away. "There's a killer out there, preying on girls like you. Don't you want me to call your parents? Don't you want to go home?" There had been a story in the paper just that morning about the latest girl, found near the French Market, her young body carved up. Just another teenager thrown away, not missed and with nobody to mourn or care. She was the tenth one in the last eight months.

Molly looked back at him with eyes suddenly old and tired. "Sometimes home is more dangerous then the streets, Father."

He'd taken her hand, rough and dirty with the nails painted black. "Please be careful, and know you can always come here. We minister here to homeless kids, Molly. You can always come here, get some food, take a shower, get cleaned up." He gestured back to the office area at the rear of the chapel. "I can get you a list of shelters…"

"And sometimes shelters are just as dangerous as home." She shook her head, the multicolored dreadlocks swinging. "But a shower would be cool."

"But where…" He shook his head. Sometimes there was

nothing he could do for them. "Come with me." He stood up and started walking toward the front.

It was after hours, and against the rules, but he used his keys to open up the shower area and get her a fresh towel. Father Soileau would not be happy, but there was no need for him to know or find out. Besides, even if Father Soileau did find out, the most he would get would be a reprimand, and not a strong one for that matter. Father Soileau depended on him too much for the work he did with the teenagers, and it would be hard to replace him. *Who wants to work for the pittance they pay me?* he thought bitterly as he handed her a towel and shut the door behind him.

While she showered, he heated a can of soup for her, found a package of crackers, got her a fresh bottle of water.

She was so pretty with the dirt scrubbed off her face. So like Carla. He watched her as she slurped down the soup, crunching the crackers into the broth, and gulped down the water. There was a wounded innocence about her. She wouldn't tell him where she was from or where she'd been. And when she was finished, she patted his hand in thanks before slipping out of the church and back into the night.

He'd prayed for her that night, and every night since.

He prayed she'd come back.

He found himself coming back to St. Mark's every night at the same time, hoping she would show up. Sometimes she did, most nights she didn't. He didn't ask questions he knew she wouldn't answer. It almost became a kind of routine on those nights when she would show up. He would get her a towel, and while she showered he made her something simple to eat. While she ate, they'd talk about little things, nothing important. And when the food was gone, she would slip back out into the night.

He worried sometimes that Father Soileau would find out. It wasn't beyond the realm of possibility that he would be fired. Rules were rules, and the Church was very big on rules. He knew that very well. It was why he wasn't a priest anymore. "But I've done nothing wrong!" he[d begged them as the archbishop up in Chicago had shaken his head.

"We cannot take that risk, Father Michael." The archbishop shrugged. "We have to release you from your vows. Even the slightest hint of impropriety must be avoided. But there's a place you can make yourself useful, down in New Orleans. There's a small church just outside the French Quarter, St. Mark's. They minister to homeless teenagers, the kind of work you enjoy. The Church will get you a small place to live, and pay you a small salary, and you can continue your work."

"But the boy is lying…"

It didn't matter. They'd shipped him off to the foul-smelling little apartment in New Orleans, sent him to work for Father Soileau, and the anger burned in his heart. But he was working with the teenagers again, the ones who needed him, and while he'd been released from his vows, he kept them.

But Molly…Molly changed everything.

She made him feel like a man again. She awakened the feelings, the emotions, that had lain dormant for so long.

He prayed for guidance, but none came. He found himself thinking about her, worrying about her while he attended mass. He found himself going to confession at St. Louis, unwilling to confess his feelings to Father Soileau. He received his penance, said his prayers, counting the beads as he repeated the words over and over again. And he worried about her, where she was sleeping, what she was doing for money. So many of them sold their bodies to strangers for a warm bed and a twenty-dollar bill, for something warm to eat. They were so fearless yet somehow wary at the same time. But there was pained innocence in her eyes, and he longed for her to tell him her story, what had led her to the streets of the French Quarter. He warned her, over and over again. There was a killer stalking the alleys of New Orleans, mutilating young girls, raping them and then mutilating them. He begged her to go home, to call her parents. The streets were not safe at night.

She would just smile and shake her head. "The streets are as safe as anywhere."

Was that what the dream had meant, he thought as he stared into the rain. That Molly was in danger? That Molly was dead?

He went cold and sank to his knees in front of the crucifix again. *Please, God, watch out for Molly, she is just a child, for all her bravado and airs. Hers is an innocent soul. Protect her from the evils that lurk out there in the night and the rain, bring her safely home…*

He was climbing out of the shower when the knock came on the door. He wrapped a towel around his waist and peered out at a tall black woman in a dove gray suit, shaking off a dripping umbrella with one hand. He opened the door without removing the chain. "Can I help you?"

She smiled, flashing a badge at him. "Michael O'Reilly?"

"Yes."

"Detective Venus Casanova, New Orleans police. May I come in and talk to you?"

He felt a wave of nausea, the coffee he'd drunk burning an acidic hole in his stomach. "I just got out of the shower, I'll be a moment while I get dressed, is that all right?"

"Take your time." She kept smiling as he shut the door again.

He dressed hurriedly, his mind racing. This was how it started back in Chicago, the police showed up at the rectory with the boy's accusations, their knowing smiles. *Calm down*, he told himself as he finished buttoning his shirt. *There's no need to be afraid.*

He walked back to the door and opened it. He smiled. "Sorry, I was..." He stood aside to let her in. "Come in. Would you care for some coffee?"

She shook her head, giving her umbrella one last shake. "No, I thank you, though." She walked in, glancing around the apartment and then giving him a big smile. She was beautiful, her hair cropped close to the scalp, with strong cheekbones and strong white teeth. Her face was unlined, and she could have been any age between thirty and fifty. "I'll try not to take up too much of your time, Mr. O'Reilly." She sat down in the worn thrift-store reclining chair. "This rain is something, isn't it?" She shook her head. "Everyone complains about the heat and humidity, but I just hate rain."

"It's depressing, isn't it?" he replied, and his voice sounded false, forced.

Detective Casanova nodded her head. "Yes." She reached into her bag, removing a small spiral notebook and a pen. "Have you been reading the newspaper, Mr. O'Reilly?"

He shrugged and felt his hands start to shake. He grabbed the sides of his own chair. "Sometimes."

"Then you know we have a serial killer here in the Quarter preying on teenage runaway girls?"

"Yes, I work with the street kids over at St. Mark's, so I know about it, yes."

"There was another murder last night. Another runaway girl, couldn't have been older than fifteen. Unidentified, of course." She clicked her tongue. "She was found this morning in Pirate's Alley, right beside the cathedral."

Like in my dream! he thought, biting his lower lip. "Sweet Jesus," he whispered.

It was Molly, it had to be Molly, why else would the cop have come to him? *Father, why hast thou forsaken me...*

"I've just been by St. Mark's, and Father Soileau sent me over here." She reached into her bag again. "He thought maybe you knew her." She pulled out a Polaroid and handed it over to him. "Do you recognize this girl?"

He took the photograph, his hands shaking, and forced himself to look at it. He let out his breath in a rush. This girl had black hair, no dreadlocks, her face pale and eyes closed. *Thank you, Lord...* "No, I'm sorry, I don't know this girl."

She took the photograph back and slipped it back into her bag. "Each one of these murders has something in common, besides the fact that each is a runaway teenage girl. Something we haven't allowed the press to catch on to." She gave him a searching look. "You do a lot of good for these kids, and I know you care about them—and obviously, they aren't too interested in talking to me or the police. Has any of the kids you work with said anything? Do they talk to you about this?"

He shook his head. "Only in general terms."

She reached into the pocket of her jacket. "Each one of the victims had one of these in her hand." She held up her hand.

A strand of black rosary beads dangled from her fingers.

"And between her breasts, a cross was carved."

The beads swung in her hand, and he felt bile rising in his throat. He glanced over at his own rosary, still on the scarred coffee table. "That's—that's just sick." He closed his eyes and took several deep breaths. "It's blasphemy."

"I think it's some kind of religious freak," she said slowly. "Someone who sees these poor girls as evil—most of them are working as prostitutes, after all, and he is cleansing the world of their sin by sending their souls to God, and probably thinks he is saving them as well." She shook her head, standing up. She placed a business card on the coffee table. "I've taken up enough of your time. If any of the kids who come by St. Mark's say anything—anything at all, no matter what, please give me a call right away. We have to catch this guy." She walked to the door. She shook his hand. "You'll call me?"

"Yes, of course." The moment the door shut he ran to the bathroom and threw up. He splashed cold water on his face, brushed his teeth again, and stared at his red eyes in the mirror.

He watched for Molly all day, hoping that she'd break her usual pattern and come into St. Mark's during its normal hours. As he ladled soup into bowls, cut sandwiches, handed out towels, he listened to the kids talking. No one was talking about the latest victim—maybe they didn't know yet, which would be unusual. Usually, that kind of news spread through the street kids in no time flat. No, there was talk about the usual inane things—good corners to ask for money, places to avoid, business owners who chased them off and others who were good for some money or something to eat, a great place to get cheap clothes, and on and on and on. He looked at them with their multiple piercings, tattoos, and wild hairstyles and hair colors, and wondered, as he often did, what drove them to the streets? He opened his mouth a few times to ask about Molly, but then closed it and said nothing. She never came in during this time, and who knew if they would even know her as Molly?

He walked home after closing, the rain still coming down, the gutters full of water spilling over onto the sidewalk. By the time he got back to the miserable little apartment on St. Philip Street, his pants were soaked and he was shivering. He pulled off his pants, toweling his legs dry and slipping on a pair of sweatpants. He sank to his knees in front of the crucifix and prayed again for Molly. As he clicked off the beads, nagging thoughts kept coming into his mind, interfering with his prayers.

It's just like before...surely that police detective was just grasping at straws, trying to get information and help from wherever she could... it's silly to be afraid of the police just because of what happened before... stop thinking like this, you're supposed to be praying, communing with the Lord...but I can't go through that again, the boy lied, why wouldn't anyone believe me?

He opened his eyes and placed his rosary back on the coffee table.

He walked into the kitchen, ignoring the roaches as they scurried off the counters, and made a peanut butter sandwich, glancing at the clock. Only a few more hours until her usual time.

The boy lied.

Joey Moran. A pudgy boy of thirteen with an acne problem and thick glasses who always seemed to have a running nose when it was cold. Shy and introverted, the only child of a shrew of a mother, overprotected and hovered over. He cried often and easily, and the other boys at St. Dominic's made sport of him, taunting and teasing, tripping him and knocking the books out of his hands in the hallways of the school. He'd felt sorry for the boy—with that horrible mother, his life had to be miserable—and tried to make friends with him, tutoring him and trying to protect him from the other kids. Until that day when the police officer came by the rectory and told him what the boy's mother was saying. It was like being punched in the face. "Lies," he'd told the cop. "I never laid a hand on that boy."

The knowing smirk on the cop's face. The endless meetings with his superiors until the archbishop himself had called him in, and no one, no one believed him.

"We've reached a settlement with Mrs. Moran," the archbishop said, frowning at him. "She will drop the charges on condition that..."

No one cared that it was all a lie. *For the good of the Church, it's best that we do this...we're releasing you from your vows, but we've found a job for you...it's best that you leave Chicago...of course I believe you, Michael, but we just can't have another one of these scandals, and it's just better to resolve things this way...you've met the mother, you know what she's like, she's threatening to go the papers and you know what will happen then, other families will smell blood and a chance to get money out of us... it's best this way.*

Best for everyone but Michael O'Reilly, he thought angrily, glancing over at the crucifix.

The boy *lied.*

He started trembling. He picked up his beads and started praying for strength, for serenity, for peace.

The string snapped in his hand.

He sank to his knees and wept.

❖

He waited for Molly for over an hour, watching the cars drive by in the rain. Finally, he gave up and walked back home through the deserted streets. Where could she be? Was she safe and warm and out of the rain somewhere? The worry bubbled within him as he unlocked his door and stepped out of the rain. The rosary beads were still scattered all over the floor where he'd left them. He knelt down and started scooping them up into his palm. He glanced up at the crucifix just as a flash of lightning lit up the room.

Jesus' eyes seemed alive, glittering and angry. Unforgiving.

"Forgive me, Father, for I have sinned..." He began reciting the words.

❖

"Fallen priest, fallen priest..."

His eyes snapped open. He was lying on the floor in front of the makeshift altar, the votive candles burning and flickering in the dark. The room was cold, very cold. The rain was still pounding away on the roof, he could hear the dripping water in the kitchen. He was trembling, his heart pounding in his ears. *I fell asleep and had the dream again*, he thought, glancing over at the clock. Almost midnight. He struggled to his feet, his knees stiff, his back and neck aching from lying on the hard floor.

She was in danger.

He had to save her.

He grabbed his raincoat and his umbrella, blowing out the candles and grabbing his keys. He took a deep breath, opened his door, and stepped outside. The rain was pouring, the water gushing off the roof. The street was underwater, swirling dark water carrying debris, rising halfway up the tires of the cars parked on the streets. The streetlamps feebly tried to illuminate the night but only succeeded in giving off a dull yellow glow. She was out there somewhere. He opened the umbrella and went down the creaking wooden stairs and took a few hesitant steps into the night.

"Hail Mary, full of grace," he muttered as a car went by, throwing up a sheet of dirty water, continuing the prayer as he started down the sidewalk, not sure of where he was going.

There was a thick mist, and the streets were silent, except for the rain and the hissing of streetlights, and the mist moved and swirled like lost souls, dancing the dance of the dead in the stillness. He began to walk down toward the waterfront, knowing somehow that that was where she was, and there was danger, danger for her, some madman with rosary beads and a knife wanted to wipe her off the face of the earth, send her soul to God...

He tasted blood in his mouth, could smell it in the wet air.

He began to run.

His footsteps echoed in the mist, the sound bouncing off the buildings that stood so silent and reproachful, almost contemptuous in their silence. The mist continued to dance as he ran, and he was sweating despite the cold, and he threw away the umbrella that was doing him no good, only slowing him down, into the gutter, thinking *I'll pick that up later*, not realizing how foolish the thought was, all he could think of was her, and he continued praying as he ran, *please God, oh heavenly Father, save her save her save her, let me be in time she is young she is innocent do not take her...*

He heard a scream. "No, mister, please, don't..."

He ran harder, and still the screams continued and his lungs felt as though they would explode, and he was crying as he ran, and the prayers and pleas were running together in his mind *forgive me Father for I have sinned and yea though I walk through the valley of the shadow of death hail Mary full of grace our Father who art in heaven please protect her let me save her...* he saw them, through the mist, as though the dancing souls were parting for him, and he closed the gap and grabbed the man's upraised hand, the hand that held the dripping knife, and just like in his dreams it was flashing blue fire, it was the knife, the sword of the Lord, the sword of the righteous...

"Forgive me, Father, for I have sinned," the man with the knife said softly, then shrugged him off. He stumbled, falling down into the water with a splash, and it was cold. The man swung the knife at the girl again, and it flashed fire, a holy pure fire, and the girl screamed, and he could hear the sound of bones splintering as the knife tore at them, and it was Molly, or was it Carla, the mist was confusing him, and he lunged for the lunatic again, trying to grab his knife arm, shouting, "Run, Molly, run!" as he struggled, trying to get the knife, to protect her, and then...

He heard her giggle again.

He stopped fighting.

"What?" He turned and looked at her, and her face changed, she was Molly, she was Carla, and she was Molly again.

"False priest, false priest," she chanted, dancing a jig in the mist, her feet throwing up water, and she was laughing.

He rubbed his eyes, her face was like liquid, changing shapes and then reforming again.

"Save her, Father, heavenly Father, she is good and innocent, save her." It was his voice, coming from behind him, and he turned and stared at the man with the knife. It was his own face, beneath the rain cap, smiling at him. It was spattered with blood.

And then it changed into Father Soileau's face.

Then the archbishop's.

And Joey Moran's.

Back to his own.

He took a few steps backward.

"False priest, false priest."

"Save her, Father, save her, oh God save her, protect..."

"...priest, false priest..."

"...heavenly father, save her..."

"...false priest..."

"...father..."

"...priest..."

He started screaming.

❖

It stopped raining just before the sun rose, and the pumps, which had been straining for days to keep up, finally managed to drain the water from the streets. Throughout the French Quarter, people were getting up, getting ready for work. Businesses were unlocked, lights turned on, and everyone breathed a sigh of relief that the rain was finally over. The sun beat down, evaporating the water, and the air thickened.

"Have you tried to get the knife away from him?" Venus Casanova asked the beat cop as she sipped at her coffee, her eyes taking in the scene, the girl's rain-soaked dead body, her shirt open to reveal the cross carved between her breasts, the rosary beads dangling from her left hand. Her eyes were open and staring up at the blue cloudless sky, her mouth frozen in a scream. Venus shuddered. *You never get used to it,* she thought as she turned her attention to the mumbling man holding the knife.

"I haven't tried, we thought it better to wait for you," the cop, who couldn't have been more than twenty-five, replied with a feeble grin. Two other uniformed cops stood safely out of reach on either side of the man, their guns carefully trained on him.

"What is he mumbling?" she asked.

"Prayers," the cop replied. "Hail Marys and Our Fathers."

Religious mania, she thought, as she walked over and knelt down. "Michael?"

He stopped mumbling and slowly turned his head toward her. His eyes were wide, bloodshot, and empty.

"Can you put the knife down?"

It clattered to the ground.

She breathed out a sigh of relief and nodded to the other officers, who moved in, grabbed him by the arms, and raised him to his feet. They cuffed him and moved him over to a squad car, and she could hear them reading him his rights. He was docile and didn't say a word as they put him into the back seat. She waved the crime lab guys over, and they started their work.

She glanced over at the body and shook her head. It was over.

She looked up at the sky.

It was going to be a beautiful day.

LIGHTNING BUGS IN A JAR

"No, no, no! The lightning bugs weren't a metaphor for the family, they were a metaphor for *humanity*!"

Each word came roaring out in an exasperated lisp, accompanied by the thump of the antique mahogany cane with the brass lion's head at the top on the floor, undoubtedly leaving marks on tile supposed to look like hardwood but not fooling anyone.

It was Aptos. No one here had real hardwood floors.

Celia picked up a couple of abandoned wineglasses, dregs of white sloshing around in the bottom of one, red in the other. No one was paying any attention to her—no one ever did when the Great Man was talking, lecturing, gifting them with pearls of genius that other literature students would sell their mothers into slavery to hear in person.

The party had gone on longer than Philip's parties for the new students in his section of the MFA program usually did. Every semester the new students in his graduate seminar on Modern American Novelists were invited over to meet and genuflect before the Great Man who'd anointed them with oil, feeding their ambitions crumbs from his table while they fed his insatiable ego.

Or maybe it just seemed like the party was running long. It wasn't like she hadn't heard his bon mots before at least a hundred thousand times, and if she had to hear the discussion about what the stupid lightning bugs in his best-known novel symbolized one more time…

"We're all lightning bugs in a jar," she mouthed the words as he said them, "that some child has captured, watching. And that's what they symbolize, man's futile struggle against forces he cannot control, just like the lightning bugs flying inside the jar, unable to be truly free."

Just like that stupid wrecked concrete ship down at the beach is a metaphor for my marriage. Yes, kids, the Palo Alto is our marriage, me and the Great Man's. Sunk just offshore and broken into pieces, something that once had value and now is just...

No, that didn't quite work, did it?

That's why he's the Great Man and...I'm just the wife.

Just the wife.

There were murmurs of approval, and she resisted the urge to roll her eyes, reminding herself to be grateful they didn't burst into applause.

Couldn't they tell they'd overstayed their welcome, were becoming unwanted pests? At least only three were left now, two men and a woman in their early twenties, eyes shining as they listened to Philip pontificate, drinking in his wisdom like the expensive wine they'd been slurping up like Kool-Aid all night. Drunk and stoned—the marijuana smoke hung in the living room like a fog rolled in from the sea in the early morning. *I should probably care how they're getting back to campus from here but I don't. I didn't choose to live out here in Aptos,* she thought as she turned her back to the swinging door leading into the kitchen, pushing it open with her backside. *His students, not mine. They're not my problem. I've got enough problems of my own, thank you very much.*

Was it all that long ago I was one of them, when my biggest worry was my grades?

"You don't have to stay," she said to Lupe, her cleaning woman. Lupe was washing dishes and ashtrays and glasses, her hands submerged in gray soapy water. Finger sandwiches on dishes wrapped in cellophane sat on the avocado kitchen counter. A large black trash bag was sitting on the floor open, red strap ties hanging limp. "I can finish everything from here, thanks."

"You sure, Señora Blackburn?" Lupe asked in her accented English, wiping her hands on a worn dish towel that had been a wedding gift a million years ago, maybe from the Styrons? She couldn't remember. It didn't matter. "I don't—"

"You've already stayed later than I asked you to." Celia forced a smile onto her face. She reached for her purse and pulled out the hundred-dollar bill she'd gotten from the bank that morning. She always paid Lupe in cash, in case she wasn't legal—no paper trail in case ICE ever came after her.

Lupe frowned. "You sure?" she asked, taking the bill and folding it, slipping it into her front pocket. She reached for her purse, tucked away by the microwave.

"I'm sure."

Lupe nodded, flipping the backyard light switch as she started out the back door. The light didn't come on, the backyard remaining wrapped in darkness. "I should change the lightbulb—"

"It can wait. Can you see well enough?" Celia had switched out the lightbulb last week for a burned-out one she'd kept hidden away in a drawer. The yard had to be dark, she needed Lupe to tell the police the backyard light was burned out when asked. The light from the kitchen windows provided just enough illumination so the backyard wasn't all inky blackness, but the gate at the back was still hidden in darkness. It opened out onto Trail Wood Way, where Lupe always parked her old Honda. "Do you want me to walk you out?"

"No, no." Lupe shook her head. "I'm not afraid of the dark."

She watched Lupe go, slinging her purse strap over her shoulder as she went. Celia bit her lower lip and looked at her Fitbit. It was almost a quarter till nine.

He shouldn't be out there yet. God forbid Lupe see him—the last thing they needed was someone to see him skulking on the road behind the house, something to remember later when questioned. She'd wanted Lupe to leave around eight, like originally agreed, but there was too much to be done with the grad students lingering, the little get-together meant to be a little happy hour with wine and simple mixed drinks and finger sandwiches and sliced vegetables with ranch dressing for dipping dragging out longer than she'd assumed it would.

After all these years, she should know better.

She'd have to hurry them out, and that would be remembered later, too.

It was a chance she'd have to take if they didn't leave soon.

She swore under her breath as the gate shut behind Lupe. If he was early...no, Lupe would be rushing, wanting to get home as fast as she could. But someone walking their dog or jogging...

So many things could go wrong.

The night was quiet, very quiet like every night in Aptos. She hadn't wanted to move there, wanting something like one of the Victorians in the older part of Santa Cruz, close to the boardwalk and the funky shops, closer to the water.

And as always, what she wanted hadn't mattered. Aptos fit Philip's pretentious snobbishness better, even if it meant surrounding her with soccer moms and women in yoga pants who drove SUVs and drank lattes while yakking on their iPhones.

She hated Aptos.

I'm going to sell this place.

She closed the door and glanced back out the window again before letting the curtain drop back into place.

They had to be gone by nine.

She couldn't use her cell phone, either.

Who did you call at nine, Mrs. Blackburn? the cops would ask.

She rinsed the wineglasses out, put them on a towel with the others to dry.

She could hear them, laughing, in the living room, and gritted her teeth. They were gathered close around his well-worn easy chair, on the edge of their seats, wineglasses in hand, drinking in his wisdom, paying attention to every word coming from his lips like the sycophants they were. Chosen by the Great Man himself, after sifting through essays and applications and recommendation letters until the wee hours of the morning, every last one of them feeling special for being picked by THE Philip Blackburn.

She had, in fact, been one of those wide-eyed, fawning, adoring, sycophantic students once, not all that long ago.

It seemed sometimes like it had been at least a million years.

Her welcome-to-the-program cocktail party hadn't been here, of course. He hadn't been at the University of California-Santa Cruz then. Philip was riding high on his National Book Award shortlisting and was writer-in-residence at Louisiana State University then, angling for the Robert Penn Warren chair. She'd been so thrilled, so delighted, so honored, to be selected for the Great Man's program back then, having read every word he'd written, every short story and essay and novel. Bashful, with her own hopes and dreams, she remembered how she'd blushed when the Great Man had turned his attention to her, making sure she had wine and food, keeping her there talking about Art and Literature and the Written Word after the other students had long gone, just the two of them left in that big empty, dusty house just off the campus on Highland Avenue, just past the fraternities and sororities and hideous student apartment complexes that looked like something, he told her with a sad shake of his head once, like something out of Eastern Europe from before the Iron Curtain fell.

She'd been the Chosen One that semester, and hadn't she felt special?

Special enough for him to marry, right?

Special.

Yeah, she'd been special, all right.

She poured herself another glass of wine and walked to the door to the front room of the big house she'd hated almost on sight. Built as part of a development in the 1970s, houses for upper-middle-class professionals on streets with adorable names like Quail Run Road and Lori Lane and Trout Gulch Road. It was a bigger house, at the end of a dead-end lane, on a bigger lot than its neighbors, with the big fenced backyard opening out onto the sidewalk of another street with slightly smaller, less expensive houses. The creek in walking distance, the redwood hiking park perfect for jogging and getting back to nature, if you liked that sort of thing. She pushed the door open, standing in the doorway, looking at the tacky living room with the furniture he'd picked, the faux wood floor tile, the never-used fireplace. He was seated, of course, in the enormous thronelike chair carved from mahogany he'd found in a secondhand shop in San Francisco and always lied was a family heirloom. He'd filled it with overstuffed pillows, the matching mahogany cane with the brass lion's head he had to use now leaning against the throne's right arm. He'd had it when she had been his student, but back then it was an affectation, a prop he used for his role of Great American Author. He was good in his role, she had to give him that, even now that she hated him. Once she'd looked at him just as adoringly as the young woman in the blue cable-knit sweater, plaid skirt, black tights, and thick glasses was now, her unruly dark hair pulled back into a severe ponytail, leaning so far forward on the edge of her chair she was in danger of pitching face first onto the floor.

The two boys looked impossibly young to her, not old enough to be in college, let alone MFA students. *Was I ever that young?* she wondered, as she took another drink. They didn't look much older than Dylan had when he—

She pushed away that thought. She couldn't think about Dylan now. That would—no, she couldn't.

Unnoticed, she walked back into the kitchen. It used to bother her they never noticed her, didn't pay any attention to her, when she was younger and first married to the Great Man. Of course, back then she still had hopes and dreams, when she spent hours hunched over the kitchen table writing in a notebook or later, at the keyboard, trying to make Art, and always failing.

And then she'd gotten pregnant.

She was three months along when the LSU Board of Regents made it clear that not only was he never going to get the Robert Penn Warren chair, they didn't want him on campus anymore.

Or in Baton Rouge, for that matter.

She pushed aside the curtain over the window in the back door and peered through the gloom. Her heart was racing. *Calm down,* she told herself, *you have to stay calm. That's how people get caught.*

She wasn't going to get caught.

She wasn't a fool.

She let the curtain fall back into place. He was out there, like they'd planned, and he would just have to wait longer. Patience wasn't Alejandro's strength, but he wasn't stupid.

Not entirely stupid, anyway.

That was part of his charm.

The Great One was shouting, thumping on the floor with his cane again. She could hear his voice rising over the others. "David Foster Wallace was not a genius!" She didn't have to see his face to know it was reddening to purple, his eyes were bulging, and there were flecks of spittle flying from his mouth.

Maybe he'll have another stroke. I should be so lucky.

It had been two years since he'd had the first stroke, when he'd fallen off his throne while watching *I, Claudius* on DVDs from Netflix ("one of the only television shows worth watching"), unable to speak, his eyes open and staring at her, unable to respond to anything she said as she punched in the numbers 9-1-1 on her cell phone, her hands shaking, not believing this was happening on top of everything else, it was just One. More. Thing.

That was the first time, really, sitting in the emergency room, waiting for the doctors to come tell her what was wrong with him, clutching her cell phone in her hand, afraid another set of doctors might call at any moment, that was the first time she'd wondered what would happen should Philip die.

And actually, it seemed...*pleasant.*

Sitting there in an uncomfortable chair with her phone in one hand and a Styrofoam cup of undrinkable coffee in the other, she lost herself in a fantasy of what her life would be like if the doctor came out and told her Philip had died. Not having to deal with his students, his tyrannical needs when he was writing another book or a short story or a book review, his desperate, childlike, narcissistic, constant need for attention and approval; the freedom to watch what she wanted and do what she wanted and eat what she wanted whenever she wanted...it was lovely.

It was so lovely she felt a little cheated when the doctor came out to tell her Philip was resting comfortably, he'd had a stroke and would need some rehabilitation, of course, but there was no reason why he couldn't make a full recovery.

She'd nodded, followed the doctor back to the private room where Philip slept, thinking bitterly *of course HE is going to make a full recovery.*

Wasn't that the way it always worked?

She'd felt guilty enough about those thoughts to head down to Our Lady Star of the Sea on her walk the next morning before going down to the beach, to light a candle and ask forgiveness for her thoughts, to plead with God to not punish her through Dylan, but even as she said the Hail Marys and worked the ancient rosary beads she'd had since girlhood, she knew Philip would live and Dylan would die.

She'd known Dylan would die the moment she heard the diagnosis.

She never admitted it out loud, of course, to anyone. But the moment the doctor told her about the bone cancer, she knew her son would die. As she accepted the condolences of the other faculty wives and relatives and the people she knew that were just the Great Man's fans and not her friends, she just felt numb. She wasn't going to cry in front of any of them, not going to let anyone see her weakness. She just smiled a little bit and said thank you over and over again, the way she did at the Great Man's book signings or launch parties or events honoring him, when strangers would tell her how amazing it must be to be his wife, to share his bed, to have borne his child.

His child. The child he'd never lifted a finger to help her with. She was his mother and therefore that was her job. The Great Man's was to create Art, hers to raise their child. "You can still write," he told her after the baby came home. "He'll take naps, won't he?"

Yeah. Naps.

And then came the cancer diagnosis.

She'd been too busy to realize how much she hated, *resented*, him as Dylan died, as he went through treatment after treatment, after he learned to not cry or scream or sob from the pain in his bones anymore, as his hair fell out and he lost weight and sometimes was so weak he couldn't get out of bed. And then she had to take care of them both after the Great Man's stroke. Dylan, so weak and in so much pain, sorry to be a bother, always saying he was sorry in his breathless little voice, as opposed to Philip, so demanding and needy and insistent and nasty to the home health workers she'd hired to help, complaining always about the cost and bitching about his physical therapist. The exhaustion she could feel deep inside her bones, her joints, the tiredness that never seemed to go away.

But no, she hadn't *wanted* him dead then. No, not even then, she was still fine to be his wife, to take care of his correspondence and proofread his manuscripts and be the good little faculty wife he wanted—thought he deserved.

No, it wasn't until Dylan was actually dead that her way of thinking shifted.

It was during the after-funeral reception or get-together or whatever you want to call it, when everyone was in the big house the most concentrated efforts of Lupe couldn't quite keep clean, aware of dust bunnies and cobwebs where the sharp-eyed faculty wives and the neighbors could see them, everyone murmuring and whispering and gathering around the Great One on his throne, paying obeisance and giving him their sympathy, like he hadn't found Dylan's existence—and his death—an enormous inconvenience.

Without Dylan, the years ahead of her as the Great Man's wife stretched endlessly ahead of her.

Sipping at a glass of white wine, ignored in a corner as everyone flocked to the side of the father who should be grieving but was actually reveling in the attention he was getting as Bereft Father, she thought again about what her life would be like without him.

And just like that night in the hospital waiting room, it looked wonderful.

The question was *how?*

She looked out the back window yet again, listening to the voices from the front sitting room. It did sound like they were winding down at last, maybe the students were finally going home. She saw the flare of a red ember out in the yard, just inside the gate. Alejandro, smoking a cigarette. She wished he would quit, but you couldn't tell a twentysomething anything, she'd heard the Great Man say that enough times.

Even a stopped clock is right twice a day.

The cliché would send the Great Man screaming into the night.

She walked back over to the doorway. The girl was leaving, pulling on a jacket, the boys still seated on the floor. The Great Man was still sitting in his throne, thumping the floor with his cane for emphasis. She hated when he did that, had always hated that cane.

Had she ever loved him?

I must have, she thought as she leaned against the doorframe. *I must have loved him once. When I was young and foolish and still could dream about my future. The question should be, did he ever love me?*

The boys were also getting up now, heading for the door, shrugging their jackets onto their shoulders in that fluid way all young boys seemed to possess, thanking her on their way out the door. Philip of course stayed in his throne, not moving, not seeing them to the front door—the Great Man never would stoop to that, of course.

One of those three, she thought, *the ones who stayed behind, it will be one of those three.*

He always chose one of his seminar students to be his teaching assistant, with all that brought with it—hours of unpaid labor for one of them, but introductions to agents and editors, the possibility of breaking through into actual print with a real publishing contract...

It was no wonder so many of them were willing to do anything to get—and keep—the gig.

Philip didn't discriminate between male and female students, either.

She didn't care until Dylan died. That was when she realized, with startling clarity, that her marriage had been over for years. She'd just been too busy with Dylan to notice.

And once Dylan was gone, and she wasn't busy being mom anymore, when she wasn't rushing to doctors and hospitals and treatments, wasn't keeping track of medications and times to take them and when they needed refilling, then she finally had the time to realize just how much she hated Philip Blackburn.

"Which one of them?" she asked, walking over to the front door and locking it, slipping the dead bolt into place.

"Ashleigh, I think." His hands were folded over his bulky stomach, his head tilted back and his eyes closed.

She walked over, picking up the empty wineglasses. A joint was smoldering in one of the ashtrays. He had a medicinal marijuana prescription, of course; as soon as it was legal in California he'd gotten one from his doctor. "Always smarter to have a girl," she said, pinching out the joint with her forefinger and thumb, tossing it into the glass jar with the others.

It had been a boy who'd gotten them run out of Baton Rouge.

He didn't open his eyes, but waved one of his pudgy hands dismissively. "That won't happen again," he muttered. "Can you get me some more wine?"

"Of course," she said brightly, refilling the glass on the table next to his throne. "Empty," she announced. "Shall I open another one?"

He sounded drowsy. "No, 'sgood."

She walked back into the kitchen and rinsed out the bottle, placing it carefully into the recycling bin for glass. She eased the back door open. Light pierced through the darkness. The enormous old trees along the back fence rustled in the cold night breeze. Something out there moved—had she imagined that? No, it was him. He stepped into the pyramid of light, smiling at her.

Alejandro.

He smiled at her, taking off the black ski mask and shaking out his thick, shoulder-length bluish-black hair.

So, so beautiful.

After they'd moved here, to Aptos, whenever she had the time she'd taken Dylan with her and driven up the Cabrillo Highway, going down to the beach and taking long walks, breathing in the salty sea air, watching the surfers. The beach, those walks, had always centered her, took her to a place in her mind that calmed her. She didn't care about which of the Great Man's students he was sleeping with when she was walking along the shoreline. As Dylan got older, as he looked for starfish and shells, played in the sand, it was a time that was just for them. Sometimes she didn't have the time to drive all the way in to the boardwalk beach in Santa Cruz, and they went to the beach down in Aptos instead. But she didn't like it there—there was always the chance that one of the neighborhood women she couldn't stand would be there. She couldn't even bear the thought of having to make idle chitchat with any of those women. She liked the boardwalk, that area of Santa Cruz—she never stopped wishing Philip had bought one of the old Victorians instead of choosing a character-less 1970s development in what was basically just a suburb.

The morning after the funeral, after her only son was buried in a cemetery in goddamned California instead of back home with her family in Louisiana, she had to get out of the house. As he waddled into the kitchen for coffee, his worn old velvet bathrobe hanging open, "You should write about Dylan's death," he'd said. Standing at the counter filling his cup with coffee, as she literally shook with anger and rage at what he'd had the callous disregard to say to her the morning after she'd buried her son, he went on, "You do still want to write, don't you? I just assumed he kept you too busy."

"Yes, yes, he did," she mumbled, before walking away from him and out the front door. Blindly she walked down the sloping streets and around corners, feeling the irresistible pull of the sea, the fishy smell of the air, the need for sunshine on her face and sand beneath her feet. *You need to leave him, you need to leave him, there's no need to stay anymore, you need to leave him* playing over and over again in her head in a litany, like a Gregorian chant. But when she crossed the road, kicked off her sandals, and felt the bare sand beneath her feet, the sea breeze on her face, the gulls squawking and flying overhead, another, darker thought came to her.

You could always just kill him.

She dismissed the thought, crossed herself, said a quick Hail Mary, plopping down on the sand, wishing she had her rosary beads with her.

But she'd thrown them away when Dylan died. She'd come home from the hospital and put them inside the little box she'd always kept them in, and put them in the trash.

It was just superstition anyway, wasn't it? Philip had always mocked her for the beads. "You haven't been in a church in years," he'd say, and he was right.

Alejandro rose from the sea as she sat there shaking with anger and hurt and rage and pain. She hadn't noticed him out there in the water, but she couldn't miss him now, in his wetsuit, water streaming off him, the thick black hair plastered to the side of a face speckled with drops from the sea. He planted his surfboard into the sand not three feet from her and started unzipping himself out of the rubber, peeling it away from tight, lean muscles spiderwebbed with bulging veins, an enormous tattoo of a fire-breathing dragon stretching from his left shoulder blade over the shoulder, the neck coiled around his pectoral muscle, the head punctuated by his nipple with a breath of flame shooting across his abdomen. He was young, the same age as Philip's students.

Something long buried awoke inside her as she watched him, as his round face broke into a smile when he realized she was watching, admiring him. "Alejandro Aquino," he said simply, holding his dripping hand out to her, the fingertips wrinkled from water.

He was first-generation Filipino American, his parents fleeing the uncertainty and unrest of their native islands before he was born. They owned a mom-and-pop grocery somewhere—she was never sure where. There wasn't much money. He had his own dreams, working in their store and nights as a bartender in some tourist trap near the boardwalk.

It was maybe the seventh or eighth time they were together that she dared broach the subject of killing Philip.

And the money that would be hers.

She let the curtain drop back into place, made sure the door was unlocked, walked back into the living room.

She smiled as she sat down on the couch, crossed her legs, raised her own wineglass to her lips, and watched her husband.

Did I ever love you?

She couldn't remember.

It didn't matter anymore, really.

The plan was simple. A home invasion, several robbers with ski masks over their faces so she couldn't identify them. She'd already gotten rid of the things they would steal; her jewelry, the money Philip kept in the safe, his big stash of marijuana. She'd set out enough for the night, of course, before the students arrived, making sure he wouldn't notice anything amiss. Philip would struggle with the robbers, of course, and wind up dead for his trouble.

Just a few moments more, Philip, and you're a dead man.

The house would have to be trashed, of course; it didn't matter because she would sell the place, never set foot in it again afterward. People would understand, would feel sorry for her, whisper to each other, *first her son, then her husband, right before her eyes, poor thing, can't blame her for going away.*

The kitchen door swung open silently.

Alejandro stood there, and she closed her eyes.

She flinched at the sound of the gunshot.

She opened her eyes.

Alejandro was standing over Philip. Blood—so much blood. Running down the front of his shirt, his eyes goggling as he somehow turned his head to look at her, and she could see it, there, in his eyes.

He knows.

"Suh-suh-ceee—" he gargled, but his eyes went glassy before he could finish saying her name, and his entire body sagged in his chair.

Celia took a few deep breaths, trying to quell her stomach, the wine and finger sandwiches turning to acid and vinegar, a strange numbness spreading through her body—

Alejandro was smiling at her.

"Hit me," she finally managed to say.

The blow was harder than she'd expected, harder than she'd told him to hit her, the side of her face stinging, the taste of blood in her mouth. He reached over and tore her blouse, that strange smile on his face as he slugged her again, sending her backward onto the couch and as her ears rang and stars pinwheeled in front of her eyes she thought *he's enjoying this* and then he was on top of her again, slapping her across the face and out of the corner of her eye she saw the gun on the coffee table and she reached for it—

And pressed it to his forehead.

There was just enough time for him to realize what she was doing as she pulled the trigger.

She pushed him off and threw the gun aside and the contents of her stomach came up, wine and sandwiches and other things she didn't recognize, and she heaved, gasping for breath, that horrid sour taste in her mouth, her teeth feeling raw against her tongue as she staggered to her feet...

Alejandro's eyes were open, staring up at the ceiling, the bullet hole in the center of his forehead—

She gagged again for a moment, struggled to get ahold of herself, putting her hand against the back of the couch for balance.

She didn't look at the Great Man, dead on his throne.

"Thanks," she whispered to Alejandro and staggered over to the front door. She got it open and started screaming for help.

Maybe I'll write about this, she thought as she screamed, as front lights on neighboring houses came on and curtains were pulled back. *That was great advice, Philip. I'll write about it and that will help.*

In the distance, she could hear a police siren.

They would believe her story.

She kept screaming.

SPIN CYCLE

My alarm woke me from the dreamless sleep of the truly content.

I smacked my hand down on it—it was a reflex. I opened my eyes and sat up in my bed. I could smell brewing coffee from downstairs. I yawned and stretched—I couldn't remember the last time I'd slept so deeply, so peacefully. I reached for my glasses from the little table next to the bed and slipped them on. Everything swam into focus, and my heart started sinking the way it did every morning when I started coming to full consciousness.

Still in the goddamned carriage house, I thought, getting out of bed with a moan, *and no commutation of the sentence in sight. Stupid fucking Katrina.*

But there was silence outside, other than birds chirping in the crepe myrtles.

No hammering or sawing. No drilling.

I smiled.

I slipped on the rubber-soled shoes I had to wear upstairs. I avoided the carpet nails jutting up from the wooden floor on my way to the bathroom. The floor slanted at about a thirty-degree angle to the left. It used to disorient me but I'd gotten used to it in the nine months I'd been sentenced to live in this pit. I looked at the bags under my eyes while brushing my teeth and washing my face. No need to shave, I decided. I wasn't going anywhere or seeing anyone today.

In fact, I'd finished a job and didn't have to start the next for a few days.

I was at loose ends.

I pulled on purple LSU sweatpants and a matching hooded sweatshirt before heading downstairs to get some coffee.

I was on my second cup, surveying the stacks of boxes piled in practically every available space. It was the same routine every morning. Drink some coffee, look around and try to figure out if there was some way to make this fucking place more comfortable, more livable. I had yet to find one, without renting a storage space and getting everything out.

And every morning I came to the conclusion there wasn't a way.

I closed my eyes and took deep, calming breaths.

Maybe I should just rent the storage unit and be done with it, I said to myself. *You don't know how long you're going to be stuck in here before the work on the house is done. Imagine not having all these towering stacks of boxes collecting dust in here. Imagine not having this soul-deadening reminder everywhere you look—*

A knock on the front door jolted me back into the present. I crossed the room and opened the door. "Yes?"

The tall black woman in a gray business suit standing there flashed a badge at me. "I'm Venus Casanova with the NOPD. I'm sorry to disturb you, sir. I was wondering if I could talk to you for a few moments?"

"Sure, come on in." I stepped aside to let her in. "Have a seat. Would you like some coffee? I just made some."

She flashed me a brief smile as she sat down on my rust-colored love seat. "No, thank you. I've had more than enough this morning already." She slipped a small notebook and pen out of her jacket pocket. "The label on the buzzer out by the front gate said J. Spencer. Is that your name?"

"Joe Spencer, yes," I replied. "What's going on?" I sat down in a green plastic chair. There were two of them on either side of a matching table. They were patio furniture, meant for the outdoors. Before the flood, I would have never had such things inside my house.

But as I kept telling myself, it was only temporary.

If you could call nine months and counting temporary.

"How long have you known Mr. and Mrs. Lafour?"

"Bill and Maureen?" I thought for a moment. "Just a few months—he started working on the house back in March. Nice couple, a little odd. I thought Bill was a little old to still be doing this kind of work by himself, but then I'm not paying them." I laughed, to take the sting out of the words. "So, what's going on? Why are you here, Detective?"

"I'm afraid I have to tell you Mrs. Lafour is dead." Her voice was calm, her face without expression.

"Oh, no! Bill must be—oh, how awful. How absolutely awful." I shook my head. "I assume it was her heart?"

She tilted her head slightly to one side. "Why would you assume that? Did she have a bad heart?"

"Well, I don't know about that," I replied. "But she was pretty old. Older than Bill, but I'm not for sure how old he is, to be honest. But she told me she was in her late seventies…and since he's doing construction work, I figured he couldn't be much older than sixty-five. But I do know she's his fourth wife."

Her right eyebrow went up. "His fourth wife?"

I shrugged. "Yes, he told me once he'd buried three wives and would probably bury Maureen too. He laughed about it—which I thought was kind of creepy, frankly. I mean, I guess when you've had three wives die on you—I don't know. It's just not something I'd think you would laugh about."

"So, did you know them well?"

"Not well. I mean, I talked to him more than her. Mostly about the house stuff, how it was going, things like that. He'd stop by every once in a while and give me a progress report, and of course he's always outside working whenever I come or go, you know?" I took another drink from my coffee mug. "They're a little odd."

"Odd?"

"Odd. I mean, they're friendly enough, but I always got an odd vibe from them. I didn't like to be around them, they made me uncomfortable. It's nothing I can put my finger on and say for a fact…but yeah. There was just something about them." I shivered a little. "Something not quite right, do you know what I mean?"

Before she could answer, there was another knock on the door. I smiled and got up. "Let me get that." She smiled and nodded. "Yes?" I asked.

The man standing there was handsome, and I couldn't help the involuntary smile. He smiled back at me. "Excuse me, sir, but I need to speak with Detective Casanova." He flashed a badge at me.

She came up beside me. I stepped away from the door but could still hear them as I refilled my coffee. "Yes, Blaine?" she asked, lowering her voice.

"We're going to take Lafour down to the station while the lab finishes processing the apartment. Do you want to talk to him before they take him?"

"No, have someone take his statement. I'll finish interviewing Mr. Spencer and head down."

"All right."

She shut the door and sat back down on the love seat. "Sorry about that, Mr. Spencer." She flipped through her little notepad. "Where were we? Oh yes, you were saying there was something about the Lafours you didn't like?"

I took another drink from my coffee. "I wish I could be more specific but I really can't. I remember when Mildred—the lady who owns the property—hired him, and they were moving into the house…he worked on gutting my side of the house during the day and was fixing up a few rooms for them to live in on Mildred's side…"

"So, you're a renter?"

"Yes, I've lived on the 1367 side of the house for about six years. The property owner, Mildred Savage, lives on the other side. Well, not now, obviously. She and her husband are living with some friends down on Jefferson Avenue. And I'm living here in the carriage house, until the house is done. Bill's doing my side first." I gestured around the small room, the piles of boxes. "This place is kind of cramped, as you can see." I gave her a small smile. "I know I shouldn't complain—at least I have a place to live."

"This neighborhood didn't flood, did it?"

"No, our roof came off." I laughed, shaking my head at the irony. "Unlike most people, we had water from above, not below. I lost everything on the second floor—all the furniture and everything was ruined, my clothes—my bedroom was upstairs." I waved at the piles of boxes. "Everything I was able to salvage is in these boxes."

"You evacuated, I gather?"

"Yes. I went and stayed with my sister up north. Indianapolis—a horrible place." I made a face. "I couldn't wait to get back here as soon as possible. And the carriage house was open, so Mildred let me move in here while the house is being worked on. It was very kind of her, otherwise I'd have been stuck up there for God knows how long."

"How long have you been back?"

"I came back on October eleventh. There was still a lot of debris from the roof around. I cleaned it all up and moved whatever I could salvage out of my side of the house in here. It's a little cramped. Cozy, I guess. Are you sure you don't want any coffee?"

"I'm sure."

"Well, excuse me while I get some more." I got up and refilled my cup. "If I don't drink a pot every morning, I'm useless for the rest of the day." I sighed. "And I have some work to do today—a deadline."

"What do you do for a living, Mr. Spencer?"

"Well, I'm a photographer—that's my real passion, but I mostly make my living from doing graphic design work," I said. "I work from home, and this place is so small I can't really...I've thought about renting office space somewhere, but...I keep thinking the house will be finished and everything will go back to normal."

She nodded sympathetically. "So, the Lafours moved onto the property how long ago?"

"About three months or so ago." I shrugged. "March? Yes, it was March, I think...since Katrina I can't keep track of dates and things—which is a problem when you work on deadlines." I took another sip of coffee. "But like I said, at first they seemed nice, but you know, I'm not really used to being around people much." I laughed. "I've always worked at home, and do most of my communication with clients over the phone or through email. I didn't really leave the house much before the storm...but since the storm, being the only person here on the property and the rest of the block being deserted, I felt kind of lonely, you know? I never felt it before the storm. Only after."

"I understand what you mean. The storm changed everything, didn't it? The way we look at things?"

"Exactly. I remember the day they moved in...it was a nice, sunny day. Mildred had called and told me they'd be moving in—I couldn't believe anyone was willing to live in the house the way it was—but they did! At that age, they were basically living like squatters while he redid the walls and floors in the back bedroom and the bathroom and the kitchen..."

❖

The sound of hammering drew me out of the carriage house with my coffee mug. It was a gorgeous March afternoon—seventy degrees or so, white wisps of clouds drifting across a blue sky, and a warm breeze rustling the crepe myrtles running along the property line fence.

The Lafours had moved in three days earlier, and my mood was good. After six months in the carriage house, there was an end in sight.

At last.

I walked to the back door to Mildred's side of the house. The door was open, and I could see Bill hammering at the moldy walls in what was Mildred's utility room at one point. The room was now empty—everything in it had been ruined. He looked up as I climbed the four wooden steps to the doorframe, a big smile on my face. "Hey there, Joe, what do you think?" He put the hammer down and put his hands on his hips. He puffed his chest out.

"I just thought I'd look in and see how things are going. Wow." I whistled. "You certainly have gotten stuff done around here."

"I like to work." He preened a bit. He was wearing dirty overalls with a red flannel shirt underneath.

"Where's Maureen?" I leaned against the doorframe.

"The Laundromat. That woman sure likes to do laundry."

"She drags the laundry down to the Laundromat?" I gaped at him, not believing my ears.

"Yup, she sure does." He gestured me to follow him into the next room. The sun shone through the windows into what used to be Mildred's kitchen. He pointed proudly at the new plasterboard. "Look at these walls! Now that's some quality workmanship, don't you think?"

"Yes, yes it is." I touched the wall closest to me and returned his smile.

But I couldn't get the image of the old woman dragging a laundry bag down the sidewalk out of my mind.

"This is the kind of work I'm doing on your place. Should be done gutting everything tomorrow, got some Mexicans coming to help haul the shit out. Once that's out, I've got the electrical guys and the plumber coming out to get all that fixed up nice. Then I can start on your walls."

"That's great," I said, my heart starting to lift. *I'll be in my home in no time,* I thought happily, finishing my coffee—and made a decision. "Bill, you know—I'm a little worried about Maureen. She shouldn't have to go to the Laundromat. I mean, that's a long way for her to go, dragging loads of laundry down to the corner. And she's not—" I hesitated.

Bill threw his head back and roared with laughter. "You can say it, son. She's not young. I know that, son, I'm married to her, you know! She's seventy-eight."

"And she shouldn't be dragging the laundry to the corner," I insisted.

"She has a cart, Joe. Don't worry about her. She's fine. She's like my second wife—"

"Your second wife?"

"Yup, that's right, Maureen's my fourth wife. I've already buried three, son, and I'll probably bury her, too." He laughed again. "I'll just find another one when that day comes, I suppose. A man needs a wife, don't you think?"

"Yes, I suppose."

"Why aren't you married, Joe?"

"I was." I stepped out onto the back stairs. "Well, I just wanted to stop by and say hello."

"Stop by any time you like."

He started pounding at the walls again as I went down the stairs.

My mind was made up.

❖

"So, you offered to let her use your washer and dryer? That was kind of you." Venus smiled at me.

"I couldn't stop thinking about her dragging it all the way down to the corner. I couldn't get that image out of my mind all night. She was a seventy-eight-year-old woman, for God's sake, and I couldn't understand why he would let her do that, cart or no cart. She had one—I saw her with it the next morning, bringing in the groceries from her car. You know, one of those old-lady carts with four wheels that you can load up with just about anything? I mean, Mildred's washer and dryer were damaged—I dragged them out to the curb myself. But mine was in the back just beyond the kitchen, and they worked just fine. I used them all the time. And so the more I thought about it, the more it really bothered me...so I decided the next time I saw Maureen, I'd tell her to just use mine..."

❖

The very next day, I ran into Maureen at the front gate. I'd run some errands and had stopped to get some things at the grocery store.

"Morning, Joe!" She beamed at me. Her iron-gray hair was wrapped up in a babushka. She was maybe five four in her white Keds. She was wearing a pair of jeans and a sweatshirt.

"Good morning—um, I see you're off to the Laundromat."

"Yes, it sure does seem to pile up. I swear, I'm doing laundry every day, it seems!" She laughed. "Good thing Bill bought me this cart, I'd hate to have to carry a basket all the way down there. I mean, sure it's just the corner—I'm sure a handsome, strong young man like you could easily carry a laundry basket all that way, but an old lady like me—well, good thing I've got the cart."

"Yes, well, I've been meaning to tell you—"

She cut me off. "Where've you been? You're usually not out and about this early!" She peered at my grocery bags.

"I had to mail some things, and I had to pick up some things at the Sav-a-center." I smiled back at her. "Maureen, I've been meaning to tell you—you know, you don't have to take your clothes to the Laundromat."

"They aren't going to wash themselves!" She guffawed loudly at the thought of it.

"There's a perfectly good washer and dryer in my side of the house, just sitting there. You know you can use them instead of going to the Laundromat. I mean, I don't use them that much myself, and well, I just hate the thought of you—"

A smile spread across her wrinkled face. "Oh, thank you, Joe! That's so nice of you! I told Bill what a nice young man you are, and that is so kind! I swear, I won't be a moment's trouble. I won't make you sorry you offered! That would be so much easier—I wouldn't have to sit there and wait for the clothes, you know how they always say at the Laundromat they'll throw unattended clothes right in the garbage, can you imagine that, and I just can't see telling Bill his best shirt was thrown away, you can only imagine the temper that man has, no sir, so I sit there and wait for the clothes. Oh, thank you thank you, thank you!"

I winked at her. "You can start with that load, Maureen."

And I walked back to the carriage house.

❖

Venus perked up. "She told you he has a temper, did she? Did she sound like she was afraid of him?"

"Well, that was the first time I heard about it. But I used to hear him yelling at her sometimes, late at night. Well, late at night for them. They were usually in bed by nine."

"Was this frequent?"

"She didn't have a heart attack, did she?"

"If you don't mind, Mr. Spencer, I'll ask the questions."

"Did he kill her?"

"Mr. Spencer—"

I crossed my arms. "I'm not answering another question until you tell me what's going on."

"Someone killed Mrs. Lafour, yes." She inhaled. "We're gathering evidence, Mr. Spencer, and that's why you need to answer my questions."

"Murdered. Someone killed her. Murdered." I shivered. "My God, the door to their rooms is just twenty feet maybe from my front door...did someone break in? Climb the fence? Oh my God, oh my God!"

"Did you hear anything last night? Anything out of the ordinary?"

I thought for a moment. "No, no I didn't. But I was upstairs in the bedroom watching television, and I'm afraid I had the sound up rather loud...it was really windy last night...the tarp on the roof was making a lot of noise, and so I turned the television up."

"Did you see either one of them last evening?"

"I saw her, I don't know, around six maybe? I was down here working at my desk, trying to get a rush job done. He was sanding things—you see where he has the sawhorses set up, right near my front door?—so I was having difficulty concentrating, but he finally stopped around four o'clock, I think. I finished the job right around six, and I happened to look out the window and saw her walking around the back of the house—heading for their door. I guess she was over doing some laundry on my side of the house."

"Did you see anything out of the ordinary?"

"No, I pretty much saw her every day around that time. Actually, seeing her come around the house was a regular thing." I laughed. "Doing the laundry—it was like a fetish for her."

"A fetish?" Venus looked puzzled.

"I know that sounds crazy, but it's true. She was constantly doing laundry."

"Surely you're exaggerating?" Venus smiled.

"No, I actually wish I were…"

I climbed the steps to the back door, carrying my laundry basket. I could hear the dryer running, and moaned to myself.

Sure enough, Maureen was turning the dial on my washing machine. She pulled the dial out, and I heard water start rushing into it. I closed my eyes.

"Why, good afternoon, Joe! Wanting to use your washing machine, I see!"

"Well, um, yes."

"'Fraid I beat you to the punch, there, Joe! I just put in a load!" She laughed, winking at me with her right eye.

"But you were doing laundry this morning…I thought you'd be finished by now," I said slowly.

"Oh, it just piles up when you're not looking, doesn't it? You've got to stay on top of it, you know, or you'll be doing it for days on end!"

"But you were using the washer all day yesterday…I really need to do a load of clothes, Maureen. I don't have any clean underwear or socks."

"It does pile up when you let it go for a while, doesn't it?"

"But the reason it's piling up for me is because you're always using my washer."

She laughed again. "Well, Joe, there's the two of us, you know. We dirty up twice as much as you do."

"But at the rate you're using my washing machine, you and Bill would have to be changing clothes every hour."

"Oh, Joe, you are the funny one! Talk to you later!" Still laughing, she went out the back door.

I bit my lip and set my laundry basket down on the floor. *What the hell is she washing all day, anyway?* I asked myself. I walked over to the washing machine and opened the lid. I stared down in disbelief.

There were two dish towels floating in the sudsy water.

"What the—" I could not stop staring at the towels. I slammed the lid down, and the machine started agitating again.

Is she insane?

I bit my lip, reached for the dryer door, and opened it.

An LSU baseball cap nestled in the bottom of the dryer.

A baseball cap.

"Dear God in heaven, what is wrong with that woman?" I said out loud.

❖

"She was doing a load of just two dish towels? And another load that was just a baseball cap?" She clearly didn't believe me—it was written all over her face. "You're exaggerating a bit there, aren't you, Mr. Spencer?"

"I wish I was, Detective." I leaned back in my chair. "I sat on the back steps until I heard the washer stop, and then I went in and put my load in—I took the dish towels out and left them sitting on the dryer. I was working on a job, so I came back here and lost track of time. About forty-five minutes later I realized my load would be done and I could put it in the dryer, you know, start my second load. So I walked back over." I sighed. "You'll never guess what I found?"

"What, Mr. Spencer?"

"I heard the washer running when I went in the back door, you know? I was puzzled—it had been almost an hour since I started my load, you know—the baseball cap should have been finished." I shook my head at the memory. "My wet clothes—my *underwear*—was sitting on top of the dryer. I opened the washer and there was another load—two bath towels—not mine—my laundry basket with the next load was still sitting there on the floor. She took *my* clothes out, put them on the dryer, and even though she could see I needed to do a second load, she started a load with just two towels. *Two towels!*" I took a deep breath, trying to keep the rising anger down.

"That must have been incredibly frustrating for you—"

I cut her off, the frustration and anger bubbling up all over again. "I didn't know *what* to think. I was shocked at the total lack of concern for my needs—especially since there were MY MACHINES, which I bought and paid for—and she just blithely ignored that I needed to do my own laundry, after I had told her—and then took MY stuff out of MY goddamned washer SO SHE COULD WASH TWO FUCKING TOWELS?"

"Mr. Spencer, please calm—"

"I'm so sorry." I interrupted her again, taking a few deep breaths. I smiled at her. "I just don't understand whatever happened to common courtesy. I mean, here I was, doing her a favor, and she was putting me into the position of having to BEG to use my own appliances!"

"No good deed goes unpunished, Mr. Spencer?"

"Exactly. So, I decided to try talking to her again."

"And how did that go?"

❖

I hesitated at the back door. I could hear some big band music playing and Maureen humming along to it. I knocked, but there was no response. I gritted my teeth and knocked louder.

The back door swung open, and Maureen smiled at me, wiping her hands on her jeans. "Oh, hello, Joe. I was just washing up some dishes."

"I'm sorry to bother you—"

"It's no bother at all. Now what can I do for you?"

"It's about the washing machine, Maureen."

"Is there a problem?"

"Well, I need to use it, Maureen."

"Well, go on and use them it!"

"I've been trying to for the last couple of days."

"I'm afraid I don't understand you."

"Every time I try to do my laundry you're doing yours."

"But, Joe, you said I could use your washer and dryer whenever I wanted to!"

"Yes, yes, I did. But—"

"I'm just doing what you said."

"But, Maureen—"

"First you said I could use your machines whenever I wanted to. I did what you said and now you're acting like I did something wrong. I really don't understand you, Joe. That doesn't make any sense to me."

"Maybe what I should have said was you could use them whenever I wasn't."

"But, Joe, you're never using them when I go over there. They're just sitting there, empty."

I took a deep breath. "Maureen, the point is you're using them constantly. *Constantly.* I went over there this afternoon and you were doing a load that was just a dish towel. So I waited, and when it was done, I took it out and put a load of mine in. When I went back later, you'd taken my clothes out of the washer, were drying the dish towel, and had started another load—with two bath towels, while my laundry basket was sitting there and you could clearly see I had more laundry to do."

"Did you want me to do your laundry? Is that what this is about?"

I stared at her in disbelief. "No, that isn't what this is about. What this is about, Maureen, is me being able to do my laundry."

"Because I'm not going to do your laundry."

"I'm not asking you to!"

"I don't understand."

I counted to ten in my head, trying not to lose my temper. "Maureen. I am telling you that I also need to do my laundry. You and Joe aren't the only people on this property who need to wash clothes. Has it never occurred to you that I might need to do mine?"

"But, Joe, like I said, the machines are never in use—"

I cut her off. "What do you think it means when there's a load of my clothes, wet, in the washing machine and a laundry basket with more clothes in it on the floor, Maureen?"

"But you just left the clothes in the washer and I had things that needed to be washed, Joe. I mean, that wasn't very considerate of you especially when I had some things to wash. Did you just expect me to wait around all day for you?"

"Maureen, you had two bath towels. That could have waited until I was finished with mine, is all I'm saying."

"But I can't just wait around for you all day."

"I really don't care, Maureen! ITS MY WASHER AND DRYER! If you want to use them you need to be more considerate of my needs!"

"But you said I could use them whenever I needed to!"

"Maureen, if you have a load that can't wait and my clothes are in the washer—and I don't care if they've been sitting there for three fucking days—you can take your load of two towels to the goddamned Laundromat on the corner if they can't wait! That's why I bought a washer and dryer! So I could use them whenever I want to! I don't want you touching my clothes!"

"But it would be silly to spend the money to wash two towels at the Laundromat."

"So if you want to save that money, Maureen, you need to be more considerate of my needs. You use my machines twenty-four seven. They're running practically day and night. You're going to wear them out. Are you going to replace them when you do?"

"You said I could use them."

"Okay, let me explain this to you one more time. I have another load of clothes to do. You are not to touch the goddamned washer and dryer until all of my clothes are finished. Is that understood?"

"It's not fair, but okay."

"In fact, I don't want you using my washer and dryer again today. Tomorrow's fine. But today, no."

"Okay." She nodded, and shut the door.

❖

"I'm surprised you were able to hold your temper. That must have been incredibly frustrating."

I laughed. "You have no idea. It was like there was a synapse in her brain that wasn't firing, you know? It was like in her mind I was being an ass by trying to restrict her access, I was being unfair and unreasonable. But I was able to get my clothes washed. Later on that night, I was actually feeling a little guilty about the whole thing, and I decided to apologize if I was rude the next time I saw her."

"That was really nice of you."

"I'm a nice guy. But before I saw her again, Bill stopped by that night to talk to me. He'd been drinking. I'd noticed him walking around outside before with a beer or a drink in his hand, but I'd never thought much about it. It was about nine o'clock, and I was upstairs..."

❖

I came running down the stairs. "I'm coming!" I shouted. Someone was pounding on my door, hard angry knocks. I unlatched the door and swing it open. "Bill! What are—"

He reeked of alcohol, and his eyes were half-closed. "Can I talk to you?"

"Sure, I guess. Come in." I shut the door behind him. He plopped down on my love seat. I crossed my arms and leaned against the door. "What can I do for you, Bill?"

"Hear you had a little run-in with the wife today." He laughed. "You're never been married, have you?"

"I was."

"Me, I always need a wife. They keep dying on me, though. When the last one died—it was kind of unexpected, kind of fast, dropped dead right out of nowhere—I wasn't sure what I was going to do. Then I found Maureen, and I married her. Don't know what I'm going to do when she's gone. Guess I'll find another one."

"I don't really—"

"I know she's a bit much, Joe, but she's old. She's not quite right in the head, you know. It's starting to go on her. And being here while I work on the house is hard on her, you know. Back up in Monroe, she'd watch her stories and Oprah all day while I was working. Here she ain't got nothing to do. We don't got a TV here. So she cleans. She don't like to be idle—idle hands and the devil, you know how that goes, don't you, Joe?"

"Yes, I've heard that before. But I don't see—"

"So she's a little bit nuts about the laundry. Can't you cut her a break?"

"Bill, I don't care if she does laundry from sunrise to sundown. Every day, all day, I don't care. But when I need to do mine, she needs to let me. And I don't have a lot of free time—so it's enormously frustrating—"

"I know, Joe. That woman would try Job, I swear to God. There are times when I just want to give her a good smack, see if that'll shake the brains free a little, knock some sense into her. But you got to remember she's an old woman. Her brain don't work like it used to. And doing the laundry—keeping busy—makes her happy. And that makes me happy."

"Like I said, Bill, I don't care if she uses the washer—"

"She can't be hauling the laundry up to the corner. She's old, Joe. And if she can't keep busy she won't be happy here. And if she's not happy here, I'm not going to be happy here. And then we're going to have to back to Monroe, if you catch my meaning."

"I think I do."

"And then Mildred's going to have to find another contractor. And that ain't going to be easy—there's more work here in New Orleans than there are contractors. No telling how long it's going to take Mildred to find another contractor. And you're not happy living here in the carriage house, are you?" He got up and walked over to me, leaning into me until his face was inches from mine. The sour alcohol on his breath made me a little queasy.

"No, I'm not."

"So that's just going to delay you're getting back into your house, isn't it?"

In that moment, I would have gladly killed him. "I understand what you're getting at, Bill."

"Good!" He clapped me on the back, his face wreathed in a smile. "I'm glad we've come to a kind of understanding. You want to come over for a drink?"

"No."

"You sure?"

"Quite sure."

I shut the door behind him.

❖

"So, basically he was blackmailing you?"

"Exactly. I had to let her do as she goddamned well pleased with my washer and dryer, and just suck it up and not say anything, or he'd quit. And you know as well as I do it could have taken months before Mildred could find someone else to work on the house."

"Contractors are scum."

"They certainly are! Did you have problems with one?"

"I lived in New Orleans East. There was no saving my house. I took the insurance money and sold it as is. But in my line of work—well, let's just say there are a few honest contractors out there doing good work, and a lot of criminals who should be strung up. The stories I could tell you—"

"I'm sure. I read about some of the scams in the paper the other day. Really makes you wonder what the world's coming to, doesn't it? You sure you don't want some coffee?" I got up and refilled my cup, emptying the pot. "I can make more—it won't take two seconds."

"No, I've had plenty today." She winked at me. "Trust me."

I sat back down in my easy chair. "So, no, it really doesn't surprise me he'd kill her, you know. Like I said, she was a pain in the ass. And he drank so much…"

"Did you ever talk to Mrs. Savage about the situation?"

"I did a few times, and she was sympathetic, but she never did anything about it." I shook my head with a sad little laugh. "I can't hardly blame her. I mean, here I was living under my own roof, really, while she and her husband were staying with friends. I know she just wanted to get back on the property as soon as she could… who wouldn't? She would just tell me to be patient, she'd have a chat with them, but nothing ever changed, you know? I even tried setting up a schedule. I sat down with her and told her she could do the laundry every day, but I would do mine on Wednesday and she would have to respect that."

"More than reasonable, I think."

"Yeah, you'd think, wouldn't you? But she was crazy. Absolutely crazy. After we set the schedule, the next Wednesday morning I got up and went over there, and sure enough, she had a load going in the washer. I thought my head would explode."

"You're kidding!"

"I wish I was. I was so angry I was ready to kill them both." I laughed and gave her a broad wink. "I guess I shouldn't say that to a cop."

"Should I consider you a suspect, Mr. Spencer?" She smiled at me.

"Like I'd kill someone over using my washing machine!"

"You'd be surprised what will push someone to kill…but no, at this moment you're not a suspect. It seems pretty cut and dried to me. Did you hear them arguing last night?"

"No, like I said, I've gotten used to turning the television up really loud, so I wouldn't hear them."

"Do you know what they used to argue about?"

"No, I mean, I never could make out what they were saying. All I heard was the noise—and it was definitely angry noise, if you know what I mean. His drinking and her—well, whatever it was—I always thought it was a potentially lethal combination."

"What time did you go to bed last night?"

"I guess it was around ten thirty, or just after. I always watch *The Daily Show* before I go to sleep. What time did he…" I swallowed. "You know?"

She didn't answer my question. "How did they seem yesterday to you?"

"I didn't really talk to either of them…Maureen did stop by for a moment."

❖

There was a frantic look on her face when I opened the door. She was clearly agitated, looking from side to side, shifting her weight from one foot to the other. She was wringing a dish towel in her hands. "Why hello, Maureen." I smiled at her. "Is everything okay?"

"Where is my laundry?" Her voice shook.

"How would I know?"

"I took a load over there half an hour ago and it's not there!"

"Maureen, dear, are you sure?"

"Joe, I took a load of towels over this morning, I know I did. I remember going over there…"

"Then where could it have gone?"

"I was hoping you knew."

"How would I know, Maureen? I haven't been over there since two days ago when Bill showed me how the place was coming along."

"You're sure you don't know?"

"No, I don't, Maureen. Just like the other day when you accidentally put the red dye in with your whites."

"I don't remember doing that…why would I do that?"

"I don't know, Maureen. It doesn't make any sense. I guess you were just a little confused," I said soothingly.

She nodded. "Confused. I've been really confused lately."

"Why don't you go lie down for a little while and get some rest?"

"That—that might be a good idea."

"Why don't you just go take a nap and forget about it?"

"Oh, oh, okay."

I shut the door and smiled to myself. "Stupid bitch," I said to myself as I walked behind a stack of boxes. I picked up Maureen's laundry basket—two towels—and walked back over to my door. It was almost too easy, I reflected, as I opened the door and walked around to the front of the house. Bill was sawing some plywood, set up on two sawhorses. "Bill?"

Bill stopped the saw and smiled. "Oh, hi there, Joe." His eyebrows came together. "Why you bringing your laundry around to the front?"

"It's happened again, Bill." I set the laundry basket down on the ground. "This isn't my laundry, it's yours."

"What happened this time?"

"Maureen just came by, extremely upset, because her laundry had disappeared. She said she took the load over and put it in the washer, but when she went back to put it in the dryer it was gone. She thought maybe I knew what happened to it."

"Go on."

"So, I told her to go lie down, and I went over to the laundry room. Bill, the basket was sitting there on top of the washer. If it was a snake it would have bit her."

"Dear God."

"It's getting worse, Bill. I mean, what's going to happen next? Is she going to leave the stove on when she goes to the grocery store?"

"She wouldn't do that," he whispered.

"Well, a week ago she wasn't putting red dye in with the whites, either. I had to run three cycles of bleach through the washer to get that dye out, Bill. She's not getting better, and you know it. She needs help. Aren't you afraid what might happen if you go to the hardware store or the lumberyard and leave her here alone?"

"I—"

"I mean, it was one thing when she was just forgetting things. But this is really serious." I sighed. "Well, I've said my piece. I'll leave the laundry basket where I found it."

❖

"So, she was getting even more forgetful?"

"I guess he just lost patience with her one last time. It's sad, just terrible." I got up to answer the door. I shrugged as I turned the knob. "She really went downhill quickly, Detective." I opened the door and smiled. "Detective Tujague, was it?"

"That's right."

"Come in. You want to speak to Detective Casanova?"

"Actually, I want to ask you something."

"Me? All right."

"Did you see Lafour last night?"

"No. I was just telling Detective Casanova about the last time I saw him. It was about two or three yesterday afternoon. I can't be more specific than that, I'm sorry. Why do you ask?"

"Lafour says that he came over here last night and you two had drinks together and talked about the situation with his wife. He got tired, and you helped him back to his apartment, and that's the last thing he remembers before waking up this morning next to his wife's corpse."

"I'm sorry, but he's obviously mistaken. I don't drink. So he doesn't remember killing her?"

"Well, that's his story. You're certain he wasn't here?"

"I couldn't be more certain. I don't drink. You can do a blood alcohol test on me if you like. But he was not here last night."

"Okay, thanks. Venus?"

"That's about all I need. Thank you so much for your time, Mr. Spencer."

"If I can be of any help…"

"We will need you to come down to the station at some point and make a statement."

"Just let me know when."

"Thank you, Mr. Spencer." Venus smiled at me as she walked outside. "I really appreciate your help."

I closed the door and leaned against it. I exhaled.

They don't suspect a thing.

❖

Bill had come over, around nine thirty. I invited him in, and he took a seat on the love seat. He was carrying a plastic go-cup.

"Hi, Bill. How is she?"

"She was almost hysterical. When she gets like that, man, she really drives me to drink. I told her to take one of her goddamned pills and lie down, she was giving me a headache."

"What are you drinking?"

"Whiskey. Tonight's a whiskey night. Man, that was a tough one. After she went to sleep I called her daughter. That one's a real bitch. Didn't want to hear a word I was saying. Wants to fly out here and see for herself. I told her I don't need her permission to put Maureen in a facility, thank you very much, and to try to keep a civil tongue in her goddamned head. Just like her mother, doesn't know her place. No wonder that one couldn't keep a man."

"I'm real sorry about all of this, Bill."

"Well, you know, Joe, that's mighty kind of you to say. I know you had some trouble dealing with the woman, and I want you to know how much I appreciate your going out of your way to keep her happy. You didn't have to do that."

"Well, I couldn't have you quit the job before the house is finished."

"Oh, I would have never done that. I might have sent her back up to Monroe, but I believe a man always finishes what he started. Once I give my word I don't go back on it."

I stared at him. "Well, you sure had me fooled, Bill!" I somehow managed to keep my voice friendly and light.

All these weeks—all of this frustration and irritation, that I've put up with—for nothing?

He laughed. "Just trying to keep the peace and make the best of a bad situation. I do appreciate everything you've done though in the last few days. She really went downhill fast."

"Went?"

"What's that?"

"Nothing. Here, let me refill your drink."

"I thought you didn't drink."

"I always keep good liquor around—just because I don't have a drink doesn't mean everyone else has to be on the wagon."

"Say, that's some good stuff!"

"I always believe if you're going to get something, get the best." I put his cup down on the counter and reached up for the Wild Turkey bottle.

And right there, sitting on a lower shelf, were the sleeping pills. They'd been prescribed for me after the storm.

I shook out two of the capsules and opened them, pouring them into the bottom of his cup. I smiled.

It was all falling into place.

I put some ice in his cup and poured the Wild Turkey over it, watching as the granules dissolved into the alcohol. I smiled and carried the cup back over to him. "There you go, Bill."

"Thank you." He took a long drink. "Ah, that's some good stuff. I never get much chance to drink the good stuff."

"So, you think she's going to have to go into a facility?"

"Like you said, I can't watch her all day." He sighed. "I can't be without a wife, Joe."

"But—"

"I don't know what to do. I guess I'll have to divorce her. Damn. I never thought I'd see the day come when I'd be getting a divorce."

"All your other wives have died?"

He yawned. "Yes, I've put them all in the ground. I figured I'd be burying Maureen, too—but this? Sorry," he yawned again, "I don't know why I'm so sleepy all of a sudden."

"You've had a draining day—all that work on the house and Maureen..."

"Yeah. I'm sorry, Joe, I guess I'd best be getting to bed." He fell back against the back of the love seat. "I don't know what's wrong with me."

"Let me help you up." I helped him to his feet and put his arm over my shoulders. He reeked of whiskey and sour sweat. "Just lean on me, Bill, and we'll just get you to bed."

"I...don't...understand...why...that...whiskey...hit...me...so...hard..."

"Don't worry about it. It happens to everyone."

"I can...barely...keep...my...eyes...open..."

He was practically dead weight by the time I got him back inside the main house. I eased him down onto the sofa. His mouth fell open and he started snoring.

I stared down at him contemptuously.

"Idiot."

All I'd wanted was for her to be put away. I wanted her and her insane laundry fetish gone, out of my life for good.

It would be so easy, I thought, looking down at his open mouth, to just put a pillow over his face—

In the other room, Maureen gurgled in her sleep.

I turned away from him and walked over to the bedroom door.

She was on top of the covers, sleeping on her back in a floral nightgown. Her glasses were on the nightstand next to the bed.

I looked back at Bill on the couch.

I never go back on my word, I heard him saying in my head again. I smiled.

I walked over to the bed and looked down at her.

"Maureen? Maureen? Can you wake up for a minute?" I said softly, reaching down to shake her shoulder. "Maureen? Can you open your eyes?"

She shifted on the bed. "Go 'way, leave me alone." Her voice was drowsy.

"Can you open your eyes for me?"

They fluttered open, and she blinked at me, squinting. "Joe? What?"

"Bill had a little too much to drink and I had to help him home."

"Okay, thanks."

"Goodbye, Maureen."

I reached down and my hands closed around her throat.

She thrashed against me, but I put my weight behind my hands. And finally, she stopped.

I let go of her throat and smiled down at her. "You look so peaceful, Maureen."

I went back to my own apartment.

From my living room window, I watched them lead Joe away in handcuffs.

He looked upset, confused.

They always say that criminals are stupid. I like to believe only stupid criminals get caught.

I hadn't planned on killing her. No, all I wanted to do was get rid of her, have her locked up in a home someplace where she'd never bother me again.

But it all just fell into my lap, and who am I to say no to opportunity?

And he was just as bad as she was, wasn't he?

All that time, he knew she was making my life hell and didn't do a fucking thing about it—actually, he *helped* her.

But to give him credit, he'd been bluffing and I'd been afraid to call him on it.

But I won the hand, didn't I?

A strangled wife, a hungover husband reeking of whiskey? And the sad neighbor, telling the terrible story of how they fought almost every night, yelling and screaming at each other? "No, Officer, he was never here." His word against mine—and really, what motive did I have for killing his stupid old wife? Like I told Detective Casanova, no one would kill someone over a washing machine.

Stupid annoying old bitch.

And that's that. They have him dead to rights, anything he tries to say will just be seen as a lie calculated to get him out of a murder rap.

Stupid, stupid people.

Note to self: Never, ever let someone use your washing machine again. Ever.

COLD BEER NO FLIES

D ane Brewer stepped out of his air-conditioned trailer, wiped sweat off his forehead, and locked the door. It was early June and already unbearably hot, the humidity so thick it was hard to breathe. He was too far inland from the bay to get much of the cooling sea breeze but not so far away he couldn't smell it. The fishy wet sea smell he was sick to death of hung in the salty air. It was omnipresent, inescapable. He trudged along the reddish-orange dirt path through towering pine trees wreathed in Spanish moss. The path was strewn with pine cones the size of his head and enormous dead pine needles the color of rust that crunched beneath his shoes. His face was dripping with sweat. He came into the clearing along the state road where a glorified Quonset hut with a tin roof stood. It used to be a bait and tackle until its resurrection as a cheap bar. It was called My Place. It sounded cozy—the kind of place people would stop by every afternoon for a cold one after clocking out from work, before heading home.

The portable reader board parked where the parking lot met the state road read *Cold Beer No Flies.*

Simple, matter-of-fact, no pretense. No Hurricanes in fancy glasses like the touristy places littering the towns along the Gulf Coast. Just simple drinks served in plain glasses, ice-cold beer in bottles or cans stocked in refrigerated cases at simple prices hardworking people could afford. Tuscadega's business was fish, and its canning plant stank of dead fish and guts and cold blood for miles. Tuscadega sat on the inside coast of a large shallow bay. The bay's narrow mouth was crowned by a bridge barely visible from town. A long two-lane bridge across the bay led to the gold mine of the white sand beaches and green water along the Gulf Coast of Florida. Tourists didn't flock to Tuscadega, but Tuscadega didn't want them, either. Dreamers kept saying when land along the gulf got too expensive the bay shores would be developed, but it hadn't and Dane doubted it ever would.

Tuscadega was just a tired old town and always would be, best he could figure it. A dead end the best and the brightest fled as soon as they were able.

He was going to follow them one day, once he could afford it.

Towns like Tuscadega weren't kind to people like Dane.

Dane unlocked the back door of the bar, turned off the alarm, and flicked on the lights. He clipped his keys to a belt loop of his khaki shorts. He put in his ear buds and selected his Johnny Cash playlist, and mariachi horns rang in his ears.

He got to work. My Place opened at five.

He moved from table to table, taking stools down. Some tables weren't level and wobbled a bit. The overwhelming scent of pine cleaner didn't quite mask the stench of stale beer and week-old cigarette smoke. Once all the stools were down, he made sure every table had a clean black plastic ashtray in the center. He sang along with Johnny Cash. He'd learned how to play guitar listening to Johnny Cash music when he was a kid, picking out the chords to "Sunday Morning Coming Down" over and over until he had them right, singing in his high-pitched kid's voice. He'd loved that guitar until his father had smashed it to pieces in a drunken rage.

He'd never touched another guitar.

He sprayed cleaner along the bar counter and ran a towel over its length. There was always dust, no matter how many times he wiped down the damned bar. It was everywhere, an endless battle that aged his mother before her time. Sometimes he wondered if it was his father's drinking that got her to leave, or the dust. She complained about both. One day when he came home from school she was gone, no note, no goodbye, no nothing. Some of her clothes were gone, a couple of things precious to her, and her car. Gone like she'd never existed in the first place, never to come back, never to call, never a Christmas or birthday card. She'd just walked away and never looked back.

One day he'd do the same.

There was a rumble of thunder as he started stocking the glass-front refrigerator cases with cans and bottles of beer from the stockroom. "Ballad of a Teenage Queen" started playing as rain started drumming on the tin roof. It took about three songs before he was done, and moved on to filling the ice. The muscles in his shoulders and back strained as he lugged buckets of ice from the storeroom behind the bar and dumped them into the bins. He checked the kegs. Both were at least half full. He glanced at his watch. He had fifteen minutes till My Place opened for business.

Dane turned on the sound system and hit this week's designated playlist. The boss paid a deejay from one of those bars in Fort Walton Beach popular with the spring break crowd to come up with a playlist for the bar every week, and Dane hated every last one of them. He went behind the bar and lit a cigarette.

The bar didn't get busy until about nine thirty or ten. There was a small rush from guys stopping in for a beer on their way home after work, but the real busy time was those last two and a half hours before closing. It wasn't a bad job. Sam McCarthy was a good boss, and Sam trusted him to open the place five nights a week. It wasn't a bad gig for a twenty-year-old. He made minimum wage plus tips— and the tips more than made up for the low hourly wage. Working at My Place beat working at McDonald's, where he worked before he turned eighteen and Sam gave him this job. It was better than working at Walmart, like so many of the jerks he'd gone to high school with did, and he'd be damned if he was going to work at the cannery, come home smelling like fish every damned day and never getting that smell out of his clothes or the house, like his father.

Fuck his father.

He'd be twenty-one soon. If everything worked out the way it should, he'd be able to get out. He'd started looking at apartment listings in Pensacola online. Once he'd moved over there, he'd get his GED, maybe take some classes at Pensacola State, get his degree. Sam said accountants never had to worry about getting work, and he'd always been good with numbers. He could get a job at a club in Pensacola—it was never a bad idea to have some extra cash, just in case things went bad.

Wasn't that how his mother managed it? Scrimping and saving and taking in people's laundry and sewing and putting aside every cent until she had enough to go?

That might be the best lesson he'd ever learned from her.

Maybe he could even work at one of the gay bars in Pensacola.

He'd never been inside one—the gay bars were strict with ID, and he'd never bothered to get a fake one. His experiences with other guys were limited to meeting guys on apps or online—local men with wives and kids, guys who weren't gay and would kick the shit out of you for even saying the word.

Like in high school.

The biggest bullies were the ones who had the most to hide.

Like Billy Werner.

Nah, that wasn't fair, was it? Billy had never been a bully. Billy had been his friend…at least until—

He put the cigarette down in a black plastic ashtray and wiped sweat from his face with a bar rag. No matter how many times he explained to Sam it was cheaper to keep the air going overnight, Sam just couldn't wrap his mind around it. Considering how Sam pinched every penny he touched, Dane thought it weird Sam never figured out how to lower the power bill at the bar—or that someone in his business office didn't figure it out. The clock behind the counter turned to five o'clock, so he unlocked the front door, turned on the OPEN light.

A couple of leathery-faced older guys came in after about ten minutes, ordered bottles of Budweiser, took them to a table back in the far corner, back near the open patch of concrete drunk couples sometimes used as a dance floor on weekends. None of his regulars came in, probably because of the rain. Rainy nights were always slow. He made himself a cup of coffee with the Keurig machine he'd talked Sam into buying.

Closing time seemed hours away.

He was making a couple of screwdrivers for a pair of women still wearing their Walmart smocks and name tags around seven when Finn Bailey walked through the front door. He was wearing his police uniform and looked tired. Finn was in his late thirties, kept his body fit and trim with regular workouts. His wife was the teller at the bank where Dane had his checking account, always was friendly and nice to him. He was the cop who'd come to the high school the day his bullies had kicked the crap out of him in the locker room, busted his lip and cracked a tooth and a couple of ribs.

His last day at Bayside High School. He hadn't gone back.

Finn had the decency to come to his house and apologize to him about there being no charges filed. He also had the decency to look like he felt guilty about it. Finn checked in on him from time to time, made sure he was doing okay, tried to talk him into going back to school.

Guilt was a wasted emotion, Dane realized, unless you could use it.

"Get you a beer, Finn?" he asked as Finn put his cap down on the bar, climbed up on one of the barstools. He was going gray, Dane noticed, cobwebs of lines radiating from the corners of his eyes and mouth.

Finn wiped sweat from his forehead with a cocktail napkin, leaving little paper crumbs across his forehead. "On duty, can I get a Coke instead?" His voice sounded as tired as he looked.

Dane dunked a plastic cup in the ice bin and filled it with the hose, put it on a cocktail napkin, waved his hand when Finn pulled out his wallet. House rule: Never charge a cop in uniform. Dane felt a trickle of sweat under his arms. *Calm down*, he reminded himself. *He can't know. He's just a dumb hick cop in a dumb hick town. Besides, he feels guilty about you. Always has.*

"Did you hear Kaylee Werner went and got herself killed this morning?" Finn slurped down the Coke, gasping for air when he finished, muffling a burp.

"Did she?" He kept his voice even, flat.

"She was in your class, wasn't she?"

"Yeah, I think so. I didn't much mix with the cheerleaders and them. So, what happened to her? Finally pep herself to death?"

Finn put the cup down, popped a piece of ice in his mouth. "Left the gas on, I guess. When she woke up this morning and lit her cigarette, kaBLAM." Finn crunched the ice with his teeth. It sounded like bones cracking. "Smoking is hazardous to your health, I guess."

Dane shook a cigarette out of his pack. "That's what they say."

"The weird thing is Billy didn't come home last night." Finn tilted his head to one side, a knowing smirk on his lips. "You know anything about that?"

Dane inhaled. "Why don't you ask him?"

"I stopped by the Firestone and talked to him. He said—" He paused, looked from side to side, and took a deep breath. "He said you knew where he was. He come in last night?"

"He was here. Until closing."

"You served him?" He raised his eyebrows, looked surprised.

Dane flicked ash. "He's not a minor. And what happened in high school was a long time ago. Billy's been coming in here for a while. His money's as good as anyone else's."

"And you're okay with that?"

Dane crushed the cigarette out. "I'm okay with that. Like I said, high school was a long time ago, Finn. Besides, like the district attorney said, I had it coming, didn't I? Someone like me?"

Finn had the decency to flinch. "I never believed that, or said it, either, you know that, Dane."

"I know. Any other questions?"

Finn slid down off the barstool. "He said he didn't go home last night, and you'd vouch for that."

"He was too drunk to drive home, yeah." Dane shrugged. "I let him sleep it off on my couch. That a problem?"

"He was on your couch all night long?"

"He was there when I went to bed. He was there when I got up this morning at seven to go to the gym." Dane shrugged. "I didn't hear his truck start. I'm a light sleeper."

Finn just looked at him for a moment, then shook his head. "You're sure?"

Dane held up his right hand. "Swear to God."

"I hope you know what you're doing."

"I appreciate your concern."

"Thanks for the Coke. If you think of anything—" Finn turned to go.

"I'll be sure to let you know."

Dane watched him walk out of the. He lit another cigarette, and this time his hand shook.

Billy Werner had come in the night before, around nine o'clock, a purplish bruise on his forehead. He'd been wearing a white ribbed tank top and a tight pair of jeans worn through in places—the knees, the cuffs, just under the curve of his left ass cheek. He'd always been sexy, even in the seventh grade all those years ago when Dane used to sneak looks at him in the shower. His dad was a minister, and part of his ministry was *your body is your temple to God*, so all of his kids exercised, lifted weights, jogged. Billy had abs you could slice your finger on when he was thirteen, a bubble butt, veins that bulged over the lean muscles of his arms. He also had an acne problem, so despite the strong jaw with a dimple in the center and the bright blue eyes, the lightly tanned skin and the body, Billy never had much luck with girls. Being the son of a minister who also owned a used-car lot didn't help much either. He was a nice kid, not too bright, but when Dane was alone in his bed at night he'd think about the way

Billy looked in the showers, in the locker room, in his underwear, until he ached down there and had to do something about it. He'd always watched Billy, marveling at the graceful way he moved, how he walked on the balls of his feet so he kind of bounced with every step.

And Billy wasn't the ringleader. He wasn't sure Billy even hit him.

He was just...there.

"What'd you do to your forehead?" Dane asked, opening a bottle of Bud Light, Billy's usual. Billy had taken to coming in to My Place a couple of times a week. It had been a little awkward that first time, sure. How do you serve one of the guys who gay-bashed you back in high school without it being a little weird? But Billy had never bullied him, Billy had never called him *fag*, Billy had just gone along with the other guys...

He'd just been there.

It was easier to believe that, wasn't it?

Billy had always...always been nice to him.

And it had just been a little kiss.

"Hit it on an open cabinet door." Billy took a drink and grinned sheepishly. "You know me, clumsy as ever."

"Kaylee didn't hit you with a frying pan?" He was joking, but only a little bit. He didn't put much past Billy's wife.

Kaylee Werner had a temper, always had, even back in high school. She had a mean streak, would get a glint in her eye that spelled danger for whoever had provoked it.

Dane always believed it was Kaylee behind it all.

He and Billy had been friends since they were kids.

It was just one little kiss...he thought she'd seen it that night on the beach but couldn't be sure. She'd called hello, and they'd sprung away from each other. She didn't say anything, just smiled, eyes glittering, as she took Billy by the hand and led him away, gave him a little wave as they disappeared behind a sand dune.

He wasn't sure until some of the guys on the football team—and Billy—cornered him that day in the locker room.

He thought they were going to kill him.

But Billy—Billy just looked sick when they threw him up against the lockers so hard it knocked his breath out, his head slamming against the metal. As they started kicking and punching and he slid down to the ground, Billy just stood there.

He hadn't said anything, didn't throw a punch.

But he was there. He hadn't tried to stop them, either.

He hadn't gone back to school after the janitor found him there in the locker room, called an ambulance, repeated his story through bruised lips and broken teeth again and again, and for what?

No charges filed. They didn't even get suspended.

No, he'd dropped out and gone to work at McDonald's. He'd see them here and there, Billy and Kaylee, spoiled princess in her yellow Mustang with her prize driving around town. He missed Billy, missed his old friend, remembered that night on the beach in the moonlight when their lips had touched for just a moment...

Kaylee got pregnant their senior year, and they got married at City Hall right before graduation. Her parents disowned her, and Billy was stuck married to an angry, bitter woman who hated her life and blamed him for everything. And Billy got a job as a mechanic working at the Firestone, changing oil or fixing tires.

The town was too small for Dane not to know everything that was going on with them. Everyone knew everyone and everyone knew everyone's business.

So, it wasn't an accident that first night when Billy turned up at My Place. He knew that as sure as he knew Billy's beer was $3.75.

It took several visits for Billy to start telling Dane his woes.

It took several more before Dane stopped enjoying hearing about Billy's pain and started feeling sorry for him.

And it didn't take long for him to feel his old attraction to Billy again. It hadn't ever gone away. Despite everything.

And thinking maybe, just maybe, Billy felt the same way, maybe he always had. He'd only pulled away from the kiss all those years ago when they heard Kaylee calling. He'd closed his eyes and kissed back, hadn't he? Dane wasn't remembering that wrong.

"No." Billy laughed but looked away, wouldn't meet his eyes. Which meant she *had* gotten violent again.

It wasn't the first time. She'd hit him before, thrown things at him, and there was a scar on his side where she'd come at him with a knife in one of her rages. "Why don't you leave her?" Dane had asked when Billy had pulled up his shirt to show him that scar, noticing the lightly tanned skin, the still-defined abdominal muscles, how deep the line from his hip bone heading into his groin was before it disappeared into the jeans. Billy shook his head. "She's on the outs with her parents, but they want her to leave me," Billy said mournfully. "She'll get everything if I walk out on her. Her dad will see to it. And who'd believe me?" His face flushed. "I mean, what kind of man lets a woman hit him?"

What kind of man lets a woman hit him.

Dane poured out a shot for Billy, slid it across the bar to him. "You need this."

"No, man, I can't. I've got to be able to drive home."

"You can't go back there, man. She's going to kill you one of these times."

Billy looked at him for a long minute, then picked up the shot glass.

"You can stay at my place tonight." Dane held up his hands. "You can sleep on the couch, or I can. Nothing more than that, man. Just a place to stay the night."

Billy downed the shot and turned the glass upside down, snapping it down on the bar. He looked Dane right in the eye and said, "That's not what I want and you know it."

It was raining the first night Billy was too drunk to drive back home. Kaylee was on a girls' weekend with some of her old friends, off to a beachfront condo in Panama City Beach with some of her buddies, who felt sorry for her in the dead end she'd wound up in, too stubborn to admit she'd made a mistake and go back to her parents, "bitches," Billy had slurred over his fourth or fifth beer, "who're too good to set foot in our house. They make her crazy, you know, they always make her feel bad about herself and then I'm the one who has to pay for it." He'd taken Billy's keys from him around midnight, told Billy he could crash in the trailer that night.

Maybe he'd known then what would happen that night. Maybe he'd hoped, maybe he'd planned, maybe.

He'd never forget how Billy looked when he took his wet shirt off in the trailer, the way the overhead light made the beads of water on his smooth, muscular chest glisten like diamonds, the way he'd almost fallen over taking his jeans off, how hot his skin had felt to the touch when Dane caught him to keep him from falling.

Later, Billy said he'd been drunk, hadn't known what he was doing, was sorry and it could never happen again.

In a way, Dane thought as he got another beer from the cooler for Jed Mathews, *Kaylee was my fault. If we hadn't gotten drunk that night on the beach when we were camping, if we hadn't kissed and gotten caught, he wouldn't have been so scared, he might not have stayed with*

Kaylee to prove he wasn't like me. Wouldn't have slept with her to prove he wasn't like me.

But he was like me.

And there was the insurance. Kaylee made sure the insurance on the house was paid every month. They had a gas stove and an old gas hot water heater. Billy was always complaining how old the lines were, how dangerous they were.

Almost—almost like he was hinting.

Billy was snoring softly when Dane slipped out of the bed that morning. The moonlight coming through the blind made slashes of blue light across his torso, and he knew he shouldn't do this, but it was what he wanted, wasn't it?

And the money—the money could make such a difference. For them both.

He picked up Billy's truck keys off the kitchen table. He worried the sound of the starting engine might wake Billy, but there was no sign of life through the trailer windows once he turned the ignition key. He drove over to the little cinderblock house on Bayshore Road Kaylee had inherited from her great-aunt, the moon reflecting on the smooth waters of the bay out past the backyard. Not only was there insurance, but the land was worth a lot because it fronted on the water, some Yankees would pay a lot of money for that plot of land, and there was insurance on Kaylee, too, Billy had told him that not so long ago one night he had life insurance on her.

Letting things slip, here and there. Letting him know.

Accidents happened every day, didn't they? That's what insurance was for.

The house was dark and he'd been there before, another weekend when she'd gone off to visit one of her old friends from high school, taken her beat-up little car and driven down to Gainesville. He used the pencil flashlight to unlock the door and slip inside. She was snoring in the bedroom, an empty bottle of Jack Daniel's on the kitchen table next to an ashtray filled with lipstick-stained cigarette butts. She was passed out, dead drunk.

He made his way over to the stove. He knelt down and, with his pencil flashlight, found the pilot light and blew it out. He stood back up and turned all the burners on.

He turned them back off.

That wouldn't work. They might be able to tell that the burners had been on.

No one would believe she killed herself.

He walked through the kitchen to the Florida room and shone his light around. The hot water heater was hidden behind a screen. All the jalousie windows were closed tight. He moved behind the screen and shone his light down on the gas line. He pushed it with his foot. It looked frayed. He started to use his pen knife on it, but stopped.

No, turning the oven on made the most sense. He carefully shut the door between the rooms and turned the oven on, up to 400 degrees. He could hear the ticking of the gas line. He opened the freezer and yes, there was a frozen pizza. He carefully opened the box, put it down on the table next to the bottle, and placed the pizza inside the oven. He could already smell the lethal gas.

The house reeked of cigarettes, sometimes he could smell them on Billy's clothes. She'd light one when she woke up and...

Billy would be free.

She got drunk, put a pizza in the oven, and passed out, never noticing the pilot had gone out.

He got up at seven to go to the gym, and when he got back Billy was gone. There was a note: *went to work, have to be there at eight.*

He dropped it into an ashtray and lit it with his cigarette lighter.

He spent the day cleaning the trailer and doing his laundry, eyes on his phone. But it never rang, never chimed with a text. And then he'd come to work.

Dane handed Jed his change. Jed pocketed the money, no tip. The cheap old bastard never tipped.

Kaylee was dead now. She'd never hit Billy or cut him again.

He remembered how her eyes had glittered that night she came up on him and Billy on the beach.

She'd gotten those boys to beat him, he'd never doubted that. It was the kind of thing she did and laughed about later.

He closed the bar at one, half-heartedly went over the floor with a broom, counted the money, and dropped it into the safe. He'd only made about fifty bucks in tips that night, give or take, but that was fine. He locked up and walked the path back to his trailer.

Billy was sitting on the steps. He stood up when Dane came around the bend. "What did you do?" he whispered hoarsely.

Dane dropped his cigarette into the sand, unlocked his door, and held it open. "What do you mean?" he said, watching Billy's ass flex in his jeans as he climbed the steps and went into the trailer. "Seems like your house blew up this morning."

"What did you do?" Billy's face was pale, his eyes bloodshot, his hair greasy and slicked back. He nervously ran one of his big hands through it, shaking his head.

"You were here with me all night," Dane said, sitting down and lighting another cigarette. "I told the cops you slept on my couch and you were here when I went to the gym at seven. Kaylee was a drunk, everyone knows it. It's not a surprise she'd blow herself up like that."

"Why?"

"I did it for you, Billy." *NO, I did it for us, but this isn't going the way I wanted it to. What's wrong with him?*

"I didn't ask you to."

"No, but—"

Billy got up. "I've got to get out of here."

"Billy—"

The door slammed against the side of the trailer and bounced back, not shutting, swinging as Billy ran down the sand path.

Dane stubbed out his cigarette.

He'd come back.

He always did.

Besides, he had that picture he'd taken of Billy's truck out in front of the house at four in the morning.

He was getting that money one way or another.

He smiled.

ANNUNCIATION SHOTGUN

I swear, I didn't mean to kill him!"

If ever a person was meant to come with a warning label, it was my tenant, Phillip. He'd been renting the other side of my double shotgun in the lower Garden District for two years now, and while he was a good tenant—always paid his rent on time, never made a lot of noise in the wee hours of the morning, and even ran errands for me from time to time—*chaos* always seemed to follow in his wake. He doesn't do it intentionally. He's actually a very sweet guy with a big heart and a great sense of humor, and he's a lot of fun to have around. Every morning, before he went to work, he'd come over for coffee and fill me in on the latest goings-on in his life. I usually just rolled my eyes and shook my head—there wasn't much else to do, really. The kind of stuff that would drive me absolutely insane seemed to roll off him like water off a duck. For all his good heart and good intent, somehow things always seem to happen whenever he's around. Bad things. He attracts them like a magnet attracts nails.

I knew I should have evicted him after the hurricane when I had the chance.

I looked from the body on the kitchen floor over to where he was standing by the stove and back again. *I don't need this*, I thought. My evening was planned to the second. My new book, the latest (and hopefully biggest selling) suspense thriller from Anthony Andrews, was due to my editor in three days. I was finishing up the revisions, and when I was too bleary eyed to stare at the computer screen any longer, I was going to open a bottle of red wine, smoke some pot, and throw the third season of *The Sopranos* into the DVD player. A very nice, pleasant quiet evening at home; the kind that made me happy and enabled me to focus on my work. After a long day staring at the computer until the words started swimming in front of your eyes, there's nothing quite like some pot and red wine to help shut your mind down and relax. When Phillip had called, panic in his voice, demanding that I come over immediately, I'd thought it was a plugged toilet or something else minor but highly annoying. I'd put my computer to sleep and headed over, figuring I could take care of whatever it was and be back in front of the computer in five minutes, cursing him with every step for interrupting my evening.

A dead body was the last thing I was expecting.

"Um, we need to call the cops." I shook my head, forcing myself to look away from the body and back over at Phillip. I felt kind of numb, like I was observing everything from a distance and was not a part of it. Shock, probably. Phillip's eyes were still kind of wild, wide open and streaked with red, his curly hair disheveled, his face white and glistening with a glassy sheen of sweat. "We need to call the cops like right now." I raised my voice. "Are you listening to me?"

He didn't move or answer me. He just kept standing there looking down at the floor, occasionally shifting his weight from one leg to the other. There was a bruise forming on his right cheek, and his lips looked puffy and swollen. I looked back at the body. I hadn't, in my initial shock and horror, recognized the man sprawled on the floor with a spreading pool of blood underneath his head. "You killed Chad," I heard myself saying, thinking *this isn't happening, this can't be happening, oh jesus mary and joseph, this isn't happening.*

Chad was his scumbag boyfriend.

"I can't call the cops. I mean, we just can't," Phillip replied, his voice bordering on hysteria. "Please, Tony, we can't." His voice took on that pleading tone I'd heard so many times before, when he wanted me to do something I didn't want to. He was always convincing, dragging me out to bars against my will, urging me on until I finally gave in. He could always, it seemed, wear me down and make me go against my better judgment. But this was different.

A *lot* different.

This wasn't the same thing as a four in the morning phone call to pick him up at the Bourbon Orleans Hotel because he'd somehow lost his pants. Or to come bail him out of central lockup because he'd pissed in public in a drunken stupor. Or to help him buy his car out of the impound lot where it had been towed. Or any number of the minor crises that seemed to be constantly swirling around him like planets orbiting the sun.

Chaos.

"What happened?" I asked. I was starting to come back into myself. I've always managed to remain calm and cool in a crisis. Panicking never makes any situation better. A crisis calls for a cool head, careful thought, the weighing and discarding of options. I started looking around for the phone, cursing myself for not bringing my cell phone with me. We had to call, and soon. The longer we waited, the worse it would be for him.

"You didn't hear us?" Phillip stared at me. "I don't see how—you had to have heard us, Tone. I mean, he was yelling so loud…" He shuddered. "Are you sure you didn't hear anything? He came over, in one of his moods, you know how he gets—*got*—and you know, just started in on me. I was making him dinner…" His voice trailed off and he made a limp gesture with his hand toward the top of the stove.

I noticed the pot of congealing spaghetti floating limply in starchy water and the other pot with skin starting to form on what looked like red sauce sitting forlornly on separate burners on the stove. "We've got to call the cops, Phillip. We don't have a choice here."

"He started hitting me." He went on as if I hadn't said a word, starting to shake again as he remembered. "Yelling and screaming. You didn't hear? You had to have heard, Tony, you had to have heard."

"I was working. I had the headphones on." I always put on the headphones when I was working so I could shut off all external distractions and focus. The littlest thing can distract me from my work, so I try to avoid all outside stimuli at all costs. The iPod had been a huge help in that regard.

"And I just pushed him away and he slipped and hit his head on the table." Phillip started to cry. "Oh, Tony, what are we going to do?"

"We have to call the cops. Where's your phone?"

"We can't call the cops!" His voice started rising in hysteria again. He buried his face in his hands. "I can't go to jail again. I just can't. I'd rather die than do that."

I looked at him, starting to get exasperated. Even now, in a panic and terrified, he was handsome, with his mop of curly brown hair and finely chiseled face with deep dimples and round brown eyes straight out of a Renaissance painting of a saint. He was wearing a tight sleeveless T-shirt that said *NOPD—Not our problem, dude.* Philip always wore T-shirts a size too small, to show off his defined arms, strong shoulders, and thickly muscled chest. I'd been attracted to him at first when he moved in and even considered trying to get him into my bed for a few days. Seeing him shirtless and sweating in the hot August sun as he moved in certainly was a delectable sight; almost like the opening sequence of one of your better gay porn movies. Yet it didn't take long for me to realize, as sexy and lovable as he was, I just couldn't deal with the chaos that followed him around like a dark cloud. No, I'd spent most of my adult life getting chaos out of my life, and I wasn't about to let it in again just so I could fuck the hot guy who lived next door. I didn't mind listening to his tales of woe every morning—but that was as far as I got involved. Just listening to him some mornings was tiring enough. "So, what do you suggest? We dump the body in the river?"

Phillip let out a big sigh and smiled. "Oh, I knew you would understand! You're the best! I knew I could count on you!"

I stared at him. He could *not* be serious. "That was sarcasm, Phillip." I looked down at Chad again, and my stomach lurched. I'd never liked Chad, couldn't understand what Phillip saw in him, and every day for the month or so they'd been dating I told Phillip to dump him at least once. He was a jerk, an arrogant ass that thought because he was handsome and had a nice body he was better than other people, as though spending hours in the gym every week somehow gave him the right to treat people like something he'd stepped in. He'd been awful to Phillip almost from the very start of their relationship. He seemed to take great pleasure in tearing Phillip down in front of people, and I could only imagine what he was like in private. After a while, I gave up trying to get Phillip to wake up and see Chad for the loser he was. I just wanted to scream at Phillip, "*Get some goddamned self-esteem!*" After he hit Phillip the first time, I was ready to kill the son of a bitch myself—but ultimately decided he wasn't worth it.

And now, as I looked down at the congealing blood under his head, I realized I wasn't sorry he was dead. The world was a better place without the arrogant son of a bitch. "I wasn't serious."

"Come on, Tony, we can't call the police." Phillip shakily lit a Parliament. "You know what that's like. And even if they believe me, that it was self-defense, and an accident, it's still going to be a big mess." He shuddered again. "That night I spent in central lockup— Tony, if I go back there, if I have to spend one night there again, I'll kill myself. I will. And you know how the cops are. You *know*."

He had a point. I didn't blame Phillip one bit for not having any confidence in the New Orleans Police Department. No one really did after the hurricane and all the allegations of police looting and car thefts and so forth, whether they were true or not. Their reputation hadn't been great before the storm to begin with. And he was probably right—getting the police involved would probably only make matters worse. Phillip needed to protect himself. They'd been pretty awful when he'd been arrested that one time. And, as it later turned out, he'd spent the night in jail for something that was merely a ticketing offense. He'd been a hysterical mess when I bailed him out. I'll never forget the look on his face when they finally let him out, and the stories he told me about that night in jail made my blood run cold. "We'll call the police and then call a lawyer." It sounded reasonable to me. "I won't let you go to jail," I said, as though I had any control over what the police would do. The more I thought about it, the less I liked it.

"I can't afford a lawyer." Phillip worked at the Transco Airlines ticket counter out at the airport. He made a decent living—always paid his rent on time—but there wasn't a lot of money left over for extras. I was loaning him a twenty now and then when he fell short. "And what if they *don't* believe me? What if they arrest me? I don't have bail money. I'd lose my job. My life would be ruined."

"We can't just dump the body somewhere," I replied, it finally beginning to dawn on me at last he was completely serious. *He wants me to help him dump the body.* "They'd find out, and that would just make things worse." I shook my head. "Phillip, this isn't something we can just cover up, get rid of the body. They always find out…and then they definitely wouldn't believe you."

"You've said a million times anyone can get away with a murder if they're careful." He crossed his arms. "I mean, you write about stuff like that all the time, right?"

I looked at him. "Murder? I thought you said it was self-defense?" I chewed on my lower lip.

"We could dump it in the Bywater." Phillip went on as though I hadn't said a word. "We could make it look like it was a mugging, couldn't we? How hard could it be?"

"Phillip…" I sighed. I could think of at least a hundred reasons off the top of my head, minimum, why that wouldn't work, but there wasn't time to go through them all. Besides, I knew Phillip. He wasn't going to listen to any of them. "We can't dump him in the river. We need to call the police." I looked back down at Chad's staring eyes and noticed the congealing blood again. "Oh my fucking God, Phillip! *How long has he been dead?*"

He bit his lips. "Um, I didn't know what to do! I freaked!"

"How long has he been dead?" I gritted my teeth.

"Maybe about an hour." He shrugged. "Or two."

My legs buckled and I had to grab the edge of the table to keep from falling to the floor next to Chad. We couldn't call the cops. It had been too long. I could hear the homicide detective now, see the look on his face, "And why did you wait so long to call us? Why didn't you call 9-1-1?" It looked bad. And what if Phillip hadn't died instantly? What if they could have saved him? *What if he had bled to death?*

And once the history of physical abuse came to light—and there were any number of Phillip's friends who'd only be too glad to tell the cops all about it, not realizing that they were sealing Phillip's indictment, thinking they were helping by making Chad look bad, like he deserved killing.

Phillip was going to jail.

Jesus FUCKING Christ.

I was going to have to help him.

"What are we going to do?" he asked, his voice hinting at hysteria on the rise. "I'm telling you, Tony, we can't call the police! I can't go to jail, I can't." He suddenly burst into tears, covering his face with his hands, his shoulders shaking.

"Well, the first thing is you need to calm the fuck down," I snapped. My head was starting to ache. I definitely didn't need this shit. I was on deadline—I couldn't exactly call my editor and say, "Sorry, I need a few more days, I had to help my tenant dispose of a dead body and come up with a story for the cops." I raced through possibilities in my mind; places to dispose of the body where it might not be found for a while. Almost every single one of them was flawed. Seriously flawed—but an idea was starting to form in my head. "Is Chad's car here?"

Phillip wiped at his nose. "Uh-huh."

"Well, we're going to have to get rid of that, too." I refrained from adding *dumbass*, like I really wanted to. But there was no sense in getting him all worked up again, since he seemed to finally be calming down. And if we were going to do this—and more importantly, get away with it—I needed him calm. "Give me a cigarette." I'd managed to finally quit a few months earlier, but I needed one now. *Get a hold of yourself, look at this as an intellectual puzzle, shut off your emotions.* I lit the Parliament and sucked in the bitter smoke. I took a few deep breaths and decided to try one last time. "Phillip, we really should call the cops. I mean, if this was self-defense—"

"What do you mean, if it was?" Phillip's brown eyes narrowed. He pointed to his cheek, which was purple. "He slugged me again, Tony. He threw me against the wall—I can't believe you didn't hear him screaming at me."

I hadn't, though—no shouting, no crashing, no struggle. Sure, I had the headphones on, but—no, it was probably self-defense, there was no reason to doubt Phillip. Chad was an egotistical bully with no problem using his fists whenever he decided Phillip had looked at him cross-eyed. I looked down at the pale face, the sticky pool of blood under his curly brown hair. His eyes were open, staring glassily at the ceiling. He was wearing his standard uniform of Abercrombie & Fitch sleeveless T-shirt and low-rise jeans, no socks and boat shoes. "What exactly happened here, anyway?" None of this made any sense. But then, death rarely does.

"I don't know, it all happened so fast." Phillip's voice shook. "Chad called and wanted to come over. I said okay, even though I really was kind of tired. So I started making spaghetti. He came in the back way"—he gestured to the door I'd come through—"and he just started in on me. The same old bullshit, me cheating on him, me not being good enough for him, all of that horrible crap." He hugged himself and shivered. "Then he got up and shoved me into the wall and punched me"—he touched his cheek again—"and was about to punch me again when I shoved him really hard, and he fell back and hit his head on the edge of the counter...then he just kind of gurgled and dropped to the floor." He gagged, took some breaths, and got control of himself again. "Then I called you."

Two hours later—what did you do for two hours? "Well, good enough for him," I finally said, stubbing the cigarette out in an overflowing ashtray on the counter.

"Are you going to help me?"

"Give me another cigarette and let me think, okay?"

The plan was simplicity itself. Once I'd smoked two or three cigarettes, I'd worked it all out in my head. I looked at it from every angle. Sure, we'd need some luck, but every plan relies on luck to a certain degree. The lower Ninth Ward above Claiborne Street was a dead zone. Hurricane Katrina had left her mark there, with houses shifted off foundations, cars planted nose down in the ground... and bulldozing had recently begun. I'd clipped an article out of the *Times-Picayune* that very morning on the subject, thinking it might be useful on my next book. Out in the shed behind the house I still had the remnants of the blue tarp that had hung over our roof after the one-eyed bitch had wrecked it on her way through. I had Phillip help me get it, and we rolled up Chad into it. We carried the body out into the backyard, and then we cleaned the entire kitchen—every single inch of it with bleach. I knew from a seemingly endless interview with a forensic investigator with the NOPD for my second book the bleach would destroy any trace of DNA left behind. I made Phillip wash the pots and pans and run them through the dishwasher with bleach. When the kitchen was spotless and reeked of bleach, I checked to make sure the coast was clear.

The lower Garden District, before Katrina, had been a busy little neighborhood. We weren't as fabulous as the Garden District, of course; when she still lived here I liked to tell people I lived about "six blocks and six million dollars" away from Anne Rice. We didn't have the manicured lawns and huge houses you would see above Jackson Avenue; we were the poorer section between I-90 and Jackson. Around Coliseum Square were some gigantic historic homes, but most of the houses in our neighborhood were of the double shotgun variety, like mine. Our section of St. Charles Avenue—about four blocks away from my house—was where you'd find the horror of chain stores and fast food that you wouldn't find farther up the street. But I liked my neighborhood. There'd always been someone around—kids playing basketball in the park down the street, people out walking dogs, and so forth; the normal day-to-day outside ramblings of any city neighborhood. The floodwaters from the shattered levees hadn't made it to our part of town—we were part of the so-called sliver by the river. When I'd come back in October, the neighborhood had been a ghost town. And even though more and more people were coming back almost every day, it was still silent and lifeless after dark for the most part. Tonight was no different. Other than the occasional light in a window up and down the street, it was still as a cemetery. We carried Chad out to his car and put him in the trunk. The way things were going it would be just our luck to have a patrol car come along as we were forcing the body in the blue tarp burial shroud in the trunk, and I didn't stop holding my breath until the trunk latch caught.

No one came along. The street remained silent.

Then Phillip got behind the wheel of Chad's Toyota and followed me through the city. "Make sure you use your turn signals and don't speed," I'd cautioned him before getting into my own car, "don't give any cop a reason to pull you over, okay?"

He nodded.

I watched him in my rearview mirror as we drove through the quiet city. There were a few cars out, and every once in a while I spotted a NOPD car. The twenty-minute drive seemed to take forever, but we finally made it past the bridge over the Industrial Canal without incident. I turned left onto Caffin Avenue and headed into the dead zone past the deserted, boarded-up remnants of a Walgreens and a KFC. It was spooky, like the set of some apocalyptic movie. We cruised around in the blighted area, my palms sweating, before I found the perfect house. There was no front door, and there were the telltale spray paint markings on the front, fresh. It had been checked again for bodies, and the three houses to its right had already been bulldozed, piles of smashed wood and debris scattered throughout the dead yards. Several dozers were also parked in the emptied yards, ready for the demolition to come the following morning.

I pulled over in front of it and turned off my lights. I got out of the car and lit another cigarette. We wrestled the body out and lugged it into the house. The house stank of decay and mold, rotting furniture scattered about as we made our way through the dark interior. We found the curving stair to the second story and carried him up. The first bedroom at the top of the stairs had a closet full of moldy clothing.

"Okay, let's just put him here in the closet," I said, panting and trying to catch my breath. Chad weighed a fucking ton. "But put him down for a minute."

Phillip let go and the body fell to the floor with a thud. I had the body by the shoulders, and I staggered with the sudden weight. The tarp pulled down, exposing Chad's head, and then I couldn't hold him anymore and he fell, dragging me down on top of him.

"FUCK!" I screamed, looking right into Chad's open eyes. His mouth had come open, and in the moonlight I noticed something I hadn't seen before.

There were bruises on his neck. Bruises—that looked like they came from fingers grasped around his neck, choking the life out of him.

A chill went down my spine. *What the fuck—*

I looked back up at Phillip. I heard him saying again, *You've always said anyone can get away with murder...*

No wonder he hadn't wanted to call the cops.

It hadn't been an accident. It hadn't been self-defense.

It was murder.

And I'd helped him cover it up. I was an accessory after the fact.

And even if I cooperated, testified against him, I'd have to serve time myself.

Does he know? I thought, my heart racing. *Can he tell that I saw? It's awful dark, and I only saw because my face was right there by Chad's.*

"Are you okay? Jesus, I'm sorry!"

He doesn't know I know.

Thank you, God.

Phillip grabbed me under the arms and lifted me up to my feet without effort. He started dusting me off. "Are you okay?" In the gloom I could see the concern on his face.

"Didn't know you were so strong," I said. I forced a smile on my face. "I'm okay."

"Don't you want to put him in the closet?" he asked. "Or can we just leave him here?"

"No, he needs to go into the closet, just in case. Let's do this and get out of here." I said, managing to keep my voice steady. *I can't let him do this, I can't let him get away with this, but I've got to get out of here, think, Tony, think, there must be something I can do...I've helped him commit the perfect crime...*

We shoved him in, standing up, and wedged the door shut.

"All right," he said, "now we have to get rid of his car, right?"

He gave me a smile. "This means so much to me, Tony, you have no idea." He gave me a hug, almost squeezing the breath out of me. *Oh, I bet I could hazard a guess or two, but damn, he's strong. Why have I never noticed that before now?* Aloud, I said, "Well, maybe we could just leave it here after all." I shrugged. "I mean, they probably wouldn't think anything about it, really."

Phillip raised an eyebrow. "But you said—"

"No, no, I know, we can't leave it here." I gave him a ghost of a smile and tried to keep my voice even, even as I thought, *I am alone in an abandoned house in an empty neighborhood with a killer.* "I'm just a little—this is a bit much, you know." I tried to make a joke. "This isn't exactly my normal Tuesday night routine." I gave a hollow laugh. "No, we can't leave the car parked out in front."

"Okay."

"We'll leave the car in the Bywater." I went on, my mind racing, trying to think of something, some clue, to leave behind. If they didn't find the body, he'd get away with it, but how to tip them off and leave myself out of it? "With any luck, within a few days the tires and everything will be stripped. And if and when the cops finally find it, the body will be gone, and Chad will have just disappeared from the face of the earth."

"Won't they check the house for bodies before they bulldoze?"

"They already checked this house—they marked the house as clear." I'd picked the house just for that very reason. I felt sick to my stomach. Oh, yes, the plan was clever. I'd outsmarted myself, that's for damned sure. Tomorrow morning the bulldozers would level the place into a pile of rubble, and when the backhoe cleared the rubble into a dumpster, if no telltale body parts fell out, that was the end of it. Nope, Chad would be off to the dump, hopefully to be incinerated, and all Phillip would have to do was pretend he'd never seen or spoken to Chad again. Sure, they'd check his phone records and see that Chad had called, but all Phillip had to do was say they'd argued and Chad said he was going out in the Quarter. Besides, it would probably be days before anyone even noticed Chad was missing—and it wasn't like the post-Katrina police force wasn't already spread thin. Even before the storm, they weren't a ball of fire.

And Phillip was obviously a lot smarter than I'd ever given him credit for.

We left the car on Spain Street on a dark block on the lakeside of St. Claude. I'd told Phillip to leave the windows down and the keys in the ignition. Someone would surely take that invitation to a free car. The police wouldn't be looking for the car for days, maybe even weeks—if ever. Maybe I could report the car stolen?

But that wouldn't lead them back to Phillip.

Phillip got into my car and we pulled away from the curb. "Some adventure, huh?" Phillip said, rolling down his window and lighting another cigarette. "Thanks, man." He put his free hand on my inner thigh and stroked it, giving me the smile I'd seen him use a million times in bars. I knew exactly what that smile meant, and my blood ran cold. "Do you really think we'll get away with it?"

"As long as you stick to your story and don't freak when the police come by to interview you—if they ever do," I replied, knowing that he wouldn't freak. Oh, no, he was much too clever for that. If the body disposal went as planned, it could be days, even weeks, before anyone even notified the police. Chad worked as a waiter in a Quarter restaurant, and from all appearances, never seemed to have any friends. Who would miss him? He wouldn't show up for work, they'd write him off—people tend to come and go quickly in New Orleans, especially now—and that would be the end of it. Unless a family member missed him, filed a missing persons report, and really pressed the cops—which wouldn't do much good, unless they were wealthy and powerful.

You have to hate New Orleans sometimes.

As we drove down Claiborne, the one thing I couldn't stop thinking about was those bruises on Chad's throat, and the two hours Phillip had waited before he called me. His story was a lie. No one freaks out and stays alone with a dead body for two hours. And I hadn't heard anything. Sure, I'd had the iPod on pretty loudly, but I'd heard their fights before. As for the bruise on his cheek, the cut lips—maybe he'd done that to himself somehow as he tried to figure out a way to get me to help him. Chad had come over—there was no way I would ever know what had finally pushed Phillip over the edge, why he'd decided that Chad had to die rather than just breaking things off with him. Or maybe the story he'd told me was partially true—maybe Chad had hit him, he'd fought back, knocked him down and Chad had hit his head on the table on the way down. But Phillip had definitely finished him off by choking him—that was obvious.

And like an idiot I fell for his story, worried as always about poor dumb Phillip in a jam, and now I am an accessory after the fact.

As I turned the car onto Calliope, I reviewed several past experiences with Phillip dealing with stress and pressure.

No, that was the other Phillip. The cute guy who always needed help, who always seemed to be in the middle of some chaotic mess.

Not the cunning stranger sitting next to me in the car who'd conned me into helping him cover up a murder.

I parked in front of the Annunciation shotgun I'd called home for the last five years.

Phillip gave me that look again. "Thanks, Tony. You really are a good friend." He leaned over and kissed me on the cheek. "Whew. Some night, huh?"

"Um, yeah."

He got out of the car and stretched, the muscles flexing. "Man, I'm beat." He gave me that smile again, and this time it curdled my blood. "Mind if I come in for a while? You have any pot? I could use some."

The last thing in the world I wanted was more quality time with him, but my mind failed me. I couldn't come up with any valid reason not to let him in. So I just nodded and climbed the steps to my side of the house. I unlocked the door and walked into my living room. The lights were still on; I hadn't turned them off when I'd rushed over there. My computer screen glowed, the pipe and my bag of weed still sitting there on my writing table where I'd left them.

"I'm really sorry, Tony," Phillip said as I walked over to the table and picked up the pipe. "You're such a good friend. I don't know what I ever did to deserve you."

That makes two of us, I thought as I loaded the pipe, my back to him. *Just smoke some pot and get the fuck out of my house.*

That's when his arms came around my waist, and I felt his lips on my neck.

I stiffened, my entire body rigid. "What are you doing?"

"Just showing my appreciation for everything you've done." He started kissing the back of my neck.

"Phillip, *don't!*" Adrenaline coursed through my body as I remembered how strong he was, much stronger than me. I turned around, planted my hands on his chest, and shoved with every ounce of strength in my body...

He stumbled backward, opened his mouth, his face shocked, and said, "Hey!" just as the back of his legs hit the coffee table.

I watched. It seemed as though time had slowed down, as though the entire world had somehow moved into slow motion.

He fell, his arms pinwheeling as he tried to catch himself, but he kept falling.

The back of his head hit the edge of the mantelpiece with a sickening crunch.

And then he was sprawled on my floor, his head leaking.

He let out a sigh and his entire body went limp, his eyes staring at the ceiling.

"Oh. My. God," I breathed, as I stepped forward and knelt down, putting my fingers on his carotid artery.

No heartbeat.

He was dead.

"I swear, I didn't mean to kill him!"

I sank down onto the floor in a stupor.

Who was *I* going to call?

QUIET DESPERATION

The fishing camps on Lake Catherine were deserted. I'd hoped they would be. That was why I was driving my three-year-old Honda CR-V east along Chef Menteur Highway at almost three o'clock in the morning. This old highway wasn't used much since I-10 was built less than a mile to the west. I could see the twin spins out the driver's window, the lights of cars and trucks heading to the north shore glowing like lightning bugs in the darkness. When I was finished, I'd head north across the Rigolets bridge and catch I-10 west back into New Orleans without being seen out here.

That was the plan, at any rate.

I pulled over onto the shoulder opposite Lake Catherine just before the road curved slightly to the left. Two fishing camps about two hundred yards ahead of me sat dark and silent on their stilts on the lake. I turned off the headlights and killed the engine. Bayou de Lesaire was just on the other side of the underbrush. I didn't know if there were alligators in Bayou de Lesaire. It would be great if there were, but it wasn't important. It wouldn't be optimal if someone found the body in a few hours, but even so, I figured I'd still have a day or two.

And then I would be home free.

I clicked the key fob to unlock the hatch.

"You just couldn't leave it alone, could you?" I said to the rolled-up rug as I started pulling it out. "You couldn't just take no for an answer."

Would I have started all of this had I known it would end this way?

Maybe.

The whole thing had started as a joke.

And now someone was dead.

The great irony is Hunter would have enjoyed the joke most of all.

Hunter had now been dead nearly two years, found in a suite in a mid-city Manhattan hotel by the maid. Ruled an accidental overdose by the coroner, the wonder was he'd lasted as long as he had. He'd always drunk too much, done too many drugs, had too much sex. He was always, as he slurred to me once over the phone at three in the morning, "up to his elbows in drugs and booze and boys."

He was one of those people who came out of the womb in a glitter shower, wrapped in a rainbow, riding on the back of a unicorn. There was money on both sides, his mother the sole heiress to a fortune made from something to do with the working parts of flush toilets, his father the last of a cadet branch of a tobacco family. His parents also drank a lot—his taste for liquor was genetic. He was from Savannah and never lost that soft drawl despite growing up in some of the most exclusive and expensive boarding schools in New England. He followed his father to Princeton and from there to the Iowa Writer's Workshop. Money was never an issue, and he'd been blessed with a talent for stringing sentences together into complicated paragraphs expressing complex thoughts. He left Iowa for New York already signed to a top agent based on one hundred pages of a novel that had everyone in the industry talking, soon signed to a contract with the publisher where I'd managed to get a low-paid job in PR after graduating from a nothing college in the middle of nowhere.

I was assigned to him when the book was being prepared for publication. Everyone thought *Shadow People* was going to break big. The higher-ups were talking National Book Awards, Pulitzers, and movie deals worth a high six figures. I wasn't sure why the vice president of publicity—a workaholic from Long Island who thought the three main food groups were nicotine, caffeine, and martinis—assigned him to me. *Shadow People* was a big novel set in the gay community with an openly gay writer—and the kind of advance Hunter got was rare for that combination. Gay novels were usually published by a house like ours as an attempt to show how hip and diverse we were—they'd throw some money at it, a couple of thousand copies would sell, it would get remaindered, and in a couple of years no one would remember it existed.

I was spellbound when I read the galley proofs. It was set in a world I didn't know—one of anonymous hook-ups, and parties and drugs and being fabulous, of gyms and bathhouses and clubs and Fire Island houses in the summer and Palm Springs condos in the winter, of bored, wealthy, talented gay men who talked about art and beauty and love and life and thought Great Thoughts, who'd never give a low-paid PR person the time of day.

It was a great book. Not the kind I would write, but a great book.

Of course, he insisted on meeting for the first time in a bar, rather than at the office. Given the choice, Hunter always wanted to meet somewhere alcohol was available. When he arrived, I stood up nervously from my table where I was sipping soda water and going over my notes and waved.

Hunter was almost ridiculously good looking, in that WASP-y white-bread-went-to-private-school kind of way. His white-blond bangs flopped perfectly on his forehead. It was all effortless; the flawless skin, the chin, the dimples, the icy-blue eyes, the proportioned frame...of course, he went to the gym regularly, but he never watched what he ate, never cared about fat grams and carbs and everything everyone else has to worry about. I've always suspected some of his enormous success as an author was because he was ridiculously good-looking. His author photos were works of art. Photographers lined up to shoot him. He could have supported himself easily as a model...over the years I've lost track of how many features in magazines like *GQ* and *Vanity Fair* and *Street Talk* there were, all shot by some major photographer.

But Hunter didn't want to talk about himself or his book or anything business-related that day. He focused those ice-blue eyes on me and wanted to know about me. About my life, my past, my dreams, why I was working in such a crappy job in publishing, finally getting me to admit for the first time I dreamed of being a writer. He was actually interested...for a brief moment I thought, flattered myself, his interest was something more than what it was, but I wasn't his type.

We became friends, and he helped me, pushed me to write, gave my books blurbs, introduced me to people who could help my career. I never would have made a living doing this were it not for Hunter. "You're just as good, if not better, than I am," Hunter said once when we were stoned and drunk, celebrating me landing an agent, "but you don't have the back story, which just goes to show how bullshit this whole business really is."

And when he died in the arms of an Eastern European hustler named Yuri, he left me everything. His copyrights, his papers, his money, his Greenwich Village apartment—everything he could legally leave to me, he did. The trusts and things from his family reverted back to the family, of course, which is how old money stays rich. His family never cared about his writing. To them it was an eccentricity, like being gay, something talked about over cocktails in a hushed voice.

I put the crates of his papers in my spare bedroom, meaning to get to them eventually. I honestly meant to. They were important, Hunter was important. I intended to find the right college to donate his papers to—they really belonged to scholars and history—but I just never could find the time to go through them.

And when I tried to make the time, I would look at the pile of boxes and give up without trying.

You see, I knew without even having to open one that there would be chaos inside. Hunter just shoved things into boxes and then wrote on them with a Sharpie, things like "first drafts" and "contracts" and "articles" and other vague things like that—sometimes more than one—so there was no telling what was where and what was even there.

I just couldn't deal with it.

And there was a small part of me that refused to believe he was gone. If I started working on his papers, that would be it. I'd have to admit he was dead, not just off on a colossal bender somewhere to resurface and regale me with tales of his wild adventures.

I loved him, and I missed him. He was my best friend.

And then one night I had a random thought that struck me as funny. I may even have laughed. I was sitting there in my easy chair streaming some lame television show someone with little to no talent was getting a fortune for writing and yes, feeling sorry for myself. I don't mind admitting that when you're a writer, shitty day after shitty day can lead to drinking too much wine and smoking too much pot and wondering why you even bother and maybe it was time to just give it all up because it's never going to happen and you've wasted way too many years of your life chasing this elusive dream, that after years of working hard and pushing yourself and doing everything your agent and your editor and your publisher ask you to do, no matter how humiliating, you still find yourself not making the kind of money where you won't have to worry every month about paying your bills, taking gigs you don't want to but you need to pay the bills.

That particular day I'd lost a ghost-writing gig. I'd written ten of the twenty or so books in a series for "tweens" about a bunch of slutty, privileged girls at a private school over the last three years and was hoping to write at least another three this year until I woke up that morning to an email from my agent telling me the publisher had decided to "go in another direction with the series," whatever the hell that meant, and so they were going to hire a fresh batch of ghost writers.

Don't worry, though, Barry, she'd closed with, *I'm sure something else will turn up soon. I'll start sending out feelers—don't get upset! Something will turn up.*

Feelers.

Something will turn up.

Great.

Adding insult to injury, about an hour later I'd gotten an email from an editor about a short story I'd been asked to write for an anthology. I'd gone through two rounds of edits with the editor, making all the changes she wanted...and then, out of nowhere, *I'm so sorry I'm not going to be able to use your story after all. But I might be able to use it if I get to do another volume...*because yes, of course, by all means, please sit on my work for some more time without paying me for it because *maybe* you might use it another time.

Yeah, that and two hundred bucks will pay the power bill.

I'd stopped myself from writing the blistering, bridge-burning response I wanted to send and just deleted her email unanswered.

I gave up on getting anything done. If it was only one o'clock, so what? I opened a bottle of Chardonnay and rolled a joint and turned on the television and spent the afternoon turning my mind into mush, trying to forget the fifty grand or so of income the loss of the series meant and wondering how I was going to keep paying the bills.

There was still money owed to me out there, and it would be spring royalty season soon. But my bank account was dwindling, more going out than coming in.

And that's when the joke came to me.

I should dig out that old manuscript and send it to Hunter's agent. I bet he could sell it for several hundred thousand, at least, with Hunter's name on it.

It was funny, wasn't it? Trying to pass off my old manuscript as one of Hunter's?

What a great joke it *would* be if I could fool his agent.

Hunter had been dead less than a year that night.

Hunter. My old friend and good buddy Hunter Sloane.

Six-figure book deal within a month, I thought, pouring another glass of wine. *If not a bidding war.*

Hunter's agent, Lester Doheny, had been pestering me about Hunter's papers since the day they arrived. I knew there wasn't anything unpublished in there, no secret lost manuscript like Lester was hoping. Hunter hated writing and never wrote anything not under contract. All those papers were just versions of novels and short stories he'd refined down and eventually published. Lester should know that better than anyone. But still, he held out hope.

People always thought I resented Hunter, his acclaim and success.

Nothing could be further than the truth. I *never* resented Hunter. Sure, I envied him. *Everyone* did. But Hunter was my friend, you know? And he wasn't, like so many others who hit the jackpot in the game of life, a dick about it. He was a nice guy, and smart. He just made a lot of bad decisions and choices in his life, which was why he wound up dead in his mid-forties. He never gave a thought to the future and never regretted his past. Hunter was all about the present, savoring every second.

I laughed a little bit as I reached for the pipe for another hit.

Fireflies was the name of the manuscript. My attempt at the Great American Novel. I'd written and rewritten and paid editors to give me opinions and sent it to agents and used their feedback and no one wanted it. It was the book I'd thought would get me out of the world of ghost-writing books for long-dead authors and turning audio recordings of D-list celebrities into memoirs or writing novels for them for a five-figure check while they banked seven figures and went on talk shows. Oops, signed confidentiality agreements for all of them, so let's just pretend I never mentioned any of that. I've written science fiction, thrillers, cozy mysteries, you name it. Hunter once told me "your blessing and your curse is that you can write anything."

The more I thought about it, the funnier it became. But Hunter's agent Lester would see through it, wouldn't he? Lester and I could laugh about it over drinks sometime when I went up to New York to sign something for the estate. Hunter only wrote three novels. The second two didn't sell nearly as well as his first one, but that first one sold and sold and was still selling and won enough awards and got taught at universities and always made lists of great American novels.

I do miss Hunter, you know. So much.

Our friendship endured even after I moved to New Orleans, where I could sit in my crumbling yet aristocratic garret in the lower Garden District and write. Hunter was so supportive, giving me advice, reading my stuff and critiquing it with his smart point of view. He never could understand why he was so admired and respected, while the books I published under my own name were virtually ignored by reviewers and awards committees and readers. It drove Hunter crazy I had to ghost-write.

"It's not right," he would always say angrily, "that you have to whore yourself like this. You are just as talented as I am."

I just didn't have his pedigree.

Hunter found the whole business of publishing ridiculous.

In my drunken, stoned stupor, I could hear Hunter telling me to do it.

I stumbled into my kitchen, sat down at my computer, and typed out an email to Lester:

> *Lester:*
> *I don't want to get your hopes up, but I've found a couple of pieces of a manuscript in Hunter's papers—I just started going through them. I will, of course, keep an eye out for the rest.*
> *Best,*
> *Barry*

After I hit Send, I had a moment of buyer's remorse.

I could always pretend I never found the rest, couldn't I?

I went to bed.

I woke up the next morning, not certain I'd really done it, that I'd just imagined doing it, until I saw Lester's response:

Barry:
> *Terrific news! Do keep me posted. If there's at least two-thirds of a manuscript, I can find someone to finish it. I can't tell you how thrilled and happy I am! There's no telling what other treasures you might find in his papers—short stories, even the memoir he kept talking about writing! I'll put out some feelers to see how much interest there is.*
> *Talk soon,*
> *Lester*

I can find someone to finish it rankled.

Why would Lester ever consider asking ME to do it?

Because Hunter was the only person who ever believed in you.

That was the moment I decided that I was going to revise *Fireflies* in Hunter's style and send it to Lester.

Fuck you very much, Lester.

Because even after all this time, after so many times…it still stung to be dismissed like that.

If I hadn't lost that ghostwriting gig. If the short story hadn't been pulled. If Lester hadn't been such a dick in his email to me.

If, if, if.

I pulled up the old manuscript and started reading.

I spent the day reading the electronic file, making notes. *Fireflies* was a much better book than I remembered…some of the rejections it got had been pretty nasty.

And undeserved.

It would be so easy to make it look like Hunter wrote it.

I shut down my computer and went to bed, completely believing I would wake up the next morning and change my mind.

But the next morning…I shouldn't have done it, I told myself not to do it, but I opened Lester's email again and read those words one more time as I drank coffee and ate my morning oatmeal. There was a dull throbbing behind my eyes.

I was going to teach Lester a lesson.

I was going to teach the whole goddamned industry a lesson.

And so I started revising the manuscript, refreshing Hunter's writing style in my mind by thumbing through his books. It was particularly galling to realize my style—the style I'd always wanted to use—was actually very similar to Hunter's.

Hunter had hand-delivered *Fireflies* to Lester twenty years ago, and told me later that night over a joint, "I told him he could thank me later for giving him his next big star."

He'd turned it down, of course.

Lester wouldn't remember it, not after twenty years.

After about a week of nonstop work, I was nearly finished. And I got another email from Lester.

Hi!

Any luck finding more pieces of the manuscript? I've put out some feelers, and I think we might get over seven figures for this. There's a LOT of interest. We might even have to take it to auction.

Thanks,
Lester

PS. You'll be hearing from a writer named Jack Sapirstein. He's an associate professor of literature, and he's interested in writing a critical biography of Hunter, isn't that great? But he'll need access to Hunter's papers.

That scared me into almost stopping. If I let someone have access to Hunter's papers...then I'd have to admit...yes, that was when I should have pulled the plug.

But I was committed to it, wanted to see what Lester would say. I could always admit it was mine if he liked it.

The next morning, I emailed him the revised manuscript. I sat there, my cursor over the Send button for a long time. I remembered Hunter, saying over and over *You're just as talented as I am, you should be even more successful than me, you can write anything, any style, any voice, which is both your blessing and your curse.*

I got up and walked into the living room and looked at the bookcase with copies of all the books I'd written. The three trade paperback novels under my own name, published by a small press for a couple of thousand dollars up front, ignored by reviewers, selling just enough copies to earn the advance back but little more than that, falling out of print quickly. The shelves and shelves of ghostwritten books, mass market paperback thrillers and cozies and space operas and romances, using house names or pseudonyms, the slutty private school girl books, the hypnotic eye of a Real Housewife staring at me from another spine.

I walked back to the computer and hit Send.

I could have told Lester the truth when he called the manuscript "Hunter's crowning achievement." I could have stopped Lester from taking it to auction. I could have admitted the truth before it was bought for seven figures. Even then I could have not signed the contract as Hunter's literary heir...but it was an awful lot of money, and my own agent wasn't having any luck finding ghostwriting gigs for me and I didn't know what else I could do. The money I had set aside was running out so much faster than I'd thought.

I was going to run out of money for the rent in about three months.

Seven figures.

Just because it had Hunter's name on it.

I'd never have to worry about money again.

I signed the contract, telling myself that was the end of it. It's not like I could find *another* manuscript. It was a one-off, my revenge on the publishing industry and all the snubs thrown my way all those years, being told I wasn't good enough.

I was just as good as Hunter. I was. And now I'd finally proved it, even if I was the only one who knew.

Jack Sapirstein was the only fly in the ointment.

He kept emailing and calling. I was running out of excuses for not giving him access to Hunter's papers. He was persistent. And I was beginning to think he didn't believe that Hunter wrote *Fireflies*.

That made him dangerous.

The first part of the advance was already in my bank account.

I thought about moving out of the country and just disappearing. Lester could just have the money wired into my account whenever royalties or other payments were due. I started planning.

Jack Sapirstein wasn't going to go away.

The only reason I answered the door was because I was expecting a package of advance reading copies.

"Jack Sapirstein," the man standing there said, sticking out his hand. He was very short, no more than five feet four at most, with a thick head of long hair parted in the center and falling to his shoulders. His teeth winked at me through a forest of facial hair, and his brown eyes were shrewd, intelligent, piercing. "I took a chance on just showing up." He pushed past me into my apartment.

"I'm sorry to be so pushy." He flashed his teeth at me again as he sat down on my battered old sofa, which I was donating to Goodwill. "But I'm impulsive and was getting frustrated with our email exchanges and I thought, hey, what the hell, I haven't been down there in years, so why not?"

He was younger than I'd thought he'd be, maybe in his early thirties. I'd checked him out online, of course, but couldn't find any pictures. He'd published a lot of pieces on Hunter and other gay writers of the late twentieth century in academic journals, considered himself an expert—wrote with the kind of arrogance that set my teeth on edge.

"This really isn't a good time—"

He cut me off before I could finish. "I'm not a beat around the bush kind of person," another flash of teeth, "but I have to see his papers. I have to."

"They're really in no condition for an academic to look at—"

"He wanted to leave his papers to Columbia," he cut me off again.

"He never said anything about that to me." How did *he* know what Hunter wanted to do with his papers?

"And he never wrote any book called *Fireflies*." That flash of teeth again as he crossed his short jean-clad legs and leaned back into my sofa. "You know it, I know it, and the whole world is going to know it soon."

I felt sick to my stomach, could barely breathe. I heard myself saying, "I was his best friend, you're being ridiculous, I certainly knew him better than you did," even as I wondered if Jack was—I don't know—maybe one of Hunter's boys? Hunter had always liked his men to be young, preferred them to be for hire. Hunter wasn't interested in having a relationship, it was only about sex for him. He usually liked his young men to have an Eastern European, almost Slavic look to them, bright blond hair and pale skin and blue eyes and *tall*.

Jack was totally the wrong type for Hunter.

So how could he know?

"I should think Lester would have noticed," he was saying, "But all Lester sees is dollar signs. Did you write it? Is that where the manuscript came from?" And he started telling me things he noticed in the manuscript that weren't Hunter-like, and about how he wasn't *really* interested in writing a biography of Hunter but he'd wanted to see Hunter's papers and Lester, whose daughter he'd dated in college, told him about the new manuscript and he *knew* it had to be a fake so he wanted to see the papers because he knew Hunter kept a diary and if there was no mention of the manuscript in the diary—

The diary.

My palms were sweating.

I didn't think anyone else knew about the diary.

I interrupted him. "How—how do you know so much about Hunter?"

His eyes narrowed, and he brushed the long hair out of his face with his fingers again. "Because I don't look like a Jan or a Stefan or an Alexi?" He laughed. "Yeah, I knew Hunter. And I also know he didn't have a manuscript stashed away somewhere." He shook his head. "Did you really think you'd get away with this?"

"What do you want? Money?"

He got right in my chest, tilting his head to look up at me. "I don't want anything from you. I just wanted to see for myself the kind of person who would try to profit off a dead man. You were supposed to be Hunter's best friend." His voice was dripping with contempt. "Yeah, Hunter told me all about you, the best friend, the only person he could really trust, the guy with all the talent who was so unappreciated and unrecognized and what a crime it was that you didn't get the glory you so deserved—"

As he spat each word at me my mind disappeared back within itself, my skin crawled and the hair on the nape of my neck rose.

I don't remember hitting him.

I don't, and I've tried in the hours since I did it. I don't remember knocking him down and sitting on his chest with my hands around his neck.

I don't remember.

When I came back to myself, I was sitting on his chest. His face was reddish-purple, eyes bulging. His hands fell limply away from my wrists. Drool was running from one side of his open mouth. There was blood beneath his head, his hair smeared into it.

I don't remember killing him.

I also don't remember the next hour or so. I was in a panic, of course, that much I do remember, as I tried to figure out what to do, ideas rushing through my mind, coming and going so quickly I couldn't make sense of them, couldn't decide which was the right one.

None of them involved calling the police.

Who knew he was coming here? Did he take a cab or an Uber? Was there a rental car parked out on the street that could be traced here? Did Lester know? Was there a lover, friend, family member who knew he was coming to New Orleans to confront me?

Someone had to know.

I couldn't get away with it that easily, could I?

I found the car key in his jeans pocket, and when I clicked the key fob there was a corresponding chirp from the street. I slipped out the front door. It was a Honda Accord, with a rental license plate. In the trunk was a suitcase. A shoulder bag in the passenger seat contained a folder, with a printout of a reservation at a French Quarter hotel—*idiot, you never rent a car in New Orleans if you're staying in the Quarter*—a laptop and phone charger. I grabbed the shoulder bag, locked the car, and went back inside.

I had to get rid of the body.

I had to get rid of the car.

How? Where?

There was an old rug in my storage attic I'd been meaning to throw away. I sealed his head inside a garbage bag, using duct tape to close it around his neck. I rolled him into the rug, tied it with twine, and dragged it over to a corner of the living room. I got out my bleach and my bucket and cleaned the floor where he'd bled, making sure to pour the bloody water down the sink and scrub out the sink with bleach.

I sat at my computer and cleared my mind.

The city was surrounded by water, swamps. The swamps had alligators. I could take the car out there, dump the body…but how would I get back home? It wasn't like I could summon an Uber out to the Manchac Swamp, or to Lake Borgne. I couldn't leave a record behind, something the police could find. Getting rid of his rental car would be easy. I could park it somewhere in the Quarter and it would get towed.

That would take days to sort out—the city's inefficiency would work to my advantage there.

So I drove the rental to the Quarter. I found an open spot on

Dauphine Street between St. Philip and Ursulines. I parked, wiped everything down, casually walked to Canal Street, and caught the streetcar home.

Getting rid of the body wouldn't be that easy.

I waited until dark to put down the back seat of my Honda CR-V. After midnight, I slung the rug over my shoulder, staggering beneath his dead weight, carried him down the front steps, and put him into the back of the car. At two thirty I drove out of my neighborhood and took I-10 and got off at Chef Menteur Highway, heading to New Orleans East. I knew exactly where to go. I'd researched the area for a ghost-written book years ago. There were fishing camps out on Lake Catherine, where Chef Menteur was bounded by the lake on one side and Bayou de Lesaire on the other, with Lake Pontchartrain just a little farther away. Bayou de Lesaire emptied into Lake Pontchartrain right before the Rigolets pass to Lake Borgne. The receding tide, with luck, would sweep the body out to the Gulf.

I set the carpet down and cut the ties.

I could see the glowing red eyes of alligators floating in the water as I rolled the body out. I removed the garbage bag from his head. I gave him a shove. He tumbled down the slope into the water. As I stood there panting, two of the gators started gliding across the top of the water in the moonlight, toward where his body floated.

There was some splashing and I turned my head away.

I left the garbage bag there and rolled up the rug.

I went over the back of the car with bleach and water, just to be sure.

When I was finished, there was no sign of the body in the water, and the alligators were gone like they'd never been there.

As I drove back, car windows down to get rid of the bleach smell, I worried.

I wasn't going to get away with this.

I'd been crazy to think I would.

The fraud was bad enough, and now I'd killed to cover it up.

But it was…it was a lot of money.

And once all the money was in my account, I would leave the country.

If anyone asked, he never showed up at my house.

If I was lucky, he'd never be found, just another tourist who came to New Orleans and vanished, his rental car towed from the Quarter, suitcase still in the trunk, his shoulder bag missing.

And I would be rich.

It was just a joke, you know, when the whole thing started.

Now it was criminal fraud for several million dollars, and someone was dead.

When I got back home, I again checked on countries without an extradition treaty with the United States.

Switzerland first, to open a bank account, and then Andorra.

Andorra sounded lovely.

Kind of like home.

THE WEIGHT OF A FEATHER

It was one of those buildings that went up right after the war, slapped together in a hurry because the city needed more living space. The soldiers were coming home with their grim memories and the city was booming. People needed places to live if they were going to work in the city, and there was money to be had. It was an ugly building, yellow brick and cement and uniform windows, with no charm, nothing that made it any different than any of the other apartment buildings that had gone up, that were still being built.

The Christmas lights winking in some of the windows didn't make them look any cheerier.

It was starting to snow, big wet flakes swirling around his head and sticking to his dark coat. There was no sign of life from Rock Creek Park at the end of the street. Max had walked past a small diner on the corner, a few lone customers behind windows frosted from cold. He'd thought about going in, getting coffee, but it was too risky.

Best to get it over with.

He buzzed the apartment, and the door buzzed open. There was a big Christmas tree in the lobby, empty boxes wrapped underneath. The white linoleum floor was already showing signs of wear and tear. He ignored the elevators and headed for the stairs. It was hot inside, steam heat through radiators making him sweat under his layers.

The third-floor hallway smelled like boiled cabbage and garlic and onions. He raised a gloved hand to knock on 3-L.

The man who answered the door smiled. Special Agent Frank Clinton was in his early thirties at most, cold gray eyes, his face battered from boxing Golden Gloves as a teen. He was wearing twill pants held up by suspenders over a white ribbed tank top. He looked up and down the hall. "Get inside, Sonnier," he said in his thick Boston accent.

Max stepped past him inside. Clinton smelled of cheap cologne, like always. The small apartment was spartan. A single bed. A table with a bottle of open whiskey. A small two-shelf bookcase. Beige walls, beige curtains. The tiny kitchenette with a gray coffee percolator on one of the burners. The little bathroom opening off the closet.

Clinton shut the door. "You brought the money?"

Max held up the attaché case. "And the pictures?"

Clinton smiled. It was an ugly smile. He crossed over to the small two-drawer beige filing cabinet that served as a nightstand for the bed. He knelt down, unlocked it, and pulled out a file folder. He tossed it contemptuously on the bed. Black-and-white 8x10 pictures spilled out across the blue coverlet.

"And the negatives?"

Clinton shoved the pictures back inside the folder, pulled out a tiny clear envelope of negatives.

"And those are the only copies?"

"I told you. I play square."

"You did." Max put the attaché on the small table, opened the snaps. He reached inside and pulled out the gun with the silencer already screwed onto the end.

"Hey—"

That was all he was able to say before Max fired twice. Both shots went into Special Agent Clinton's chest. He fell backward onto the bed, the shock frozen on his face as the blood began to run down the front of his chest. Max sighed and tossed the gun back inside the attaché case. He crossed quickly over to the bed, grabbed the folder with only a cursory glance at Clinton's sightless gray eyes. He shoved the folder inside the attaché case, dropped the gun into his coat pocket.

Sweat dripped into his eyes as he pulled open the top drawer of the file cabinet. He pulled out the first file. He didn't recognize anyone in the pictures. But he'd been right. Frank Clinton was a blackmailer, and he wasn't his only victim. He pulled out a few more folders, tossed them on the floor, letting the pictures spill out.

Panting a bit, he stood back up. Clinton's service gun was inside the file drawer. He put it in the other pocket of his jacket and carefully let himself out of the apartment. He went back down the stairs and back out the front door. There wasn't anyone on the street to see him head into the park. He walked down the path quickly to the little stone bridge over Rock Creek.

He took a deep breath and looked over the side.

The creek looked grayer and deeper than he remembered. The strong current swirled and splashed its way through the park on its way to the Potomac. There was thin ice by the banks, much like the glaze on the donut he'd choked down for breakfast. The park was silent, other than the rushing water beneath the stone bridge. He felt like he was in the middle of a forest somewhere instead of a park in the nation's capital, a short walk from civilization. The trees poking up through the snow were stark and bare and uninviting. There was no sign of life no matter which direction he looked. No couples out for a walk on a cold winter's day, no runners in gray military sweats, no birds or squirrels, no one out giving their dog exercise before heading back to the warmth of home.

Just do it and get it over with.

Someone could come along at any moment, and that would be a disaster.

Max Sonnier looked back down at the dark water. The gurgling noise it made sounded almost like a beckoning voice, inviting him to swing a leg over the side of the bridge, close his eyes, and let go.

Everything will be so much easier if you just let go...

But he knew the creek was too shallow, no matter how deep it looked. Even if he stood on the bridge's slick stone side, the fall would be at most ten feet—he might just break a bone, and really, wouldn't his survival instinct prove too strong in the shallow water for him to keep his head under long enough to drown?

Besides, he had too much to live for. Wasn't that why he'd done it? Why he was here? To keep his life together, protect what was his, what he didn't want to lose?

His jaw set. If he gave up now, his entire life, all the sacrifices made, would be for nothing.

Suicide wasn't an option any more now than when he'd first thought about it, in college.

If he'd missed any evidence, well, the creek water would ruin it.

And someone would have to *find* it, wouldn't they?

The water might be shallower now, in the dead of winter, but when the snow melted in the spring the creek would rise. No one would see it resting on the bottom of the creek, and there was a chance that the current from the higher water in the spring would lift it off the bottom and sweep it out to the Potomac.

Maybe carry it all the way out to Chesapeake Bay.

Besides, even if someone somehow did eventually find it, the trail wouldn't lead back to *him*.

It was the only answer, Max, what else were you going to do? What else could you have done? Did you really have a choice?

He closed his eyes. *There's always a choice*, he heard his mother's voice saying. *And there's no such thing as a wrong choice—you just have to figure out what is the BEST choice. Some choices are just better than others, that's all—but you always have to live with the consequences of the choice you make. There's no escaping them, so always make sure you make the RIGHT choice.*

He opened his eyes and took a deep breath, looking again furtively from side to side. He was still alone, no one in sight. He couldn't even hear cars on the nearby road. The bridge was far enough down the sloping hillside so it couldn't be seen from the road. He put his right hand into the pocket of his black trench coat and tossed the gun over the railing before he could give it another thought. It fell much faster than he'd thought it would, hitting the surface with a splash and vanishing in seconds.

It was done.

He turned and walked back up the path to the road. The wind was blowing harder, and snowflakes danced around his head as he repositioned his muffler to cover up the exposed skin on his neck. The wind was bitter cold, cutting right through his layers of clothes and his skin to the bone. He walked faster, putting as much distance from the creek as quickly as he could without breaking into a run.

It was the best choice, he reminded himself as he walked, the cold wind somehow finding chinks in the heavy armor he'd bundled himself into. He hated the cold, hated the way the leaves changed in the fall and how everything turned gray and the snow came in the winter. He hated seeing his breath, hated how cigarettes didn't taste as good when he smoked them through gloves, hated how he never really felt warm again until spring came. Ten years living in DC, and he still hadn't gotten used to the winter. He didn't think he ever would.

As the path got closer to the exit on Sixteenth Street NW, he could see a parked police car. A young man in uniform with broad shoulders and narrow hips leaned back against it, talking to a young woman whose hands were shaking slightly as she tried to drink from a paper cup of some steaming hot liquid, most likely from the little greasy spoon diner there on the corner. He kept walking steadily, making sure his glances over toward them weren't frequent enough to be noticeable.

They're just flirting, it's a first date and it's cold, that's why her hands are shaking, it has nothing to do with you.

He must be inconspicuous. If anyone noticed him, he couldn't do anything that would make them remember him later.

"You're just out for a walk, that's all, nothing more, getting some exercise, not wanting to be trapped inside all day," he muttered under his breath, lowering his head against the wind and making his face—his mouth already covered by the muffler—even less recognizable.

Not that his face was all that memorable in the first place.

Besides, it was far too soon for anyone to have found the body, wasn't it?

You shouldn't have taken so long to throw the gun away. How much time did you waste on that bridge? You should have just tossed it over the railing the minute you got there and got the hell out of there. You should already be home, everything taken care of, getting ready to leave town on the train tonight, long gone before the police get involved.

It had been a mistake to stay in the park so long.

Mistakes were how people got caught.

A mistake was why he had to go to the park in the first place.

He'd been so careful. He'd always been careful, even in New Orleans where he didn't need to be as much, where everyone just turned a blind eye as long as you didn't rub their faces in it, where so many other men he knew would sometimes head downtown to the French Quarter to satisfy their *baser* needs. No one talked about it, of course—that just wasn't done in polite society.

And those nights in the French Quarter made his marriage to Bitsy so much more tolerable, so much more bearable.

He wasn't sure he was completely safe now. He wasn't sure he'd ever feel safe again.

He couldn't be sure Clinton didn't have another set of pictures hidden away somewhere, but that was the chance he'd had to take.

But if the whole thing had been a trap designed to catch him…

Isn't that how Hoover operates?

He pushed that thought away. *You're just being paranoid. No one's interested in you. You haven't had access to anything anyone would want in years.*

But…it couldn't have just been about cash.

He needed to believe Agent Frank Clinton had been working alone, that no one else at the Bureau knew, that there were no telltale notes hidden away somewhere that would surface and point to him. He had to believe that the negatives and prints he carried in his attaché case were it, and those—those would be destroyed as soon as he walked into his home and could throw them into the fire.

He had to just get there.

He nodded to the police officer and the young woman as he walked past them. The cop was young and relaxed, far too relaxed than he would be if he'd been called to a murder site. So the police hadn't been called yet. He resisted the urge to walk faster, to get away from the apartment building as quickly as he could. But he couldn't do anything that might make them remember him once the body was discovered.

He had to be nondescript, forgettable.

Just another man out for a walk on a cold snowy day, that's all he was.

This is how people get caught. You know that. Just keep walking and acting normal.

And after today, it was important to act like nothing was different, like everything was just the same as it always had been, before that day a few months ago when Aleks walked into the grungy, dimly lit bar in the seedy part of Washington.

He hadn't been to that bar in years, not since Bitsy got pregnant the last time and warned him if he didn't give up his inversions she'd leave him and get a divorce and "tell people things." Bitsy didn't come right out and say *what* things she was talking about, but she didn't have to—she never liked actually saying it, and only did when necessary, contempt on her face and her voice shaking with self-righteous loathing.

But she'd always known, even before they were married, about his little bachelor's studio on St. Philip Street in the French Quarter just up the street from the blacksmith shop. She knew about the parties, the sailors and artists and soldiers from Jackson Barracks who would stop by for a cocktail on a hot Saturday night, sultry nights when everyone's skin had a slight sheen of sweat, nights when cold drinks filled with melting ice were just the thing to press to your hot forehead before everyone else left other than the night's guest, who would be snoring in the damp sheets when the musician across the street would come out onto his balcony at four in the morning and play mournful notes on his saxophone wearing only his underwear because it was too hot to wear anything else, his creamy coffee skin glistening in the light from the streetlamps below, with the ceiling fan blades spinning overhead pushing the thick night air around in a futile attempt to make it cool enough to sleep.

She knew and looked the other way, because she was getting old enough to be called a spinster behind her back, and marrying a younger man with a bright future in politics was better than turning into the old, bitter spinster aunt everyone else in the family pitied and whispered about after she left the room.

Ten years later the bright future in politics had turned into an important-sounding but essentially meaningless job in the State Department where he pushed papers around and tried not to fall asleep at his desk, with a town house in the Dupont Circle neighborhood and three children who looked nothing like him that he only felt a slight degree of fondness for, most of his free time spent feeling trapped and wishing he could escape. That was why he'd gone to the bar that night, while Bitsy and the children were in New Orleans visiting her family, his hat pulled down low and his jacket collar turned up high to hide his face from any watching eyes. The bar always smelled of sour alcohol and sweat and desperation. He sat down on a warped stool at the scarred bar and ordered a gin and tonic while the Andrew Sisters sang "Bei Mir Bist Du Schoen" on the jukebox. He was halfway through the drink when a young man sat down next to him.

"Buy you another?" the young man said with a thick accent, inching closer so that his knee was touching Max's.

Max felt the rush he always got when another man would approach him, hinting at desire and excitement and furtive fumbling in the dark to come. He nodded and turned his head slightly, seeing the young man's face in profile, recognizing him in that moment with an even bigger thrill.

Aleksander Smorodnikov's defection from the Soviet Union had been big news a year or so earlier. He'd been with a lesser Russian ballet company—not the Bolshoi—but one that had been allowed out from behind the Iron Curtain to make a tour of the

US, as tensions grew over Berlin. Aleks had been the principal male dancer. He'd somehow managed to escape from his heavy guard and ran to a nearby police station, begging for political asylum. Someone else Max knew at State had dealt with the resultant mess, and eventually Smorodnikov was granted asylum and landed a gig with the Washington Ballet, eventually fading from the headlines. Max wasn't a fan of the ballet but had been curious about the handsome Russian whose face had been on the front page of the papers for those troubling weeks, and so he took Bitsy to see a performance of *Don Quixote*. Smorodnikov's body, in the skintight flesh-colored tights, was magnificent and he couldn't stop staring, even after Bitsy had noticed and pinched his thigh so hard he'd winced.

Max couldn't believe his luck that night in the bar, even as Aleks led him back to an apartment, which was actually only a short walk, maybe three blocks, from the town house Max called home.

That was how it started, that evening—and with Aleks living so close by, the affair was so incredibly easy to continue…even after Bitsy and the kids came home from New Orleans.

All he needed to say was he was talking a walk, going for cigarettes, anything.

It never occurred to him that maybe it was too easy until the day Agent Frank Clinton showed up at his front door.

The timing was, again, almost perfect. Once again Bitsy and the kids were in New Orleans, this time for the Christmas holidays; as soon as the older kids were released from school Bitsy was in a taxi with them on the way to the train station. She hated DC but would never admit it and was happiest back in New Orleans, surrounded by the vapid girls she'd gone to McGehee with and her equally empty-headed family. He would follow later, of course, but was looking forward to the two weeks of freedom from them, free to pretend he'd never married his wife or had children, free to spend his evenings in bed with Aleks.

Bitsy had left for the train station not an hour earlier. He was enjoying a Scotch and the blissful silence of the empty house, just waiting for Aleks to get home from his rehearsal and call, when he answered the knock on the front door.

A fortyish man in a gray trench coat, a felt fedora pulled down low over his forehead, with small beady black eyes and thick eyebrows, stood there with a nasty smirk on his face. "Good evening,

Mr. Sonnier," he'd said in a deep, throaty voice with just a hint of smugness in his tone. "Won't you invite me in?" He flashed his FBI badge.

Wordlessly, his stomach twisting, Max had stepped aside and let him in.

"Do you know a Russian named Aleksander Smorodnikov?" Clinton asked, sitting down on the couch and placing his dirty boots on the coffee table.

He already knows, so don't deny anything—he wouldn't be here if he didn't.

"Yes. Yes, I do." Max sat down in a chair, trying to remain calm, to keep his hands steady and his voice even.

"How long have you been involved in a perverted homosexual relationship with him?"

"I don't know what you mean," Max said, his heart rate increasing, his stomach filling with bitter acid.

In answer, Clinton reached inside his jacket and tossed a black-and-white 8x10 photograph on the coffee table.

Max glanced at it but didn't reach for it.

"He's a Russian agent, you know," Clinton went on, his voice pleasant. "So, I suppose the proper question is what information have you been feeding him? You are working with him?"

This isn't happening to me, Max thought, unable to form words, unable to say anything at all.

"Weren't you a friend of Alger Hiss? You worked with him when he was with the State Department, didn't you?"

Alger Hiss—a name he'd never wanted to hear again. "I've already been interviewed about that and cleared," he replied, wiping his sweating palms on the arms of the chair.

But on it went, question after question, Max stammering out answers as his armpits and hands and forehead became slick with sweat, glancing at the phone in terror that Aleks might call in the middle of all of this, feeling the noose of circumstance closing around his throat.

He'd been questioned, of course, like everywhere who'd known him or worked with him in the department, after Hiss was accused of being a Soviet agent, but that had been the end of it. He'd had no idea whether Hiss had been a Soviet agent, a Communist, or if he wasn't. The questioning had been horrific, absolutely terrifying.

What if they didn't believe him? What if there was money somewhere he couldn't explain? What if something innocent was perceived as something bad? Had he said something that had been misconstrued?

Bitsy's snide voice, "Are they going to find out about your perversions, Max? Because if I am humiliated publicly, I may kill you myself."

It had been a horrible few weeks before he'd been cleared, with apologies and pats on the back and smiles.

That fear, though, had never gone away completely. It had always been there, in the back of his mind.

And now—here it was again.

And this danger—this danger was much worse.

"I'm sorry?" He stared at Clinton, not certain he'd heard the last thing the agent had said correctly, the smirk on his face perfectly in place.

"I said I don't think you're a Soviet spy," Clinton went on. "You're a pervert, of course, I have lots of proof of that, and you're consorting with a spy in a way that turns my stomach." His face twisted momentarily with disgust. "And for that alone, I could ruin you." He snapped his fingers. "The pictures alone would ruin you. I checked you out," he went on, the smirk getting wider. "And your wife, she has quite a bit of money, doesn't she? You've got some, too, but your wife, she has a lot more." His big yellow teeth looked like a shark's as the nasty smirk turned into a predatory smile, almost like his head was going to tilt back and he was going to somehow swallow Max whole. "I can make this all go away—for a price, of course."

He'd heard, of course, that the FBI was corrupt—everyone knew about Hoover and the parties he threw at his home that were invitation only, and that the moral corruption at the top of the bureau had filtered its way through the ranks to even the lowliest of agents. "You want money?" he said, not quite believing this was happening to him yet.

"Five thousand should do it," Clinton said, standing up. "You have a week. I'll be in touch." He pointed at the picture on the table. "I'll leave that for you. Just touching it makes me feel dirty. I'll see myself out. Men like you make me sick."

He heard the front door shut. He didn't know how long he sat there, staring at the black-and-white photograph on his coffee table before picking it up and tossing it into the fireplace, watching as it burned.

He sat down and drank several glasses of Scotch before Aleks finally called, wanting him to come over, angry about something that happened at rehearsal, his outrage only requiring that Max grunt occasionally until Aleks's anger ran its course and he began purring, longing for Max to come over. He had, walking through the fading light the three or four blocks in the cold, wondering if Aleks was a spy, wondering if Aleks had set him up, was in on the entire scam with the crooked FBI agent. Aleks didn't notice, didn't seem any different than he usually was, pouring wine and walking around without a shirt in the overly hot studio apartment, his pale marble skin glistening with sweat he occasionally wiped off with a towel. Aleks was keyed up, the way he always was after rehearsal, his bare feet sore and bloody in places, but he was so used to the aches and pains in his battered feet he didn't even notice it anymore, dismissed it as nothing if Max mentioned them.

Max didn't mention Agent Clinton until much later in the evening.

And the gun was Aleks's idea.

"You have to kill him," Aleks said, blowing cigarette smoke toward the ceiling as they lay together in his twin bed, their sweaty bodies entwined. "They always come back. Is never enough money for these peoples, and you'll never be safe. *We'll* never be safe." He shuddered. "What you think they do with *me?* They send me back, that's what they do with me. Cannot happen. You know what they do to me if I get sent back?" His ice-blue eyes widened. "A defector? Who likes other men?" He shuddered. "The gulags would be a mercy."

He was right, of course, Max realized.

Unless Agent Clinton was silenced once and for all, neither of them would ever be safe.

He'd drank more Scotch when he got back home that night as he made up his mind that he would indeed have to kill Agent Clinton.

There was no other choice, unless he wanted to lose everything.

Are they going to find out about your perversions, Max?

He sat there in his chair, smoking and drinking, until past midnight.

By Tuesday morning his plan had come together in his mind.

But the gun—where to get the gun?

Aleks solved that problem later that night, by putting the gun into his hands.

"Russians can always find guns," he said matter-of-factly when Max asked the obvious question, his face blank and expressionless. He gave a shrug. "I asked around with the other Russians. One was bound to turn up." He smiled, a sly look on his face.

Max flinched as a police car came roaring around a corner, its siren blaring and lights flashing. *They've found him, then,* he thought, willing himself to keep up the same pace as the police car went past him, heading down Sixteenth Street NW toward Rock Creek Park, to the grim apartment building where Agent Clinton lived.

Had lived.

But the threat is always going to be there, hanging over my head like the sword of Damocles, he realized as he turned the corner at Q Street. Maybe some of the pictures were in someone else's hands, there was no way of knowing. Sure, he'd gotten the negatives—but he'd never be able to relax completely ever again.

But at least the cops won't be looking for me, he thought, a smile playing at the corner of his lips as he walked up to the beige brick building Aleks called home. He slipped his key into the door and walked into the lobby, heading for the stairs instead of the elevator. *There are so many files in that cabinet, so many damning pictures of other men in pictures that could destroy them, dangerous negatives that are going to destroy a lot of careers on the Hill and in the District. But mine won't be one of them. They're not coming looking for me.*

He knocked on Aleks's door, one sharp rap of his fist against the door. The door swung open and he stepped inside quickly as Aleks shut and bolted the door behind him. His big blue eyes were wide with excitement. "Is done?" Aleks said in a half whisper, his cheeks flushed and red.

Max nodded, not saying a word.

Aleks flew into his arms, showering his cold cheeks and neck with kisses, hugging him tightly. The little apartment was hot, the windows steamed up and Aleks's thick black curls damp with sweat. He picked Aleks up, and Aleks's legs went around his waist, and Max carried him over to the bed.

Aleks's eyes glinted as Max set him down on the bed, sitting down on the edge himself. He reached for a pillow and placed his hand inside the case.

Aleks looked confused as Max raised the pillow.

He pulled the trigger, and the feathers blasted everywhere, but the pillow muffled the gunshot.

Aleks fell backward, a surprised look on his face as the dark red blood began to trickle slowly from the round hole in the center of his forehead.

"I'm sorry," he whispered, tossing the gun onto the bed next to Aleks's body.

As he searched the apartment, looking for anything and everything that might tie him to Aleks, every so often he glanced over at the bed.

The other men, the ones in his past, there had never been any kind of attachment to them. They had just been lovely bodies with handsome faces, passing through his life without leaving any marks.

He had thought Aleks was different.

This is what you get for being a fool, he castigated himself as he carefully went through everything in the desk drawers.

The search didn't take long. It was only a studio, even smaller than Clinton's, a 300-square-foot-room with a little kitchenette and a bathroom.

There was nothing.

Max walked back over to the bed. He reached down with a gloved hand and stroked the pale cheek one last time.

His eyes filled with tears for a moment, but he shook his head and walked to the door.

He made sure to lock the door before closing it behind him. The hallway was empty. He headed back for the staircase.

Ten minutes later a fire was roaring in the living room of his town house, and he watched as the negatives and what he hoped were the only pictures of him and Aleks in existence burned to nothing.

They'd identify Agent Clinton's gun, of course.

He sipped his Scotch. They'd think Agent Clinton had killed Aleks, maybe in a lover's quarrel of some sort, and who knew who the police would think killed Agent Clinton? There were at least thirty people in his file cabinet with a motive to kill both him and Aleks.

He'd so hoped Aleks wasn't involved—but every set of photographs, every picture of two nude men locked in a sexual embrace of some sort—the only thing they had in common was that Aleks was one of the men.

He picked up the phone to call Bitsy in New Orleans. As he waited for the operator to put the call through, he closed his eyes again and reminded himself of his little studio apartment in the French Quarter.

Never again in Washington, he told himself as he finished the Scotch. "Bitsy? It's done...I miss you and can't wait to see you... yes, I've packed and will be heading to the train station in about an hour..."

MY BROTHER'S KEEPER

C ottonwood Wells still stank twenty-five years later.
    I'd forgotten about the smell from the oil refinery just
north of town, near the oil fields where my father had worked. It
hung over the town like a shroud, poisonous and foul. When the
wind blew from the north the stench was almost unbearable. The
trailer park where we lived was close to the refinery, so there was
no escaping it. I never got used to it. I learned to tolerate it, like so
many other things I learned to tolerate growing up in that town.
    And like those other things, I never liked it.
    There was a Best Western now at the exit from I-10, with
a Days Inn just across the street. I pulled into the Best Western
parking lot because it was easier to turn right. I got my briefcase
and rolling suitcase from the hatch of my Subaru Forrester. In the
distance, on the far side of town, I could see the flaming stacks where
excess gas was burned off at the refinery. What used to be fields just
on the way into town from the highway was now the enormous
parking lot of a sprawling Walmart Super Center, with a Lowe's
on its other side. Like everywhere else in America, Cottonwood
Wells had fallen victim to the plastic commercialization of the chain
stores. There was a Whataburger and a McDonald's on the other
side of the highway, and a couple of gas station/mini-marts. I could
see the fast food signs lined up like soldiers on the way into town:
Burger King, Arby's, KFC, Taco Bell, Pizza Hut. All we'd had when
I was a kid was a Sonic Drive-in downtown on the main drag, and
a McDonald's.
    I walked into the lobby. It was a standard Best Western, a little
worn but not to the point of needing to be redecorated yet. There

was a hotel bar called the Mustang Ranch to my right that looked empty.

The woman at the counter wasn't aging well. She was wearing a cream-colored blouse and one of those weird female ties underneath a blazer that matched her skirt. She was wearing too much makeup and her hair was dyed a color that doesn't occur in nature. She was a little too thick in the middle for her blouse. She didn't look familiar, but Cottonwood Wells was a small town where everyone knew everyone, and people can change a lot in twenty years. "You have a reservation?" she asked without looking up from her computer screen.

"No."

"How many nights?"

I considered. I didn't know how long I was going to be in town, but I knew it wasn't going to be a minute longer than necessary. I was already sorry I'd come. "Let's say two."

"Just you?"

"Yes."

"King bed?"

"That works."

"Driver's license and credit card."

All this without even looking at me once. I slid both across the counter at her, waiting for the inevitable New Orleans conversation once she saw my license. Instead, she looked up. "Chanse MacLeod? Class of '94?"

Her name tag said Marla.

Marla. There was only one Marla in our class. Marla Quinn. She'd been one of what my sister used to call the "not girls"—not cheerleaders, not popular, not poor, just kind of in the middle with everything. I remembered her as not being particularly nice, either. There was always a mean, sly look on her face. She was the kind of girl who didn't want anyone to think she was mean but never had anything nice to say about anyone, and she'd always make it seem like an accident. She looked up at me, and I could see the meanness was still there. "I suppose you're here because your brother's in jail? He's gonna fry, you know."

Apparently, we were skipping passive-aggressive and going straight to aggressive. "Maybe." I shrugged. "It's amazing what a good lawyer could do." I wasn't about to pay for a good lawyer for my brother, but she didn't need to know that.

"Yeah, well." She smiled, her voice smothered in syrup. She leaned forward and lowered her voice to a whisper that still carried. "Bobby Cassidy was a well-liked and well-respected member of this community. Can't say that about anyone in your family."

I remembered Marla mocking my sister when we were in junior high school, what was that about? I couldn't remember, but I did remember my sister stiffening in pride, holding up her chin while her cheeks flushed red and her eyes filled with bitter, angry tears. I wanted to do something, but my sister grabbed my arm in a death grip and whispered, angrily, "Don't."

I smiled and held out my hand. "My room key?"

She flushed and handed me back my credit card and license. She didn't look at me as she activated a key card. "You're in 233. Turn left when you get out of the elevator."

I didn't answer her.

The room was clean, smelled of pine cleaner with maybe a hint of lavender. It was decorated in all the shades of brown. I unpacked my bag, put the clothes away in the battered-looking dresser, stored the bag in the closet, put my shaving kit in the clean little bathroom. I pulled out my phone and called the public defender. "Hey, it's Chanse MacLeod. I'm going down to see my brother. Maybe we should talk first?"

Her voice sounded tired. "Yeah, that'll work. There's a Starbucks on Arkansas Street, at Seventeenth. I can be there in about ten minutes."

"See you there."

The Starbucks was where a gas station used to be, and as I parked on the street a few doors down I wondered if the big gasoline tank had been removed or if they'd just built over it. I used to buy gas at that station sometimes. Some of the stoner kids, the ones with the black heavy-metal T-shirts and tight jeans, used to hang out there. By the time I was driving I was a football star, and most of the kids who'd made my life hell when I was a kid left me alone. But I still remembered their names, still remembered their faces. I remembered one of them, Stinky Parrish, even worked at the station. Maybe that was why they hung out there. He probably let them buy beer or slipped them cigarettes or let them have whatever they wanted. I bought gas there because I wanted to see if they'd have the balls to ever challenge me, try to bully me again.

They never did.

A pretty young woman, maybe thirty, got to the front door at the same time I did. From the way she was dressed—business attire, hose, skirt, matching jacket, pumps, silk blouse, hair pulled up into a bun it was trying to escape—I took a leap as I held the door open for her and asked, "Siobhan O'Connor?"

She looked at me and smiled. She wasn't wearing a lot of makeup, or it had worn off over the course of the day. There were circles under her brown eyes and her lips were a little chapped under the lipstick. "Chanse?" She shook my hand. "You're—you were a football player, right?"

Which, I supposed, was a kind way of commenting on my size. I nodded. "Used to be."

She gave me a weak smile. "People still talk about those state championship teams," she said as we walked to the counter. "I guess those were the last good times this town had."

"Those times weren't that good," I replied as a shiny-faced girl with Mercedes on her name tag greeted us. We both ordered a small dark roast of the day—I always refuse to use their pretentious size names, my little way of sticking it to the corporate man—and I paid for both of us.

We carried our cups of too-hot coffee over to the condiment bar. I watched her sprinkle a heavy layer of vanilla powder on the top, add a couple packets of pink sweetener and a dollop of half-and-half. She stirred the potion with a wooden stick and we headed to a table as far away from the counter as possible. There was no one else in the place, and the bland middle-of-the-road crooner's voice singing jazz standards through the speakers hanging from the ceiling was making me miss silence.

We had a good view of the drive-thru from our table, which was doing a fair business, cars full of teenagers backed up all the way to the street. I recognized the black-and-red letter jackets, the white chenille CW letters outlined in red thread and sewn onto the left side. I used to have one of those jackets. My sister sewed my letters on, our mother too drunk on cheap gin and too busy watching her afternoon stories to be bothered. My jacket was probably in a box in my storage space, the same box that held things like my high school yearbooks, my fraternity composites, and all my football memorabilia from LSU.

Yeah, I needed to clean out my storage space.

"So, my brother is supposed to have killed this Bobby Cassidy?"

I said while watching her stirring her coffee, trying to dissolve the vanilla flakes. "Why would he do that?" My brother had always been getting in trouble. He could lie with the brightest, most sincere smile, lie right to your face even though you both knew he was lying. But it was always penny-ante stuff, shoplifting a candy bar here and there, breaking and entering, moving on to some minor drug dealing—never anything stronger or more dangerous than marijuana. He'd always been a good-looking kid, had probably grown into a handsome man.

And don't ever believe for a minute that good-looking people don't get away with things less attractive people can't.

"It's pretty open and shut. Me representing him is just a legal formality." She nodded, blowing on her coffee before taking a tentative sip. "They argued, he grabbed a butcher knife and stabbed him. No premeditation, no other fingerprints on the knife other than your brother's. I'm hoping to plea it down to manslaughter. The DA seems open to avoiding a trial." She gave a little half-hearted shrug. "I'm sorry. There's a witness, and he confessed—not much of a confession, to be honest, just says that he did it. There's not really much for me to do besides get the best deal for him I can."

"I appreciate your calling me." A Mustang pulled into the drive-thru, a good-looking blond kid behind the wheel, his arm draped around the pretty redheaded girl in the passenger seat. They kissed, and I looked back at Siobhan. "Why was he over there in the first place? Was Ash working for Bobby?"

My brother was a carpenter, claimed he was a good one. It was hard for him to get bonded because he'd been arrested any number of times over the years for possession. He never did time—the charges were always dropped, and he claimed he just dealt a little to pay for his own weed habit. But it was enough that no one would bond him, and that made getting work hard. That was the last I'd heard, so who knows? He may have moved on from dealing a little weed to heroin for all I knew.

"No, he'd been laid off from his last job, was just drawing unemployment," Siobhan replied. "I guess—I don't want to get into a lot of this—but the Cassidys had apparently split up. Your brother was seeing Mrs. Cassidy." She made a helpless gesture. "Mr. Cassidy stopped by the house when your brother was there, and it got ugly. That's all I got."

"Thanks." I got up. "Thanks for meeting me, and for helping my brother. I appreciate it."

"Thanks for the coffee." She gave me a weak smile. "I wish I could do more. I just have this gut feeling your brother didn't do it, Chanse."

I resisted telling her that she wouldn't be the first woman my brother had fooled.

The Cottonwood Wells police department was still on Prairie Street, according to my phone, and the building looked pretty much the same, only more tired. The whole town looked more tired than I remembered, the boarded-up windows of the stores on Commercial Street and the empty parking spaces more apparent. I made a game out of trying to remember what the now-empty stores used to be. This one used to be the shoe store, that one was a diner, and that one used to be a sporting goods place. Now they were empty, forlorn For Lease flyers stapled to the plywood covering the windows.

The police station smelled like stale sweat and lost hope.

I told the tired-looking woman at the desk I wanted to see my brother. She looked at me warily when I told her his name and showed my ID. She directed me to have a seat and to help myself to coffee. I did and regretted it.

"Chanse?"

I got up and put down the *Texas Monthly* I was reading. The man who'd said my name looked vaguely familiar. He was wearing a white dress shirt and an ugly maroon tie. There were wet spots at his armpits. He had what I used to think of as the redneck body, big upper torso and belly, narrow hips and scrawny legs. His brown polyester dress pants had seen better days, and he had an enormous belt buckle underneath the swell of stomach. His cowboy boots clicked on the tired linoleum floor.

I didn't recognize his face, blasted brown by the sun and deeply lined, the small brown eyes alert. The overhead lights reflected off his brownish-red scalp. He held out his hand and took mine in a tight, hard, dry grip, shaking it vigorously. "You're looking good, man," he said in his East Texas accent. "Me, I let myself go. Nothing to do about it now but wait for death." He grinned, crooked yellow teeth slightly masking the smell of stale coffee and cigarettes. "Aw, you don't recognize me, do you?"

"Sorry."

He dropped my hand but the smile stayed in place. "Well, I've changed a lot. Larry Michalak."

To say the years hadn't been kind was an understatement. Larry was older than me. We grew up in the same trailer park. My mother used to give him a buck every now and then to keep an eye on us while she went to the liquor store. I'd forgotten he'd become a cop once he was done with high school. His mom waited tables at the diner on Commercial Street and his dad had run off when he was a kid. He'd always been nice to us, I remembered, letting us watch whatever we wanted on the television, willing to throw a football around with me.

He was one of the few good memories of my childhood. Back then he'd been skinny as a rail, rangy, all loose energy and live nerves.

"Good to see you, Larry."

He nodded. "You're here about your brother, I reckon. Come on." He used his ID badge to unlock a door and I followed him into a back hallway painted beige. I followed him into an office with bare paneled walls. It was sparsely furnished, a big metal desk, a couple of file cabinets, some uncomfortable chairs. There was a file on his desk. He waved me into one of the chairs. It was even more uncomfortable then it looked. He sat down behind the desk and opened the file, put on a pair of cheap reading glasses.

"It's pretty cut and dried, Chanse, I'm sorry to say." He didn't look up. "Your brother admitted it, had Bobby Cassidy's blood all over him, and his fingerprints were on the knife."

"What kind of knife?"

"A butcher knife, from the set in the kitchen. We don't think it was premeditated, just one of them wrong place at the wrong time situations that got a little out of hand. The Cassidys were separated, Bobby was staying at a place in one of his apartment buildings he owned on the other side of town. Bobby stopped by the house and caught Ash with his wife, and words were exchanged and things escalated."

"Ash was having an affair with Mrs. Cassidy?"

He looked at me over the top of his reading glasses. "I know you haven't been around much, Chanse, but how much do you know about your brother?"

It was supposed to sting, I guessed. It didn't. "Other than calling to say Merry Christmas every few years, I haven't spoken to Ash since I left for college. And yes, this is my first time back in town since then."

"But that's been almost twenty years!"

"Twenty-four, to be exact. Next year is my twenty-five-year class reunion. We weren't exactly a close family."

He didn't know what to say to that. He cleared his throat. "So, are you here to bail him out? The bail was set pretty high."

"I'm not bailing him out." Siobhan had mentioned the half-million-dollar bond on the message she'd left for me. I leaned back in the chair, which had no lumbar support. "I'm just going to ask some questions, find out if he did it or not. And then I'm going back to New Orleans."

"Just like that?"

I nodded. "Just like that." I didn't add that I'd regretted coming as soon as I took the off-ramp from I-10, or that every exit along the highway since New Orleans had triggered an internal debate about turning around and heading home. "I don't know my brother anymore. You could tell me he was head of a huge international drug cartel and it wouldn't surprise me. Ash always had an abusive relationship with the truth. But something doesn't sit right with me about this, and that's what brought me here. So, Ash was having an affair with Mrs. Cassidy?"

He nodded. "Ash and Becky Harlan go way back—"

"Becky Harlan is the Mrs. Cassidy in question?" I whistled. That changed everything. Becky Harlan.

Now it all made sense.

I remembered Becky Harlan. The Harlans also lived in the Hook 'Em Horns Trailer Park where I'd grown up. An image of a little blond girl with pigtails following my little brother around like a puppy dog when she couldn't have been more than eight years old flashed through my mind. She had a little sister, too, but that name was lost to the years. I remembered her mother used to sit around and drink sometimes in the afternoons with mine, while they watched *One Life to Live* and *General Hospital* and *Edge of Night*. It usually fell to us to take care of Becky and what's her name. "I don't remember Bobby Cassidy."

"He wasn't from here." He rubbed his eyes. "Come on, follow me." He jangled his keys and opened the door he came out of, gesturing for me to follow him. I did, into a long hallway of yellowed linoleum and fluorescent lights, down past some doors and then another door he had to unlock, talking the whole way. "Bobby came to town about twenty years or so ago, had the Arby's franchise out by the highway. He bought some land, put up apartment buildings, made some investments, did pretty well for himself. He married Becky about sixteen years ago. She was bartending at Sam's Place. Caught everyone off guard when he married her. She and your brother had been off and on for a long time, and Bobby swept her off her feet, I guess, during one of the off times. They've got a couple of kids. Best we can figure it, her and Ash started back up again when Bobby moved out, maybe even before. Becky's not talking much about any of this, other than saying Ash did it. Bobby walked in and caught 'em together, Ash stuck a knife in him." He made like he was washing his hands of it. "Open and shut."

I sat down in an uncomfortable brown plastic chair at the table. There was a mirror against one wall, which I assumed was one way. I only waited for a few moments before he led my brother in. He was wearing an orange jumpsuit and was shuffling; his wrists and ankles were cuffed, and they were connected by a long chain in the front. He grinned at me as he slid into a seat.

"I'll be right out here when you're ready," Larry said. "Just knock on the door when you're done."

"It won't be long," I replied.

"Nice of you to come," Ash said. "Been a while."

Ash and I looked alike, always had, even when we were kids. He had the same brown hair, the same gray eyes, the same frame. He was just shorter than me, never been inclined to sports. He'd always been too lazy. Our parents hadn't been the best parents—but he'd been the baby. He always got away with murder, just by letting his gray eyes fill up with tears and making his lower lip tremble.

Well, he wouldn't get out of it that way this time.

"What brought you back this time?" Ash asked. "Suddenly you care?"

"Curiosity, I suppose, more than anything else." I folded my arms. "You going to plead out?"

"That's what everyone seems to think I should do."

"That's not what I asked."

"I did it." He held up his shackled hands. "You and Rhonda have been bitching at me my whole life to take responsibility, so I am."

I looked at him. "Something doesn't make sense to me." I

leaned across the table. "Don't get me wrong, I'm glad you're taking responsibility for something you did wrong for the first time in your life, but I'm not sure you did this. And I don't understand it."

He gave me a sour look. "Larry, we're done here," he yelled.

I waited for Larry to get back from taking him to his cell. As Larry walked me out to the lobby, I said, "Looks bad, doesn't it?"

"Probably won't even go to trial, unless Ash gets stubborn. The DA's looking to plead him out."

"Ash always was stubborn." I shook his hand again. "Thanks, Larry, for your help." I opened the door to the lobby, stopped, and looked back at him. "Didn't it strike you as a little bit odd that the only fingerprints on a kitchen knife were my brother's?"

He looked at me, confused.

"Not many knives in many kitchens don't have any fingerprints on them." I smiled at him. "It's like it had never been touched or used, isn't it?"

I shut the door as that sank in and walked back out to my car.

The Cassidy place wasn't hard to find. It was out near the country club, across the street from where my old friend T. J. Ziebell had grown up. I stopped at the foot of the Cassidy driveway and looked over at the Ziebell place. It looked different. It took me a minute to realize there was an addition on the left side, and the house had also been expanded over the three-car garage. The little trees and bushes his mother had planted in the front yard had grown, and there was now a fountain bubbling in the front lawn. The mailbox said O'Reilly now. I wondered what ever had happened to ole T. J. He'd been my best friend and my first crush.

And that had ended badly.

I turned into the Cassidy driveway and pulled up to the front of the house. Like so many other Southern people who'd come into money, Bobby Cassidy had built himself a replica of an old Southern plantation house, complete with the obligatory enormous columns and a veranda that ran around the whole house. There was an upper gallery as well, disappearing around the corners of the house. The Cassidys didn't have a fountain in their front yard, but there was a summer house off to the right of the house and the driveway also curved around to go back, which was where the garage was probably located. I got out of the car and climbed the steps.

A teenage girl about sixteen or seventeen answered my knock. She was pretty, with long blond hair falling down her back, a snub nose, and bluish-gray eyes. She was tan, with darker freckles sprinkled across her nose and below her eyes. She wasn't wearing makeup, and from the disappointed look on her face when she saw me, she was clearly expecting someone else. She looked familiar to me, but then, I knew her mother.

"Your mother home?" I asked.

"In the den." She gestured with her head toward a door off the hallway. "Come on."

I followed her into the den, where she said, "Someone's here to see you, Mom," and disappeared down the hallway before I could say anything.

Becky Harlan Cassidy was sitting on the sofa wearing a loose-fitting University of Texas T-shirt and a pair of black yoga pants. Her feet were bare, and from the state of her toenails I'd say she was about a week overdue for a pedicure. She was holding a glass of what looked like bourbon and melting ice in her right hand. Her hair was pulled back from her face into a tight ponytail, and I doubted the blond color was the same shade her genetics had given her. She didn't stand up, nor did she invite me to sit down.

I sat down anyway. "How you holdin' up, Becky?"

It looked like it took a great effort for her to turn her head and look at me. She took a drink from the glass. "Chanse. I wondered if you'd come." She took another drink, finishing the glass, and held it out to me. "Will you be a dear and pour me another? The Wild Turkey's out on the bar. Just a couple of ice cubes. Help yourself to whatever you want." Her words were slightly slurred, barely noticeable unless you were listening for it.

I was tempted to tell her I wasn't her servant, but I wanted her to talk. I got her a fresh drink and poured myself a glass of sparkling water.

She didn't thank me when I handed it to her. "You saw Ash?"

"Yeah," I replied.

"You're not a good brother."

"You weren't a good wife."

That got her attention. She looked at me, blinked a few times, and put her glass down on the table, ignoring the stack of coasters. "You're not going to post bail?"

"I'm not putting up a half million when there's no guarantee Ash won't run," I replied. "And from what I know of Ash, I don't trust him not to. He certainly won't appear in court because he owes me anything. In fact, I think he'd get a good laugh out of leaving me on the hook for half a million bucks."

She started to say something, then just nodded. "Yeah, you're probably right."

"You could bail him out, but that would look funny, wouldn't it? The grieving widow bailing out her husband's killer?"

"I love Ash." She picked up her glass again but didn't drink. "I loved my husband. He was good to me and the kids. But I always loved Ash more. Maybe I shouldn't have married Bobby."

"Then you wouldn't have all this." I waved around the room. "And what's a husband you don't love in exchange for all this?"

"Watch your mouth."

"How'd you get him to take the fall, Becky?"

"He killed Bobby."

"No, he didn't." I got up and walked back over to the bar, put my empty glass into the little sink there. "Ash is…Ash is a lot of things. He may not be the smartest guy, he may bend the rules here and there, skirt the law, but I don't believe for one minute he stabbed your husband to death. I don't believe for one minute that your husband caught the two of you in bed and Ash stabbed him with a butcher knife. From your kitchen. From the set of knives on your kitchen counter."

"That's what happened."

"And his were the only fingerprints on the knife."

I waited to see if she'd make the connection that any decent lawyer, any decent cop worth his salt would have, but she didn't. Becky was sly, but she wasn't smart. "So, no one ever used that knife before? It sat there in your kitchen unused until Ash grabbed it and used it? No one touched it?"

"It got washed."

"So, if I have the handle tested for DNA only Ash's will be found?"

"I—"

"I don't suppose any of your daughter's DNA will show up, will it?"

"There isn't any need to test for DNA!" she burst out.

"Jade is Ash's daughter, isn't she?" I said softly. I sat back down on the couch and leaned forward, looking into her panicked face. "I recognized her when she answered the door. She doesn't look much like Ash did, but she looks a lot like my sister did when she was that age. Is that what happened, Becky? Does Ash know?"

She nodded, her lips pinched together and sucked in between her teeth. "Bobby never knew."

"You never wanted Bobby to know, did you? But you wanted Bobby gone, didn't you? But you didn't want to let go of all this, and you didn't want Jade to know. So, you killed Bobby, didn't you, and you called Ash and got him to take the blame?"

"No!"

"Ash wouldn't take the blame for you, would he, but he would for Jade." I stood up. "You told him Jade did it, didn't you? You got him to wipe the blade down and put his own fingerprints on there. To protect his daughter."

Her eyes narrowed. "You'll never prove it."

"Daddy wasn't my father?"

We hadn't heard her walk back into the doorway. She was barefoot and the floor was carpeted. She was holding her cell phone in one hand, and her face was drained of color. "*You* said I killed Daddy?"

"You two have a lot to talk about," I said, getting to my feet. On my way out of the room, I stopped and looked down at my niece. "I'm sorry, Jade. You deserved better."

I got back into my car.

I couldn't put Cottonwood Wells in my rearview mirror fast enough.

I dialed Siobhan's number. "About my brother's defense..."

DON'T LOOK DOWN

Jase shifted the Fiat's engine into a lower gear as he started up the steep hill. He hadn't driven a standard transmission since college, but he did remember hills required downshifting. As the Fiat started climbing he passed two handsome, tanned men on mountain bikes, sturdy thighs straining against their brightly colored Lycra casing. According to the directions, he would be in Panzano when he reached the top of the hill. There was a parking lot off to the left, and just beyond that he could see a stone wall. The hill—or mountain, he wasn't sure which—dropped off into a valley to the right, vineyards and olive trees spreading out to the next sloping hill. A low stone wall hugged the right side of the road nearer the crest of the hill, with barely enough space for pedestrians or mountain bikes. All the roads had been incredibly narrow since he'd left the highway, with many sharp blind curves as the road weaved in and out and around and along mountains. At one point an enormous bus coming the other way had almost forced him onto the shoulder, missing the black rental car by inches. He glanced up at the directions tucked into the sun visor. At the crest of the hill there would be another sharp, almost ninety-degree turn to the left, and to his right would be the triangular town center of Panzano-in-Chianti. Because of the narrow one-way streets, he'd have to circle around the town center to get to the little hotel.

The sunlight breaking through the clouds in the valley was beautiful.

Philip would have loved this, Jase thought. *He always wanted us to see Italy.*

He felt a twinge of sadness, which was an improvement. Just a month ago he would have broken down into tears. He was healing.

And getting away from the apartment, the neighborhood, seeing Philip everywhere he turned, everywhere he looked was the best thing for him.

And what could be better than two weeks in Italy?

The trip wasn't about *forgetting* Philip, anyway. He'd never forget Philip but needed to get on with his life. Taking this trip was the first step. It was *doing* something instead of just moping around feeling sorry for himself, being lonely, missing him. Sure, he'd kept working—the bills didn't stop coming due because your partner dies—but he couldn't work all the time, and when he was home the apartment loomed so quiet, so empty. The trip to Italy they'd talked about but never gotten to take together was a positive step forward, getting past the grief, a way to finally say goodbye and maybe move on at last. He'd thrown himself into plans for the trip, scouring websites and guidebooks and looking at flight and train schedules, deciding finally on Florence and Venice, with side trips to Padua and Pisa and Siena and Lucca.

The Fiat continued climbing. He saw the sharp turn ahead and slowed. He was tired. He hadn't slept much on the overnight flight from JFK to Pisa. He could never sleep on planes, and even the lorazepam, which always helped at home, hadn't worked. He'd dozed a bit, waking up whenever someone walked past in the aisle or when the person sitting next to him shifted in her seat. He'd felt a rush of adrenaline when he'd gotten off the plane that carried him through getting his suitcase and going through customs. That adrenaline kept up as he picked up the Fiat from Hertz, dropped his suitcase in the back, and caught a bus into the city. It was drizzling a little, the sun hidden behind clouds as he went inside the cathedral, climbed the worn marble steps winding around the leaning tower, slick and slippery with water. Now that he was almost to Panzano, he was starting to crash, the adrenal thrill of actually being in Italy wearing off.

There was a coffee shop near the hotel, he remembered. An-official-made-in-Italy cappuccino to boost his energy before checking into the hotel was probably just what he needed. He made the sharp left and saw his right turn just ahead. The town square was actually slightly triangular, just as it looked on Google Earth. There was a parking place in front of the small restaurant. He zipped into it easily and got out of the car, stretching, his spine crackling and popping. The sun came out from behind the clouds, bright and strong, drenching the village in light. He locked the car. There were benches and trees and an enormous pond in the little park, inside a small stone wall. Caffe Terzani was on the other side of the little park. Some old men were sitting on benches in the shade of one of the trees, smoking cigarettes. They nodded at him as he walked by. He smiled and said *ciao*. The little pond was murky green, choked with water lilies and plants. An enormous golden koi fish swam to the surface, blinking at him. He crossed the street quickly—that blind curve was nerve wracking. He went inside under the gelateria awning and smiled at the older man behind the counter.

"Cappuccino, *grazie*," Jase said, and pointed it at a sort of pastry sandwich with whipped cream and strawberries as the filling, the top of the pastry sprinkled with powdered sugar.

The man nodded. "American?" he asked in a heavy accent. "Have seat, we bring to you."

"Thank you—*grazie*."

Jase sat down at one of the black wire tables and rubbed his eyes. There was a soccer game playing on the television, and the only other person in the café was an old woman, dressed all in black, reading the Florence newspaper, *La Nazione*. He suppressed a yawn. Hopefully the cappuccino would give him a jolt of energy.

He didn't want to—*couldn't*—make a bad first impression.

He heard the grinding of beans, the hiss of the steamer for the milk. He wasn't able to suppress another yawn, and when he opened his eyes the old woman was looking at him. Her brown eyes were intense and bloodshot, the whites yellowish. She pushed her chair back and stood by his table. "American?" Her voice was deep and throaty. Her long iron-gray hair was braided and coiled around her head like a crown. The lines on her face were deep, and her right eye was a little milky. She was a little bent from age, and slender. She pointed a slender, crooked finger at him, the bones of her wrist poking through the papery skin.

A little repulsed, not knowing what to do, he smiled and nodded. "Good afternoon."

"Panzano not good for you," she said, bowing her head as she made the sign of the cross. "You need to go. Go on to Florence, Venice, Padua, anywhere but here. Panzano not good for you."

Jase gaped at her. "I—"

"He is with you." She closed her eyes and crossed herself. "He is with you now."

He felt the hairs on his arms and neck standing up. "I—I don't know what you mean."

She crossed herself again, gathered her fingers together and kissed the tips. "He watches over you in death as he did in life."

"Philip?"

She nodded slowly, closing your eyes. "You need to leave Panzano. He wants you to go, insists. He worries." She made the sign of the cross again. "Is not good for you. There is danger here."

"I'm only here for two days—"

"Billy Starr." She spat the words at him. "He's a curse. He will be your death." She pointed her finger at him. "You go, or you will be sorry."

She turned and shuffled out of the café, her flat black shoes scuffing along the tiled floor. Jase stared after her, his mouth open. As she passed a middle-aged man coming in the door, he made the sign against the evil eye behind her back.

The counter man placed his coffee cup, resting in a saucer, and a small plate holding the pastry on the little wire table, the receipt tucked under the plate. The man gave a helpless little shrug. "Signora Agretti," he said, apologetically. He tapped the side of his temple with a forefinger. "They say she has second sight. I say she not right in head. Ignore her." He went over to her table, crossing himself before picking up her dirty dishes and newspaper.

Jase stirred a packet of brown sugar crystals into his cappuccino. His phone chimed in his pants pocket. He took a sip of the cappuccino and moaned a little. It was the best he'd ever had. He checked the message. It was from Billy.

How close are you?

He typed back, *Stopped for a cappuccino. Need to check into the hotel. Be there shortly.*

Great. I'll wait by the pool. I was starting to worry.

Billy Starr.

I'll text you once I'm on my way. Shouldn't be much longer.

How could the old woman have known he was here to see Billy Starr?

Get a grip. Jase took another sip of the cappuccino. It was a very small town and he had a reservation at the hotel. Billy probably mentioned to some locals that a journalist was coming to visit, to interview him. They probably didn't get many Americans in Panzano, and she'd heard him talking to the counterman.

It didn't take second sight to figure out who he was and what he was doing in Panzano.

Still—it was a little unsettling.

And the Philip stuff was just creepy. How could she—

I don't believe in second sight. There's no such thing.

But...she *knew.*

Nonsense. She didn't know anything. Fortune tellers read body language, how people react to what they say.

All she said was "he." She didn't say his name. She was just trying to maybe shake you down for a couple of euros.

He drank the cappuccino and took a bite of the pastry. It was delicious. The whipped cream was fresh, and so were the strawberries. *Forget the old woman, you're on vacation. You're finally, at long last, in Italy. Enjoy it.*

And he was starting his trip by doing Billy Starr's first interview in almost twenty years.

The mention of Billy Starr got a blank look from most people these days. Billy Starr's short stardom had coincided with Jase's puberty, when his body began to change, feeling urges and desires he didn't quite understand, his body doing things it hadn't done before. Those images of Billy Starr, pants drooping down to show his underwear, his flat, defined stomach and thick round pecs and bulging biceps, and arms road-mapped with swollen veins, brought him to terms with his own sexuality; he knew, unequivocally, he was gay at age twelve. He'd wanted Billy Starr, worshipped him; wasted as much time as he could examining Billy's pictures, recording his music videos and every television appearance to watch over and over until the videotapes wore out. He dreamed about Billy, erotic dreams where the jeans came all the way down, the white underwear barely encasing Billy's excitement, waking up with a start and a shudder with his own underwear sticky and wet.

Jase knew Billy Starr's actual talent for singing and dancing was fairly limited. Having an older brother in the boy band currently hot with young teenage girls had gotten him his first exposure in one of their videos, dancing shirtless in baggy jeans with his tighty-whities showing, baseball cap turned backward on his head. He stole the video right out from under his brother's boy band and began developing a following of his own. MTV played him up, having him guest-host video countdown shows without a shirt and wearing his trademark drooping jeans. He started turning up on the covers of

Tiger Beat and *16* and other fan magazines targeted at teenage girls and their baby-sitting money. It was inevitable he'd get a recording contract, with the same manager as his brother's band. The record company rushed out a single and a video, with nonsensical, almost juvenile lyrics, designed to make the girls squeal: "Be My Girl." He had a limited, at best, vocal range, but the song hit number one and stayed there for a couple of weeks. The video displayed his body, the camera lovingly lingering over his muscles, as he sang and danced, some of the shots with him in the rain, the white underwear becoming more revealing the wetter it got, the water dripping off his muscles, running in streams down his definition, playing up his odd combination of boyishness with adult male sexuality. He was a bad boy, the kind your father didn't want you to date or be alone with, the one who might talk you into going further than you planned, his pouty lips and slashing blue eyes. Then came the moment that catapulted him into the stratosphere, even if it was only for a short while: doing a live performance on MTV, he was dancing, and while doing some highly choreographed pelvic thrusts with his backup dancers, the baggy pants slid off his hips and past his knees into a puddle of denim around his ankles. He didn't stop dancing or miss a beat. He was wearing tighty-whities and sporting the kind of bulge that made screaming girls' parents uncomfortable. He fluidly kicked the pants off completely and kept performing, his muscular legs and a hard, round butt flexing as he moved, the girls in the audience screaming louder with every pelvic thrust, every shake of his ass.

And of course, it became a scandal, a cause célèbre, parents complaining about the sexuality of it all being too much for the girls in his target audience. Apologies were made, it was claimed to be an accident, MTV talking heads debated whether he was just that gifted a dancer to keep going despite the wardrobe malfunction or if it had been planned.

Defiantly, he dropped his pants again at the MTV Music Awards performance to a standing ovation from the audience, claiming in his thick South Boston accent it was now a "free speech" issue.

But it wound up becoming as much of a gimmick as him not wearing a shirt. He had a couple more hits, some videos in heavy rotation, but his star was already sinking. There was that minimal talent thing, and he got some shade from other performers who basically said he was nothing but a glorified male stripper. Jase didn't care—he loved seeing Billy dancing on his television in his underwear, surreptitiously buying all the teen magazines with the tear-out posters of Billy showing off his superb body. But like any controversy, it stopped being interesting and people stopped talking about him.

Billy Starr dropped his pants again, yawn, no big deal, did you hear what Madonna did on her tour?

By the time the second album was released, his audience had grown up and moved on to rappers or grunge rockers, and that period of teen idolatry was over. Billy's second album sank like a stone, disappeared without a trace, came and went with most people—other than Jase—not even noticing. His management team managed to get him an underwear modeling gig with a major design company, plastering his underwear-clad body over billboards and magazines. They also tried to keep the music career alive, selling him to his gay fans, booking appearances in gay clubs—where the audience chanted for him to drop his pants. Washed up before he turned twenty-one, Billy made some homophobic comments and there had been a backlash, canceled bookings, the underwear contract not renewed.

Billy Starr vanished as quickly as he'd appeared, just another flash in the pan, not even enough of a blip to make it into *where are they now* articles and shows.

When he paid his bill, the counterman said, "Enjoy your stay in Panzano, ignore Signora Agretti. *Loco.*" He made a circle with his index finger near the side of his head, smiling broadly.

Jase grinned back and nodded. *"Grazie."*

He got his bags and checked into the hotel, determined to forget the old woman. The young woman working at the counter was friendly, her English good, and the view from his room on the second floor was stunning. The valley beyond the mountain slope Panzano-in-Chianti perched on was even more gorgeous than he'd thought from stealing quick glances from the car.

And the light…he understood the Renaissance so much better now.

How could you not being inspired to create more beauty when surrounded by it, the vivid colors? He could stare at the view for hours and never be bored.

Philip would have loved this light, he thought.

It almost felt like—Philip was there with him.

He shivered and pushed that thought away, reminded himself

to forget the old woman. He texted Billy: *I am heading down from the village now.*

He drove around the triangle and headed down the one-way road, narrow as it headed down the side of the hill, the houses and buildings in the village pressed up against the sidewalk. He could see the sharp drop-off in the small spaces between buildings, where cars were parked on the dirt. He reached a stop sign, with arrowed green signs pointing to Siena in one direction and Firenze in another. The directions here were to turn right.

This road, which was a two-way, seemed even narrower than the one-way through town. He hoped he didn't meet an oncoming car. There was an enormous stone wall on his right, a lower one on the other side, barely enough room for two cars to squeeze past each other. *Those walls have been there for hundreds of years,* he thought, marveling at the view of what looked like miles and miles of vineyard to his left in a small valley. He was so focused on the road and the view he almost missed the turn. He slammed on the brakes, forgetting to engage the clutch, and the Fiat jerked a few times before stalling.

Idiot, he swore. The directions clearly said the sign would appear suddenly after the stone wall on the left ended; he should have slowed down. The sign wasn't large; just a white post with a board painted white with Villa Stella carved into it, the letters painted red. The lip of the paved road hid the gravel road from view; in the far distance he could see it climbing a hill on the opposite side of a vineyard. He started the Fiat and turned, the bottom of the car scraping on the gravel. The road sharply angled down, at an almost sixty-degree angle. Enormous trees lined the inside of the stone wall, so the small grassy area to his left was completely shaded. Another gravel road went off to his left, just past the grass.

This, per the instructions, was the driveway for Villa Stella.

He drove slowly along the gravel driveway. Behind another tall hedge on the left was a parking area, with the three enormous recycling bins mentioned in the directions. He parked next to a black Mercedes. The driveway continued up to the enormous stone house. Just past the recycling bins was an opening in the middle of a weathered wooden fence. A path was worn into the grass from the parking area to the opening. He locked the car, stretched and yawned again, his heart beating faster.

Maybe it was just the cappuccino, or the excitement of meeting his former teen idol in the flesh.

Don't make an ass out of yourself.

He could see the sparkling blue water of a swimming pool before he reached the opening. As he stepped through the fence, he could see a man lying on a deck chair in the sun wearing nothing but a very tiny black Speedo and sunglasses.

Jase felt like a little starstruck preteen again. He hesitated, almost afraid to make his presence known.

It was ridiculous, he knew. He'd worked for *Street Talk* magazine now for over fifteen years; had interviewed far bigger names than Billy Starr before. Britney and Madonna and Meryl and Beatty and Nicholson and Jagger, just to name a few.

And yet a two-hit wonder at best from the early 1990s was the one who made him forget his journalistic ethics and his professional distance, who awed him and turned him into a tongue-tied closeted little twelve-year-old gay boy again.

Billy was becoming newsworthy again, worthy of a feature in *Street Talk* magazine because he'd made a movie, after about twenty years out of the spotlight. A low-budget art film, made by an up-and-coming young American director who'd won an Oscar for a short film a few years ago, filmed in Florence starring some unknowns the director knew from film school. Billy was the biggest name in the movie (if you could say he still had a name) but both he and the movie were getting positive buzz from screenings at some smaller film festivals.

It had been picked up by a major distributor in the United States, and now, people were talking about Billy Starr again.

There was even some Oscar buzz. Sure it was early, but Oscar talk was still Oscar talk.

A possible comeback for the mostly forgotten former teen idol was a story that *Street Talk*'s readers might find interesting.

At least, the editor-in-chief thought so.

Being called into Valerie Franklin's office was rarely a good thing. As he walked from his desk to her office, he wondered if he'd done anything that might get him fired. Sure, he'd just been phoning it in a bit after Philip died, but...

"You're going to Italy, aren't you?" Valerie Franklin asked after he shut her office door behind him. She wasn't looking at him—she never looked at anyone she was speaking to—never taking her eyes off her computer screen. That was Valerie—no greeting, no hello, no how are you—just straight to the point.

She didn't believe in wasting time on niceties.

"Yes," he'd replied cautiously. Valerie was a notoriously tough boss, wasn't above making an employee cancel a vacation to take an assignment. "I leave in two weeks."

"You're going to…?"

"Flying into Pisa, but spending most of my time in Florence and Venice."

He felt a bit of a nervous chill when she smiled, looking at him over the top of her glasses, making eye contact with him for maybe the fifth time in the fifteen years he'd worked for her. "Pisa? Perfect. Forward your ticket invoice to accounting and we'll reimburse you for it. You'll need a rental car as well; talk to Travel and have them make the arrangements for you. You'll be making a side trip to a village in Chianti—for a few days—and Travel will find you a hotel; we'll foot the bill for that, of course. You'll interviewing Billy Starr, have you heard of him? Do some research." She pressed her intercom button. "Sandy, forward that email from Billy Starr's agent to Jase, will you, and email him to let him know Jase will be doing the interview and will follow up for directions and so forth." She let go of the button. "We'll cut you a stipend check to pay for expenses and so forth." She dismissed him with a wave of her hand and turned back to her computer.

For once, she'd done him an enormous favor. His trip was now pretty much covered—he'd planned on taking the train from Pisa to Florence, but driving wasn't a huge imposition or change in plans—and what was a few days' work if it got most of his vacation expensed to *Street Talk*?

A great bargain, that's what.

Had she known what a thrill it was for him to get to meet Billy Starr, even after all these years, she probably wouldn't have given him the assignment, even though he was already going to Italy. Then again, why tell her, open himself up to her scornful glance, the cutting comments she would have made?

She was a great editor, but a lousy person.

Maybe it wasn't ethical to not tell her he'd been a huge fan of Billy during the brief flare of his career. He still had a poster of Billy from his underwear spokesmodel gig, recovered from the Macy's at the mall where his sister worked. She'd grabbed one for him when Billy had been replaced by another model and the posters were being discarded.

He'd held on to it for year before finally having it framed and mounted; it still hung on the wall of his apartment.

Philip thought it was cute the way he held on to his childhood celebrity crush.

And now, all these years later, he was standing just a few scant yards from Billy Starr, his tanned skin glistening in the bright Tuscan sun, wearing a bikini that barely covered the bulge Jase remembered so vividly, so clearly, from those underwear ads, Billy's body still as perfect and muscular and defined as it has been when he'd posed.

He flashed back to when he'd first seen Billy on his television set, gyrating and dancing, transfixed, unable to look away from the vision of masculine beauty on the screen. How often had he fantasized this moment, seeing Billy in person wearing even less than he had in the underwear campaign, close enough to touch and smell him?

He snapped out of his reverie when a shrill, high-pitched scream pierced the air.

Startled, he flinched, looking up at the wall of green vine. It sounded primal, a scream of terror from deep inside the soul.

His heart was pounding so hard he almost didn't hear his name being said.

"Jase?"

Jase turned. Billy was sitting up on the lounge chair, his handsome face relaxed into a smile. "You must be Jase Worth," he said, getting to his feet and walking toward him, his hand stretched out in front of him. He moved gracefully, the muscles in his body rippling, the bikini—*don't look down, whatever you do, don't look down.*

"Yes, I'm Jase, and you're Billy, of course. What was that scream? Should we call the police?" Billy was shorter than Jase had thought he would be, maybe five seven, smelling of sweat and musk and coconut oil. They shook hands. Billy's hand was slick with oil and sweat, warm, his grip strong. Beads of sweat decorated his oiled skin. There was some slight black razor stubble on his muscular chest, a trail of curly black hairs leading from his navel down to the tiny bikini. His legs were also smooth, the thick upper legs bulging over the kneecaps, the thick calves mapped with blue veins. His thick dark hair had a slight curl to it but was slicked down to the scalp by either sweat, water, or oil.

Billy shook his head. "There's a mental hospital up the mountain." He gestured with his head. "St. Dymphna's." He shrugged, the muscles in his shoulders flexing under the skin. "Sometimes, when they let their patients out in the yard, one of them screams. It takes some getting used to." He laughed, his perfect white teeth flashing. "It doesn't happen all the time. I barely even notice anymore."

"Good to know." *Don't look down, don't look down, don't look down.* "Thanks for agreeing to the interview."

"*Street Talk* was always good to me." He gestured for Jase to follow him, and he started walking back toward the pool. The bikini had ridden up over the tanned butt cheeks, and Jase tried not to stare. "So, I figured, when people started showing some interest in me again, why not? Valerie still the same ballbuster she was twenty years ago?"

They walked past the pool. Enormous stepping stones were set in the grass, leading to the house. "She's definitely a ballbuster," Jase replied. On the other side of the gravel driveway an enormous vineyard spread across the wide valley. "Is that your vineyard?"

"Oh, no." Billy smiled at him, dimples deepening in his cheeks. "I just own this small strip of land here, with the house. Everything on the other side of the driveway belongs to the Agrettis." He pointed, the triceps muscle in his arm tightening. "That building in the distance is where they make their wine. It's quite good. All the local wines are good."

"Agretti?" That was the name of the old woman at the café.

"Oh, God. Don't tell me you've already encountered Signora Agretti?" Billy frowned. "The old bitch hates me. Let me guess— did she tell you I killed her granddaughter?"

"*What?*"

Billy waved his hand and rolled his eyes. "Her granddaughter, Isabella. She worked for me here for a while…she became *obsessed* with me. I never touched her. I finally had to let her go. And she killed herself. The old woman blames *me*." He scowled. "You have no idea how hard it was for me to find someone else who'd work for me. Thank God for Lucia."

They'd reached the door to the house. As Billy opened the

door and walked inside, Jase hesitated. "No, she didn't mention anything about that…"

"Oh, that's a relief. Poor Isabella. I felt bad, of course but what could I have done?" He shook his head. "I hope you're not going to put that in your story!"

"Well, no, I don't see how it's relevant." *Maybe to a scandal sheet.* "But she clearly said something that's upset you." *He's not good for you. There is danger here.*

"She acted like…" How could he put it into words? "I mean, she doesn't like you, but it was more about…I don't know, like she could *see*." He paused. "I lost someone," he finally said. "About a year ago. She made it sound like she could see that person?"

"People in the village think she has second sight, if you believe in that sort of thing." Billy shrugged. "Come on inside, we'll have some wine. Some Agretti wine." He laughed. "They do make good wine."

Jase stepped into the cool inside. The floor was stone. A small wooden table and some chairs stood off to the left side, and a door on the right with stairs led down to a room at a lower level. There was another flight of stairs just beyond. Billy picked up a robe from one of the chairs and put it on, tying the belt at his waist.

"I don't know if I should have wine," Jase demurred. "I'm driving."

"You can just leave the car here and walk back, if you get a little buzz going." Billy descended down a short flight of stairs to a kitchen. Cloves of garlic hung from a hook above the sink. The window had a terrific view of the backyard and the pool. There was another wide window with a stunning view of the vineyard. "It's not that far, definitely walkable. I walk into the village all the time." He opened the refrigerator and retrieved a bottle of white wine. He grabbed a corkscrew, and in a few twists of his wrist it popped out of the bottle. "Is this your first time in Italy?" he asked as he filled two glasses.

Jase nodded. "It's so beautiful here. The drive from Pisa… wow." *Yes, you're a brilliant conversationalist. "Wow" pretty much sums up Italy.*

"Let's sit in the living room."

Jase followed him back up the stairs. The living room was just beyond the steps to the kitchen. There was an enormous fireplace, and a big stone spiral staircase in the center of the room. On the far side was another door, and enormous windows. Billy sat down on the L-shaped couch and put his wine down on the coffee table.

Jase sat at the opposite side of the couch from him.

"Valerie told me you're gay, Jase." Billy laughed. "Just so you know, reports of my homophobia were greatly exaggerated." He took a healthy sip of wine. "I should have apologized. I was an idiot. And no, I'm not going to try to pretend like it was taken out of context or anything. I said it, I have to own it, and I need to apologize to the gay community." He crossed his legs, the robe falling open. "I think this interview is a good start to making amends. Everything's on the table for this interview. I have nothing to hide." He laughed. "So, yes, I suppose if you want to put Isabella Agretti into your story, I guess you should."

Your bikini certainly isn't hiding anything, Jase thought, trying to not look at Billy's crotch, at the exposed abs, the deep cleavage.

Don't look down, don't look down...

But there was a voice whispering inside his head, *he knew you were gay, he knew you were coming, and this is how he dressed to meet you...*

Maybe he just wasn't modest. He'd modeled underwear, for Christ's sake. Maybe he was trying to prove he wasn't homophobic. European men thought nothing of wearing Speedos, of showing off their bodies, no matter what kind of shape they were in.

Maybe he wore a bikini because he was proud of his body and wanted to get as much of his body tanned as he could.

Europeans didn't have the hang-ups about exposing bare skin Americans did.

And Billy had lived here a long time.

He's not gay, Jase, drop it and don't stare. Be a professional, for fuck's sake. And don't look down.

Jase had smirked a little when he'd read that final interview with Billy in an old issue of *Street Talk* he'd found in the archives as part of his background research. "The Last Interview" splayed across the cover, Billy with his trademark backward ball cap, scowling at the camera, the muscles of his bare upper torso flexed, the oversized jeans hanging loose, exposing the deep lines from his hip bones leading to the waistband of his boxers. Sick of being called a has-been and only getting gigs in gay bars, he'd decided to retire in his early twenties. Sullen and surly with the macho toxic masculinity of the poor-kid-made-good, his response to the question about homophobia didn't go over well: "I don't get why any dude would want to suck a dick, you know what I'm saying? And I don't want any dude sucking mine, but as long as they leave my dick alone I guess I'm good."

There had been backlash, of course, but in those days before social media it kind of came and went without making much of a splash, other than some opinion pieces in the queer press. But Billy didn't respond, he just disappeared from public view.

And was forgotten, like his brief moment of stardom had never happened.

"If you need to stay longer, you're certainly welcome to stay here," Billy was saying. "There's an entire bedroom suite on the lower level. Down there you'd have your own bathroom, shower, bidet, you name it. Privacy." He smiled, and there was something boyish about it, the years seeming to shed away from his face when he grinned. The dimples, the mischievous sparkle in his brown eyes—the charisma that made him a star was still there. It was more than just the handsome face and muscular body; something about him glowed, was impossible to look away from.

Charisma, publicists called it. *Star quality.* Billy had always had that, and he hadn't lost it despite the time away.

"I have a reservation in Florence for Monday and have to return the car," Jase said, but Billy didn't seem to be listening.

"You don't have to decide now," Billy smiled. "Just know it's an option. Shall we go out back and watch the sunset?"

Ethics—he couldn't ethically interview Billy and stay in his home.

But he didn't say anything.

They took the wine back out into the yard. The sun was starting to set in the distance behind the hills, the sky a brilliant flash of colors, oranges and yellows and pinks, the shadows cast by the trees somehow more vibrant than anywhere else, the smell from the vineyards on the other side of the driveway carried on the warm, soft breeze up to where they were sitting at a wooden picnic table grayed with age and exposure to the sun.

Billy was nothing like he'd feared. He was open and easy, quick with a joke or a laugh, casual, interested. They drank more wine and talked about Italy, Jase's trip to the cathedral and up the slippery wet marble steps of the Leaning Tower, his work as a freelancer, his plans for the rest of his stay in Italy. The wine was amazing—"and it's so cheap," Billy confided with a wink as he opened a second bottle as the sun disappeared over the Tuscan mountains, after they moved back inside and were seated on the couches.

By the time jet lag caught up to him and he found himself yawning it was just eight.

"Go get some sleep." Billy smiled at him, taking his glass. "We can talk about my movie and the so-called comeback tomorrow. You're sure you're okay to drive?"

As Jase headed for the back door another scream split through the night. He looked back at Billy nervously, standing at the top of the stairs to the kitchen, an odd look on his face. "Just the mental hospital." Billy didn't smile this time, wouldn't meet his eyes. "Get some sleep. I'll see you in the morning."

As he walked across the lawn and past the pool to where he'd left his car, he felt like he wasn't alone, like he wasn't the only person out there on the lawn. When he reached the opening in the fence he looked back, but Billy had gone inside and shut the door behind him.

As he turned back, he saw something move out of the corner of his eye. It looked like—"Philip?" he asked, then shook his head. *You're tired and you've had a lot of wine. And that woman upset you. It was nothing.*

Maybe you're too drunk to drive?

But he felt more tired than drunk, despite all the wine.

And he didn't have too far to drive.

He drove through the village back to the main road, pulling into the big parking lot he'd seen on his way into town on the downward slope behind the café, and walked up the sidewalk back to the hotel. There were voices coming from the restaurant across the square, laughter and loud talk and music. As he reached for the doorknob he again thought he saw something—*Philip*—out of the corner of his eye.

But when he turned to look, there was nothing there.

Tired. He was just tired.

He undressed and climbed into the big bed. It was comfortable, the blankets soft, and he was exhausted. He turned off the light, and settling his head down on the pillow, he thought about the shadows.

You're tired. And that old woman—she spooked you this afternoon, is all.

Philip's dead.

There's no such thing as ghosts. And even if there were, how could he have followed you to Italy?

As he dropped off to sleep, he could hear Billy saying *oh, there's a mental hospital up the mountain from Panzano.*

I could never get used to the screaming, Jase thought, closing his eyes.

He woke up the next morning feeling deeply rested. As he showered, he shook his head at his own foolishness from the day before, in his jet-lagged state.

There's no such thing as ghosts. And Billy wasn't flirting with you, that was the jet lag talking.

He put on a light T-shirt and a pair of shorts. He texted Billy as he walked to the café for a cappuccino and another one of those wonderful whipped-cream-and-strawberry pastries. Fortunately, Signora Agretti wasn't there.

Italy, I'm in Italy, he reminded himself as he ate his breakfast, trying not to let his excitement show on his face as customers came in and out of the café. When he was finished, he walked out to the pond in the town center and sat down on a bench to wait for Billy.

He didn't have to wait long. Billy had his long hair pulled back into a ponytail and was wearing a very tight white muscle shirt over khaki shorts. He looked just as good as yesterday. "You want to take a walk around the village?" Billy asked, flashing his brilliant, borderline seductive smile.

Jase nodded, trying not to stare at the muscled arms, the thick legs, the handsome face.

"The market will be set up soon," Billy observed, leading him away from the center. "Local farmers and merchants, every Sunday, set up here to sell their wares. It's great to get fresh fruit and vegetables, and there's a truck that sells roast meats." Billy took him by the arm and led him away from the square, up the steeply inclining main road, showing him the gelateria, the local grocery market, and the stunning views. In some places there were no sidewalks, the houses right up against the side of the one-way road, the air fresh and everything green. Sometimes there would be a place alongside a house on the left side of the road where a car could be parked, and just beyond the parking space the mountainside dropped away, the tops of trees barely visible in the distance.

And when they got back to the square, every conceivable kind of fruit and vegetable was arranged on wooden boxes and trays.

Another truck had rotisserie chickens spinning on skewers, long pans of hot foods like fried cheese and potatoes and vegetables, the smells of food wafting across as the villagers did their marketing. Billy picked out fruits and vegetables, ordering and paying in what sounded like flawless Italian. But as they moved around, placing orders and gathering bags, Jase noticed that the villagers didn't seem to like Billy very much, scowling and turning their backs to him.

Jase asked him about it when they stepped back into the café and ordered cups of fruit gelato.

"It's the Isabella Agretti thing—her family and friends." Billy stirred his cappuccino. "She was young, I'd hired her to clean for me—you know, basic housekeeping—laundry and dishes and dusting, that sort of thing. She was engaged to a young man in Greve, the next town over—you drove through it on the way here— but she imagined she fell in love with me." He shook his head, a scowl crossing his handsome face. "She claimed I loved her, that I'd seduced her and then wouldn't marry her." He shook his head again, the bluish-black ponytail swinging. "She killed herself. It was all ridiculous, of course, but she has lots of relatives here in the town." He shrugged his shoulders, bare and tanned. "Some of them know she wasn't right in the head, others have long memories." He laughed. "In the old days I would have gotten a knife between the shoulder blades, but these aren't the old days, thank God." A cloud crossed his face. "Obviously, I'd rather that story not be in your piece, but I'm going to trust you. I feel like I can trust you. Can I trust you, Jase?"

"Yes," he replied, briefly imagining Valerie's response if knew he was agreeing to not write something potentially embarrassing for Billy. She'd fire him without a second thought.

"Thanks." Billy briefly touched his arm.

Jase tried to not react to Billy's touch. "It must be hard living here with…knowing that people blame you for her suicide." He managed to keep his voice steady, even though his mind was racing. *He touched me!*

Another old woman, wearing an apron over her black dress, crossed herself as she walked past the open door of the café and saw them before turning her back and muttering to herself.

"It's a small town," Billy replied. "And small towns are small towns. It's so beautiful here, and the people are so lovely"—he held up his hands—"for the most part, what can I do? I love the villa, I love the peace and quiet of Italy. Sometimes I wonder, do I really want to give all this up and get back into the crazy world of American show business?"

Jase picked up his cappuccino. The gelato was the most delicious ice cream he'd ever had. Everything in Italy tasted fantastic—fresh and alive with flavor. He'd never realized how homogenized and boring American food had become.

"But the part—it was too good to pass up," Billy was saying. "When the director sent it to me—I still am not sure how that all happened, to tell you the truth. I'd done such a great job of disappearing, of walking away from everything, and I was pretty certain everyone in America had forgotten me, you know? But Joe—the director, Joe Campeggio—when he read the script and signed on, he said he only pictured me in the role. And once I read the part, I had to play it. It was one of those opportunities that come along once in a lifetime, you know?"

"There's been some pretty amazing buzz." Jase took another drink from his cappuccino, deciding he was going to have a second. "There's even talk of an Oscar nomination. Excuse me for a moment." He pushed back his wire chair, ordered another cappuccino at the counter. When he sat back down, Billy was grinning, his eyes sparkling.

"I never saw myself as an actor," Billy said. "I mean, I never really thought ahead about anything, to be honest. When I was a kid, I mean, that's why I made those bad decisions that came back to haunt me, you know what I'm saying? We were poor, and then when my brother hit big in that boy band…" He got a faraway look in his eyes. "I was all, look at all the money he's making, maybe I can make it, too, and then we did the MTV thing and I took off my shirt and his manager signed me and the rest is history." His face clouded. "And then…I didn't have any real musical talent, I know that and my manager knew that, but I had muscles and a cute face and the girls liked me."

"And the gay men."

"And the gay men." He finished his cappuccino. "So stupid, I handled that whole thing all wrong, I never had nothing against gay men, you know, but the managers were trying to keep the money going and I knew my music career was already over but they were trying to beat that dead horse, you know what I'm saying? And I wasn't feeling it anymore, I knew I had to find something else, and

I acted out like a little punk—like a little bitch—and I killed the career and they dropped me. But I could have handled it all better, you know what I'm saying? I could've handled it better."

His bare leg brushed against Jase's under the table, and Jase was glad his second cappuccino was ready, so he had to get away from the table for a minute. He couldn't put a finger on what the deal with Billy was. Was it just his natural charisma, or was he actually interested in Jase? Was flirting, or seeming to flirt, so much a part of his personality he wasn't even aware of it?

Or was it just his own wishful thinking?

"Do you want to do more movies?" Jase asked, trying to keep his hand from trembling as he added brown sugar to his cup.

"If the part's right." Billy's leg brushed against his again under the table. "I mean, I got a pretty great life here in Panzano, you know what I'm saying? Florence—Firenze—is only an hour from here by bus. And the bus goes right to the train station, and I can be anywhere in Italy, anywhere in Europe, in no time. Nobody recognizes me, and that's nice. And show business?" The muscle fibers in his shoulder moved as the shoulders went up and down again. "It's such a fucking rat race, man. Everyone wants a piece of ya. I got out alive when I was a kid, so I think I can handle it now, but you never know." He grinned. "Why don't you run up and get your swimsuit? We can hang out by the pool and get some sun while we talk."

Billy kept talking as they walked down the sloping road back to the villa, out of the village. Jase couldn't help but notice more people looking at them, and their facial expressions weren't kind, or friendly, or interested. *I don't think Billy realizes just how disliked he is in this village*, he thought as they walked, the warm breeze caressing his skin.

As they reached the steps to the front of the villa, another scream pierced the air.

"Do you really get used to that?" Jase asked.

Billy scowled. "I guess I'll have to lock the doors tonight," he said as they went down the wide stone steps. This side of the villa was even more beautiful than the back. The vineyard stretched away beyond to another stone house, far in the distance, where the land started sloping back upward. So much greenery. "Someone escaped from the sanitarium last night. They'll catch her, of course—the local police are quite good about that—but until they do—"

"Does that happen often?" Jase asked as they went down the steps to the kitchen, putting the bags of produce up on the stone counter. "That would make me nervous. If the screaming—"

"I don't even notice the screams anymore, to tell you the truth." Billy smiled. "You look a little tired. Why don't you take a nap in the spare room? We can talk some more out by the pool—the jet lag will really sneak up on you. You think you're over it and then...go take a nap and I'll wake you in an hour, and we can get some sun?"

Jase nodded, going into the spare room and lying down. Despite all the sleep, despite the cappuccino, he was still feeling tired and fell asleep, yet the nap was not restful. He tossed and turned in the throes of a strange, almost fevered dream. Billy was onstage, singing his biggest hit, dancing in his underwear, sweat glistening on his defined muscles, but Jase couldn't get near the stage—no matter how hard he tried to move, he couldn't. Every so often the song was interrupted by a scream that echoed throughout the foggy gay bar, and Billy and everything would stop until the scream stopped echoing through the corners of the bar, until the cobwebs hanging from the ceiling stopped vibrating and then he would start singing and dancing again, only the lyrics weren't the same; lyrics Jase didn't recognize:

She loved me but I didn't love her,
She wouldn't leave me alone
And she died, no matter how I tried
She died no matter how hard I tried
And so many times I've lied
Lied lied lied lied about how she died

He sat up in his bed, drenched in sweat.

He got up and changed into his swimsuit, grabbing his phone and a towel as he went out the back door. Billy was already out there by the pool, in a bright yellow bikini, barely more than a couple of strings and a pouch over his genitals. His tanned skin glistened with sweat and oil in the afternoon sun. There was a bottle of white wine in an ice bucket on the metal table next to his lounge chair. "There you are," Billy said as Jase sat down on the chair on the other side of the metal table. "I was wondering if you were going to sleep all day. Have some wine. There's some sunscreen, too, if you need some."

Jase poured the wine, switched on the record app on his phone.

He slathered the tanning oil on himself and asked, "Where do you see your career going from here?"

The lazy afternoon passed, with Jase asking questions and Billy answering, as they drank the wine and shifted from front to back to front on the lounge chairs. No, Billy had no desire to get back into music—his musical career had been a novelty act, after all, and the novelty had worn off. Yes, he'd like to do more films, obviously, he seemed to be a natural actor but wanted to study it more, take it more seriously, unlike the music, so he could actually possibly sustain a career in acting, maybe even do a show on Broadway—no musicals, of course, that would just be ridiculous, his musical talents were limited. Yes, he could take voice classes, get training, but he didn't see any point in that, music was just something he'd lucked into and made enough money to retire from it, walk away from it all. Yes, he'd been a bit of a thug when he was a kid, before his brother's boy band took off, before his own one-hit-wonder career, but he'd atoned for that. He read a lot of books, history and philosophy and art, and living in Italy was the best education in both Western history and art appreciation anyone could get.

The peace and quiet and wine was relaxing. Rarely did a car zoom past on the road up above the wall, and no more screams pierced the stillness of the afternoon.

"I think I have enough," Jase said, pouring the last of the wine into his glass and sitting up. He saved the conversation on the app, turned off his phone—there was only 10 percent battery power left, he'd need to recharge it—and his skin felt warm, good, tanned. "Thanks for this, Billy. I think it's going to be a great article. My editor will, of course, get in touch with you about the photo shoot once I turn the piece in."

"Thank you for detouring out of your vacation to do this." Billy flipped the sunglasses up, winking at him. "And tomorrow you're off to Florence, right?"

"Yes." Florence was about an hour drive. The plan was to drop the car off at the airport and then take a cab to the old part of the city, where he was renting an apartment for a few days. He already had tickets for the Uffizi, the Galleria dell'Accademia, and the Medici tombs, and planned to explore the beautiful old Renaissance city on foot before taking the train to Venice for a few days. "I'll start working on the piece—"

"Don't touch it while you're in Italy," Billy insisted. "You've already given up too much of your vacation as it is."

Jase smiled back at him. He really was considerate, so much more so than anyone had a right to expect, given his past. Maybe the years of retirement had mellowed him, given him a chance to get a handle not only on who he was himself, but on his past as well.

"About the girl…"

"Isabella?" Billy's smile faded. "Jase, you have to believe me when I tell you I would have never done anything with her if I'd known how ill she was."

Almost on cue, a scream echoed down the side of the mountain to them, echoing across the vineyards.

"I don't know how you can handle hearing that every day." Jase shivered, and Billy reached out, placing his hand over Jase's.

"I don't even notice it anymore, like I told you." Billy smiled at him.

Was it a seductive smile? Or was he just making all this up in his head, his old crush, his old passion, for the boy dancing onstage in his underwear bubbling up from deep inside his memories? Remembering those days of buying *Tiger Beat* and *16* magazines at Walgreens because of the pictures of him, shirtless and smiling seductively at the camera, his underwear visible above the waistband of the jeans hanging down so low off his hips? Those magazines never were so bold as to have pictures of him in his underwear, which would be so threatening to the tween girls and their parents, because the magazines couldn't push the reality that part of Billy's appeal was how revealing the tighty-whities were, the enormous bulge he was clearly so proud of, wanted to show off, which was why he was so popular with the gay audience.

Had the homophobia of his later career been an attempt to cover up his own sexuality?

The girls wouldn't squeal so loudly for him if they knew he was gay, right?

Or was it again projection of some kind? Wish fulfillment of the worst kind?

What would Billy do if he made a move?

No, that was not only crazy but unprofessional.

"We're out of wine." Billy sat up, the straps of his bikini shifting, the muscles in his legs and abdomen flexing and rippling beneath the taut brown skin. He laughed. "One of the best things about Italy is no one judges you for drinking wine all day. Come on, let's get something to eat."

Jase followed him along the flagstones through the grass, watching the barely covered cheeks flexing as he walked, stepping from stone to stone.

A woman was in the kitchen making a fruit salad, the sharp knife flashing in the sunlight from the windows as she sliced. Charcuterie was already placed out on the kitchen table on a cutting board, another bottle of the wine opened on the table. She didn't look at them other than an expressionless glance, her eyes running up and down their scantily clothed bodies. She washed her hands, wiped them dry on a towel, and muttered something in Italian. "This is Lucia," Billy said to Jase, "she's a sort of housekeeper, comes in a few days a week for me." He answered her in Italian, straddling one of the chairs, gesturing for Jase to sit down on the other side of the table. She nodded, and climbed the steps, the back door slamming in the distance as she made her way to the steps up to the road.

"She didn't seem very happy," Jase commented as he helped himself to the fruit salad. The flavors exploded in his mouth.

"She never seems happy," Billy replied, his face grim. "They still haven't found the escapee from the mental hospital."

"Are we in danger?"

"Most likely not. The girl's probably trying to get home, to Greve. She'll turn up, they'll find her, they always do."

"Ah."

After the late lunch, they went for a walk through the village. There was a cathedral, smaller than most, Billy explained, but Panzano was a small village. But as before, whenever Billy waved and smiled or said hello to a villager they encountered, Jase couldn't help noticing how the villagers looked back at him. They seemed friendly on the surface—but there was something more to it than what appeared. There was an undercurrent of dislike, and he'd even noticed that one of the women made the sign against the evil eye once Billy's back was turned. He felt claustrophobic, afraid, and was glad he would be leaving the village the next morning. Having a mental hospital so near—Billy pointed out its high stone walls, the statue of the Holy Mother just before the gates on the narrow cobblestone road—yes, he would be glad when he could load his suitcases back into the Fiat in the morning and get on the road to

Florence, following the instructions from Google Maps app to get to the Florence airport. He wasn't sorry he came, no, he was glad, glad to be able to play a part in the comeback of his childhood crush, his teen idol, the man whose pictures he'd masturbated over so many times with the door to his bedroom closed, in that miserable house he'd grown up in.

They had dinner in the small restaurant on the town square, the fountain now shut off and not bubbling, the enormous koi in the big pond swimming up to the top looking for food as they passed by. The food was amazing, the wine delicious, but again Jase was aware of looks from the locals, something about the flamboyantly gay waiter, a slender young Italian man in his early twenties who was flirtatious with Jase but coldly formal and distant with Billy, who didn't seem to notice it any more than he noticed the cold looks, the obvious distaste.

Maybe I'm imagining it, Jase thought, maybe it's the wine, *maybe it's the claustrophobia of being in this small town, beautiful as it is.*

After they paid, as they walked out the front door of the restaurant Signora Agretti stopped them on the narrow sidewalk. She raised a gnarled finger and pointed at Jase. "Panzano not good for you. He warns you to get away before it too late."

Billy laughed and stepped around her. "Lovely to see you, Signora Agretti."

As Jase moved to get around her, she gripped his arm with her hand. "You must go," she whispered hoarsely, "before it too late." Her hand dropped away, and he could see pleading in her reddened eyes. "Go."

"Tomorrow," he whispered as she made the sign of the cross.

He could hear her muttering in Italian, glanced back over his shoulder. She was watching them, the upraised finger still pointing as they walked along the narrow sidewalk.

He felt better once they went around a corner and he couldn't see her anymore. Heading out of the village and back to the villa in the blackness of the still night, the velvety night blue of the sky above them, he tried to shake off what she said, how it made him feel. *She's just a poor crazy old woman,* he reminded himself over and over. *There's no such thing as second sight, and there's no way Philip is here with you.*

And as they walked in silence along the old road, it seemed like they'd somehow gone back in time to the past in some ways, the houses they passed silent in their darkness, no lights within other than the light of the moon overhead.

Another scream pierced the night as they walked down the steps from the road to the front of the villa.

Jase shivered involuntarily. "I could never get used to that," he said.

Billy put an arm around his waist. "It's nothing."

Jase was aware of the heat of Billy's body, aware of his own desire rising from the closeness of their bodies as Billy unlocked the front door of the house. As the door swung open, Billy turned and grasped Jase's face in both hands. Billy kissed him deeply and passionately, pressing him against the doorframe.

Jase knew he had to stop this, couldn't let it go any further, it was unprofessional and wrong, but he couldn't, wouldn't, he wanted this, he'd always wanted this.

Later, afterward, he untangled himself from Billy's naked body. Billy was snoring gently, softly, the sleep of the content.

He picked up his clothes, pulled on his underwear, shaking his head. He would get fired if this ever got out, never work as a journalist again, and yet he found he didn't care. As he slipped down the stone steps of the circular staircase to the first floor in the moonlight, he didn't care. He couldn't report on it, he couldn't ever tell anyone about it.

Billy Starr was at the very least bisexual. Or open to sexual encounters with other men.

He put his clothes down in his bedroom and went to the back door.

A shadow darted across the lawn in the light of the moon.

"Philip?" he asked, opening the door and stepping out into the cool of the evening, feeling like a fool.

The old woman sure did a number on you—

The pool surface glittered in the moonlight, the absolute still and silence broken suddenly by a face looming up out of the darkness.

The blade of the knife shone in the moonlight.

She looked like—she looked like the old woman, a younger version of Signora Agretti, her eyes flashing and her smile wide.

His neck was burning, like it was on fire, and he put his hand up to his throat.

Warm blood gushed out from the deep cut, spilling over his hands.

She laughed. "*Lui appartiene a me finocchio,*" she whispered and danced away, along the flagstones in the moonlight, running when she reached the pool, disappearing once again into the shadows.

He sank to his knees, aware of the blood running down the front of his shirt, feeling cold in his hands and feet and fingertips, unable to scream.

He heard the old woman's voice in his head again, *Panzano not good for you. You must go.*

And she was right, he thought, as he fell facedown into the grass, his hands and feet starting to get cold. *Panzano wasn't good for me.*

DIGESTIF: OUT OF THE DARKNESS

I've always been afraid of the dark.

There was always a Donald Duck night-light plugged into the outlet across the room from my bed, in my direct sight line in case I woke during the night. To this day I sleep on my left side on the left side of the bed facing where that night-light would be if I still used it. I remember waking up many times when I was a child and drawing comfort from that bizarre, yellowish-orange glow. While the dark doesn't necessarily scare me now that I am an adult, it does make me uncomfortable. When I'm home alone, I leave the bathroom light on when I go to bed, and I always leave a light on downstairs when I retire for the evening. In hotels I leave the bathroom light on. Intellectually, I have never been able to make sense of this fear, this discomfort with the darkness—the absence of light doesn't necessarily correlate to possible danger or to monsters hunting me, waiting out there in the darkness, ready to pounce and rip my throat out—but what I know *intellectually* to be true has no effect on my visceral, primordial, emotional reaction to being in the dark. It's a primal fear, coded into my DNA millions of years ago, when cavemen huddled around fires wondering what was out there in the dark with sharp teeth and claws, just waiting...

The supernatural creatures I feared as a child, the ones I imagined out there in the darkness and the shadows, the ones I read about in books or saw on the late-night movies on my television, aren't real. There are no witches or warlocks, goblins or gremlins, vampires or werewolves, phantoms or ghosts. They aren't real, they are fictions and folktales. The true monsters are human. People like Charles Manson and Richard Speck and Ted Bundy and Jeffrey Dahmer—*those* are the real monsters, hiding in human flesh, who look like everyone else, whose eyes hide true darkness, madness, a desire to cause pain and hurt others.

I became a crime writer because I was curious about that human darkness, about what turns a human being into a monster in human costume. What is it that makes the wife, after years of being beaten down emotionally by her husband, shoot him one night? Why? What was the breaking point, the thing that was just too much to be borne any further?

I am also interested in the *aftermath* of crimes: how does one who has been the victim handle it and go forward? The families of the victim?

I find the short story format is perfect for exploring morality and amorality.

The problem is that there aren't many paying markets for short stories. When you add the adjective *crime* to the mix, the market shrinks still further; adding *gay* makes it almost completely disappear. When you're a gay writer, short stories are not the direction you want to go if you're trying to make a living through your writing. I am a firm believer that writers should be paid for their work, but sometimes...sometimes you just bite your tongue and put your principles aside in order for your story to find readers. I didn't get paid for many of the published short stories in this collection, and while the *exposure* I did receive might not have made up for the time spent on the story, sometimes the satisfaction of seeing the story in print is its own reward. I am terribly proud of the stories in this collection, and I am very happy to have them—along with the new, previously unpublished stories—collected in print in the same place.

I enjoy the challenge inherent in writing short stories. When I was beginning my career, I wasn't terribly interested in telling stories about straight people; there are plenty of other writers doing just that. There weren't many gay crime short stories, and that was undoubtedly due to the lack of places to publish them. There weren't many markets for *literary* gay short stories, let alone adding *crime* to the descriptive adjectives. At the time I was breaking into print and getting paid to write fiction, the gay fiction anthologies were beginning to die out: the last volume of the *Men on Men* series had already been published; the *His* series had also finished; and as those opportunities for gay writers dried up, the print magazines interested in publishing short fiction about gay men were either shutting their doors or cutting back dramatically on what they were publishing. The only markets open to gay short stories were erotica anthologies and magazines, so I wrote—and edited—erotica. I used to call myself "the accidental pornographer"; it had never occurred to me to write erotic short fiction. It wasn't on my radar, but a friend suggested writing erotica as a way to break into print, and I was willing to give it a shot. I found myself writing short stories for *Men* magazine, and anthologies like *Men for All Seasons* and *Best Gay Erotica* and *Friction*, or putting together my own anthologies, like *Full Body Contact* and *FRATSEX*.

I am not ashamed of my pornographic past; nothing could be further from the truth. I am very proud of those stories (collected under my pseudonym Todd Gregory in the collection *Promises in Every Star and Other Stories*—pick up a copy!), and I am equally proud of the anthologies I edited. Writing erotica was an education in and of itself—an education in writing short stories better than any course I took in college.

Erotica writing teaches story structure in an easy, perfect way: two people meet, they have sex, and what happens after.

Beginning, middle, end.

Before I wrote erotica, writing short stories for me was difficult. If I wrote a good, solid story it was usually entirely by accident; I quite literally had no idea what I was doing. But after writing a dozen or so erotica stories, I found that writing short stories had become much easier. I had trained myself to follow the structure of beginning, middle, end and had done it so many times it had become almost innate, like muscle memory for exercise. That doesn't, of course, mean that I don't start short stories that never get finished because I have no idea how to finish them; I have two file cabinet drawers filled with ideas not carried to term. Sometimes I repurpose them—any number of nascent ideas that I never finished were converted and adapted to other ideas.

But in order to write short stories, you have to *love* short stories.

Like I said earlier, no one is ever going to get rich writing short stories—I remember a college writing instructor telling us that *you make your name writing short stories for small literary journals, then get an agent and write your novel.* Perhaps that's still true; maybe that does still happen. But the days when there were scores of publications looking for short stories are distant memories, and many of the ones that still do publish either pay nothing or a token pittance.

So, while some of the anthologies that published some of these stories paid nothing, I didn't mind so much. In many of those anthologies, I found myself sharing the table of contents with writers I had long admired, with best sellers and critically acclaimed, award-winning writers.

And while I am an ardent advocate of *the writer must be paid*, there's also the element that stories are written to be read.

And no one can read them if they're just electronic files on my hard drive.

When you're a writer, you have to sometimes backtrack on your principles.

I don't write short stories for the money because there would be no point. I write them because I love the form. I love trying to figure out how to tell the story in the space constraints. I love writing to theme; trying to come up with a story that, while fitting the theme, sometimes stretches and bends and turns it on its head. I love creating a new character, figuring out some moral or ethical dilemma for them to face, and figuring out how best to handle a situation.

I love wrestling with the length and the character and the setting and the motivations. I love trying to get it right. I like the brevity—although sometimes I feel like I am stretching the stories out; I have this mentality that every story should be at least between four and five thousand words. I'm not sure where that comes from—there are certainly fantastic stories out there that are much shorter. But one of my primary struggles with myself as a writer is an innate stubbornness. I get something into my head and become so attached to it that I stick to it even when it demonstrably makes no sense.

I'm not sure where the stories come from, to give an honest answer to the question that plagues authors at public events or during interviews. They come from somewhere within my brain, sometimes triggered by something I've seen or heard, something that made me sit back and think, *interesting*.

"Survivor's Guilt" began as a horror story, written for an anthology call for stories of a thousand words or less. It was originally called "Blues in the Night," and I thought it was pretty good. But the anthology didn't take it—didn't even give me the courtesy of a rejection, which seems to happen more and more as I get older and the bar of what's considered professional courtesy continues to lower. So I put it aside as a failed story and figured I would go back to it again sometime, when I wasn't limited to such a low word count. When the opportunity to write something for the *Blood on the Bayou* anthology came about, I pulled out "Blues in the Night" and rewrote it, made it longer. I had once written an opening for another story that never went anywhere, that I really liked, and so I pilfered it from that other story for this one. And as the story grew, I began to understand it more—and why it didn't work as a thousand words or less type story. I was pleased with it, and even more thrilled when it was nominated for a Macavity Award. It didn't win, but I was also short-listed with some amazing authors—Art Taylor, Paul D. Marks, Joyce Carol Oates, and Lawrence Block.

That still boggles my mind.

"The Email Always Pings Twice" was written for the MWA anthology *Mystery Box;* all stories had to be about the contents of a box. As is so often the case, I came up with the title first, and I decided to play with the theme a little bit; years ago I worked in an office where an older woman always referred to her computer as "this stupid box," and a computer is, in fact, a type of box; something that contains other things. As I played with this idea and the title, the idea of a woman starting a new life by moving in with the man she loves, only to find something in his computer that lets her know that maybe he's not who she thinks he is, started forming in my head. I also liked the idea of the double ping—her cell phone *and* her laptop letting her know she had a new email. I thought this outside-the-box thinking about the theme (yes, a bad pun, but it was there for the taking) might just get me into the anthology (they are incredibly competitive), but I was wrong. But I was very pleased when *Ellery Queen's Mystery Magazine* liked it enough to publish it.

"Acts of Contrition" also was published in *Ellery Queen's Mystery Magazine.* It was my first time in their pages, and it was one of the biggest thrills of my career when Janet emailed me that they were going to use it. The great irony of the story—which was used in a special "one year after Katrina" issue—was that it didn't begin life as a New Orleans story. In the early 1990s I was visiting a friend in Seattle and stepped out onto the balcony of his apartment to smoke a cigarette. It was raining, and through the downpour I could see a priest talking to a young homeless girl. I couldn't hear what they were talking about, but both were very animated, and the fact that both were getting soaked in a cold rain didn't matter to either of them. I went back inside and wrote what I saw down in my journal, adding *what were they talking about?* On my flight home, a red-eye that left at one in the morning, I couldn't sleep and so I wrote, in longhand, a story based on what I saw. After I moved to New Orleans, I adapted it to New Orleans—the drenching rain in New Orleans being something I'd become very well acquainted with in the meantime—and when the opportunity for *Ellery Queen* came along, I worked on the story some more.

My first crime story with a gay main character to see print was "Annunciation Shotgun." I was asked to write a story for the *New Orleans Noir* anthology by Julie Smith. The way Akashic Books' noir anthologies work is each writer is assigned a neighborhood, and they write a story about that neighborhood. The city noir series also has a diversity requirement, so I was asked to write a story with a gay main character. I had already conceptualized a story called "Constantinople Shotgun" that I wanted to use, but that neighborhood was already taken. I had to moved my story to the lower Garden District, where I've lived for over twenty years. I picked Annunciation Street because it was a long and unusual street name; the shotgun from the title is not an actual gun, but rather refers to the shotgun style of house common in New Orleans. I once described a friend as 'the kind of person who, if you call him and tell him you've killed someone, without missing a beat replies, "Well, the first thing we have to do is get rid of the body."' I wanted to write about that kind of friendship, that kind of bond between two gay men who live next door to each other in the halves of a shotgun style house; how that spatial intimacy allows you insights into each other's lives.

"An Arrow for Sebastian" was my second crime story with a gay character to see print. The narrator of the story is removed somewhat from the actual story; it's told in an observational style. He is observing the events of the story but isn't really an active participant in them. I remember the opening of the story came to me one afternoon when a friend was telling me about this horrible dinner party she'd been attended the previous evening. As she spoke, I had this image of someone trapped at a horrible dinner party, noticing the young man sitting across the table from him and wondering what his story is. The young man was accompanying a much older gay man whom the narrator dislikes. As I wrote the story, I began to see the young man and developed him more. As I got to know him better, my sympathy for him began to grow. I originally saw him as a hustler, being paid to be the obnoxious gay man's date for the evening. But as he began developing into a person in my mind, as I gave him a backstory, the story also began shifting and changing. It became more than just a crime story; it became more sad and poignant than I'd originally intended, which made the ending even more tragic. Novelists, Inc., a professional writer's organization, took the story for their first anthology, *Cast of Characters*.

"A Streetcar Named Death" was also published in a Novelists, Inc. anthology; the next year's *I Never Thought I'd See You Again*. In the late 1980s, I'd written a story called "Fellow Traveler," in which a truly awful woman is forced to take public transportation and…well, let's just say it doesn't end well. I liked the idea of the story, the basic frame of someone who doesn't ordinarily take public transportation being forced to and the story springing from that happenstance. When Lou Aronica, who'd edited the first Novelists, Inc. anthology, asked me to contribute a story to this second anthology, I remembered my story about public transportation. At this point, I'd ridden the St. Charles Avenue streetcar in New Orleans many times and was always surprised whenever I ran into someone I knew on board. Using a streetcar as the foundation for the story, and someone having to take it home from work because their car was in the shop, all I needed now was a story. I was actually on the streetcar, watching a young man board, when I wondered, *what if you ran into someone who'd harmed you many years later on the streetcar? What would you do? And what would you do if that person got off at a spot in your neighborhood? Someone who harmed you years before now lives in your neighborhood, and after that first time seeing him again on the streetcar, you see him everywhere now. And he doesn't recognize you.*

That was apparently the right premise, because the story just flowed out of me.

"Cold Beer No Flies" likewise is also one of my old stories from a particularly fertile writing period in the late 1980s. It was originally set in Kansas, at a bar I used to occasionally frequent when I was in college called My Place. In the original version of the story my bartender was a young straight woman, and someone she'd always had a crush on in high school one night shows up at her bar, miserably married to another one of their classmates, and she gets him back to her apartment that night and sleeps with him, only to wake up alone in the morning with a lot of regret. The story never worked; I thought the ending wasn't right. When the chance to write a story for *Florida Happens* presented itself, I remembered "Cold Beer No Flies," reread it, and realized what was wrong with it. I changed the straight woman into a gay man and moved the setting to a small Florida panhandle town, and it evolved from that seed. What is it like for a young gay man to grow up in the smothering climate of a rural small town where he's seen as a freak and a sinner, something slightly less than human? A victim most of his life, he has plans…and if those plans cross the line into criminality, well, what choice does a poor working-class gay kid in rural Florida have?

"Housecleaning" was written for *Sunshine Noir* at the request of the editors, Annamaria Alfieri and Michael Stanley. My mother was actually the inspiration for this story—although the only thing she and the mother in my story have in common is the obsessive cleanliness; I always joke that my mother would have thought Joan Crawford was a slob. That first sentence came to me one day when I was cleaning my apartment. I was filling a bucket with hot water to clean the bathroom, and when I added bleach to the water I actually did think *the scent of bleach always reminded him of his mother.* I laughed, thought *that's a great opening line for a short story*, and made a note of it. When Annamaria and Michael kindly asked me for a story for their anthology, I remembered the line and used it as a starting point. The narrator began to take shape for me as I wrote about the woman his mother was and how who she was impacted who he would become. It's one of those rare cases where I didn't know the ending of the story when I started, but as I wrote it inevitably led me down the path to what the ending had to be. The final version of the story is pretty close to the original draft. The only changes I made to the story were some sentence/paragraph revisions here and there to improve the tone, pacing, and wording. The plot, the characters? They didn't change one bit.

"The Weight of a Feather" was originally written for an MWA anthology about the Cold War; it, too, was rejected (getting into an MWA anthology is a bucket-list item of mine; I will keep trying until I make it), and then just sat around in my files for years before I pulled it back out and worked on it again. It was my first time writing something that could be considered *historical*. It was also my first time writing a story not set in the ambiguous present. I tried to remember that some details of modern life (like direct dial telephones) didn't exist in this postwar world of Washington, DC, that I was writing about. I wanted to write about that very real fear of being exposed as a closeted gay man working for the State Department during the time of McCarthyism, and about what it was like to *be* gay in that era. In rereading my original draft, I realized I'd stomped on the action by starting the story in the wrong place—I can be terribly stubborn about that sort of thing. While the place I originally opened the story made for an actual great opening, the result of starting there meant everything that came before had to be told in flashback, which slowed the pace down to a crawl: Nothing happened.

Sometimes it's best to let things sit so your emotional attachment to what you've written lessens and you can then see it more clearly.

The story behind "Lightning Bugs in a Jar" is an interesting exercise in rejection: It was written for a specific anthology but was cut from the final manuscript by the editor after two extensive revisions/rewrites based on editorial notes. I came up with the title years ago; when I was a kid I always used to catch lightning bugs and keep them in mason jars with holes punched in the lid with a butter knife. I've always loved that image and thought it made a great title. I've always been interested in creative couples who work in the same discipline, and how difficult that must be for married writers—the sense of support yet competition at the same time, and how the relationship can eventually go sour…and in this particular case, divorce isn't enough—not after the years of suffering the wife has been put through.

There's no loathing quite so intense as that which comes from living in close proximity to another person, is there?

"Spin Cycle" is one of my post-Katrina stories. Originally written and performed as a radio play, I turned the play into a short story for my anthology *Men of the Mean Streets*. For "Spin Cycle," I took something comical yet incredibly frustrating from my real life and used writing about it as a cathartic release. In those days after Katrina, contractors had real power over their clients—they were in short supply and everyone needed repair work done to their homes—and I've heard many stories about contractors and their employees that make "Spin Cycle" look tame in comparison. And yes, my contractor's wife used my washer and dryer, and precisely in the way described in the story. No good deed…

The final two stories in this collection, "Don't Look Down" and "My Brother's Keeper," are both originals written specifically for it. "Don't Look Down" originated as a story set in the French Quarter about a has-been music star and the gay journalist who comes to interview him on the eve of a comeback attempt, and was called "Whatever Happened to Billy Starr?" When I visited Italy several years ago and stayed in a villa in the Tuscan village of Panzano, I realized this was the perfect setting for that story. The elements of the village were perfect, and it simply made sense for the story to be set there. Once I moved the setting to Italy and started writing the story, it just continued to grow—but I couldn't find anything to cut that wouldn't (in my opinion) irreparably harm the story. While I'm very aware that people might not be satisfied by the ending of the story as written, I am very pleased with it; it does everything I wanted and intended for it to do when I started writing it.

Several years ago, I ended my Chanse MacLeod series after seven books, with *Murder in the Arts District*. I said at the time I didn't know if I would continue to write about Chanse moving forward, but I just couldn't see writing another novel at the time. "My Brother's Keeper" is the Chanse novel I never got to write, the one where Chanse goes back to the small East Texas town where he grew up, where his younger brother is in jail, charged with the murder of an upstanding local businessman. In writing this story, I realized there are still Chanse stories I want to tell—but they most likely will be short fiction rather than novels. I am working, in fact, on another Chanse short story—it might become a Kindle single, maybe I'll do another collection. Who knows? But I do like writing short stories about Chanse, and I do think I will do more in the future.

So, there you have it: my first collection of crime/suspense stories. I hope you enjoyed it as much as I enjoyed writing the stories and pulling them all together into this collection. I have a lot more stories in my filing cabinets, and I get ideas for more stories all the time. (I've come up with ideas for three more stories while writing this afterward, as a matter of fact.)

I love short stories.

Until next time.

—Greg Herren
New Orleans, 2018

About the Author

Greg Herren is the award-winning author of over thirty novels and twenty anthologies. He has won two Lambda Literary Awards, an Anthony Award, and numerous others; he has also been short-listed for the Shirley Jackson Award, the Macavity Award, and the Lambda Literary Award an additional twelve times. A public health worker by day, he lives in New Orleans with his partner of over twenty years.

Books Available From Bold Strokes Books

Survivor's Guilt and Other Stories by Greg Herren. Award-winning author Greg Herren's short stories are finally pulled together into a single collection, including the Macavity Award–nominated title story and the first-ever Chanse MacLeod short story. (978-1-63555-413-7)

Saints + Sinners Anthology 2019, edited by Tracy Cunningham and Paul Willis. An anthology of short fiction featuring the finalist selections from the 2019 Saints + Sinners Literary Festival. (978-1-63555-447-2)

The Shape of the Earth by Gary Garth McCann. After appearing in *Best Gay Love Stories*, *HarringtonGMFQ*, *Q Review*, and *Off the Rocks*, Lenny and his partner Dave return in a hotbed of manhood and jealousy. (978-1-63555-391-8)

Exit Plans for Teenage Freaks by 'Nathan Burgoine. Cole always has a plan—especially for escaping his small-town reputation as "that kid who was kidnapped when he was four"—but when he teleports to a museum, it's time to face facts: it's possible he's a total freak after all. (978-1-163555-098-6)

Death Checks In by David S. Pederson. Despite Heath's promises to Alan to not get involved, Heath can't resist investigating a shopkeeper's murder in Chicago, which dashes their plans for a romantic weekend getaway. (978-1-163555-329-1)

Of Echoes Born by 'Nathan Burgoine. A collection of queer fantasy short stories set in Canada from Lambda Literary Award finalist 'Nathan Burgoine. (978-1-63555-096-2)

The Lurid Sea by Tom Cardamone. Cursed to spend eternity on his knees, Nerites is having the time of his life. (978-1-62639-911-2)

Sinister Justice by Steve Pickens. When a vigilante targets citizens of Jake Finnigan's hometown, Jake and his partner Sam fall under suspicion themselves as they investigate the murders. (978-1-63555-094-8)

Club Arcana: Operation Janus by Jon Wilson. Wizards, demons, Elder Gods: Who knew the universe was so crowded, and that they'd all be out to get Angus McAslan? (978-1-62639-969-3)

Triad Soul by 'Nathan Burgoine. Luc, Anders, and Curtis— vampire, demon, and wizard—must use their powers of blood, soul, and magic to defeat a murderer determined to turn their city into a battlefield. (978-1-62639-863-4)

Gatecrasher by Stephen Graham King. Aided by a high-tech thief, the Maverick Heart crew race against time to prevent a cadre of savage corporate mercenaries from seizing control of a revolutionary wormhole technology. (978-1-62639-936-5)

Wicked Frat Boy Ways by Todd Gregory. Beta Kappa brothers Brandon Benson and Phil Connor play an increasingly dangerous game of love, seduction, and emotional manipulation. (978-1-62639-671-5)

Death Goes Overboard by David S. Pederson. Heath Barrington and Alan Keyes are two sides of a steamy love triangle as they encounter gangsters, con men, murder, and more aboard an old lake steamer. (978-1-62639-907-5)

A Careful Heart by Ralph Josiah Bardsley. Be careful what you wish for...love changes everything. (978-1-62639-887-0)

Worms of Sin by Lyle Blake Smythers. A haunted mental asylum turned drug treatment facility exposes supernatural detective Finn M'Coul to an outbreak of murderous insanity, a strange parasite, and ghosts that seek sex with the living. (978-1-62639-823-8)

Tartarus by Eric Andrews-Katz. When Echidna, Mother of all Monsters, escapes from Tartarus and into the modern world, only an Olympian has the power to oppose her. (978-1-62639-746-0)

Rank by Richard Compson Sater. Rank means nothing to the heart, but the Air Force isn't as impartial. Every airman learns that rank has its privileges. What about love? (978-1-62639-845-0)

The Grim Reaper's Calling Card by Donald Webb. When Katsuro Tanaka begins investigating the disappearance of a young nurse, he discovers more missing persons, and they all have one thing in common: The Grim Reaper Tarot Card. (978-1-62639-748-4)

Smoldering Desires by C.E. Knipes. Evan McGarrity has found the man of his dreams in Sebastian Tantalos. When an old boyfriend from Sebastian's past enters the picture, Evan must fight for the man he loves. (978-1-62639-714-9)